DEATH WATCH

DEATH WATCH

✦⊹ THE ⊹ UNDERTAKEN ⊹ TRILOGY ⊹✦

⊹

ARI BERK

⊹

SIMON & SCHUSTER BFYR

New York   London   Toronto   Sydney   New Delhi

SIMON & SCHUSTER BFYR

An imprint of Simon & Schuster Children's Publishing Division
1230 Avenue of the Americas, New York, New York 10020

For information about special discounts for bulk purchases, please contact Simon & Schuster Special Sales at 1-866-506-1949 or business@simonandschuster.com.
The Simon & Schuster Speakers Bureau can bring authors to your live event. For more information or to book an event, contact the Simon & Schuster Speakers Bureau at 1-866-248-3049 or visit our website at www.simonspeakers.com.
Also available in a SIMON & SCHUSTER BFYR hardcover edition
Book design by Laurent Linn
Map illustration by Drew Willis
The text for this book is set in Minister Std.
Manufactured in the United States of America
First SIMON & SCHUSTER BFYR paperback edition November 2012
10 9 8 7 6 5 4 3 2 1
The Library of Congress has cataloged the hardcover edition as follows:
Berk, Ari.
Death watch / by Ari Berk.
p. cm.—(the Undertaken trilogy)
Summary: When seventeen-year-old Silas Umber's father disappears, Silas is sure it is connected to the powerful artifact he discovers, combined with his father's hidden hometown history, which compels Silas to pursue the path leading to his destiny and ultimately, to the discovery of his father, dead or alive.
ISBN 978-1-4169-9115-1 (hc)
[1. Fantasy. 2. Fathers and sons—Fiction.]1. Title.
PZ7.B452293 De 2011
[Fic]
2011006332
ISBN 978-1-4169-9116-8 (pbk)
ISBN 978-1-4424-3603-9 (eBook)

For Robin & Kristen, always

CONTENTS

Time is now fleeting, the moments are passing,
Passing from you and from me.
Shadows are gathering, deathbeds are coming,
Coming for you and for me.
Come home, come home,
Ye who are weary, come home . . .

—from *"Softly and Tenderly" (traditional hymn)*

What candles may be held to speed them all?
Not in the hands of boys, but in their eyes
Shall shine the holy glimmers of goodbyes.

—from *"Anthem for Doomed Youth," Wilfred Owen*

Ye mournful folk, be ye of Goode Cheere! In the comforting soyle of Lichport, your dead shalle finde peace. We shalle give every consideration to the speedy restfulness of your dead and/or departed. Let us minister to your grief in the venerated and accustomed manner of Lichport, a town well known for its verie full knowledge relating to every ancient and worshipfull ritual that shalle bring peace to all deceased or wandering folk. Walk abroad upon the peaceful lanes of Lichport and finde at every turn goode ground for your kin's eternal rest. Here shall they be made welcome. Here shall they come to the sweete comfort that only our goodlie earth may give. Come ye! Come ye! To Fayre Lichport where the Dead and the Living find an Ende to Life's Toil and Worldly Troubles Are No More!

—*A Printed Advertisement distributed along the coastal and inland towns between 1792 and 1802 Written by Samuel Umber, Undertaker, Lichport*

CHAPTER 1

HOME

HE SHOULD HAVE GONE HOME.

It was after eleven, so he'd have been home already. Arguing with his wife. Lying to his son about work and the hours of his work and the kind of work he said he did back in Lichport.

Amos Umber's lies had become habitual. He would invent something about the corpse to tell his son. That's what Silas always wanted to know. The grisly details. *What happened to them? How did they die? What did it take to put all the pieces back in place?* How did he treat the flesh so the family wouldn't be reminded there was anything other than sleep waiting for them at the end of days?

It was their little ritual. Father and son. Lie stitched to lie. An elaborate collection of details and variations to make the stories he told sound real, momentarily fascinating, but also common and forgettable. Corpses and coffins, chemical order forms, and a dark pin-striped suit. So many details it almost held together if no one pulled at too many threads. No matter that his son assumed that "Undertaker" meant "mortician." No matter that in the Umber family an Undertaker was something else entirely.

Amos hated lying to his son, but he had made a promise to his wife. He'd sworn not to say anything about the Undertaken, or Wanderers, or the Restless. He'd sworn not to talk to Silas about his side of the family or the family business in Lichport, where they all once lived together briefly when Silas was a baby.

Most of what he told his son was a lie, but not all of it. No matter how many minute details he fabricated, he always tried to say something about the Peace. At the end of each evening's tale, that's what he told his son he tried to do in his work: bring peace. And at least that part, that most essential act, was true.

On nights like this one, he longed to actually live inside his story-life, just doing the easy stuff: Bag 'em. Bury 'em. Arrange the flowers, line up the chairs for the visitation, hold the hands of the bereaved. But these were not part of his calling. His work began after the funeral. Or when there hadn't been a funeral because the body was lost and rumors were making folk restless. Or because something so awful happened that folk couldn't bring themselves to speak about it at all. As sure as a curse, secrets and silence brought them back and kept them wandering. If they couldn't find the Peace . . . that's when his dark and difficult work began.

He should have gone home.

But instead of driving his car on the road over the marsh, back to Saltsbridge and the other house in the suburbs, he was walking from his office down Main Street toward the water, deeper into the old neighborhoods, and singing softly to himself as familiar houses rose up against the night sky as if to greet him. He'd never once felt at home in Saltsbridge. Lichport would always be home, and he knew it.

The Morton house stood on a street of old leaning mansions above the Narrows, and it hadn't been on his list of trouble spots. Sure, things came up unexpectedly, but not often—a quiet one might turn wakeful—but nowadays this was a rare event. That neighborhood had been peace-bound for a long time, even though the houses and the families around there were old and had troublesome pasts. Lots of the founding families had left Lichport, or died out, like the one last ancient aunt who lived with a hundred cats until someone noticed she wasn't picking up her mail anymore.

Only the families with more dignity than money still lived near the waterfront, and the Mortons were one of those, lingering quietly among their losses, generation after generation, as the whole pile continued to fall down around them. One of the remaining Morton children had written to Amos, hastily, before abandoning the house "temporarily." And now, very suddenly, there was talk of awful visitations and unsettled business, and no one wanted to walk past the house at night, and Lonely Folk were seen wandering at noon, even in the Narrows. Three people had heard the Sorrowsman on Dogge Alley. Two had seen him.

Rumors were running again in the streets of Lichport.

Even before he got to the house, even without seeing *it*, he guessed it was a box job causing the trouble, because those were the ones that came back without warning. That's why no one used boxes or tins anymore, even though it used to be common practice, because they almost always broke open or corroded, and when it came back it was always worse than before. The last box he'd read about in the Undertaker's ledger was used maybe two hundred years ago. Put it in the box, seal the box, bury the box somewhere deep. Under water. Under earth. Under stone. Many of the older sources suggested sinking such containers to the bottom of the Dead Sea, though this always seemed to Amos a little impractical.

But those boxes never stayed shut, and once the seal cracked it would start its long journey home one stride at a time, making a little progress every year, getting angrier and angrier along the way. And when it finally got home it would all start again, and that was a bad time for everyone. Amos had made quite a collection of boxes, keeping them away from people who might open one up out of curiosity, and occasionally, he'd try to set one right if he thought it could be done without causing any trouble.

All of the houses on this street roosted high above the sidewalk and peered down over the edge of land and out to the sea. Each was approached by long stairs that rose from below, ascending to carved front doors set deep within elaborate but crumbling porches and porticoes. As he looked up at the Morton place, he could see he was expected. Curtains, usually closed, were drawn away from the windows, and candlelight played out onto the casements.

When he arrived at the top of the stairs, he knocked once, firmly, on the faded door, its red paint peeling from the carved surface, and after several moments, opened it. No one greeted him. Perhaps the family had left the house for the night. This was often the case, and he never minded, because it was so much easier to be alone when he was at work. He looked back briefly over his shoulder before he entered the house to see the water out beyond the Narrows, where the moon cast a long warm shadow over the summer sea.

Somewhere deep inside the house a clock began to chime. Amos turned his head back toward the open door and crossed over the threshold. As he closed the door behind him, the last chime struck.

The rest was silence.

Outside, beyond the door, the moon had fled.

Shadowland was waiting.

CHAPTER 2

NOBODY

HIS FATHER WAS COMING HOME.

Silas Umber had been waiting all day for his dad. He'd stayed home "sick" from school that day.

"Uh-huh. Sick of school, you mean! Silas, please. Just tell me you're going to graduate," his mother pleaded when he'd told her he was staying home.

This was their usual conversation. Silas would come up with an excuse to remain home. His mother would complain. He'd try to calm her by saying he wasn't missing anything and that his grades were good enough for him to graduate high school, that he'd catch up when he went back. For the most part, Silas made good on such promises, though he could tell his mother was disappointed in him, but she was too tired most of the time to fight about it.

"Then run to the store for me, Si," she said, "we're out of a few things."

Toward dusk Silas thought he could hear his dad's shoes on the stones, could hear his father's familiar step making its way up the drive and onto the porch.

It was time for their little ritual: Silas would run to get to the door before his dad could put in the key, throw the door open, and playing the annoyed parent, yell the famous lines, *Well, young man? Where have you been?*

Although he had not yet heard the key in the lock, Silas turned the knob and swiftly pulled the door open, but no one stood on the porch. A nightbird called from the park at the end of the street, and the smell of the distant salt marsh rolled past him into the house, but his father was nowhere to be seen.

His mother called wearily from the den, the sound of her voice accompanied by bells of ice ringing in a thick, half-empty glass.

"Si? Is that your father?"

Silas couldn't answer her. He stood looking out past the certainty of the empty porch, but he couldn't imagine his father standing anywhere else. It was like listening for the phone to ring, wanting it to ring so badly you convince yourself that you can feel the person on the other end of the line, feel them dialing your number, but then you wait and wait, and it never rings.

CHAPTER 3

OUTER CIRCLE

IT MIGHT HAVE BEEN NOON OR MIDNIGHT. When Silas woke each day, only the light beyond his window gave a sense of the hour. Since he now often slept in his clothes, when Silas looked in the mirror, he saw the same person as the day before, the same costume. He had become a character in a play, same story, over and over.

With each day of his father's absence, time fell further and further away from Silas. He spent his time moving belongings across the surface of his desk, examining them. An old arrowhead, a toy gun made from PVC pipe, a book given to him by his father. Everything came from somewhere. Everything was going somewhere. Even the smallest toy was moving its way through time. Each treasured object in his collection occupied space, had weight and a story. Since his father's absence, memories became the minutes and hours of Silas's days.

He needed the quiet that attended memories.

Even common sounds now annoyed him terribly. The texture of certain noises became harsh, even unbearable: The awful scrape of his mother's butter knife across the ragged surface of a slice of toast would drive him from the breakfast table back to the safety of his room.

The sound of some words—like "school"—affected him badly. Certain words were banished altogether.

Silas refused to say the word "dead" in the same sentence as his father's name. He worried every day that he'd get the actual news that his dad had died, but he believed, absolutely, in the power of words and so, for a long time, he was careful with what he said. Growing up, he'd watched his parents throw words like rocks at each other, words like weathering tides that would tear at the shore and eat away at their lives. So he wouldn't say his dad was *dead*, even when his mother told him it was possible, even probable.

Silas knew words could have power behind them. Usually it was just a sort of bad luck. He also knew, very early on, that you could never tell when that bad luck would jump up to claim its due, so it was best to be careful. Quiet was safer. He wished his parents had been quieter when they were together. Who knew what might happen when you said something awful to someone else? It was hard to take some words back. Some words stuck and you couldn't shake them off. Silence was better than those kinds of words. Silas had learned that lesson the hard way.

When Silas was eleven, he had a real friend. Not one of his imaginary friends. This was a real kid from his real neighborhood who lived in a real house just like Silas's, although in mirror opposite with the living room to the right of the entry hall instead of the left. Tom was his only friend, and Silas's parents were pleased he finally had someone in the neighborhood to play with, someone real. Before Tom, Silas hadn't wanted to play with any other kids from his school.

When his parents asked him why, why not play with some of the kids from the neighborhood who also went to his school, all Silas would say was they looked different at school. School made them different. But Tom looked the same wherever he was, and he smiled a lot and didn't seem to mind when Silas got quiet and started talking fast about something that had nothing to do with what they had been doing. Tom would just wait him out. And when Silas looked up, or stopped rambling, Tom was still there, smiling.

It was a holiday weekend, and early Saturday morning, Tom had come to Silas's house and yelled from the lawn, "Come outside and play, Si! C'mon already!" Silas and Tom played with guns they had made from white plastic PVC pipe and black electrical tape. The battle waged all day Saturday and well into Sunday. Sometimes they were on the same team, running missions behind enemy lines; other times they each took a side, and tracked and chased each other through the neighbors' yards and through their own houses until one or the other of their parents ordered them back outside.

Silas had been hiding behind the trash cans in front of his house. He'd been waiting for over fifteen minutes for Tom to appear. Just as Silas thought Tom might have quit, Tom came around the wall of the house next door. He crouched low and moved close to Silas's hiding place. When Tom passed in front of him, Silas knocked over the cans, jumped up, pointed his gun and made a barrage of shooting noises, then chanted, "Dead! You're dead! Dead, dead, dead, Tom! You're dead!"

Always a fair player, Tom fell over dramatically, and his gun flew out of his hand and landed on the lawn a few feet away. Gracious in victory, Silas went to help him up and a few minutes later, Tom's parents called him in to dinner. The boys went home dirty and exhausted but agreed that this was the best time either could remember.

As Silas got ready for bed that night, he did something he rarely ever did: He thought about the future. Made plans in his head for sleepovers and bike rides and a dozen other adventures. He thought things might change for him. Even if his parents didn't get along any better, Silas thought he might now have something to do other than try to avoid them when they were fighting. Maybe Tom's parents would let him spend some weekends at their house, you know, when things got bad at his.

Three days later, Silas and his parents were eating dinner when the phone rang. Tom had been struck by a car and killed. Silas's mother refused to let him go the funeral, but allowed him to accompany his father to pay their respects. Silas remembered his dad telling his mom that he wanted to speak with Tom's parents, but before he could even say what it was about, Silas's mother started in on him: "Oh, leave it, Amos! Let it alone. No one here cares! When someone dies out here in the suburbs, that's the end of it!"

His parents barely spoke a word to each other for almost a month after that, and Silas grew quiet too. He kept mostly to himself, invited no more friends home, and hid the guns he and Tom had made in the back of his closet. Silas got sick a lot, or said he was sick, and stayed home more than he went to school.

Silas's mother, Dolores Umber, looked into her son's room and saw him holding that old toy gun he'd made seven years ago with that other boy, the one who'd been hit by the car. She drew herself quietly back into the hall without disturbing him. She remembered that event very well. It was shortly after the boy's funeral when she began noticing differences in her son. Silas seemed off somewhere. Absent, even when he was standing right in front of her. She'd talk and talk, and he'd stand there with a blank look; his face might have been the still glass surface of a lake on a windless day.

And now it was bad again, since Amos had vanished. Dolores even tried to cut back on the drinking some, tried to talk to Silas when he came home from school, or wherever he took himself when he ditched. He'd just look at her. Blank. Then, sometimes, maybe a few words. She tried to talk to him, but if she mentioned one of the Forbidden Things, like school, or making plans for the future, or moving on in general, he'd get mad fast and then go quiet again for days.

She thought he cared too much. Sometimes Dolores could see that her son felt what other people were feeling. He was sympathetic, she knew that. But Silas managed to make his feelings about others into another kind of absence. You'd laugh, Silas would laugh. You'd cry, he'd start crying. It was like he was tuning in to a radio station. It took a moment for the distant signal to lock in, but once it did, he'd be right in sync with you. Only when he got angry, or hurt, did the signal fail and he'd become very present indeed, and very annoyed to have his calm broken. Then it was nothing but static.

She couldn't win. Eventually, Dolores came to dislike her son's empathy intensely. She worried it would hold him back, distract him, keep him worrying so much about others he'd be unable to look after himself. Her son's empathy was just another one of his father's "gifts." Why take on another's misery when you had your own to deal with, was her feeling. But there was Silas, after she and Amos had been fighting, standing in the doorway of her room crying because she was crying without knowing why in the world either of them was crying. It was like he was trying to take the pain from her, as if anyone could. Old pain was heavy in the heart, hard to move, and anyway, Dolores Umber kept a tight hold of her pains and grievances. She thought her pain was the last thing she really owned, the last thing that she could keep all to herself. Her very own thing, and she didn't much care for the idea of someone else trying to take that away from her too.

◆ ◆ ◆

Amos Umber had been gone for three months.

It was a Tuesday.

Silas was on the porch for a change. Paint was peeling from porch rails, and he was pulling it off like dried skin after a sunburn.

He was wearing the usual, too, clothes that hung on him because they were slightly too big. He was on the tallish side, but in between more usual sizes, so the pants that fit him almost everywhere were always a little too long. His mother did no hemming, although she used to embroider years ago, so the pants Silas wore were frequently frayed along the bottom edges. This infuriated his mother, and Silas knew it. But if she wouldn't hem them, they'd stay long, a symbol of her inattention. He even left her a note on the near-empty fridge:

Things Mothers Do
1. Keep food in the house
2. Wash clothes
3. Stay sober
4. Say "I love you"
5. Hem pants

It was a stalemate Silas was willing to live with, and apparently, so was his mother. They both knew it wasn't about the hem on a pair of pants. One of them was mourning, the other was not, and their individual reactions to Amos's disappearance created a powerful tension. The air in the house was charged with it.

Silas knew, instinctively, that mourning required people. Effort. Community. Although he had been to only one funeral and hadn't at the time been allowed to participate in it fully, something deep down in him told him that sadness is best when shared out among others. His mother believed anything that caused distress was a weakness, something that might embarrass you in front of the neighbors. It was plain in the days following Amos's disappearance that whatever had happened to him, his wife and son would never be able to agree on how to handle it. So Silas grew sadder, more detached. The fatherless world he now lived in left him with no one to talk to, no one to help him see his fears as part of something reasonable, practical, or even natural. Every day Silas felt like he was standing at the edge of a cliff, and try though he might to see how deep it was below, or catch a glimpse of the land on the other side, he couldn't see anything but his own feet wavering against a chasm.

It had been six months and one week since Amos Umber had disappeared.

Silas was in his room, looking over his collections. Old things lined the bookshelves. Odd, old-timey things. He took some objects down from the shelves and lined them up on his desk. Then he'd put some back, leaving others in the desk collection. It was as if he was arranging the pieces of a puzzle without knowing what it was supposed to look like.

As a boy Silas had collected everything. It might have started because his mother would never allow him to have pets. So he brought home rocks, interesting bits of wood, books he would buy with money his father gave him. And as he got older, Silas became more and more his father's son. He had boxes of small bones he'd find among the bushes in the park. Silas would draw them and try to figure out what animal they might have belonged to.

A fox skull sat in front of him. He was watching a sliver of late-day sunlight make the teeth of the bottom jaw spread into jagged, pencil-long shadows on the surface of his desk.

Mostly he brought home books. Saltsbridge had a few bookstores, their shelves filled with new novels and cookbooks, but Silas hated these. There was only one bookstore in Saltsbridge that carried old, used books. Antiquarian books. Books with leather covers and engraved images. The owners knew Silas well and would look out for things they thought might interest him.

Looking at his bookcases, Silas saw what he loved best: books on folklore and ghost stories. Books about magic, a photocopied manuscript on medieval sorcery, a thick, broken-spined leather tome about Renaissance astrology. Books about bizarre customs, lost ceremonies. Things folks in Saltsbridge didn't care about or even know existed. If he could afford the book, Silas would buy it. Often, his father would add related titles to his growing collection, always quietly left on the edge of Silas's desk sometime during the night.

While Silas looked at the books on his shelves and stacked next to the bed, he could remember when he'd seen each one for the first time at the bookstore. Surprisingly, the local store was usually well stocked, because the owners visited the surrounding towns, small ancient seaports whose inhabitants had long ago brought books with them from across the sea, and so still had libraries with curious subjects on their shelves. These were bought cheap from desperate folks selling up and moving on. While the bookstore owners might have gotten more for such titles as *The Sworn Conjuring Book of Honorius* in a handsome translated and reprinted edition, it pleased them to see books like this go to Silas, who was so desperate for them. His eyes opened wide when he held such books and turned their stained pages. Besides, in Saltsbridge, who else was buying anything but romance novels and Westerns?

Silas looked at the empty doorway and could almost see his dad standing in it.

Sometimes his dad used to come in, spot a curious title among the stacks of books piled around the room, and sit down for a chat.

"Do you believe in this, Bird?" Silas remembered Amos once asking him, after he thumbed through a volume filled with drawings of conjuring circles inscribed with the names of spirits. Often his dad would call him "Bird," and when Silas was younger, or he was feeling fragile, "Little Bird," and it always made him feel better. When he had been really young, there was a song about birds his dad would sing him when he couldn't sleep. Silas could remember their conversations as if they'd all happened only the day before.

"Well," said Silas, sitting down on the edge of his bed to consider his dad's question, "I think it was true once. In the past, someone believed in it, and it was true to them. And maybe," he added after a little more thought, "these things might still be true, or might be real again, if someone needs them to be."

At first Silas liked the subjects simply because of their strangeness, but slowly he began to believe in the possibilities of what he was reading, in a world filled with secrets and magic. When he was younger, he'd suspected his father believed in many of these things too, so that made it easy for them to talk. As he grew older, Silas began to see the glimmers of hieroglyphic logic behind the occult. There was a reason for these oddities to exist, perhaps as strange connections between the mind and the things people feared or desired. Magic was a conversation. Ghosts were real, and they were watching because something had happened that necessitated their presence.

Silas began to see this mystery as part of a process, an arcane mechanism that fueled the inner workings of the world, but a part of the world known only to a very few special people. That made it all even more exciting. This hidden world where magic worked and ghosts walked was like a secret club. His dad belonged, and the more Silas read, the more he could belong to the club too.

There was one moment when Silas thought, *Yes, now I'm in*.

Around his neck he wore a pendant his father had given him on his thirteenth birthday. From a finely made silver chain hung a silver coin set in a sort of frame with clasps to hold it securely. On one side of the coin was a wreathed head in profile. On the other, a head with two faces, one looking left, the other looking right, a small door below them. His father told him it was a very old Roman coin.

"Whose head is that?" Silas asked immediately.

"Ah, that is, I believe, Emperor Nero," his father told him in a scholarly tone with a mock British accent—and a smile.

"No, no. Not him. This guy." Silas turned the coin over and pointed to the head with two faces.

"Oh, him," Amos replied knowingly. "Well, why don't you see if you can find out for yourself? Put a few of these books we've collected to some use."

It took Silas less than five minutes to find a name to go with the two-faced head. But when he asked his father why he'd given him the coin with Janus on it, Amos got quiet and seemed a little distressed and sad, like he didn't want to talk about it. "I've had that coin for a very long time, but it's time to pass it on. Please keep it close. Besides," he said, speaking softly now, "you never know when you're going to need a little pocket change."

Silas could feel when the pendant touched his chest that it was already warm. This was his father's thing. Silas had seen it on him, and his dad had been wearing it right up to the moment he gave it to him. When Silas looked up, he saw that his father's eyes were tearing up.

"Dad?"

"It's all too soon," Amos whispered, "but I will not take it any further. I cannot. Maybe you will be able to . . . ," but his voice broke and he trailed off. "Maybe you will be able to make something of this."

Amos put his hand to his son's chest where the pendant lay, over his son's heart. He hugged Silas and said finally, "Let it remind you that you have choices and to keep your eyes open, Bird."

"And look both ways when crossing the street?" Silas added, smiling, trying to cheer his father up.

"Yes, especially when crossing."

Since his father had disappeared, Silas hadn't gone to school more than a couple of times a week. He did his work in a perfunctory manner, and when approached by his teachers about his irregular attendance, he told them his family was having a difficult time.

He just couldn't be with people. There were a few kids he sometimes spoke with at school—at lunch, or walking home—but months ago even they had stopped trying to talk to him. Silas had no real answers for their predictable questions.

"Are you all right?"

"Don't know."

"Any news about your dad?"

"Nah."

Easier just to stay home where he could slip through most days more or less unnoticed. Not wanting to add to the family's grief, the school let him graduate without any fuss. Silas didn't attend his graduation, despite his mother asking him about it repeatedly. The day after the graduation ceremony was held, his mother brought home a cake from the market. They sat in the kitchen, each picking at their piece of cake with a fork.

When his mother asked about college, Silas looked away without answering, then left the room.

"Just glad we got through high school, right?" his mother answered for him into the air. "No real plans after today, right, Si?" she yelled after him. "No *real* plans?"

He had plans, but his hopes for higher education, like all his others, were built on "mights." He *might* go hang out somewhere, with someone. He *might* get a job and earn some money. He *might* go to college, a really old school with gray stone buildings and an enormous library. He was thinking of applying next year. Maybe the year after. He wasn't thinking about application deadlines. That sort of detail wasn't a part of his plan. Not at the moment. And why tell his mother about this anyway? It would rekindle her expectations, and she'd only start riding him again. Better to let it be. When his dad came home, they'd sort it out together.

His mother retreated into her world, Silas into his. *What a family*, his mother would say, but until now, Silas had never realized that they weren't really much of one. The names of the days retreated from them both, and soon after the school term ended, Silas was no longer sure what day of the week it was. Every morning when he woke up, he missed his father more keenly than the night before, but the details and differences of each day blurred and eventually vanished. For Silas, the passage of time became a longing ache in his heart that grew daily worse.

Twice a year, by tradition and without fail—once when the weather got warm, and again when it turned cold—Dolores sifted through the family's closets to get rid of anything beyond use, and she insisted Silas do the same. Silas had taken a blue blazer, just a little too small for him now, from the closet to throw into the "give away" box. He remembered this jacket. His mother had bought it for him for special occasions, although there were not many of those in his family, so Silas put it to another purpose. Sometimes when he ditched classes, he went to the cemetery in Saltsbridge. It was quiet, and the few people there had their minds on other things; it wasn't the kind of place anyone was likely to look for a kid cutting school.

Floral Hills was an enormous property, meant to serve the now sprawling suburbs of Saltsbridge, as well as the older town of Kingsport to the north. It was built to be a "proper" cemetery for local people after Lichport began its descent and rumors had started circulating abroad about the numerous "irregularities" in "that forsaken place by the marsh." Floral Hills, it was clear, was built by people who cared more about money than about the peace of the dead or the bereaved. It was filled with "art," the largest and most garish reproductions of the world's masterpieces. There was a poorly made version of Michelangelo's *David*, with hands far too small for the big body. There was a garden of tombs displaying a copy of the Winged Victory of Samothrace at its center. Everywhere you turned, these sculptures rose up as if to say, *Look here! I was a very important person in life! Isn't this place tasteful and cultured?*

Silas enjoyed the cemetery's visitors. Some came to pay respects to loved ones. Others were tourists, attracted by Floral Hills's garish advertisements along the highway. These people wandered the property, viewing the monuments and taking pictures, as though they were on vacation in Rome. It wasn't long before Silas found other ways to amuse himself. He started wearing his blue blazer to Floral Hills and would give tours to the sightseers. He knew the grounds well by that point, where the famous people were buried, and even knew a bit about some of the sculptures. What he didn't know he made up.

After a while, to make it more interesting, he began to invent stories about some of the people buried there, sometimes quite elaborate family histories. The storytelling lasted only a few weeks because honestly, it made him feel guilty. He meant no harm, but they were lies he was telling, and he got a sour taste in his mouth when he told them. And sometimes, when he spoke the names of the dead and attached them to things he'd made up, he had the unsettling feeling he was being watched, listened to, and hated.

It was eleven fifteen p.m.

Dolores Umber was not quite sure how many months her husband had been gone. More than seven.

She held a gin and tonic in her hand because when she tried to set things down, sometimes she dropped them. The heat of her hand would warm the drink too fast, so she sipped quickly. She was pretty sure there wasn't much gin left in the house.

Out of gin and tired as hell.

She could see her son was tired too. Exhaustion and depression floated like bruises just under the skin of his handsome face.

In her presence, Silas wouldn't retreat from the belief that his father was alive. He refused to back down, though she knew he must have *some* doubts. She knew what Silas wanted. He wanted *her* to believe Amos was alive somewhere. Silas wanted help, clinging to his hope. She knew her son. For all her dislike of how much he was like his father, she knew him. She suspected that under all his yelling about not giving up, far, far down inside him was a place where he might just barely consider that he would never see his father again. He needed to visit that part of himself more often, let it out, let it breathe a little. She knew that if he did, he might start feeling like she did: a little guilty, but relieved.

She could see Silas wasn't sleeping well, and how jumpy he

was every time the phone rang. He was tired. But what was his losing a little sleep compared to what she had lost? *She* was tired, damn it! Tired of living without for so long. Tired of living with a man who cared more about the dead than he did about how or where his family lived. And she was tired of being the sensible one, the one telling people to get on with things and to stop dreaming about what wasn't likely to happen. She'd given up her dreams a long time ago, so now it was someone else's turn.

More than anything, she was tired of looking into her son's eyes and seeing how much he wished at every moment that his dad might come back. Silas's neck was taut as a bowstring all the time. And his eyes were like headlights, wide open, staring at every corner, as if his father might be hiding somewhere and if he didn't spot him fast, Amos might slip away for good.

All day, every day, he carried the weight of his father's absence squarely on his shoulders and his alone, because Dolores knew that if she gave in, even a little, he'd be moon-eyed and stupid forever, just like his father. Amos had traded away a chance for a decent, normal life. Was it too much to ask that their son have a chance to be happy?

She was weary of fighting with her son and just wanted to start over. But whenever she tried to move something of Amos's, or worse, throw away some worthless piece of paper her husband had left lying around, even the newspaper Amos had been reading right before the night he didn't come home, Silas would blow a gasket. She usually gave in, but there was a price for her retreat. She would go right to the bottle and drink until she didn't care that her son probably hated her. She knew she and Silas didn't see eye to eye on most things, even before Amos died, when she was sober a little more often. But couldn't two people still love each other even if they didn't understand each other? *Am I thinking about Silas or Amos now?* she asked herself as she nursed her drink.

How alike they looked. At least, Silas looked a lot like how Amos did when she'd first met him. *Fine* was what she'd called Amos, back in Lichport, when their parents introduced them: *a fine-looking boy.*

Dolores didn't like thinking about the past, about how Amos used to be, because that's when the brakes came off. Lord, but she did love him in the beginning. Hard to admit it now, but oh, it used to feel so good, holding hands, just looking at each other. He'd touch her cheek and she couldn't remember her own name. Amos would set those eyes on her and there was nothing else in the world. That's what hurt the most: thinking about how much she'd loved him when they got married. But it wasn't long after the marriage that the nuptial fires began to cool, because Amos turned more and more toward his work. She'd hoped when Silas was born, Amos's delight in her might be stoked again. No luck. Once old Lichport got its hooks into him, it was all over. He took to Silas right away, but he didn't look at her very often after that. Now, when Dolores gazed at her son, she saw Amos's cold eyes looking back at her, and she could feel herself filling right up with all that old hurt and anger and jealousy. And what was she jealous of? Of Silas? Of *them*? Of those folk Amos claimed to help? *Please,* she thought, *what kind of man prefers the dead to the living? My man,* she told herself. *Mine does.*

Dolores had started grinding her teeth. She took another sip of her warm gin and a deep breath after that.

I'm not drunk.

"Comfortable" was the word she used. *Be quiet with that noise of yours,* she'd sometimes yell down the hall, *your mother is just getting comfortable.* When she was comfortable, she was more honest. Wasn't that a good thing? The way she figured it, every parent is also a person, filled with inconsistencies and human error and occasional pettiness, so what? *We're all just people*, she told herself. She assumed some parents kept the truth from their kids, learning to bite their lips and fight only when their kids had gone to sleep. She wasn't that kind of parent. She said what she meant. Here comes some honest talk from an honest woman. And if that made her a bad mother, well, just someone tell her that to her face.

She needed to be comfortable when she spoke about Amos to her son. The truth wasn't easy to say, wasn't easy to get out, so she had to coax it a little. Just being honest. The boy needed more honesty in his life, so she'd let Silas hear anything she could think of, any disappointment she'd ever had, any of Amos's shortcomings she could remember. Sometimes she thought she might have taken it a bit too far, but the liquor pulled the wall down so low it was easy to get at and share even her oldest and worst memories. She desperately wanted Silas to see his father as she had. With eyes wide open. But with every revelation she handed to him, he just distrusted her more. Like it was all her fault. Amos had lied to his son every single time he saw the boy. *Mortician my ass*, she thought, and laughed, *but I'm the one Silas doesn't trust. Go figure.*

Silas might be awful quiet except when he was hollering at her, but the boy was smart. She knew that. He'd read all those damn books. Smart and good-looking, tall and that perfect nose and good cheekbones . . . those were her gifts, and Silas was wasting them. Most days, you couldn't even see the best parts of his face behind all that hair.

Silas was clever, so why couldn't he just admit that everything she was saying was true? *See? It's okay. He's gone now, I know. But trust your mother for a while, because believe me, hon, we're better off without your father.*

CHAPTER 4

MAIL

SILAS'S MOTHER HAD LEFT THE HOUSE for two days in a row, taking a taxi both times. Each night when she got home, the drinking went on more heavily than usual, so Silas knew something was going on. At lunch the next day he asked his mom if something was wrong, and in a rare moment of clarity, she was succinct and spoke without the hint of impatience or a sigh.

"Silas, I think we are going to lose the house. We have almost no money left. Your father left no money."

"But we own our house. How can we lose it?"

"We don't own it, Silas, your uncle owns it. When your father and I got married and left Lichport, your father had almost no money. Your grandfather was furious at Amos for leaving Lichport and wouldn't help us, and my family, well, let's just say not too many of them came to the wedding. The bank wouldn't loan us the money with nothing to put down, so your father's older brother stepped in and helped us."

"He loaned you the money for the house?"

"No. He bought the house outright and your father paid him rent, though I expect that there were many months when your father didn't pay him anything at all. But your uncle is a generous and patient man, so we're still here. But with no money at all, and good prices for homes right now in Saltsbridge, and times being what they are in Lichport, your uncle can't afford not to sell this place. Not after a year of no payments from your dad."

"So he's throwing us out? I mean, just where the hell are we supposed to go?"

"I told you your uncle is generous. Well, he has come up with a solution. An idea for now. Not forever, God knows, but *for now*."

Dolores reached into her purse and pulled out a letter. Without a word, she handed it to him and walked to the kitchen. Silas could hear her dropping ice cubes into a glass.

A few moments later, Silas was still standing there, looking at the unopened letter in his hands. As though his mother could see him through the walls, Dolores said from the kitchen, "Go on. Read it, Si. Then start packing."

Silas turned the envelope over in his hand. It was heavy, good quality paper, but when he took the letter from the envelope and opened the carefully folded paper, it felt damp, and he thought he smelled something like stale candy.

Dearest Dolores,

It is my most ardent wish that you will not think ill of this intrusion, either of its timing or its sender. A year, it must be agreed, is ample time to grieve, even for a great loss such as yours.
As I know you are all too well aware, the house you and Silas occupy was partially paid for as a gift to you and my brother upon your nuptials. The remainder of the mortgage was to be paid in regular installments by my brother to me. I had hoped this arrangement would allow you both to begin your life in some comfort,

even though it meant your departure from the loving company of your families. I hoped, as you did, that your move would be the beginning of a marvelous adventure. It appears now that many of our dreams have not been realized.

In a perfect world, all would have been well and Amos would still be with us and regular payments would have been made. Indeed, had Amos followed everyone's advice and sought more gainful employment, the mortgage might have been long ago paid off. This business has been hard on everyone, and it brings me to a difficult decision. The house must be sold. I simply cannot continue to bear the financial burden of a second property as I have my own family's welfare to consider, a son beginning his first term at an expensive private college not least among them.

However, let it not be said I take and give nothing, or that I have given little thought to you or your son, my dear nephew. Kin cannot be turned out into the streets, and of course I realize you are descended from a fine Lichport family and should be, now most especially, allowed to live in a manner more in keeping with your upbringing if not your marriage. Here, in

Lichport, within my own house, there is room enough for you and my nephew for as long as you should like to stay.

Dolores, I know you hold Lichport in little regard, and the thought of returning here on the charity of your husband's kin may be less than welcome at this time. I beg you to consider your son, who is now fatherless. I would maintain him as though he were my very own. Should he make plans to attend college, I will cover the costs, yes, as though he were my own child. For the memory of my brother, I would gladly take on this sacred duty.

The day you took my brother's hand in marriage, a bond was forged between our families, for good or ill. Let me now, in friendship and with true and appropriate affection, extend to you my own hand at this, your hour of need.

It is no secret that my brother and I quarreled often over the years, and he turned away from my friendship and sober advice, choosing instead to squander his days in the pursuit of what I have always considered a distressing line of "work." Let me now, by offering you shelter, succor, and the protection of my own humble house, here, in the safe harbor of our ancient neighbors and acquaintances,

*show you the depth of my love and
affection for my family.
Your loving brother and friend,
Uncle*

Nearly everything about this felt wrong, but Silas didn't know enough about his uncle, really, to either put facts to his fretting or set his mind at ease.

His uncle's name was Charles, but he had been given the nickname "Uncle" when he was younger for his habit of playing rough with the other kids, and it stuck. No one called him by his first name. Hadn't for ages. Silas didn't like it. His dad never spoke very well of his brother, so Silas had a hard time believing this was all kindness between kin. But maybe his unease was more about his mother than his uncle. Hadn't she always aspired to better? Now here comes Uncle Umber with his big fine house. "Come on over!" Uncle calls, and his mother starts running.

But there was Lichport, and on that point, Silas felt a little differently. To imagine walking the same streets his father walked made his heart quicken. At least there, in Lichport, he might be able to find out something about his father. Maybe people had seen him. Maybe someone there knew something.

So he decided he would go and try to make the best of living with his uncle. *Think of it like being on vacation*, he told himself. At least he'd be away from Saltsbridge, and for the moment that would have to be enough.

The day his dad didn't come home, it was like a huge window over their heads had shattered, and every day they were walking through the broken pieces. Nothing fit together. Nothing made sense or seemed connected to anything else, and every step hurt.

Maybe in Lichport he'd find a missing shard or two that would help him start piecing things back together.

"Okay," Silas shouted to this mother in the next room, refolding the letter and slipping it back into its envelope.

"Okay, what?" his mother said hesitantly, coming to stand in the doorway with her hands on her hips, expecting a fight.

"We'll go," Silas said quietly, hugging his mother tentatively before walking quickly to his room and closing the door behind him. There, he began sorting his belongings into piles on the floor. All the complicated arrangements he'd created over the past year—the little altarlike clusters of books, rocks, and curios—were now being taken apart in preparation for packing as if they'd never had any meaning at all.

CHAPTER 5

PORTENTS

THE TIDE WAS FLOODING FAST, leaping up over the rocks, churning itself into spirals of foam and bladderwrack, pushing higher among the piles of driftwood abandoned above the high-tide mark left long ago by a storm.

Mother Peale stood watching the quickening flood from the wharf-side, wondering how high it might get.

"Company's comin', and that's sure," she whispered into the still evening air, and then began to sing softly, just breathing the words out into the twilight. "Who will it be? Who will it be? Shall we dig 'em a grave, or set table for tea?"

If the strange high tide was any hint, someone was coming home. In the old days, Lichport folks could always tell when a ship carrying kin was sailing into port because the tide would flood in high without a storm, without so much as a breeze. But kin ships were not all that came in on a flood tide. The portents hailed worse, things that ought to have stayed out at sea, things best not to set eyes on.

A black dog was sitting at the edge of the pier, barking.

No good, she thought. *That is no good sign.*

Someone was coming in by land, she could feel that, but this omen—the dog—told her trouble was coming on the flood, too. Looking farther out over the water, she could hear a sound, soft but sure, something like the creaking of timber and a distant cry, like someone might make from the bottom of a well if they survived the fall.

By land and by sea . . . it made her think whatever was coming from either way was no accident. Maybe connected. Maybe not. Whatever was out there on the water was a fair bit off yet. So she turned back toward the land and closed her eyes. She could see farther that way. She drew the dark night close about her like a shawl.

Yes. Yes, she thought, opening her eyes as she began her short walk home. *Let the child come home again.*

She could hear Mr. Peale hollering within the house even before she'd crossed the threshold. He was having one of his fits. Mother Peale walked in quickly and saw her husband sitting in his chair by the fire. He was covered in sweat, his wet hair plastered down onto his skull in strips and his night clothes clinging to him, yellowed and translucent.

As she entered the room, he threw back his head and yelled, "There is a shadow on the sea, my girl! Wandering it goes, yet sure it comes to harbor! The ship of air . . . the ship of mist . . . Hold fast!" And before Mother Peale could cross the room and soothe him, he jumped from his seat, his eyes still closed, and began leaping on the stones near the fire in a sort of dance, singing out,

> Hear the wailing of the crew,
> Hark! There's the tolling bell!
> Away! And weigh the anchor,
> A ship sails forth from hell!

Had it been a hundred years? Fever or no, she knew her husband could see the truth in the turning tide. The mist ship was coming into harbor, and before sailing forth again, it would take a soul with it out of Lichport and into perdition.

CHAPTER 6

CARRIAGE

IT WAS THE BEGINNING OF THE END of their time in Saltsbridge. The day before departure. It had been quiet in the house all morning. Silas and his mother were each doing their own last-minute packing, but there was a heaviness in the air. Too many boxes unfilled and unsealed. Too many things still to sort out and no time left. Silas was trying hard to ask his mother only easy questions, the kinds of things you could answer with a plain fact.

"What time are we driving to Lichport tomorrow?"

"We aren't driving," Dolores said a little smugly. "We are *being driven*. Your uncle is sending a car for us."

"Okay, then. I'll drive over myself in the car while you're chauffeured."

"That might be difficult, Silas. That car's gone."

"What? What do you mean, gone?"

"I mean it's gone. I sold it. Go look in the garage if you don't believe me. How do you think we paid for the movers?"

"What the hell are you talking about?" Silas yelled, his calm shattered. "That was my car!"

"Si, it was your father's car—"

"It *still is* his car!"

"It *was* your father's car. And when he . . . didn't come back . . . it became *my* car, and I sold *my car* so I could get some of *our* things to *our* new home and pay to put the furniture in storage because we can't just go redecorating the house of our host. You understand that, right?"

Silas couldn't speak. He was beyond angry. No car? What would he do if things in Lichport went bad, or he hated living with his uncle? He'd always assumed he'd have a way out, but, with no car, now what? Not to mention, his mother had just pretty much admitted that she thought his dad was never coming back. He ran to the garage and opened the side door. Even as his eyes adjusted, he could feel the unfilled space in the way his quick breaths echoed loudly off the floor and walls.

It was all falling away, everything he knew he could count on. All vanishing. And tomorrow he was leaving for Lichport. He'd be just another item on a growing list of things that weren't where he needed them to be.

Dolores sat on the porch, watching the movers carry all her marked boxes across the yard. Only the boxes with her handwriting on them were being stacked in the truck, while Silas's boxes of books sat idle in the driveway.

"Well?" she said as though someone was secretly questioning her. "What if there's not enough room for important things, for the valuables? I don't know why you're taking all your father's old books along. They're rubbish anyway."

"These are my books," Silas said calmly, not wanting to argue with her again today.

"They are not your books!" she insisted, and then sneered, "Your *dear* father bought most of those books or slipped you the money for them. Money that might have been better used, I might add."

"Do you see him around?" Silas asked, rising to the offer of a fight after her remark. He hadn't forgotten she'd sold the car.

She glared at him from her chair on the porch, her eyebrows and lips pulling thin as if someone were standing behind her and making a knot of the flesh on the back of her skull.

"No. You don't," Silas said flatly, answering for her. "So that makes them mine. But," he added out of spite, "when he comes back, I'll return all the books if he asks me for them."

"Besides," she called back over her shoulder at Silas, unable to let him have the last word, "haven't you washed your hands of school? Didn't you call it quits at high school? No college, right? At least, not in the foreseeable future. You'll *see*, right? So all that reading, it's just a waste of time, isn't it?"

"I *did* graduate, or don't you remember? You bought a cake," Silas said coldly. "And I'm not wasting time. Time is what my father left me, and I'm keeping a good hold on every second, even if you have made other plans for yourself and forgotten your obligations." Then he walked up to her chair and leaned over to whisper, "But it looks like you need another drink. Can I bring you something from one of the crates? Perhaps you'd like to join me in the kitchen to see if we can find a bottle that you haven't already emptied?"

Dolores didn't reply with words, but her hands, dry and chapped from days of wrapping everything she loved in layer after layer of paper, were clutching the arms of her chair like claws. Forget her obligations? Her? Run from them, maybe, but she'd never forget them. She had sunk down into herself, into a seated, crouching posture that said, *Try and get me out of this chair, and go to hell while you're at it*. Besides, she knew there wasn't a single bottle in the kitchen that had even a drop in it. The well was dry.

So she just sat there while Silas stormed back into the house, just sat, watching the men make a river of her belongings across the lawn. Down the steps and across the stone pavers set into the lawn like little islands on a wide green sea. One, two, three. The movers were timing their steps so their feet came down in the middle of each stone. One, two, and just there, under the third stone, she remembered, there was a little corpse, another thing being left behind.

In her mind she could see Silas as a boy sitting on the lawn in that very spot, carefully digging a hole. She remembered his slow, deliberate movements as he gently placed the mouse wrapped in one of her good linen napkins into the ground. She was about to start yelling about the napkin when she saw Silas take a handful of small seeds, the mouse's favorite food, and cast them into the little grave. She asked him, more annoyed at the action than the theft of the napkin, "What the hell is the food for?" And she'd never forgotten his answer, which he said so slowly and carefully, as if he thought she didn't know English—

"So he knows I love him."

She knew then, all those years ago, that Silas would be headed back to Lichport, that he was his father's son. She never would have guessed that she'd be returning with him. She could have done with forgetting a lot of things from the days when Silas was little. But gin never seemed to work quite as advertised on her. She remembered a lot. Too much, she thought, getting up to go in to get a drink, maybe from a bottle she'd hidden in the bathroom.

"You okay?" Silas asked, trying to make peace.

"Damn dead mouse," was all she said. But she thought: *A dead mouse gets to stay put, but I have to move. Christ.*

Although she had actually admitted to wanting to move into a bigger house, and knew that Charles Umber was a man of some remaining means, she didn't like to do anything because someone else's actions made it necessary. Her husband had failed to come back. Failed to support his family. Failed to raise his son properly. Failed to save them from bankruptcy and the awful but necessary charity of family. Failed to keep them out of Lichport like he'd promised when their son was born. She could blame him for these things until the day she died, and in that, she took some comfort and eased her grasp on the chair just a bit. Was it so much to just want a normal life? For things to be unremarkable, simple?

Maybe in Charles Umber's house, with all that good furniture and art on the walls, things might get easier for once instead of harder. If only he didn't live in Lichport. Maybe she could convince him to move someplace nicer. What did he have to tie him there? Unlike Silas, Uncle's son was in college, and his wife had abandoned them long ago. There. They already had something in common. She knew he was sweet on her. Always had been. She could see that in the way he'd looked at her years ago. Maybe this could turn out okay. Big house meant some money, savings. But back in Lichport. Maybe she'd get some brochures of condos in Florida, leave them around the house.

But Lichport.

Right back where you started, she told herself. *Right back in the middle of that town. You were out*, she told her heartburn. *You. Were. Out.* Her father once told her that when you leave a place, you should never go back, because no matter what the actual circumstances, it will always look like a retreat, a failure. That was sure how it felt. As the men with the boxes flowed past her chair, her mind began to make a list of things in her life for which she was now being punished. But this time there would be a fine house and someone with money looking after her.

But Lichport! Every time she so much as thought the name of that town, she felt nauseated and nervous.

◆ ◆ ◆

Silas looked at his mother in her chair. He could feel her doing that *list* thing, where she didn't speak or look at you because she was tallying something in her head. Figuring out how bad you'd messed up.

Yet, seeing her like that, he started to feel bad for having taken such a nasty tone with her. Didn't she have enough to worry about without him being such a pain and trying to pick a fight?

He looked around the living room, empty except for a few small boxes and the luggage that would go with them in the car. Where the furniture had been, Silas could see marks sunk into the carpets, footprints of the arrangement of their life here in this house. In that moment, he felt like the illusion that his family had become was held together only by the constellation of patterns left by the furniture feet set on a rug, by the runes formed in the shadows that the chair backs threw on the walls, and that once those things were moved or faded, he wouldn't know who he was anymore. All the pictures had been taken down, and the walls were scarred with the holes of rusted nails. When he passed his hands over the holes, he could feel little jets of cold air blowing into the room from the space beyond. He leaned his head close to the wall and felt a pencil-thin stream of air on his face, and the sound of it escaping from behind the walls was like one soft, continuous exhalation of breath, like the whole house was dying.

CHAPTER 7

NIGHT TRIP

FOR SILAS, LICHPORT WAS ONLY A NAME, like that of a distant cousin or a dead relative he'd never met. Familiar but abstract. Even though Amos had told his son about Lichport many times, the town had always felt far off, a place that kept his father from him. Although he'd been born there, it was like a foreign country to Silas. Now that he could feel the night wind on his face, now that the car was driving swiftly in the direction of that otherworld, Lichport was becoming more real, part of an actual landscape that he was just beginning to be able to see.

What is it about traveling by night that makes even a short journey strange and a little wonderful? Momentary lights appear and pass across the windowpane so fast they burst suddenly into view before becoming patterns of the past, stars that grow ever more distant as they follow their opposite course away from the car as it hurtles on its way through the darkness.

As Silas rolled down the window, the smell of the salt marsh and the distant sea flooded the interior. He imagined his father driving this same road hundreds and hundreds of times. He could feel his father's history like ruts worn deep in the road. He wanted to walk where his father had walked. Wanted to live where his dad had spent so much of his time. *That's how you'll find him*, he said to himself as he put his hand out of the car into the night air, feeling the wind push against his palm. His mother was dozing and didn't notice they had crossed from the town into the empty lands surrounding it. As the biting air buffeted his face, he realized he was holding his breath the way you do when going through a tunnel.

Everything was changing. Silas brought his hand back into the car and reached into his pocket, taking out a folded piece of paper, the last thing he'd taken from his desk before the furniture had been carried away. He opened it and read the words he'd written just before his dad disappeared: "Do It Now List. (1) Start on English paper, (2) CALL HER, (3) Talk to Dad about a car, (4) Get college application stuff."

Not one thing on the list had been done. He'd passively ignored any plans to pursue college during his father's absence. Silas put his hand back outside the window, holding the paper by the corner between two fingers. He watched it blow wildly for a moment in the night air before letting it go.

The car turned left down a road marked by a worn and bullet-riddled sign, briefly illuminated by the headlights as the car slowed. The sign leaned precariously toward the highway, as if it was about to fall over. The old white decorative letters could still be seen to proclaim with a misplaced funereal enthusiasm:

WELCOME TO LICHPORT—COME FOR THE DAY, STAY FOR ETERNITY!

The car slowed almost to a crawl as it drew toward dark shapes ahead. The moon was very bright and lit the town and surrounding country in a milky light. The first buildings of Lichport's main street rose up in shadow ahead. Silas could see a church steeple in the distance and a hill curving upward like a bell. He knew—but could not see—that the sea flowed away to the east beyond the far side of the town.

On the left side of the car was some open ground, a millpond with the moon reflecting on the water, and beyond it the salt marsh stretched out and faded away where a small, silhouetted line of reeds pointed up at the cold stars.

There was a light over the millpond.

As his mother softly snored, Silas saw it, flickering, hanging above the water.

"Could you stop the car, please?" Silas asked the driver, staring hard through the window.

"Sir, we'll be at your drop-off point in five minutes."

"I've gotta pee," Silas lied. "I mean right now."

The car pulled over and Silas got out. He walked past an abandoned shop, its windows long since boarded over, and made his way toward the millpond. The light was still there, like a candle flame, floating above the water. It gave no reflection, but as Silas approached, the light wavered and slowly drifted toward the bank where he stood with his feet almost touching the water. As the flame got closer, it grew brighter and smaller, a tiny star hanging low in the air, but as Silas reached out to touch it, the wind rose and the light dropped suddenly into the pond and vanished. Silas realized he had taken a step forward, and his right shoe was now half-submerged in the cold water.

In the distance, the long, searching cry of marsh birds sounded from among the reeds. As water seeped into his shoe, Silas looked down. It seemed that the bright reflection of the moon had somehow pierced the water. The small light now seemed to have settled at the bottom of the pond, where it illuminated various silt-covered shapes and a few pale sticks. A trick of the moonlight, Silas thought, and he leaned down until his face was just above the water. Something was moving at the bottom. A fish? Perhaps the rising wind rippling the water's surface was stirring the silt on the bottom. The water seemed pretty shallow. Again, maybe a trick of the light, but Silas thought he might be able to reach the bottom. He put his hand onto the cold surface of the water. He was about to stretch his hand below toward the objects that reflected the glow of the bone-white moon, when from behind him, the driver's voice called out, "Sir? Sir?"

Silas walked quietly away from the millpond.

Below the surface of the water, something stirred, awoke, and watched him walk away.

CHAPTER 8
THE WHITE THINGS
THAT ARE MINE

ABOVE THE WATER, SOMETHING LOOKED.

Below the surface something saw.

She could feel him.

She wanted him and began to stir her mind up from the murk
and mud.

> *I am here, where I was*
> *I am Be.*
> *The high torches bring shadows*
> *grasses turn, weave about, fold and flash, leaves above,*
> *some sink down*
> *bright leaf, dark leaf, catching the torchlight.*
>
> *Even in dark nothing is still*
> *little crabs move along all the white branches and I can-*
> *not sleep*
> *eels thread through the hard sticks that are mine and I*
> *cry because I am not with him*
> *not warm*
>
> *when jewels are in the water weeds it is quiet*
> *nothing breaks the high still glass above*
> *he has not been*

once a time
anyone is not there
is not saying my name
I want to be
I want to be
I am again
but now and there on the glass
his dark moves
moves for me to be
to be with him
the dark on the glass is Solace
we will be
now in the bright time
he puts his face down to the glass
looks low for me
he is looking
looking down for me to be with him
he was again
I did not see before when my own blood men took the
thyme he gave me and put me in the cold bed and I
thought he left and always
forgot the thyme he gave me wild
from the mountain time
there was another
But I did not forget
that one did not want to be with me
But I did not forget
Even when the crabs and eels and the white things that
are mine were before my eyes and I saw little in the glass.
But again
he wants to be with me

my Solace

the low places will be high places he will give me thyme
again
he will make cold bed into crystal fountain like the words
he gave me and upon it he will pile all the flowers of the
mountain
I will go
I will go
I hear that song again
he looked upon the glass
looked for me
I will go
I will Be
I will go and will hold thyme again
the thyme he gives me
our time will be
I want to Be
I will comb my hair
I will rise up
I will Be
and he will be with me
and I
will not
come back
to this
cold bed
alone.

CHAPTER 9

SIDEWALK AND STATUARY

THE CAR PULLED UP TO UNCLE'S HOUSE on Temple Street, and the driver removed the suitcases from the trunk and took everything up to the porch before opening the car doors for Silas and his mother. He told them good night without looking up, got back in the car, and drove off. Silas could see confusion on his mother's face. Maybe Dolores had been thinking the driver was in Uncle's employ, which they could both now see was clearly not the case. So much for Dolores's hopeful plans of chauffeured shopping trips in the far more fashionable town of Kingsport.

Silas didn't really care who had hired the driver, but he was wondering now if anyone, *anyone*, in his family owned a damn car. Didn't people travel? Run errands? Maybe Uncle had a garage around the back and kept his car in there.

The house was crisscrossed with shadows from the high trees, and the moment Silas took a step toward his new home, he felt dizzy. It was like the time when he was young and had a high fever, and the margins of the room and the world disappeared. There were no walls, no floor or ceiling, just some infinite plane stretching out from him. He stood there, waiting on the sidewalk, convinced that when he took his next step, he would fall into empty space.

"Silas?" his mother said impatiently. She had already stepped onto the columned porch.

"Coming," Silas replied. He took one step and held fast. He paused another second, while he waited for the earth to fall away from his feet. When it didn't, he began to walk slowly up the steps to his uncle's house, where he saw the massive front door open like a giant's mouth. The iron door was ornate but impractical, and Silas could see the frame had long ago been reinforced to support it on large hinges. It certainly was much older than the house. His mother looked different in the light pouring through the doorway. Her back was straight. She walked right in like she lived there, without hesitating even a moment on the threshold.

It was long past dusk, but a whip-poor-will in the tree next to the house continued making its call, over and over, filling the night with its name.

To this lonely song, Silas slowly climbed the seven steps up to the porch of the house where his father was born. He paused at the threshold. His senses were floundering for associations, something to tell him, *You belong here.*

Silas stepped inside and heard the heavy door close behind him. To his right in the parlor, he could see that the windows looking onto the street had decorative shutters across them, with just a thin line open at the top to allow some moonlight in.

Uncle stood proudly in the center of the front hall, ready to welcome his kin, and he filled the room with his posture of ownership and a big, forced smile. Silas looked away to better study the details of the house, but then Uncle made a grating sound that pulled Silas's attention right back to the center of the hall. It was hard not to notice that his uncle's jaw moved back and forth slowly, as the top and bottom teeth ground together.

Just as suddenly as the grinding sound started, it stopped, and some other part of his uncle's body began moving and twitching.

It seemed as though a part of Uncle was always in motion. Maybe he was excited to see them, or just nervous.

Uncle must have noticed Silas staring at him, because he stared back now, seemed to lean into the stare, as he extended his neck out like a probe. He walked toward Silas and put his arms around him briefly and stiffly, in a perfunctory hug.

"Welcome home, my boy."

Then he moved across the room to where Dolores stood, and Silas continued his quiet assessment of his uncle's looks while the two made small talk.

Uncle was well dressed, but Silas wondered what the occasion was. Was he trying to impress them? Who wore a dark business suit to celebrate his bankrupt relatives coming to live with him? *Maybe he's just a little vain*, Silas thought. People with money and houses like this sometimes were, he assumed. Uncle wore a tie, looked like he always wore one, and the knot was pulled tight as a bead. From his cheeks, his face drew down to a point at the chin, and he had a way of holding his head with his neck forward and dropped slightly so that the point of his chin appeared to be balancing on the knot of his tie. He seemed to smile a lot, but under the lines of his face, muscles strained. His suit, which Silas was pretty sure was his favorite because it was a little worn at the elbows and pant cuffs, was pressed, although not too neatly, because Silas could see there were little wrinkles on it that had been pressed flat, almost like the fabric was really dark striped skin. The tips of the lapels were not flat, but curled up slightly, as if they were peeling away from his uncle's body. For the most part, Silas found his uncle's appearance more comical than strange.

Silas turned his attention to the front room next to the hall where they stood. Looking in, he guessed this was the drawing room, where guests had been received in the past, and the family would gather to entertain themselves. Silas's initial impression was that it might be okay in here. It was clean. His uncle kept a lot of books. He liked that. There'd always be something to read. There were stacks of books by all the chairs and sofas.

The rest of the house was very quiet, hollow-sounding, almost, but there was an antiseptic smell Silas didn't like.

Many of the objects on display were very old, or seemed so: chipped stone carvings, animal and anthropomorphic forms maybe from the East that were wrapped in ancient stained bandages. Alabaster jars with the heads of animals. But his uncle waved for his attention, back in the front hall, and said there would be time for a real tour of the "collections" later.

Although Silas was attracted to the museum-like clutter, the closer he looked, the stranger and stranger his uncle's house became as it revealed its contrasts and tensions. It was like a movie set, meant to look real, but something about the light wasn't quite right. Silas couldn't put his finger on it. So many old things, crudely preserved, oddly shaped, but so carefully displayed. At the foot of the stairs stood some kind of stuffed monster with the legs of a small hippo, the body and fur of a lion, and the head of a crocodile. Silas was sure it had been mummified.

"Ah! You have an excellent eye, Silas!" His uncle beamed as he stood next to the grotesque statue. "You like my Eater of Souls? Egyptian. Exceedingly rare. When the Egyptians died, they came before Osiris, the god of the dead, to have their hearts weighed. If the heart was found, well, lacking, then the soul was devoured by Ammit, the Eater of Souls. Isn't that extraordinary? No afterlife, merely an eternity of dissolution within the belly of our friend here."

"It's great," Silas said, both intrigued and disquieted by the statue. On the one hand, he wondered what kind of person would keep such a thing on display in his house. You'd have to look at it every day as you descended or climbed the stairs. On the other hand, a part of him was very curious about his uncle's love of the past. An Umber trait, it seemed. But the "Eater of Souls" made him uneasy, not just because the thought of a sculpture made from stitched-together animal parts was gross. Silas was thinking about its story—what it *ate*—what owning such an object said about his uncle's . . . interests.

"Why don't you let me show you to your rooms so you can freshen up a bit, and then I'll have Mrs. Grey bring a little light supper up to you, as it's rather late? I must apologize, but I have some important work I must finish tonight. Let us all plan then on a good night's sleep, a lazy day tomorrow, and a nice family supper, all together. Indeed, let that be our family ritual each night, supper together to share our news of our daily adventures. Shall we?"

Not waiting for an answer, Uncle started up the stairs, and as he mounted the first riser, he let his hand slowly brush across the top of the Ammit, as though he were petting the head of a child or a dog. Silas could see his uncle must have done this a lot, because the bandages on the statue's head had long since been worn away in just that one spot and the ancient, pitted skin of the crocodile was showing through.

CHAPTER 10

BRING HOME THE CHILD

MRS. BOWE WAS POLISHING HER CRYSTAL, although she didn't know why she bothered. No one called anymore, so there was hardly any need to set the table. It had been ages since anyone had come to see her and even longer since she'd left her house. There was just no need anymore, especially not since Amos had disappeared. She suspected that after so long, folks got tired of always having to come to her. Groceries were delivered. Mail, too. And she could always rely on the bees, from which much news could be gotten so long as she remembered to share her news with them in return. Sometimes folks walked by and she might say hello from the porch. Or seeing her sitting by the open window, they'd call to her from the street. *Good afternoon*, she'd say, as if she were about to alight from the house and come down to the sidewalk for a chat. Other days it felt like she was the only person living in Lichport. Regardless, she couldn't bring herself to leave the house. Not unless there was a funeral, but even then, she'd hurry back, almost running. Otherwise she'd only come out to walk in her garden, or work in its well-tended beds, hidden behind a stone wall and high gate, or to hang up the laundry because she would only wear clothes that had been washed by hand and set to dry in the open air.

She deeply disliked being so fearful, but had actually grown rather comfortable over the years with disappointing herself. She used to try. Just leave the house by the front door once a day. Then, after a while, she'd try for once a week. Then once a month. Then, *Why bother?* she thought. *Let the world come to me, and I'll set out a little lunch.* What she hated most was that she'd become one of *them.* Another Lichporter grown self-indulgent and eccentric, the subject of sidewalk gossip: *Oh, her, Mrs. Bowe . . . yes, yes . . . so sad. She doesn't leave the house, you know, unless there's a you-know-what, not unless someone D-I-E-S.*

But there was just no need to leave the house. Out the door and down the steps there was only trouble waiting. And here, among her things, there was only good. Good memories. Love. A dearly beloved past that still attended her and kept her feeling safe. Here, in this house, her recollections glowed like embers on the hearth, and each night, in their warmth, she'd take a memory or two down from the shelf and dance with them for a while.

Of course, it was easier when Amos had lived there in the house attached to hers. She liked having a man close by who could help her from time to time, or talk with her. She still would not venture down the front steps on her own, but he was always coming and going, bringing news from outside, although some-times no news might be better than the kind of news he had to share. But she knew about his work and helped him. That was traditional. To assist the Undertaker, and only for that, would she make her way down those steps, and only with Amos by her side. A woman of her family always helped the Peller, as he was once called, although Amos Umber never cared for the term "Peller," or "Expeller," preferring simply "Undertaker." Even long ago, back in Ireland where her mother's people came from, even in the small villages, there was always a woman like her there, at the time of passage. Dark work, but needful, and she was proud of her name and the work that came with it.

She had taken each piece of crystal out of the carved cabinet and had arranged them all on the large mahogany dining room table, where the moonlight could fall on them as it passed through the window. Then she gently picked them up, one at a time, and slowly wiped over the surface with a piece of soft cloth to remove the dust. When she finished one piece, she set it back on the table and picked up another, a small sphere of smoke-hued quartz. One of her mother's folk had brought this crystal with her across the sea when the Bowe women came first to Lichport, and her own mother had used this crystal more than any other. The stone was very clear, only a few veils and fissures inside it to catch the moonlight and make it dance when she turned the stone and then looked into its depths. It was hard not to look. How the light swam inside it! How the smoke swirled within! And before she could look away, the veil drew aside and she could see a scene play out in miniature pantomime before her eyes, down deep within the stone.

At first it was like looking at something at the bottom of a river. Then slowly the vision became bright and clear, and because of its sharpness, she knew that she was seeing something that was happening at that very moment, here, in the present. The past was cloudy, indistinct, blurred along all its edges. The future was even harder to see, often very dark, like sifting through murky water for something lying at the bottom, and just as soon as she could begin to see what it was, it slipped from her hand and was below the surface, hidden in the mud again. In and out of focus, never still. That was the future. But now, before her eyes, the vision was clear as you please, like looking out a window.

Within the stone, a woman stepped out of a car and toward a house, followed by a young man who paused, waiting on the sidewalk. As Mrs. Bowe had been taught to do, she "pushed" at the vision with her mind and the details grew smaller, but she could then see more widely, as though a camera were pulling back from its subject to reveal more of the world around it. She knew that house. And she knew whose house it was, with its high roof and black eye windows and strange columned temple at its side. This was local. Here. In Lichport. Just a few blocks away from where she was sitting.

She drew the stone up to her eyes for a closer look. She was now looking right into the woman's face. She did not recognize it immediately, but after a moment she began to remember someone she used to know, but had not seen in a long time. Was that Amos's wife? In Lichport? This made no sense to her, for of all the many people who'd left Lichport, here was one she was sure would never come back. Back in the stone, a tall man stood by the open door of the house, then walked up to the woman, to Dolores Umber, and seemed to welcome her into the house. As they stood in the light of the doorway, they cast long shadows down toward the street and looked like they had been cut out of black paper, so bright was the light coming from inside that house. What reason could she possibly have to be calling at the Umber place? Perhaps some family arrangements were being made. He was family, after all. Had something happened? Was there news of Amos? Had he been found? Had he come home?

But then the tall figure stepped onto the porch again, coming back into focus, and it took all of Mrs. Bowe's remaining fortitude not to drop the stone at the sight of Charles Umber. That was a face she did not wish to see. He lived just a few blocks from her, but safe inside her home, it might as well be a thousand miles away. She'd have preferred that. She tried very hard never to think of him, although they'd been close enough once. Her father had even once thought that Charles would—No. Let those days stay out of reach of her mind. But who could forget such a person, or what he'd done, or—*Enough*, she told herself. *Don't let him in. Look away from* him, *but* look again.

Look again.

And for a moment the scene in the crystal tilted, and she was looking up the side of that house and at a window set high in its wall. Then a cloud began to draw across the stone, pulling a shadow between her and the window. She pushed again with her mind, and suddenly a mouth flew open inside the stone in a silent scream and she nearly dropped the crystal. Regaining her composure, she fanned her hand across the stone's surface as if brushing aside the awful image of that pained, distorted face. Oh, God, she thought, was it Amos? No. Surely she would have been able to see him more clearly, feel his presence. Enough.

Look again.

The scene returned to the sidewalk.

She could see the young man very clearly now, though a mist was rising in the stone. She thought she had never seen him before, yet how familiar he looked. A little awkward, stooping slightly as he waited outside the house, but handsome. His Roman nose, an Umber trait, so familiar, and the hair worn long and in his eyes. So like Amos.

In that instant she knew who the young man was, and she choked back a sob. Of joy or fear she couldn't tell.

Amos's child had come.

Amos's son.

Come now, to that dark house. She felt cold from the ground beneath the floor climb up through the boards and up her spine like a rising damp.

"Holy Mother," she said, setting the stone back onto the table and closing her eyes, "Holy Mother, watch over him."

The moon was up and bright. She wrapped a shawl about her shoulders and went quickly toward the back door that led down to her garden.

The bees would have to be told.

CHAPTER 11

QUIET VOICES

UNCLE ENTERED A SMALL CHAMBER on the second story and locked the door behind him, one lock after another, seven in all.

With his company arrived, Charles Umber felt, finally, a little hope, but care would be required. He had become very used to doing whatever he pleased in his house. Now he would be sharing it with others, and accommodations would have to be made. Alterations to the routine. Circumstances had already been changing in the Camera Obscura—his name for this chamber, because once, long ago, he'd used it as his dark room. Now his photographic equipment had been moved into the outer chamber, and the Camera served another purpose.

The room had had many uses over the years, even before he began spending so much of his time here. The oldest objects, pushed under tables and stacked in the corners, were the kinds of things one might find in an attic. More recently the room had been used as a nursery, a bedroom, and a playroom, although the walls, padded, hanging with manacles and various restraints, belied any visions of a joy-filled childhood.

Uncle's eyes were rimmed with fire from weeping and lack of sleep. He was exhausted from having spent much of the last two days scrubbing the room from ceiling to floor, and for the first time in years, it didn't smell like piss.

Under the table, a few forgotten toys had escaped his notice.

The more Uncle looked, the more reminders of childhood he could see hiding in the corners. Hardly a room for a grown man, he thought. Perhaps it was best things had ended when they did. Now there would be a change.

A change!

He spoke to the other in the room:

"Metamorphosis . . .

"We can begin again.

"Company is here. Your family is here. We'll be all together. Won't that be something? All together. They have made their way to us from afar, driving across the black land to our little patch of sunshine! You'll hear their voices through the walls and floors. Everywhere, the sound of family. Your family. Our family. Won't that be fine!"

Uncle's mouth turned down just slightly. He was telling himself a story. He wanted to be hopeful. This last year had been unbearable. He still had to keep this door locked to keep the other in. Further measures had been required because the room's occupant was so strong. Locks. Bindings. The inner door was covered with chalk drawings that seemed to be working. No more escapes. No more mad scenes in other parts of the house. Everything was calm now. Contained.

Charles Umber looked forward to the future.

There would be metamorphosis. A rite of transformation, a rebirth. And a new thing is so like a child. So much easier. Excitement began to rise in him again, and, unable to control himself, he spoke once more into the room.

"You are safe. Rest awhile. Your life was all hardship. Be at peace and prepare. Prepare. The worlds divide. The form remains. The spirit rises purified and reborn, a child of gold! Oh, creature of shared blood, be cleansed! Endure! War no more with thine own flesh, for it is preserved in peace and is now a holy place, a hallowed shrine. . . ."

He stopped just as his voice began to rise, remembering himself and the houseguests who now occupied bedrooms in the east and west wings of the house. Better to assume that he would never have the complete privacy to which he was accustomed. He looked at the massive door. The locks would keep them out, and it was a large house. But the house had many hollows behind the walls, gaps between the floors and ceilings, and sounds ran through such spaces like scurrying mice. It would be hard to know just how far his voice, or any other sound, would carry.

"So you see? We shall have to make some accommodations. Quiet voices. *Sotto voce*, if you please."

Uncle had been spending more and more time in the Camera Obscura, and that would have to change too. One of the chains on the wall shook against its rusted bracket. "Yes, I'll still be here, but I can't sit all day in this room," he said, feeling guilty. "I must prepare. Please understand. No matter where I am, I am always thinking about you. Always."

Across the room, several books fell to the floor with a loud thud, as though they had been pushed from their dusty shelves.

"And that is precisely what I am speaking of. Please trust me. I need a little time."

Uncle stacked the books into a pile. He paused to hold a small volume between his hands like an open Psalter, as his eyes ran over the lines of a favorite page. Then he closed his eyes and said, quoting aloud,

> "Broken in pieces all asunder,
> Lord, hunt me not,
> A thing forgot,
> Once a poor creature, now a wonder,

A wonder tortur'd in the space
Betwixt this world and that of grace . . ."

"Yes," Uncle said with concern, "it has been all affliction for you, but rest assured, a change is coming. Metamorphosis. Resolution and the rising soul!"

He looked through the thick glass.

Its eyes were closed. No. One eye was open just slightly, and Uncle knew it was looking at him. Seeing him through that gray eye, somehow. Hearing his words. Waiting for his words, assurances, promises of what was to come . . .

"Be easy now," Uncle said soft like a song.

"You are home.

"You are home.

"You are home."

CHAPTER 12

NEW DIGS

THE NEXT MORNING SILAS AWOKE to a quiet world. He could just hear the sound of running water downstairs, but the rest of the house was silent. Outside, not even a car could be heard.

He got dressed and made his way down to the kitchen. He enjoyed the way the thick wool Persian carpets throughout the house felt on his bare feet. It was like walking on warm moss.

When he reached the kitchen, he saw a woman bent over the sink as she washed pans. She was dressed in a faded blue dress and wore thick-soled shoes. She didn't look up, but said, "There's a plate of breakfast in the oven for you, Master Umber. Real eggs. Fresh."

Being called "Master Umber" seemed much too formal to Silas, so he replied politely, "My name is Silas. Please, call me Silas."

"I know your name, Master Umber. I knew your father when he was a young man." The woman turned to face him and stared Silas up and down. "You have your father's look about you, and there's the truth," she said. She opened a cupboard and brought out a jar of peaches.

"Have you seen my father recently?" Silas asked very suddenly. He knew it wasn't polite, or proper, but he was interested in her reaction.

The woman's hand must still have been wet from the washing, because the jar of peaches slipped from her grasp and shattered on the floor. Thick syrup pooled out from among the fruit pieces, most of which were now shot through with shards of broken glass.

"I'd prefer not to talk about your father, Silas, if you don't mind. I am much saddened at his loss. He was a good man, although your uncle wouldn't care for me saying so."

Silas felt the little hard edge to her voice. She was uneasy. Maybe because of his comment, or maybe something else. Her face was the surface of a stone and revealed nothing. Silas couldn't even tell quite how old she was. She was stooped a bit and her face was careworn, her eyes circled with lines and arcs, but she might easily have been sixty or eighty.

"May I ask your name?"

"You may. I am Mrs. Grey."

"Have you worked for my uncle for a long time?"

"I have worked *for this house* for many years. I knew your grandfather."

When she said "this house," Silas could tell she wanted him to know that she didn't consider herself her uncle's employee, but instead, somehow, was part of the house itself, like the carpet or the roof.

"So you are to live here now," she said without any question in her voice. The sink faucet dripped as they talked, one quick drop after another, like the mechanism of a clock.

"Yes, but, well, I'll have to weigh my options," he answered wryly.

"That's good," she said quietly, "for the danger lamps are lit all the time now, and there's the truth of it."

The kitchen door opened to reveal Uncle in the doorway. Mrs. Grey turned quickly back to the sink as she quietly resumed her work. Uncle ignored her.

"Good morning, Silas. Excellent. Do take your breakfast where you please. I thought the fresh eggs would be a treat. Now, your choice: the den, or the parlor? The porch is warm this morn-ing. It looks to be fine weather. I shan't join you, as I've a little work to do in my study. Do forgive me. But if you like, shall we meet in a couple of hours for a little informal tour of the house? That will give you some time to unpack your things. I'll fetch you at, say, ten?" His eyes were wide as he spoke, like an actor onstage presenting a well-prepared monologue.

He waited for no reply before he turned quickly and left the kitchen. Silas could hear his uncle's footsteps on the stairs.

"You see, Silas," said Mrs. Grey, as she turned toward him again. "You can see it in his eyes. The lamps. The danger lamps are lit." She looked at the empty doorway where Silas's uncle had just been. "You be sure you don't spend too much time locked away in this house. Plenty to see. Indeed there is. Plenty to see in Lichport. You be sure to get out when you can. You understand me, Master Umber? Get out when you can."

Silas smiled at her, but suspected there was great precision and meaning in her choice of words.

"I'll just eat in here, if you don't mind, Mrs. Grey."

"Your uncle won't like to know you're spending so much time in the kitchen, but you must suit yourself."

From a high-backed chair perched near the rail of the second-floor landing, Uncle had been watching and listening to Silas's movement downstairs for some time. He liked this chair with its heavy carved lion's-paw feet. In it, he felt as though he was resting at the very center of the house. He could see the wide hall below and through the doorways into the front rooms. He could, by craning his neck, look down the entire length of the north wing. A simple sweep of his head one way or the other revealed to him both the east and west wings.

He saw Silas come from the kitchen—where he had obviously

eaten his breakfast—and watched him make his way to the parlor, where he paused—mostly out of view—for twenty-two minutes, perhaps reading? From there, Silas crossed the hall again and opened the front door, rather tentatively, and enjoyed twelve minutes of sunshine on the porch before coming back inside. He then stopped in the hall and had a good look at the mummified Ammit. Uncle watched the boy regard it from several angles. *He is intrigued*, thought Uncle. *This is good.* He stared quietly at his nephew, then coughed lightly to make his presence known and descended the stairs just as Silas had begun to pull gently in an exploratory manner at some of the ancient linen bandages.

"A natural archeologist!" Uncle exclaimed, startling his nephew who quickly pulled his hand away from the wrappings.

"Shall I show you a few more things that might interest you?"

"Please," said Silas.

Quiet. Reserved. Inquisitive. *Good*, thought Uncle.

Uncle led his nephew into the drawing room.

"Please. Do look more closely."

Uncle watched as Silas rose up on his toes and bent over to examine the contents of all the shelves he could reach. Sometimes he nodded, as if he might know what an object was. With others, his nephew simply turned a particular specimen over and over in his hands, both mystified and apparently fascinated.

"I see you are intrigued by Egyptian funerary sculpture."

Silas had been looking at a small ceramic statue in the shape of a wrapped mummy. It was no more than ten inches long, glazed bright blue, with a short inscription carved down the front length of its body and a longer text incised down its back.

"I am here," Uncle intoned.

Silas was amused at this, and replied, "I know. I am here too. We're both here."

"Ha! What a wit you have. No, no. That is what the little man says: 'I am here.' The Egyptians believed that when one read the inscription, the figure would come to life in the tomb to serve its master, because in order for some to enjoy eternity, others must perform a service. Reasonable enough, no? Surely you see the wisdom of such a doctrine? The honor of enabling the immortality of your betters. Isn't that wonderful? Your father, forgive me for saying so, could never see the elegance of such a practical philosophy. If only I could get it to work! This house hasn't had a full staff for years."

"Did you collect all these yourself?" asked Silas with genuine interest, ignoring his uncle's attempts at humor.

Uncle wondered if the boy might not be a little resentful at the cost of adding to or maintaining such a collection while he and his mother were, in essence, homeless.

"Oh, no, Silas. Much of this collection goes back a very long time. And this is by no means all of it. Your father, I think, spirited away a number of intriguing pieces over the years, although I suspect they were sold. What you see here is the work of many generations of Umbers. Some of these specimens were brought over the sea with the first of our ancestors who came to Lichport. And, of course, through my business, I have been able to add many excellent objects to these shelves."

Uncle walked to the end of the drawing room and opened his favorite cabinet. Here he kept what he called the "experimental" pieces.

"Look here," Uncle said, as he beckoned Silas over to him with one hand and held up a large bottle of blue glass. "Herein, tradition and the auction record assert, a homunculus was grown in the eighteenth century."

Uncle could see his nephew was unfamiliar with this term and elaborated.

"Homunculus . . . a little man. Certain preparations were

made, all very secret, some say involving mandrake root, others insist . . . well, on even more obscure methods. All manner of ingredients were put into this bottle, which was then buried in dung, for warmth, for the span of thirty days. When that time had passed, a little man would have formed within the glass. Wondrous. Fed on honey and milk. When grown, it would protect its maker and might live forever."

Uncle handed the bottle to Silas, who held it up to the light and peered inside. Uncle could see him scrutinize its contents. Had the boy perhaps noticed the small pile of dust encrusted on the bottom or that tiny, partially formed bone? Uncle gently took the bottle from Silas's hands and returned it to the shelf.

"It is my hope you will enjoy studying the objects collected here, Silas. This is your house now. These things were all collected by your relatives. So now, you and I, we are the keepers of these sacred things. It is our job, indeed, our obligation, to learn as much as we can about them and their secrets."

Uncle saw his nephew's eyes glimmer with what appeared to be pleasant surprise at being tasked with such a responsibility. "What else would you like to know about?" Uncle asked him.

"Everything," Silas said, staring at a bowl filled with carved jade cicadas.

"Would you believe that in ancient China, these were inserted into the corpses of the elite to insure their place in the after-life? The cicada was seen as immortal, the human body merely a cocoon, a requisite prelude to eternity brought about by the metamorphosis of death. Why, did you know, in Persia they . . ." He paused momentarily, smiled at his nephew's obvious fascination, and said, "Perhaps we should find you a notebook."

CHAPTER 13

PRESERVES

SILAS WAS HUNGRY. He had spent all day in the drawing room taking notes, listening to his uncle, and making his own small drawings of some of the ancient things. He was still resolved not to like his uncle, but now that Silas knew he was part owner, in a way, of everything in that room, he was determined to enjoy his share of the "inheritance," even if it all technically belonged to someone else.

His mother hadn't cooked at all in the weeks leading up to the move, so both of them had made do on canned soup and whatever else they could find in the pantry. Now on the table in front of him, set out on an intricately worked but yellowing lace tablecloth, was more food than he'd seen in one place in a long time. Strange, though, Silas thought, because little if any of it that he could see was fresh or cooked. Maybe this was the custom in Lichport? There were several kinds of pickled vegetables and preserved fruits, olives swimming in little china bowls of brine, salted nuts, some kind of smoked fish, and a silver platter of thinly sliced cured meats. The room smelled like vinegar and melting wax, which was dripping from numerous tall candles set into tarnished silver candleholders. There were so many candles burning that the room felt warm. Maybe his uncle thought his mother looked better in candlelight.

"I hope you are fond of preserves. These days, who knows where things come from or who might have handled them. The eggs were a bit of a treat for your welcome breakfast, but I think you'll find our usual fare far more sustaining, in the long run."

Looking out over the table, Silas's stomach knotted with appetite, but he couldn't bring himself to eat. More than anything, suddenly, all he wanted was fresh food. How long have those olives been around, he wondered. Everything that comes from the earth must return to it. Everything. Yet here was a dinner of *remains*. So even when his uncle invited him, saying, "Sample anything you like, be at home here, my boy," it only made Silas feel worse. It was as though eating even a single mouthful would have been the signature on some kind of unspoken bargain between him and his uncle. Although his uncle hadn't asked anything of him, Silas knew one bite would let some other world inside him, into his mouth and stomach, and the thought sickened him. He told himself he was just tired, that it was too much too soon; that it was all too new. After all, he'd enjoyed exploring the museum in the other room, and breakfast had been good. Why should he feel so differently when it came to this food? *Enough*, Silas told himself, *enough. Give the place a chance. . . .*

"Do you have any fruit?" Silas asked in a low, queasy voice.

"Oh, Silas!" his mother exclaimed, clearly embarrassed.

"I'm sure there's something, maybe a jar of peaches, in the kitchen," his uncle said, as he strained to keep the tight, sharp edges of his mouth pulled upward in a not particularly pleasant smile.

"I think you're out of peaches."

"Really? There must be more in the cellar. But I see by your hesitancy we've offended you already. Well, we shall all have to become accustomed to one another's ways, I think. In the fullness of time, in the fullness of time! In the meantime, let me see what I can find for you."

"Don't trouble yourself!" his mother called after Uncle, but he was already up from his chair and headed into the kitchen.

A minute later Uncle returned, beaming, holding a small silver tray with a single red apple perched precisely in its center. He set this down in front of Silas with mock ceremony, smiling all the time, and returned to his dinner, which, never having been cooked, had not cooled noticeably in his absence, but smelled as though it had warmed slightly in the heavy air of the dining room.

Silas thanked him and looked down at the apple. He picked it up to take a bite. It felt soft in his hand, and as he turned the apple around, he saw the other side was brown and bruised with rot. Uncle seemed to smile with self-satisfaction as Silas returned the apple quickly to the tray and rubbed his hand on his napkin.

"You see? Preserved is always best. Lasts nearly forever that way. No nasty surprises. Now," Uncle said, apparently prepared to mount the aforementioned expedition to the cellar for dessert. "Who wants jarred peaches?"

Silas chose to restrict himself mostly to nuts and olives because they seemed somehow safer, more natural than the strips of translucent meat. He had been eating slowly, as he watched the two of them talk for over an hour, and what a script. His uncle appeared almost gleeful as he talked about the other families in town who were dying out, or leaving, as if he wanted the town all to himself. There was an edge to his uncle's tone that seemed arrogant and a little mean: a note of superiority.

His mom and Uncle then turned to Amos as a topic of conversation. Although they were clearly being careful about what they said, trying to be pleasant, cordial, respectful, every now and again one of them said something that proved neither of them had much esteem for Amos Umber. Silas looked down at his plate while they spoke, chasing olives around with a fork.

"Always undependable," one said.

"A little weak when it most mattered," replied the other.

"Youthful temperament, even later in life."

"Soft."

Silas pretended to be distracted, allowing them to continue talking freely as if they were alone.

His uncle and his mother seemed to agree on everything they said about his dad, but there was something different about the tone of their comments. Silas tried to read the rise and fall of their voices, the angles of their necks, the arch of their eyebrows, and after a while, he thought he saw what the difference was. His mother was pretending, trying to convince herself that Amos was dead and she knew what had happened to him. His uncle, Silas suddenly felt, was lying and rather enjoyed doing it. Uncle knew something about his father. And worse, Uncle seemed to take pleasure from knowing things other people didn't. Silas did not like thinking this about the man who'd given them a place to live, but there was a sort of smirk hidden inside his uncle's words that made Silas feel like he was being laughed at. He knew that tone. He'd heard it often enough from kids at school, from the ones who'd look at you like you weren't worth talking to, from the ones who looked at your unfashionable clothes, or the shape of your face, and told everyone else that you were a freak. Silas was scared of those kids, because usually, those were the ones who didn't think that normal rules applied to them, the ones who thought they could get away with anything.

Eager to be thought a pleasant conversationalist, his mother had been asking a string of questions as the candles at the dinner table burned lower and lower in their tarnished silver candelabras. Uncle answered everything cordially, although Silas could see him gently steer his mother away from certain topics, like his wife. It was clear to Silas that his uncle didn't care much for that topic when Uncle said merely, "Oh, I hardly think of her anymore. I mean to say that a man can only endure so much heartache and then must either expire, or do the best he can and not look back." Dolores looked impressed with his answer and so continued on, obviously enjoying having a man's attention on her, especially when there was candlelight to improve her complexion.

Silas tried not to look at his mother, because she had this simpering smile plastered across her face every time she gazed across the table at Uncle.

"And what of Adam? Still off at school, is he? You must be so very proud of him. A son at college in Europe! What parent wouldn't be bursting with pride at such a child?"

Silas deliberately ignored that question, which he knew was as much for him as it was for Uncle. It was going to be one of those nights where she'd sink her teeth into a topic and keep chewing and chewing at it.

Uncle looked up just briefly and then replied, "Oh, goodness yes, though that boy is costing me a fortune in upkeep! Not to mention tuition. But I don't begrudge it. When he graduates, he'll have his pick of careers. He'll move in the best circles. He'll have a life I never had."

Silas lifted his head at this. "You seem to have done all right for yourself, Uncle."

"You mistake me, Silas. Yes, I have done well and am comfortable here, but I have, on occasion, longed for a life somewhere else. Though I have been fortunate in Lichport. I have had several businesses. At one time, as I think you know, I dealt in antiquities, and still sell the occasional piece. There was an excellent market for such things here, once, and I sold to galleries and collectors all over the country. Again, this was some time ago, but I have invested well and have remained immune to the town's general decline. Perhaps you are not aware, but this town has seen more vibrant days. I have, once or twice, thought of leaving, wondered, *What if?* But this is my place, and I am at ease with my fate. And now that you have come, we might make a new life for ourselves, together." Uncle gazed across the room, over both their heads, perhaps at his reflection in the window. Somewhat dreamily he said, "Having you here, Silas, well, it's like getting to live with the son I never had."

What the hell did that mean? thought Silas. *How long has Adam been away at school?*

"Of course," said Uncle, as he adjusted his posture and looked at Silas again over laced fingers, "I mean, having a young man in the house again will just be so pleasant. It will make it feel like a real family is here, all together again." He looked now, very deliberately and as if on cue, across the table at Dolores, who still had that smile pulled across her face, even as she chewed.

"My dear nephew," Uncle said, "I know the move must be awkward. I suppose you will miss your friends back in Saltsbridge?"

Before Silas could reply, his mother leapt in.

"What friends?" she said through a full mouth. "The only friends he spent any time with were the ones he made up. Oh, mind you, there were plenty of those. I used to remember all their names. Had to, or the little prince wouldn't speak to me for a week. There was this one time—Amos was away, of course—Silas was maybe seven. Guess this was the first time he took it in his mind to leave school. But he just up and walks out of class, right past his teachers and out into the hall. No one noticed. No one knew he was gone. It was like he was invisible, like he lived his whole life at noon and cast no shadow. Well, why would they notice him? Head in a book all the time, drawing those weird pictures on everything, and never caring for anyone other than his father."

At first Silas didn't look up from his plate. Just kept eating. Fork to plate to mouth to plate to mouth to plate. But then he couldn't hold it in and spoke, again without looking up.

"As usual, you have your facts mixed up. I was *always* invisible. That started at home. Remember how you hardly ever spoke to me or asked me how I was? Remember how when you and Dad would start screaming at each other, I never seemed to be around? Just invisible. But I heard every word."

Uncle had stopped eating as he watched what was unwinding between Dolores and the boy. By his posture, Silas could tell Uncle was fascinated.

"But when you made me go to that school, that's when I learned how to take it one step further. It wasn't hard. I'd just repeat over and over, 'Look right through me, through me, through me. I am not here. I am not here. I am not here.' And pretty soon, I just wasn't. I could sit right in front of the teacher and she'd never even see my hand go up. It was magic. I could just disappear. My first spell."

"You pushed them away, Silas. No one will keep trying forever when you just sit there with your head down on the desk."

"Maybe, but when you're sitting right in front of someone and they can't see you, refuse to notice you—I mean, what was I supposed to think?" he asked more forcefully, as he looked directly at his mother. "Of course," he added, "you could make things disappear too, right? One glass after another would just vanish." Silas could see that one struck home, and for just an instant, he could see sorrow and shame in his mother's eyes as she looked back at him, but then the challenge took over again and her back went straight and she slowly turned her head, looking past Silas to Uncle.

His mother shifted the topic, but only slightly, and evaded her son's stare. She said to Uncle, "And if you could have seen the pictures he made. You know how most children draw the same things: houses, suns, flowers, animals? Not this one. Boxes with eyes. Tunnels. Old men with two heads. Whole pictures painted black."

"There were people in that picture, but it was nighttime. Duh. All you had to do was ask where they were and I could have pointed them out to you. Dad always asked."

Dolores looked back at her son as she tried to bring a kindness into her voice that she clearly didn't feel.

"Silas—and hon, I don't say this to be hurtful—it was easier not to ask you anything, because, let me tell you, some of the things you'd say, about people who weren't there, about things living in the basement, about your drawings, about what you saw looking in the window after dark—let me just tell you I couldn't sleep at night for your *wonderful* imagination."

His mother watched him, but he didn't respond. Silas remembered those days, and how he would talk about these "friends" in such detail that sometimes his mother would think someone was with them in the house. "More of your father's nonsense," she would say to him as she quickly closed the drapes or hid his pictures in a drawer.

"Anyway," Dolores said, returning to the present, "we hardly spoke at home, anyway. In the door you'd come, and right up into your room. All day long, in that room, with *them*. And how he'd talk and talk into the air."

"A wonderful imagination indeed," Uncle said, weighing in.

"Yes," said Silas, his face beginning to redden with

embarrassment and anger. "You needed an imagination in my house. Dad worked long hours and probably didn't want to come home, because someone had spent the day drinking and stank of it by dinner. I mean, it took an active imagination to keep from killing yourself in a house like that."

Dolores threw her silverware down on the table and pushed back her chair. Silas said, "Don't bother. I'm going upstairs to my room now."

He rose, thanked his uncle for dinner, and left the room, but he paused on the other side of the door to hear what they'd say behind his back.

"Shall I assume these little flights from the dinner table are to become customary?" Uncle asked Dolores. When she didn't answer, but only closed her eyes and sighed, he continued.

"It's all right, Dolores. A passionate consistency is not unacceptable. A little supper, a little light conversation, a little attitude, a little defensiveness, a little walk around the block to clear one's head. It is good for a man to be regular in the governance of his day's business. That leads, eventually we may hope, to regularity in the habits of the mind and body. Yes. Eventually. So you see, Dolores? Even in such trying moments, there is hope for improvement. He is a remarkable person, I think. Yes. I think he may eventually prove extraordinary. He has important work ahead of him. Be assured of that."

Instead of going upstairs, Silas left the house without even getting his jacket.

CHAPTER 14

FALLING WATER

BEATRICE HAD BEEN WANDERING THE TOWN since before the rain began, following the paths he had walked. She wanted her feet to follow his feet, although she did not go down the lanes of the Narrows, even though she could strongly feel he'd been there or would be going there. Some days past, present, and future were hard to reckon. Anyway, she didn't want to see the ocean. Too much water, and how wide it was. The deep endlessness of it made her feel hopeless. So she was keeping to the little side streets around the square. It must have been late because there was no one out, no one else walking, not that she could see. Something was beginning to pull at her, and without thinking she turned south down Fairwell and walked along the large avenue that would eventually lead to the gates of Newfield Cemetery, drawn by the sense that where she moved, he had moved before, and if she stepped where he'd stepped, they were walking together . . . in a way.

The year was turning. She could feel that much. Strong winds would rush by, briefly blowing the mist aside, and there were the trees that reached up with long arms and fingers, and burning orange leaves setting all the branches to flame. *Like my heart*, she thought. *Just like my burning heart.* She needed to love someone again. Longing gave her back a sense of herself.

She kept walking, farther than her usual and habitual boundaries. It felt good to be away from the millpond, where everything always felt so stagnant. She was following a sound she could barely hear. Like a distant drum, or a heartbeat. But just below the thump, there was pain and anger. Every time the beat came, there was a cry that tore its way up the street toward her like some mad thing running just because it could. And this sound had something do with *him*, with the one who'd looked down to see her. It was connected to him, close to him. That much she could feel.

She wasn't sure how long she had been walking, but when she looked up, she found that she was standing outside a house on Temple Street, and knew that he was here, that he had slept in this house, and that he was in it now. She also knew some of his relatives lived there because she could feel the common blood song inside the place, the chorus of ancestors moving about in familiar constellations. It was late and the house should have been quiet, but as she stood in the street looking up at one of its high windows, a rising howl was making her head throb.

The house seemed to be shaking too, like all its walls were being hit with hammers. If she closed her eyes and just listened to the crying, she thought she could see a figure through that high window, although it was a dark night, and the glass was black. This figure was in one of the upper rooms, and repeatedly threw its head and upper body against the wall of the house, and each time it did, it cried out and screamed, a long, awful, lonely wail. Buried in the piercing volume of the cry she thought she could just detect a word.

"SSSSIIIIIAAHHHSSS . . . SIIIIIAAHHSSS . . ."

It was calling out for someone with whom it shared something, and it wanted that person so much it hurt. She knew how that felt, but this was . . . horrible, a siren of anguish and fear and loneliness.

The rain was coming down harder now, but it couldn't keep

the mist from rising. She should go back. This was not one of *her* places, and she didn't like this street or this house, or that sound, and the longer she listened the more she was forgetting why she'd come here. As she turned away from the house, the front door was thrown open and a tall man staggered out onto the porch with his hands clapped over his ears. He tried to pull the door shut but struggled with it, as though someone was holding the door from the other side. Finally, whatever it was let go, and he managed to pull the door closed. The force of that, along with his pulling so hard, made him fall back, nearly between the columns and down the steps. He looked sick and scared.

He looked back at the house as another scream sounded. He threw his hands over his ears, hunched over where he'd fallen on the porch with his arms wrapped around himself, and began to cry.

"SSSIIILLAAASSSS!"

The scream drove itself out into the night, where it blended with the wind's striving rasp. It was no word at all, but when the scream rose a final time, she thought she could hear what it might be saying. It sounded like a desperate child crying for its parent, and she began to realize that it was saying a name, and the more she heard it, the more she was sure she knew what that name was: *Silas.* She went cold right through as all the recent cheer poured out of her and left her shaking in the air.

She was scared and began to run, passing through the thick ropes of rain that now fell all around her. She ran back the way she came, but instead of going left on Main, she stopped very suddenly. She needed to know that Silas was all right, despite whatever else was trapped inside that house. She turned into the mist on Fairwell once again and in an instant stood once more on Temple Street below the window of what she now knew to be Silas's room.

The wailing stopped.

She could feel Silas breathing in his sleep and focused on that steady, quiet sound. She just stood there, wet right through, water pooling around her, covering her, running over her eyes, down her body. This was familiar. She began to calm. He was all right. He was sleeping. No one else was here. The tall man had returned inside, and the fury that had wracked the house had now subsided.

All this water, she thought. *Time to go home*.

But to be so close to him filled her with such exquisite joy. She knew his name now, and she thought it, *Silas, Silas, Silas*, the name working through her like a spell. Had that always been his name? No matter. She held it in her mind like some treasured thing. She said it out loud, and as the name left her and wove itself with the wet air, she could see him, really see him. As if he had been there all along, waiting just for her. Then and now. Only for her.

Asleep in his room, Silas threw his head from side to side, in the grip of a bad dream that was trying to settle its business before morning. He could hear rain, somewhere.

He knew that he was dreaming and that water was rising all about him. He knew that he was drowning in his dream. There was a girl there. Below the water. She was wet and beautiful and she kissed him as he screamed, and his mouth instantly filled with water.

At that, his eyes opened and went wide, and he sat upright, although for a moment he could see only the distant distorted features of a room, as if through rounded glass, as if he were still underwater.

Beatrice smiled.

It was almost dawn. She liked the morning. As the sun rose, things seemed to make more sense to her. She could remember more, although not all her memories brought her joy. Old thoughts rose up inside her too, and inhabited her again, like fish in a net, blurry and distant but quickly becoming clearer, plainer, more certain as they were dredged up from the bottom. She remembered the last one, the last little fish. How he watched her, and how he would look for her. She remembered how she had followed him and how he had liked it. She remembered how they never spoke, but were often together. Then the last one was holding a child. A boy. How interesting that was, watching father and son, knowing then it might never end, one fish following another, on and on and on. Always someone to love her. She felt an unfamiliar warmth at the endings of her body—fingers, toes, knees, the very top of her head. But the last one—*Amos,* she remembered now—he saw her looking at his child and his face changed, as if he'd just realized there was a knife on the floor and he needed to snatch his child away from it. The father turned very quickly, and the air seemed to close behind him. The mist drew in about him, and she could barely make out his body. But over his shoulder, the child's face was clear and bright, a little sun shining through the clouding mist. The baby looked at her, she could feel it. The child looked right at her and smiled.

And here he was again. But at least now she could remember his name: Silas. Grown and fine and handsome. Like always. She had waited, and at last he'd come.

Then, before she knew it, Beatrice was standing by the edge of the millpond, her feet where Silas's feet had made impressions in the wet earth. In her memory, she watched Silas walk away. When was that now? Then she thought of what might come next. *Tomorrow night. Or the next*, she thought. *We must be careful. Love is fragile and rare and cannot live long in open air.* She remembered her father berating her, her brothers' harsh words the last time they discovered she had a paramour. What was it they said? They were always looking down at her. She remembered being frightened, but now, it all seemed so very far off. Never mind. So long ago. *Let the past fall away, fall away, fall away from me. . . .*

And it did.

Oh, Silas! she thought. *Here you are! Our time has come.*

It was all so familiar now, so right. They would meet here, in the quiet solace below the trees, though many of the trees she once knew were gone. But he was here. He was here. Silas. And she would be with him. She was still mostly cold. She turned away from the water. The fog was receding, and she could clearly see the path to town.

Silas's name was everything, and now she could remember almost nothing of the past. Now was all she had. Suddenly she could no longer recall that it always began this way. Each and every time, no different. And always the same ending. By the time she took her first step toward town and away from the millpond, she had forgotten the awful ending to her own story entirely.

CHAPTER 15

GRAND TOUR

SILAS HADN'T SEEN MUCH during his post-supper pacing on Temple Street last night. It already was late when he departed the dining room. He'd left the table angry, storming out of the house without his coat, so he'd returned not long after, once the cold, hard rain began. The ground floor was quiet when he returned, though he heard people moving about above. Later, from his room, after he thought everyone had gone to bed, Silas heard the sound of running on the stairs, then heard the front door open again, and later still, he heard Uncle muttering to himself as he paced the long upstairs gallery. Boards creaked. The house and its occupants were restless.

Silas awakened early the next morning with a strong desire to see more of Lichport. The street was quiet in the pale light and he was filled with nervous excitement as he stepped from the porch and set off to walk the town. Although he was only partway down Temple Street, he already felt more alive, more himself with each step.

He was fascinated by the variety of the houses, the way they all seemed to come from different periods. In Saltsbridge, everything had looked new and had to be kept that way: brightly lit streets and malls, freshly painted houses built out of things that didn't decay, and they all looked the same, with residents who worked hard to keep them looking pristine, with carefully maintained lawns and tightly pruned trees. "Candyland," he had called it.

Here in Lichport, everything appeared neglected, forgotten, but still somehow sort of wonderful.

When he looked down Garden Street, Silas saw tall, high-peaked houses, each trying to outdo its neighbors. Farther on, there were rambling mansions that overlooked the sea, built up over the years by successive generations. There were entire homes covered in ivy. Many houses had broken windows, and shards of glass remaining in their window frames caught the light and glinted against the blackness behind them. Occasionally he'd hear muffled noises from inside one of the houses or a hidden garden, so he knew that even some of the most dilapidated houses were still occupied. *Who would live in houses like that, with the whole place falling down around them?* Silas wondered. *People with secrets,* he told himself.

On Lichport's streets, the trees were very large and strangely shaped, and he guessed that most had been planted well over a hundred years ago. Most looked as though they had not been pruned in decades, their wildly growing branches reaching higher than the houses. The trees had dropped many limbs—every street was covered with them, and along some of the streets, the branches formed large, brittle hedgerows along the curbs.

Most of the houses, small and large, had what Silas thought of as the "Lichport lean," some oddness of angle, or curvature perhaps caused by settling, that made the neighborhoods look as though they were drawn by children. Many buildings were boarded up; there were several whole streets like that. Fine high houses with their front doors covered over with planks.

On the north end of town, at the entrance to Fort Street, beyond the overgrown hedges, the upper windows of the large houses were dark eyes that looked out over the street. Strange, Silas noticed, that none of the windows on that street had been broken as was the case with the other abandoned homes. He felt uneasy here. Watched. He turned around and went back the way he had come.

All over town, through the overgrown bushes and tall weeds, he began to notice the cemeteries. At nearly every turn of the various streets, a portion of a cemetery could be seen. Practically every corner or lane had some plot with a family name, and as Silas approached the end of Fairwell Street, which dominated the southern end of Lichport, there lay before him what appeared to be a vast necropolis.

At the gates of Newfield Cemetery, an enormous lion stood guard, fashioned out of bronze. Silas climbed up the body and sat between its paws. The warm, smooth bronze against his back was so comfortable that for the first time since arriving in Lichport, he felt the tension in his shoulders unknit. From the lion's view, he stood up and looked into the cemetery, where the crowded plots of Newfield formed another city entirely: a vast city of the dead.

Silas climbed down from the lion and walked up to the far end of Fairwell, toward the town's center again. At the corner of Fairwell and Main, he saw a large, handsome Victorian building with a warehouse attached and a sign that read:

BOWE'S MORTUARY EMPORIUM

MR. EDWARD BOWE, MORTICIAN AND PROPRIETOR

The emporium appeared to have been closed a long time, lock rusted, boards across the door, filthy windows, everything sealed up. Silas wondered if his dad had been associated with it, and the more he thought about it, the more confused he became,

e thought Amos would have been the "Mortician and
"

...he mortuary emporium was attached to a large house that
was itself connected to a second sizable Victorian dwelling. Silas
walked through the park between Garden and Main, around the
back of the houses attached to the emporium. As he got closer to
the gate that ran around the property, he could hear bees, some
of which buzzed past him. He figured that he must be near a hive.
As he tried to find a gap in the foliage, Silas thought he heard a
voice say his name. As far as he knew, he didn't know anyone else
here, so he shrugged it off.

He walked quickly away from the fence and went up Coach
Street, which ran alongside the other boundary of the large,
gated property. He turned again onto Main. A few old cars drove
back and forth, and a truck piled high with boxes turned right on
Coach Street and headed back the way he'd come, likely toward
Lichport's only real grocery store. He passed high yew trees on
his right, and then the front of a fine old house rose up alongside
him, and as he walked by, he heard the voice again, which seemed
to call from behind a high gate covered with vines and climbing
roses.

"Silas Umber!" the voice called, laughing. "Don't you dare
walk off again!"

A little door in the gate swung open, and hesitantly Silas
walked through it and into the garden. A woman held it open as
he entered, and then closed and locked it behind him. Though her
gray hair was tucked up under her hat, Silas thought she might be
in her late sixties. She wore a long sundress and a wide-brimmed
straw hat, and there was a basket of cuttings at her feet. Her gloves
and apron were covered with dirt. She had a kind, inviting face,
and although he'd never been too willing to trust anyone right off,

he was drawn in by her voice. She had enough joyful runes lining her face that Silas knew she was a kind and good-natured woman, that she smiled and laughed a lot. Worry can pull a person's face into a mask of anxious lines, and he could tell she'd had some of that, but even worried folks could laugh.

"Silas, I am Mrs. Bowe, and although I have not seen him in over a year, I am your father's good friend."

The fact that she used the present tense when she referred to his father made him like her immediately.

"I am so happy to see you, though I must tell you, I am concerned about the company you've been keeping," she said, chiding him in a joking tone, and he knew at once that she bore his uncle little affection.

Silas turned to look more closely at the garden, which was beautifully kept, just a little wild around the edges, especially in the corner, where a large crypt stood with its green metal doors open.

"The women of my family are all buried there," Mrs. Bowe told him, as she followed his gaze.

"Where are the men?" he asked.

"Elsewhere."

Silas moved closer to the crypt, but a rising buzz from inside halted his progress.

"The crypt is also a hive, so you'll have to ask the bees' permission before crossing the threshold, I'm afraid."

"It's okay," Silas replied, as he retreated a few steps back. "I don't want to bother them."

Then, very suddenly, Mrs. Bowe asked, "Silas, I wonder if you wouldn't like to see the inside of the house now?"

"Um, okay, sure, if you want to show me your home, that's very kind. Maybe I could trouble you for a glass of water? I've been walking for a while."

"Oh, I don't mean my home, I was referring to your father's. Though you are welcome to tour them both if you like. Your father and I were very close, and nothing would please me more than to have Amos Umber's son as a guest in my house."

His father's house. His father stayed here. His heart began to beat as if, when he opened the door, his father might be standing inside, just taking a rest from the day's bright sun. He knew that was not going to happen, but his blood was pounding through him, making him nervous and anxious both.

"Yes! Oh, yes, please!" he said to Mrs. Bowe, who had already removed her dirty gloves and apron and was opening the back door.

"It'll be easier going in through my house than going all the way around the front. Our homes are connected, you see. You didn't know your father lived here, did you?"

"No, ma'am."

"Well then, here's another surprise. This won't be the first time you've been in these houses. You were born here."

Silas didn't speak, and he felt embarrassed that Mrs. Bowe could see he was becoming emotional. He wasn't crying yet, but his hands were shaking badly and he felt close to tears. She put her hands on his shoulders and said, "It's all right, Silas. This house has waited a long time to see you again. I think it's okay to feel a little . . . overcome."

"Yes, ma'am. Thank you," said Silas, his voice breaking.

She opened a door leading to a hallway with another door at the far end. "That door will let you into your father's house. I think it might be best if you see it first by yourself. This is your father's place, Silas. Part of him is still here, waiting for you. You go on in. And Silas, dear? Everything in there is yours. Everything. You take anything you want, you understand? Anything. Your father's study is just across the hall on the ground floor through the big open doors. Perhaps today, you may just wish to remain on the ground floor. I'm not really sure about the condition of the upper rooms. I'll be right here if you need anything. You just come back here to me when you're done, or give a call and I'll come to you, all right, dear?"

"Yes, ma'am," Silas whispered. He walked down the hall toward the closed door, paused only for a moment, then reached out, turned the bronze doorknob, and opened it.

Right away, Silas could smell his dad. A moldy smell. Not rotten or bad, just the smell of someone who read old books and kept a lot of them around and spent his time in old places. The smell of dust. The smell of the past after it had been put up on a shelf and left to sit for a while. If it were a cologne, it would be called Cherished Neglect. That's what his dad smelled like. Old silver, vellum pages and leather bindings, like a two-hundred-year-old suit of clothes from the attic, like a stack of magazines stored in a basement, like the lining of a steamer trunk that had been around the world, or a blazer that hasn't been laundered in a few years. That much of his father at least was still here.

The quiet reminded him of his dad too.

The waiting stillness of his father's house was so very different from the captive, subdued quiet of Uncle's. That was the quiet of a place holding its breath. Here was the stillness of a home at ease with itself. He felt safe here, surrounded by his dad's dusty things. Comforted by the presiding peace of this house, he realized that at Uncle's, he might always be a little on edge, even when reading or looking over the treasures in Uncle's wonderful collections. Maybe that would pass in time.

His father's large study was on the ground floor of the house. Although it hadn't been kept up well or painted in a long time, there were lots of carved details in the house's architecture that gave the place a feeling of history. Carvings adorned the tops of the doorways, and many of the walls were covered in faded wood paneling.

One entire wall was covered with high bookshelves that spilled over with volumes of every size. Great folios lay on their sides toward the bottom, and right up to the ceiling were shelf after shelf of leather-bound books, vellum-bound manuscripts, nineteenth-century volumes of folklore, whole runs of journals. He passed his hands over some of the fine embossed bindings as he thought, *I am a book also, words and thoughts and stories held together by flesh. We open and close ourselves to the world. We are read by others or put away by them. We wait to be seen, sitting quietly on shelves for someone to bother having a look inside us.* He drew one of the early tomes from the shelf and read its title page, *Anatomy of Melancholy.*

"Mine or his?" muttered Silas to himself as he returned the book to the shelf.

It looked like nothing had been put away or straightened up, so Silas guessed all was as it had been the night Amos disappeared. When he looked around the study, he could almost see his dad sitting at the desk. His jacket was there, hanging from the back of the chair. He wouldn't have needed it that night, as the summer had been warm. Silas took the jacket off the chair and held it up. He brought it to his nose and smelled it. He put it on, slowly, first one arm and then the other. It was worn and comfortable and it smelled like his dad. Book mold and wood grain and something of the sea.

One side of the jacket hung a little lower than the other, and when he looked in the pocket, Silas found his dad's pocket watch. He had seen the watch only a few times before; his dad never took it out in public. It was silver, fashioned in the shape of a skull, very realistic, with great attention to detail. The suture lines on the top of the skull were so carefully engraved. Despite its small size, it felt heavy in the hand. The lower jaw could be unlatched and when open, the watch mechanism, face, and dial—built into the upper part of the skull—could be read. Silas remembered his dad showing it to him the night of his grandfather's funeral.

Silas had not thought about his grandfather for some time, but now, clear as a picture on a screen, he could see him in his memory, just as he did on the day of the funeral. That day was the first and only memory Silas had of his grandfather, although surely they'd seen each other when Silas was an infant, before his mother and father moved from Lichport. At the funeral, Silas had to stand on his toes to look over the edge of the coffin and see his grandfather. Eyes closed. Skin looking like a doll's, painted and still.

A moment later, returning to his seat with his father, Silas saw his grandfather again.

Silas wasn't sure if that was the first time he saw a real ghost, but it was the earliest and best memory he had. Maybe it had only seemed true because his father had believed him. Maybe, looking back, it was just that Silas had always believed in ghosts, as long as he could remember, even before his father had told him they were real and his mother made his father start sleeping on the couch. Silas had looked up again from his chair and was staring at the coffin when his grandfather stepped into the air from somewhere behind the open lid.

Silas glanced down, then quickly back up, and the figure was growing clearer with each breath he took. It stood very still, and the space around it seemed blurred, as if the air was a pane of smudged glass. The ghost looked right at Silas and smiled. Then it put its forefinger to its lips and mouthed the words, *Don't tell.*

When the funeral service was over, he told his mom about the ghost, and she slapped him. Right there in front of everyone in the church, and without even a moment's hesitation. Silas's eyes welled up, but he didn't start crying until they were outside in the car. It was his only trip to Lichport, and he hardly saw any of it, because his mother wanted to pay her respects only briefly at the Umber home and then return to Saltsbridge as quickly as possible.

On Temple Street, at the wake, Silas was dragged swiftly out of the car by his mother and into the family house, then dragged back out and into the car barely five minutes later. His mother claimed that she wasn't up to visiting, for she wasn't feeling well enough. The truth was she wasn't sick, just angry. Angry at being back in Lichport. Angry that Amos was to receive nothing from the estate. When she demanded to know why, Amos refused to speak about why his father had left everything to his brother Charles, including the house and the rest of the family money, except to say, "Dolores, believe me, you're not the first person I've disappointed." Amos drove quietly while Dolores went on and on about it during the entire car ride home, as if complaining and yelling would somehow change the dead man's will.

"You're just going to let him stay in that house and not pay you some portion of what it's worth? Is that it? You're done? And it's not like he needs any more money, Amos! Property, investments, not to mention whatever was left of his wife's estate! Nothing left to you, and you say 'fine' and just walk away?"

"Not my decision. My brother's been caring for him and has made the house his own, has lived there with his wife while his son's been at boarding school. My brother also has money of his own. He's always been good with it, antiques and investments, I assume. I've hardly spoken with either of them in a long while, and I suspect my dad and my brother simply came to an understanding that didn't include me. Besides, there were some things on which my father and I did not see eye to eye, as you know very well."

Dolores ignored the end of his sentence, but hissed, "An understanding?"

"Yes. An understanding." And that was all his father would say on the matter. When they got home, Silas's mom went right into the house and slammed the door, leaving Silas and his dad still standing on the porch, so his dad put him back in the car and took him out for dinner.

On the way, Silas asked his dad, "Will I see them now? Ghosts?"

"No. Probably not," his dad told him matter-of-factly, but then added more earnestly, "Maybe." Amos paused a little longer, then said, "You saw my father because he wanted to see you. He wanted to say good-bye to you, Little Bird."

That made perfect sense to Silas. It seemed simple and sensible and right. Why wouldn't his grandfather want to see him and say good-bye? Of course he would.

Looking back, Silas thought that maybe his dad had thought about that moment coming and had planned to answer his son's questions with only just enough information, to answer what Silas asked about and nothing more. Not to make a big deal about it. This kind of stuff upset his mom, so his dad was always quiet about it with him. Quiet and careful.

When they got to the restaurant, Silas had asked his dad if he could give the hostess another name, a made-up name.

"Why?" Amos asked him, amused.

"It'll be fun to be someone else. Let's be other people tonight!" Silas remembered saying that because the thought of him and his dad playing a trick on the world excited him.

So Silas told the hostess their last name was "Bedlam" because he had read it in a song in one of his father's books, and because he had heard his dad use it a few times when talking to his mom. A few minutes later, the hostess called out, "Bedlam! Party of two! Bedlam, party of two," and Silas nearly squealed, he was so pleased with himself. All through dinner, he pretended he was someone else, that he and his dad were other people, from some other place where there were people named Bedlam, and the spell was only broken when they got back into the same old car to go home. Still, Silas felt better and asked no more questions about ghosts.

When they got back, perhaps emboldened by his alternate identity, Silas couldn't help but say something to his mother about what she'd done to him. He told her in a tone perhaps too much like his father that there was "no reason to hit people just because a ghost wanted to say good-bye to them." His mom really starting yelling then.

"Damn it, Amos. *Damn it!*" And from that day forward, his father hardly ever went upstairs except to visit Silas in his room.

After the funeral and the fight, Amos showed Silas the watch, maybe just to distract him, maybe because he knew Silas would come to see it eventually.

"Does it really tell time?" Silas remembered asking his father. "It looks very old."

"It is rather old," his dad told him, "but it's not for telling the time. Not really." And then Amos would say no more about it except that one day, he might show it to Silas again and talk a little more about it then.

But that day hadn't come, and now Silas sat alone with his father's strange silver watch in his hand.

◆ ◆ ◆

It was about three hours later when Silas came back through the hallway to Mrs. Bowe's house. She noticed immediately that he was wearing his father's jacket and that his right hand did not leave the front pocket.

He's found the death watch, she thought, and for a moment she paused and her breath caught in her throat.

Then she said, "Your father's jacket looks very good on you, Silas. It suits you, but it still might be a little early for it. For wool, I mean—but of course you should wear it. Of course you should."

She wasn't sure if she was doing the right thing, letting the boy leave with the watch. But Amos surely left it behind for a reason, and more and more Mrs. Bowe felt she was following a path trod out for her by another. For the time being, she was willing to play the part allotted to her. But she would keep an eye on the boy in her way. She felt everything would be easier and safer if Silas were here, in his father's house, with her.

Still in a bit of a haze, Silas quietly thanked Mrs. Bowe and said he'd come back soon. He turned to go out the back door, but she told him he might leave by the front, since he was respectable company from good family. When they reached the front door of her part of the house, Mrs. Bowe took Silas's hand and stroked it three times in the old way. He looked up, a serene expression on his face, and smiled at her. *Good*, she thought. *We have an understanding. He trusts me.* She quickly opened his hand and pressed a heavy key into the center of his palm.

"Silas," she said with a glance back toward the hall that connected the two homes, "that house was given to your father by my mother and father. Given to him outright and in perpetuity, and from where I sit, that makes it yours. That is *your* house, Silas," she said again, because he looked bewildered. "You come here anytime. This is *your* home. *Yours.*"

"Yes, ma'am. Thank you, ma'am," Silas replied.

She smiled to see his fist tightly clenching the key as though he was holding his own life in his hand.

As Silas made his way back through the garden, Mrs. Bowe called out from the porch, "That key is for all the doors, Silas. Let yourself in or out as you wish. Be sure to lock the gate behind you." And as Silas let himself out, she stepped out of the sun and into the cool shade of the crypt.

Silas walked back along Main Street, two words circling around and around in his mind: *My house. My house. My house.* Silas took the key and put it on the chain that also held the pendant his father had given him. He liked the way the extra weight felt around his neck and the press of the now warm metal against his chest.

He was happier than he'd been in a year. But fast on the heels of joy, guilt caught up to him. If he had the key to his father's house, that meant it was because his dad had no need of it. He was filling a space left by his dad. But still. He could go there anytime he wanted, and that meant not having to put up with anything at his uncle's. It wasn't a car, but it was a place to go if he needed one. Close. Safe.

Silas began to walk faster, and as he turned left on Fairwell Street to make his way back to his uncle's, someone waved to him from the overgrown patch of ground past the schoolyard and in front of the millpond.

It was a girl.

She was across the street, maybe a hundred feet away from him. She was really pretty, and she was waving at him.

So he waved back.

She waved again, then smiled at him.

Behind her, light from the late-day sun hit the surface of the millpond, making Silas squint and his eyes water a bit so that the harder he stared at her, the more she washed in and out of focus.

She must have been swimming recently, because her hair was wet. Silas thought that made her look mysterious and attractive, and then, as if she could hear him thinking, she ran her hand through her hair and shook the water off and waved again.

Silas stood trying to muster the courage to cross the street. He looked down as he stepped off the curb into the street, glancing left and right just in case a car was coming, but when he looked back, the girl was gone. *Okay,* he thought. *Someone just being nice. I'm new here, and someone waved. No big deal.*

No big deal.

But all the way back, Silas thought about what it would be like to take a date to his place and say, real casual, *Yeah, I own it. Yeah. This is my house.*

CHAPTER 16

BOOKS OF THE DEAD

LONG BEFORE THE UMBERS TOOK HOLD of the property in 1768, the street had an awkward and lingering reputation that Uncle rather enjoyed. It had been named Temple Street because the old Knights of the Eastern Temple meeting hall once stood where the house was now. Some of the meeting hall and a portion of the rotunda were still standing at the time the Umber house was built, and the large, ornate columns of the rotunda had been incorporated into the new house. It was in that rotunda that—according to the more imaginatively inclined townsfolk—the brothers of the temple were said to have enacted their secret and most blasphemous rites. The brotherhood of knights had arrived in the earliest days of Lichport and had kept very much to themselves. By the early eighteenth century, perhaps because of spreading rumors, perhaps because of the appearance of a comet in the eastern sky, the brothers dissolved their order, leaving Lichport by ship in the middle of the night. Five of the brothers of the order remained in the house. Four of those disappeared, some say leaving Lichport by night-coach, a few years later. That left only one elderly brother to live out his days in the crumbling hall, and why he remained behind no one knows. It was said he was living in the rotunda even as the roof fell in around him. He never left the house and died there in 1765. Three years later, the Umber family—who had been living in Arvale Manor, a large estate on the edge of the marshes and too close to the sea and brackish waterways to be thought fashionable—acquired the property and began refurbishing the buildings in the neoclassical style.

Of all the remaining portions of the brotherhood's ancient meeting hall, Uncle's ancestor had loved the rotunda the best and, despite its dilapidated condition, insisted on making it part of the main house by erecting walls within the older building as well as an elaborate, statue-lined gallery that connected the temple to the main house. The original structure that formed the basis of the rotunda library had been built by the brotherhood in the seventeenth century as an outdoor ornamental classical temple with high limestone columns that held up a lead-lined roof. The original limestone columns still stood on the outside, most covered with ivy, but inside, additional decorative columns of dark wood had been added by the Umbers and between those, carved oak shelves. So, from the time it was added to the house, it was meant to be a library.

Uncle was eager to show Silas this library for several reasons, primarily because he wanted Silas to spend more time in the house. A little sightseeing in town over the past few days was fine, but there was no telling what Silas might eventually find out, or who he might meet. Uncle knew the boy had an interest in books and would doubtless be impressed by the collection, so this was a way to keep him busy in his new home and curtail his wandering.

Uncle watched as Silas slowly made his way down the long gallery, looking at the faces of the statues as he went. Most wore distant expressions, and they seemed to regard his nephew passively as Silas scrutinized them. Uncle looked at his watch as Silas approached. A little late. *Good. He is comfortable here. He is sleeping well. All for the good*, Uncle thought, and with a flourish of his arm, he welcomed Silas into the library.

Uncle could see his nephew's obvious excitement, his palpable curiosity. Silas lifted his face as he entered the room, perhaps intoxicated by the smell of wood polish and old books. Around the room, between the columns, high shelves soared, connected by a thin brass rail to which was attached a ladder on wheels that could be pushed easily in front of any bookcase to access the high shelves. There were several long wooden tables in the middle of the room. Several small lamps with green glass shades were set along the length of each.

"Rumor has it that there is a chamber here, in the earth, beneath our very feet," Uncle said with a deliberate hint of mystery in his voice.

At the mention of a subterranean hollow, Silas looked quickly to the floor, turning his head this way and that, as though he was trying to see through the tiles into some vast dark space below. He put his hands out to his sides, as if to steady himself.

"It is said it was built by the brothers of the temple to house their most hallowed rites and treasured artifacts, and only the highest ranking of their initiates could enter the sacred subterranean vault."

"Is it true?" asked Silas, clearly fascinated.

"I think it unlikely, but who can say? No one in my father's time was brave enough to pull up the tiles of which your grandfather was justly proud. But just here,"—Uncle moved toward the center of the room, where one of the inlaid spokes of a large marble compass star lay on the floor—"yes, just here, come and listen." Silas moved toward his uncle, and as he approached, Uncle raised his foot and brought it down sharply on a particular spot on the floor. On the surface of the sound was the expected slap of shoe leather on the marble, but then, extending beneath that sound and beyond it, there was a low *TOOOM* that indeed suggested a large, hollow space below the floor. Silas listened carefully as the sound faded.

"Please be welcome here. This room is yours day or night. Nothing would make me happier than the sight of you reading and studying in this library. My father and grandfather were learned men, and I know your father loved learning, so I suspect you have inherited this trait. Your mother is keen for you to return to school, but I have said to her that all the learning you need may be had here. And of course, if there is some other text you require, well, I am sure we can obtain it."

"I . . . I was thinking about college before my dad disappeared, but I don't have any real plans yet. I haven't really started to—"

"It's all right, Silas. I see," Uncle interrupted gently. "Let this place be your university."

Silas looked at him with surprise and something else. Was it thanks? Uncle wondered.

"Silas, even a learned man could spend a lifetime studying in this room."

"I want to—" Silas said absently as his eyes flew from shelf to shelf.

One entire case was dedicated to books on ancient Egypt. Silas reached out and took a tall, brown volume. It was an excavation report dated 1901 from Abydos, the funerary city on the Nile. Uncle watched Silas dreamily turn the pages and scrutinize the many photographs of amulets, drawings of inscribed columns, and images of carved walls bearing sacred portraits of animal-headed gods. On one particular page, Silas's eye fixed on a portrait of Osiris, the god of the dead. Before Osiris stood the deceased, whose heart was weighed against a white plume, the feather of Ma'at, and there the Ammit stood ready to devour the deceased if its soul did not measure up.

"Please," said Uncle, "leave it on the table so you may return to it later. So much to learn from the Egyptians. Oh my, yes. They understood what it means to live forever. Truly. Theirs was a philosophy of permanence. That the soul might endure through the preservation of the body. What implications! What insights! And so long ago."

Uncle was pleased. Silas showed a sincere interest. Uncle thought that he might fish a little further to see what else might pique his nephew's curiosity.

"Of course, there are other books stored throughout the house, rare volumes on the most curious subjects. And other collections. Odder things I prefer not to exhibit in the public rooms."

"What kind of collections?"

Uncle smiled, as he ran his thumb and forefinger along the sharp crease of his lapel.

"Well, the albums containing my photographic work, for example. Those are kept in my workroom upstairs."

"That was your job once, you were a photographer?"

Without letting his smile drop, Uncle wondered how much Silas knew and to whom he might have spoken in town.

"I was. Yes. Though that part of my life seems a very long time ago now. To be honest, I think that your mother would be disturbed by the subject of my photographic work, and perhaps might not be so pleased that I show it to you."

Silas's face fell a little, just as Uncle hoped it would.

"Even so, why don't we meet in the upstairs hall after dinner, after your mother has gone up to bed, and I might then show you something more? Shall we?"

At the appointed hour, Silas and his uncle walked side by side past the entrances to the west wing where his bedroom was, the east wing, which housed his mother's, and straight ahead through the carved archway into the north wing of the house. Atop the arch, Silas could see as he passed below it, was a carving in light-colored wood of a pelican and its offspring. The pelican was piercing its own breast with its beak to feed its young on its blood. Beyond the arch, a long gallery extended in front of them. There were pictures on the right-hand walls and windows on the left.

Long ago, a gallery such as this would have been used for exercise and amusement when the weather was bad. Small tables, ornate chairs, and settees were arranged apparently randomly along both walls. With the exception of Uncle's room, all the rooms in the north wing were closed, and the doors on the right side were blocked with large pieces of furniture: bureaus, bookshelves, and highboys. Silas had found those immovable the first day when he tried to shift a high chest of drawers to get at the door behind it, where he'd imagined he heard a soft knocking on the wood. When he had opened one of the lower drawers, Silas found it carefully and tightly packed with bricks. It seemed that the only easy way into these interconnecting chambers was through Uncle's bedroom.

The first doorway on the right led into the master bedroom. The high ceiling was domed, like the library, but on a smaller scale, and long, dark velvet curtains were drawn over the windows against the light. There were paintings on all the walls, mostly nineteenth-century oils of classical scenes. Silas recognized some of the subjects. Zeus and Semele, just as the god's lightning-charged embrace was about to turn his mistress to ash. Hades and Persephone, a tear in the earth opening up and Hades driving his sable horses and red-gold chariot down in the underworld with his stolen and terrified young bride. Phaethon and Phoebus, father handing the son the reins of the sun-car that would shortly bring about the son's demise. Proud Niobe, looking over the corpses of her children.

Silas looked but bit his tongue, even though he was dying to comment. Who could sleep with such images in the room? The bed was made, but its sheets were scored with creases, and it didn't look like anyone actually slept there, merely used the bed to sit on.

Silas followed his uncle through a doorway and into the work-room, where he could immediately detect the thick, sweet smell of honey. Here, where Uncle kept his long-unused photographic equipment, was another small library. On the shelves were numerous glass jars with what appeared to be specimens of small animals. Uncle quickly explained, "These were part of my anatomical studies. So important for any artist. Even though I haven't really used them in a long time, I could never part with them. To simply dispose of them would seem . . . disrespectful. So I keep them. My pets." He laughed at his own words, but Silas could feel Uncle's eyes on him intently. Uncle was watching every expression as it flashed across Silas's face. But Silas turned away from Uncle, unable to keep his eyes from the shelves and their holdings.

On the shelves on the opposite side of the room stood numerous jars of honey. When he looked back at the specimens, Silas could see that some of them were suspended in honey and not formaldehyde, as he had previously thought. How the little jars glowed, even in the dim light. Unlike specimens he'd seen in school that were floating in formaldehyde or alcohol, these ones in honey seemed more alive, more like they were asleep rather than dead. The way the honey held them suspended kept the small corpses from losing their hair, or looking like they'd been roughly shoved to the bottom of their jars; the honey-preserved animals looked more likely to open their eyes, and there weren't any little pieces of flesh flaking off them either. In their strange way, they were lovely, little golden creatures, barely affected by death.

"Now that is an ancient custom," Uncle told Silas, his hands shaking slightly. "The Romans would sometimes preserve their dead in honey, as did the ancient Babylonians. Some cultures thought it was holy stuff, can you imagine? The food of the dead and the gods both. Of course, the dead and the gods are so similar, are they not? After enough time, the line between ancestor and deity blurs, and gods are born."

With his eyes, Silas followed row after row of jars down toward the opposite end of the room, where a very strong door, one that did not match any of the others in the house, had been set into the wall.

"That is my Camera Obscura now. My private work studio. My darkroom, if you like. One day I'd very much like to show it to you, and if you're interested, I'd like you to help me with my work."

Thinking of the knocking sound he'd heard the previous day, Silas suddenly asked, "Is there anyone in there?"

His uncle had been walking toward the door, but at Silas's question he seemed to take a small misstep and fall forward. He quickly caught himself and just as quickly stood up as straight as a pole. "No. It was the old nursery, in your grandfather's time. I am eager to return to work in there. Perhaps with a new partner?"

"C'mon! Let's have a look," said Silas, intrigued and striding across the room. But as he approached the door, he could see his uncle tense visibly, and from somewhere, Silas thought he heard a low, soft cry, not unlike a cat. The door looked heavy, and as Silas got closer, he saw that it was inscribed all over its surface. Some of the marks were clearly deep gouges, while others looked like complicated circles and lines carved carefully and deeply into the wood. Uncle tried to cover them casually with his hand as he leaned against the door.

"Had I not already told you, you might have guessed by all the juvenile markings on the wood that this door once led to a nursery."

Considering the thickness of the door and the size of the bolts on the bronze locks, Silas commented, "This is a very big door for a nursery, don't you think?"

Uncle laughed somewhat uneasily and said, "Oh, Silas, children can be the very devil!"

He held up his hand and waved it, as if trying to keep his laughter going. "But seriously, this door is an antique and came with these locks. They are ornamental, very old, and I suspect no one had the heart to remove them. I am rather fond of them."

"You sure we can't take a quick peek inside?"

"We most certainly may, but not today. I would like to straighten up the mess in there before I show it to you. Allow me my pride, I beg you. Besides," he said, as he put his arm around Silas's shoulder and led him back to the opposite side of the room, "I was going to show you my photography."

"Yeah, okay," said Silas, willing to be distracted for the moment, wanting to see more because he was beginning to suspect this was not so much a tour as it was an initiation. Like him, Uncle had eccentric tastes and liked old things. The difference, Silas was beginning to see, was that Uncle saw such objects as extensions of himself, of his body, essential, required, uniquely his. This thought made Silas uneasy.

"Show me your art," he said, as he turned away from the door, past the amber-lit flesh-filled jars, and looked back at Uncle, who had begun to bring some large leather-bound volumes down from a high shelf. He placed them onto a table inlaid with complicated marquetry designs in contrasting light and dark woods. A few he opened briefly and put back on the shelf. "No, no. So many were ill in those years, and it marred the final image." He looked over the spines, stamped with gilt dates. He chose the volume farthest along the shelf and put it on the table. "Yes, the last were my best, I think." His uncle drew two high-backed chairs up to the table and motioned wordlessly for Silas to come and sit by him.

In that moment, as he sat down, Silas felt cold, and he noticed his uncle's skin: It seemed to absorb whatever light fell on it, and the longer Silas stared at it, the darker the room appeared to become.

"My work," was all Uncle said, as he opened the first album and turned it slightly toward his nephew. He watched every move of Silas's hand as he slowly turned a page. Silas could see that his uncle was perspiring.

With great care and some hesitancy, Silas looked at one page and then another. The first few images stopped him cold, and he could not look away from the subjects of the photographs. He turned more pages, paused briefly, then kept on turning page after page, unable to stop.

There were the dead.

The photographs were exquisite in their detail, composition, and contrast. The placement of hands and the postures were perfect, always merely at rest. The expressions were more various. Many were quite lifelike, although dreamy, like a person who had paused only briefly to close his eyes for a moment, the merest pause, a comma; then he would awake refreshed, rise, and carry on with his life. But the faces of the living captured in bereavement for their dear departed always gave away the illusion—their expressions spoke of death's presence. Their posture described an angle of mourning, while their eyes seemed to glance somewhere off to the side, as if they might be looking for something they'd lost.

Slowly, Silas turned the thick pages of the album.

A picture of a mother cradling a dead child, her arms framing the body of the baby, mother and child still one being, maybe more so now, arranged in death.

Two children. One lying on a small divan, eyes closed, holding a doll. Kneeling behind the little sofa, another child with another doll that she holds tightly next to her head. Looking not at her dead sister, but beyond her, perhaps at her ghost waiting just out of frame.

Mother and child again. But this time the mother is dead, yet skillfully propped upright with her right arm around her child's body. The mother's eyes are very flat, eyelids not quite halfway down. The child's arm is wrapped about his mother's neck, and his other hand rests very tentatively on her chest, as if his mother's body is made of air. The little boy seems well aware that his mother is not present. This is not my mother anymore, he thinks. He knows. He is weary of the farce, the small corners of his mouth are beginning to pull down. His remarkable composure is about to fall apart.

"They're beautiful," was all Silas could say, and he meant it. He looked up briefly at Uncle with awe. There was no denying Charles Umber was an artist of a very high order. Silas quickly looked back down at the extraordinary photographs that had captured his attention.

Uncle exhaled softly, said nothing, but put his hand gently on Silas's shoulder.

Silas could barely look away from any of them. He slowly realized, *These are all Lichport folk. These are my people, my ancestors, my neighbors, and I love them.*

Toward the end of the album, Silas noticed an alteration in style, subtle at first, but disturbing. There was a growing fascination with particular parts of the bodies. In some photos, veils had been drawn over certain features of the body so that others could be highlighted. Finally, some had no faces at all, thick crepe wound about the head so only the white neck showed, or a portion of the chest and clavicle. These were not memorials, not people anymore. Under his uncle's eye and careful deliberate manipulation, they had become objects. Looking at these pictures, Silas began to perceive a side of his uncle that seemed something less than human. For the first time since he had arrived in Lichport, Silas thought about his uncle with fear.

At the end of the album, Silas came to the strangest picture of all. This photograph was very dark, not because it was underexposed, but because there was a lot of black fabric that surrounded a single hand at the center of the picture. The hand almost glowed, it was so white. Silas at first thought it was the hand of a child, because it was fine and very smooth, but the length of the fingers and the delicacy of the bones told him it belonged to a woman. Who was she? More importantly, *where* was she?

There was no face in the photograph. Black crepe had been wrapped around and around the entire head, and more fabric had been drawn across the body and the arm so that only the single hand appeared to float against the dark background. Silas guessed that no relative of the deceased had ever been shown this photo. This was something Uncle had done for himself. It was an extraordinary thing, beautiful and awful both, and it raised bumps on Silas's skin and turned his stomach. He could feel his uncle's eyes, long ago, on this dead woman's body, could feel him arranging her, caressing the hand, placing it in an unnatural relation to the body by covering the face and all the other parts. It was almost as though in taking this picture, his uncle had severed the hand from her body, as though the hand was a trophy.

As if he didn't want her to see what he was going to do to her.

"What was her name?" asked Silas very quietly, as if the woman in the picture were asleep in the next room and hearing her name spoken out loud might wake her.

"Whose name?"

"The woman in the photograph."

"I certainly can't recall. This was taken years ago. Anyway, it is of very little consequence. She was buried and forgotten in Newfield with all the rest of the rabble. This picture is what remains, what shall remain." Silas thought that Uncle's face seemed troubled.

"Most people give little enough real thought to their own mortality. Oh yes, they gabble on about heaven and the bosom of Abraham, but really, they are weary of life almost from the time they're born, and are only waiting for it all to end. They live their days quietly, obscurely, and underneath their daily toils, they long for oblivion.

"But we can be eternal, Silas. We must be ready to embrace that possibility. Through sacrifice, and art, and meticulous study, we may join the gods in their bowers. Do you believe that is so? That death on deathless substance has no force, even on the body, if the seeker is prepared?"

Silas was fairly sure his uncle was mad, at least to some degree, and as Uncle continued to speak, Silas thought, *He is sleepwalking. Don't wake him.*

"I have never thought about it quite that way, but I suppose it might be possible for someone to be remembered forever."

"Not quite my point, but it is a beginning." The eerie mood was broken when Uncle tousled Silas's hair as though he were a dog that had brought a stick back to its master.

"Ah, I remember now," Uncle said as he slowly slid the book around so he could see the image more clearly, as if the woman's name and history were somewhere inscribed on the photo.

"There's a story about her well worth remembering," Uncle said, as he took a deep breath and half closed his eyes.

"Two children died. Their mother, this woman, lost her arm to infection a year later and, you may find this fascinating, buried the arm with her children in the earth. Of course, she was a God-fearing woman, and she would need that arm when the great horn sounded and the righteous were called. If you believe in such nonsense. But everyone in town knew her true purpose and why this strange action brought her such comfort. A part of her would be with them now in that low, lonely place. She could hold those children in her arm until she could be laid to rest beside them. Now isn't that a curious thing, Silas? A great testament, I suppose, to a mother's love. Yes, you can even go see the stone. You'll see there is just one stone for the two children—this was common—and she even had the headstone amended, so that her arm might be carved above the little cherubic heads of the children. A portrait of the arm that she put into their grave. All true."

"There were, at the time, many stories about her," Uncle continued. "She was, I now recall, rather remarkable. A large family, and so well loved by everyone. A strong presence among her kin."

Silas thought about the many ghost stories he'd read where the dead come back for things: treasure, unrequited love, a golden arm, to watch over their children.

"Were there any stories about her, you know, *coming back*?" he asked Uncle, his eyes never leaving the photograph.

"Who knows? Well, I suppose she might have become a ghost. I never heard any stories to that effect, but I mean to say, after the business with the arm, I shouldn't be surprised. Ghosts are always a little needy, incomplete, if you take my meaning."

He smiled at his nephew. "Like the living, they are always looking for something or other that they've misplaced, no?"

Uncle was lost momentarily in his thoughts, but then cleared
his throat quickly.

"Perhaps I should be getting back to my work, and surely
some work of your own awaits you in *our* library?"

Silas understood that he was being dismissed, and after what
he'd seen, he was eager to make his way back downstairs into a
part of the house where at least some of the windows were open
and uncovered and let in just a bit more light.

CHAPTER 17

LITTLE CREATURES

"We live on immortal shores, Silas."

To the right of the massive carved mantel, Uncle's living room boasted a tall wooden case carved with ivy vines and leaves. Behind its glass doors were numerous shelves of fossils. Before dinner, Uncle postured next to the case. "Did you know, Silas, the seacliffs of Lichport are filled with fossils, though many of these here have come to me from the far corners of the world."

While Silas listened, he looked carefully at the ancient skeleton of one of the small reptiles, preserved in pale yellow sandstone, revealed as if a blanket had been drawn back from the bed of stone in which the creature had been sleeping without its skin. There were many urchins and shells, which most resembled themselves as they had been in life, now turned to stone. There were curled ammonites, some black, others with pearled surfaces; one on the floor was over three feet tall and leaned against the mantel.

Uncle had walked up quietly behind Silas and began to speak over his shoulder. Silas, surprised by the proximity, knocked his head to one side, trying to get a little distance between his ear and his uncle's mouth.

"Rotting is so common," Uncle said in a low voice, "so communal. But certain creatures, some forms, because of either some unique qualities they possess, or because of some extraordinary pains taken on their behalf or Nature's, do not succumb, do not lose form. Instead, such fortunate souls continue into eternity by virtue of their enduring form. How wonderful are these little sigils of immortality, are they not? The dross, the physical body of the creature begins the process, but for the fortunate, it ends in eternity, in the endurance of the soul."

"Are you suggesting a mollusk has a soul?" said Silas, and laughed a little. He picked up one of the specimens from the case and turned it over in his hands.

"Not, I think, in the way you mean it. It is very complex and, of course, not all wonderments occur on the physical plane. Calcination, fixation, solution, distillation, sublimation, separation, projection. Those are the keys and as much part of the soul's preparation as the body's—" Uncle's eyes seemed to glaze over for a moment, but then he looked at Silas again, leaning toward him.

"That said, even a mollusk has an enduring *principal element*. All living things do, although most never consider the possibility of the continuation of spirit I am speaking of, because they are simply incapable of doing so. For those ignorant souls, the world is not unlike a hospital, a place to lie idle and then die. And after their body's demise, they may watch silently from the gallery the tedious dumbshow of their corpse's decay, followed by the yawning epilogue of the soul's dissolve into nothingness. But it needn't be so. Many of the ancient people of this world turned their great minds to just such a problem and discovered the truth, the same truth hinted at by this simple fossil. With the body preserved, we bind ourselves to an eternal present. We may retain the use of the immortal soul. No forgetfulness. No oblivion."

Silas paused, with the fossil still in his hand, as he tried to puzzle out the implications of what Uncle was saying and why he might be saying it.

"But Uncle, don't you think there's a simple elegance in death? In just letting the end come and then joining hands with your ancestors who have gone before? In letting go? I think people who worry too much about the kinds of things you're talking about end up trapping themselves in some way. I mean, I haven't really thought about it like this before, but what you're saying just sounds, well, *wrong* somehow." Silas was thinking especially about his uncle's later photographs, about how it seemed now that they might be fledgling attempts at the bizarre process Uncle was trying to explain to him. Although that was many years ago, Uncle had had a long time to think about it, to refine his philosophy and his technique. *What was he experimenting on now?* Silas wondered.

"Ah!" Uncle exclaimed as he forced a smile. "His father's boy, indeed! How wonderful! But perhaps you will allow me, sometime soon, to explicate the matter a little further for you, to actually *show you* what I mean?" There was a cold light in Uncle's eyes, and Silas didn't like it, but he stayed polite, deferential, because he knew it would keep things on an even keel and there was still dinner to get through.

"Of course! I'd be honored. I know there is so much I can learn from you." Silas hoped he didn't sound as insincere as he felt.

"Wonderful. Just wonderful. By the way, how tall are you, Silas?"

"About five-eleven," he answered without thinking. "Why?"

"I was just wondering if some of my old clothes might fit you, some jackets, or perhaps something more appropriate for a young man of letters such as yourself?"

"Um, sure," said Silas, who did not intend to part with his father's jacket, which he had taken to wearing all the time now.

His mother sailed into the room, stroked her son's cheek as she passed by him, then perched next to Uncle. She took his waxy hand in hers and held it affectionately.

"Isn't your uncle wonderful, Si?" Dolores said, running her hands over a new dress of purple velvet accessorized with a small hat and veil. Presumably a gift from Uncle.

Silas said, "It's a little much for dinner at home, isn't it? You look like a silent movie star."

Dolores seemed not to notice her son was being anything but complimentary, and she smiled as she fussed with an imaginary wrinkle on the fabric. "Doesn't your uncle just think of everything?"

"Indeed I do," answered Uncle before Silas could proffer an opinion. "Dinner?" he asked, ringing a small silver bell.

The dinner ritual was the only part of Silas's days that had any structure. He spent his time investigating the house, or reading, or wandering portions of the town, but he knew that every night at six, he had to be in the parlor ready for dinner. While he found it overly formal and didn't particularly look forward to it, having one thing to do every day kept him aware of the passage of time. *Only an hour until dinner, better get home. Three hours since dinner, must be nearly nine.* This was something his life in Saltsbridge had lacked completely, and so each depressing day there had blurred into another until, by the time they had left for Lichport, Silas wasn't even sure what month it was or how long his father had been gone. But in Lichport, he had an easier time staying focused. He knew it was dinnertime and it was Wednesday and that it was September, and that his father had been missing for one year, two months, and twelve days.

Everyone was expected to contribute to the dinner conversation, and Silas found asking questions easier and usually less annoying than answering the questions put to him. So he asked his mother where her side of the family lived in Lichport.

"All gone," she said, not even looking up.

"But houses must still be there. The house where you lived? Your grandparents? Cousins?"

That seemed to get her attention, and she snapped her head up suddenly and barked at Silas, "Keep the hell out of those old houses! You'll fall through a floor or some damn thing and we'll never find you!" She caught herself and suppressed her annoyance. "This is a new start for us, Si. No need to go digging around in the past."

"Don't worry," said Silas. "If I fall somewhere and die, I'll make a point of floating back to say good-bye."

"Jesus Christ, Silas!" Dolores rose abruptly and stormed into the parlor to compose herself.

"He only wishes to know something about his new home and family, Dolores. It's only natural," said Uncle over his shoulder, in a soothing voice.

"Indeed I do," said Silas, imitating Uncle's calming tone. "And there is something I'd like to ask you about, if you don't mind?"

Uncle nodded, as he chewed a piece of dried meat.

"I saw the building belonging to the mortuary. And I saw a sign saying a Mr. Bowe was the mortician?"

"That is correct. Mr. Bowe was the town's mortician, and once my employer, my partner, really, until we parted company. He has been dead for some time."

"So my dad has been the town's mortician since Mr. Bowe died?" Silas asked.

Dolores came back into the room and sat down at the table, apparently more or less recovered. She looked hard at Uncle, then shrugged and nodded as if to say, *Go ahead. Do it.* As if they had already discussed the possibility that this topic would arise.

"Not at all. Your father may have worked *from* Mr. Bowe's house, but he was not a mortician, not by training or inclination."

Silas couldn't let the question go.

"But my dad *was* a mortician. He told me about it all the time. Do you mean he worked *for* Mr. Bowe? That Mr. Bowe was the mortician and my dad helped him? Was my dad just his assistant?" Silas began to feel as though he was trying to fit a square peg into a round hole.

"Silas, your father was, how shall I say it? Self-employed. I assure you, my boy, if your father had become the mortician, I would have known about it. Indeed, I might have taken up the reins from Mr. Bowe . . . why, I once even thought of asking for his daughter's hand. But in the end, I found her somewhat plain, and thought better of it. Silas, I am very sorry to be cast in this role as the exposer of lies, but I can only be honest with you. Your father was a tremendous disappointment to this family, and to your mother. He was a person of some promise, but he chose to squander the gifts God and family bestowed on him and spent much of his life in a world, in a fantasy, to which he alone had the key."

Silas didn't want to hear any more and stood up from the table.

"You know what, *Uncle*," he said, the sarcasm unmistakable, "I don't think you knew my father very well at all. He hardly spoke of you, and now I see why. You think because you've helped us out, because you've got money and a nice house, that you're what, the head of the family? My new dad or something?"

Far above stairs, a loud, sickening banging had begun, as if someone was hitting the floor over and over with a sack full of rotten fruit.

Uncle looked up suddenly, his eyes wild, then looked back at Silas with an unfocused gaze. After a few labored breaths, he seemed to be himself again.

"Silas, I am sorry that I have offended you. Here, you finish your meal. I will yield." Uncle smiled thinly as he waved his white napkin and said, "Truce."

He threw the napkin down on the table as he stood up. Without explanation, he walked quickly to the staircase and took the steps two at a time, in a hurry to reach the second floor. Silas could hear doors being unlocked in the north wing, opened and closed, and after a few moments, his uncle shouted something and the walls of the house shook once, and the banging stopped.

Dolores put her face in her hands.

"Oh, Red . . ." She sighed, invoking Silas's least favorite childhood nickname.

Silas sat back down at the table, picked up his uncle's untouched glass of wine, and said to his mother with a forced smile, "Love you, too."

Dolores left her son at the dinner table and retreated to her room.

Though she liked lingering downstairs with a drink as the candles burned down, tonight all she wanted was to go to bed. She stood before her dressing mirror in a long robe and looked at herself and the room about her in reflection. Behind her, the wood-paneled walls glowed in the low lamplight. The large bed held aloft a velvet canopy, and the furniture was gilt and grand. That all felt right. Even so, she was weary. If only Silas would trust her a little more. Or at least be more willing to see things through, wait them out, see what might come next. It wasn't in her son's nature to be trusting. She knew that. She brought a small cotton square up to her mouth. As she wiped and wiped the soft cloth across her lips, the rouge came away a little at a time.

Silas used to trust her. Christ, how they'd play when he was younger and Amos was hardly ever home, hadn't yet taken a hold on Silas. She'd called Silas "Red" sometimes, not because of his hair, but because of their fairy-tale game. She had this game she'd made from Little Red Riding Hood. She would get in her bed with her clothes on and draw the bedding up around her, covering most of her face. Silas would knock on her bedroom door, and she'd say in a high voice, "Come in, come in, my dear." And Silas, oh, he was maybe six or seven at the time, would come in very slowly, dressed in his red-hooded jacket. He knew all his lines because they'd read the story together many times. Dolores liked that story. Men were wolves and practical women took the knife to them, and those wolves, those sharp-toothed men, they didn't come back after that.

"Grandmother, what big eyes you have."

"All the better to see you with, Red."

"What big ears you have. . . ."

"All the better to hear you with, my dear."

And with each line, she'd call him closer and closer to the bed with her eyes. She'd laugh in her throat at how nervous Silas would get, and by the time he got right next to the bed, he'd look like he was about to piss himself, thrilled and nervous both. She'd pull that sheet up over her mouth, and as she spoke, he couldn't see her say the words, though the sheet moved a little with the in and out of her breathing. Sometimes Silas would start to shake toward the game's end, like maybe somewhere in his mind he thought that under the blankets his mother had changed into something else, something that wasn't his mother anymore. So she'd drop the sheet a little toward the end, down to her chin.

"What big teeth you have."

And at this she'd laugh and leap from the bed, hollering, "All the better to eat you with!" She'd grab him and he'd laugh too, but his eyes were wild, like an animal in a corner, looking rapidly this way and that for a way, any way, out.

She liked this game, liked the weird tension of it. Sometimes she'd call him "Red" for the rest of the day. She did that until it became a habit, a regular nickname for him. Silas didn't like it, maybe because the main character was, in the story, a girl. Maybe because when he heard it, it reminded him of a part of him that scared more easily. Maybe because his father called him "Bird," which he liked much better. Either way, one day when she called him from the bed, he said he didn't want to play that game anymore if she was going to call him Red. She didn't hesitate. Just jumped up out of the bed, straightened her clothes, and said loudly so he could hear her through the door, "Your way or no way, huh? Okay. Your way."

And that was the last time they played together. Though every now and again, when Silas failed to finish something, or she wanted to chide him, she'd call him Red, even though she knew he wouldn't respond and would ignore her for it, sometimes for days after.

Thinking about it now as she stepped away from the mirror and sat on the edge of her bed, Dolores thought maybe this hadn't been such a great game to play with a little kid.

Later that evening, after everyone had retreated to their rooms, Uncle came downstairs, unable to sleep, and sat in the quiet dark as he pondered his options. If he was lucky, he would fall asleep in his chair for an hour or so. The house was at peace for the moment, and dawn was not far off.

Dolores had gone upstairs to her room after dinner and had not come back down. Silas might have gone to bed as well, although for all Uncle knew, his nephew could be wandering the town. *Brave, that one. Intrepid.* How like himself, he thought. It was becoming clear that Dolores had little if any discernible maternal instinct. That would not serve the purpose for which he'd brought her here. Not at all. Two failures—the father and now the mother—both unsuitable. Uncle tried to comfort himself by remembering that this was, after all, an experiment, and setbacks were to be expected. And really, two errors could be considered two steps closer to eventual success. Dolores wouldn't be any trouble, though. No need to take any action yet. She might prove useful in unexpected ways. When she drank, she was in her own little world, usually quiet and detached from the daily noise and doings of the house and blissfully uninterested in the long hours he spent above stairs dealing with the other occupant in the north wing.

From the side table, he picked up the fossil of a small, domed, star-marked urchin that Silas had left there earlier. As he held it in his hand, Uncle wrapped his palm and fingers about it like a protective nest.

"Did you have a mother, I wonder?" he said to the fossil's stony, rippled surface. How permanent and individual it seemed, how it appeared to have been made exactly as it was, a little immortal thing waiting down the ages. He admired those qualities.

"Never mind," he said to the fossil, putting it gently back on the shelf. "Hardly matters now what's become of *her*, does it?"

CHAPTER 18

LOCALS

EVENING AT UNCLE'S HOUSE became a ritual set in stone. Reliable. Unchanging.

Dinner at six. Candles lit as usual and melting onto the tablecloth. Uncle and Dolores, at opposite ends of the table, gazed at each other while they chewed and dabbed the edges of their mouths with linen napkins. Occasionally, Dolores would drop a hint about a trip to Florida or going shopping in Kingsport. Then Uncle would say how lovely that would be if only his work would allow him such indulgences. Dolores never asked Uncle to elaborate on how he filled his days.

While they talked, Silas looked out the window at the amber light. It was about an hour before dusk, and he loved how the town changed at twilight. He wanted to be outside, rambling among the long shadows on the streets, watching the little candles being lit in the windows of houses he had thought were abandoned the night before.

Also, Silas wasn't sure how much more he could stand of watching his uncle watch his mother. Uncle's eyes moved over his mother's arm as it lifted food to her mouth. Uncle's eyes eagerly watched her empty her glass, and looked hopeful each time she tipped in a little more scotch.

Tonight Silas excused himself from the table before dinner was quite finished. Said he felt a headache coming on—a trick he'd learned from his mom—and that a little fresh air would do him good. He left the dining room without waiting for a response from either Uncle or his mother. He went directly to the front door and out into the street. It wasn't quite dark yet, but the air of the approaching evening was coming in off the sea with the promise of a cool breeze.

He walked slowly up Fairwell Street, feeling that the entire town was his. There was a particular gravity in Lichport, a sort of pull he could feel, as if the town's streets and stones were continually calling him. Or maybe it was just the comfortable weight of his father's watch in the front pocket of his jacket.

He passed by a gate on his left that led to another of the town's many family cemeteries. Atop the gate, iron was twisted into calligraphic letters spelling: UMBER.

The Umber family plot.

Just over the name "Umber," also in iron, was a head of Janus, much like the one on his pendant. He opened the gate, and it whined in protest. Silas entered the overgrown little graveyard and looked around. He noted with interest that a number of stones had the same image either carved into them, or as an ornament on the gravestone.

Here are my people, he thought proudly.

In the very middle of the cemetery, there was a large granite mausoleum in the classical style, surrounded by briars at its back and sides. At first the bronze doors seemed locked, the handles unwilling to budge. But Silas kept turning them this way and that, and eventually, the door creaked open.

The light from the low sun, though fading fast, hit the stained-glass windows on the west wall so the inside of the tomb glowed in jeweled light: ruby, emerald, amber, and sapphire. There were numerous engraved plaques that marked the hollows in the walls that held some of his more ancient ancestors, and he could easily follow the names back well beyond the few he knew. Near the still-open chambers nearest the door were the coffins of his grandfather and grandmother, his father's father and mother. And there, just beyond them, were the coffins of his paternal great-grandparents. Tradition seemed to be that the most recent dead were left out for the continuance of mourning, but after a time, their coffins would be set into the walls and covered over so as the coffin dissolved, it was done out of sight of the curious. It also appeared the custom had been abandoned or forgotten, since clearly no one had been in the mausoleum since his grandfather died.

So, Silas thought, for all Uncle's formality, he clearly didn't cling closely to tradition. The light was fading, and as much as Silas liked being around any family other than his uncle, he didn't much care for the idea of being in the mausoleum after it got dark.

As he exited through the bronze doors, he saw her standing just inside the gate, under his family name. She looked at him and tilted her head to one side as if offering an invitation, but she didn't speak.

Silas was nervous. Maybe she'd think he was weird skulking around the cemetery at night, so he sort of waved an arm around and said, "These guys are my family." *Idiot*, he thought instantly after that. *Idiot*.

But she was smiling now. *Good. She likes weirdos*. Or maybe she felt sorry for him. Silas was okay with either reason. He looked at the pale skin of her face and at the bright aquamarine of her eyes and guessed that he and she must be about the same age.

"You're Silas," she said, calling him over. It wasn't a question.

"Yeah. Silas Umber. I just moved here." He looked down and

tried not to smile too broadly, which was hard because he thought she was the prettiest girl he'd ever spoken to.

"I know who you are," she said, looking up at the word "Umber" over the gate.

"How do you know?"

"It's not a very big town. Word travels fast," she said, waving her arms around at the graves, imitating him.

"Have you lived here long?" said Silas. He hoped she wasn't making fun of him.

"I come and go."

"But you live in Lichport now."

"Yes. My family's been here a long time."

"I think I saw you the other day near the millpond."

"That's where I live."

"Which house?"

"The dark one."

"Which one?"

"It's one of the older houses. Maybe I'll show you sometime." The girl ran her hand over her hair from her temples to the back of her neck. "Don't you want to know my name?"

"I really do."

"Bea," she said so softly Silas could barely hear her. "I am Beatrice."

Silas smiled and bowed slightly, then opened the gate for her, and they walked out of the cemetery and onto the sidewalk.

"Where are you going, Silas?"

"Don't know. I thought I might walk along the river," Silas said, as he realized that he hoped she'd want to come along.

"Oh, I've just been swimming," she said, seeming a little sad. "Tell you what, why don't I meet you here another time?"

"How will I find you?"

"I'll find you. You kind of stand out here," she said. With that, Beatrice turned and walked off up the street.

Distressed at her quick departure as well as the sketchy nature of the plan, Silas called out, "But what if I want to find you?"

"Just look for me at the gate. Or whistle, if you like, and I'll come to you."

And as Beatrice walked away, Silas saw that she was still wet from her swim, and in her long hair, among the chestnut strands, green weeds were woven; and where she'd walked, he could see the trace of wet footprints. He pulled his collar up against the evening breeze. He hoped she didn't catch a cold on her way home.

Silas walked absently along Main Street, and then down Coach until the lights of the general store were glowing before him. Silas hadn't yet visited Peale's General Store and Mercantile, and so, not wanting to go home yet, he entered. Little bells rang from a string on the back of the door. A woman in her fifties stood behind the counter and beamed at him.

"Silas Umber! Have you finally come to see me about a job?"

"Sorry?" Silas said, distressed that while he knew no one, people in Lichport generally seemed to know him.

"No, no. I'm sorry to tease you," she said, still smiling warmly. "I'm Joan Peale, and this is my father, John." She hugged an elderly man, maybe in his eighties, who was sitting next to her. Silas could tell Mr. Peale wasn't well, even though the man smiled at him from his chair. For an instant, as Mr. Peale looked at Silas, he seemed to be looking right through him into a room that wasn't there. But after his daughter gently tapped his shoulder, Mr. Peale reached out a shaking hand to Silas and said, "I hope to see you again soon, Mr. Umber."

"We all knew your dad very well," Joan said, "especially my

mom. I was wondering how long it was going to take you to sneak out of your uncle's house and come to see us."

An older woman came through a back door and into the shop. She was wearing a long apron over a faded dress, and her head was covered with a sort of loose bonnet like women wore centuries ago.

"Silas," said Joan, "this is my mother. But you can call her 'mother' too. Everyone does."

"How do you do, Mother Peale? I am Silas Umber," said Silas, as he extended his hand to her.

Instead of shaking hands with him, the old woman grabbed his wrist and pulled him toward her, then threw her arms around him. Silas could feel her walking stick pressing against his spine. She laughed heartily as she hugged him, then held him out at arm's length and looked at him very carefully, studying, it seemed, all the features of his face in minute detail.

"So you're back then?"

"Back? You mean back home? Because I was born here?"

"I mean because Umber folk always come back, and we Umbers and Peales keep finding one another. Little things like time and generations don't matter very much with good friends who are fond of each other's company."

She squinted at Silas now, as she looked closer and closer at his face.

"Of all the faces I've looked on, I was curious which one you'd have. Yes, it is very much like your father's, but there are differences, in the right light. No. I've not seen your face for a very long time."

"How long is that?" asked Silas, enjoying what he thought was a game.

"Oh, ages it feels like. And not perhaps on this land. But good friends and kin always find each other, don't you find?" she asked with a hoarse laugh. "Anywise, we are who we were, so everyone's always coming back, that's how I see it. And here we are, all one in the moment, for the moment, if you take my meaning, Silas Umber."

"I'm not sure I do, ma'am."

"Well, well, let it be then, until you've settled in and remembered yourself."

"What can I get you today, Silas?" asked Joan.

"Just looking really," said Silas, as he gazed with wonder at the oddly stocked shelves.

There were the sorts of things you'd expect: flour, sugar, cereals, bread, canned fruits and vegetables, coffee, chocolates, and other staples. However, most of the shelves were filled with things Silas had never seen, with labels he either couldn't read or couldn't understand. There were things he was not accustomed to seeing in cans, and packets of things no one ate anymore. Someone obviously liked something called Jell-O Spoon Candy, because there was a whole shelf of it. There was canned milk and canned apples and lots of lard and something called "graisse de canard." One can appeared to contain some kind of stewed chrysalis from Asia. There were cans of jellied eels and cans of haggis from Scotland. There seemed to be every kind of canned fish, which seemed absurd considering Lichport was a seaside town.

On a high shelf, Silas saw a can of roast veal and gravy marked 1824. He looked at the can, and then at Mother Peale.

"You're looking hard at my shelves, Silas Umber," she accused.

"Just curious. What is all this stuff?"

"Old families, Silas. Old families. Stuck in their ways. They like things as they were, and some of 'em, I can tell you, go back a long ways. Folks just like what they've always liked and what their parents liked and back and back . . . and so I try to get it for 'em. And I'll have you know, cans of veal and gravy sailed with Captain William Edward Parry when he went to find the Northwest Passage!"

"Who would buy a can of meat from 1824?"

"Hm," Mother Peale admitted, "I can't say it's been flying off the shelf."

Silas looked at the kind old woman, at the deep lines of her face and the small hump on her back. "I have heard of you, you know, Mother Peale," said Silas. "I remember my father mentioning you when I was young."

"Well, I would not be surprised," said Mother Peale. "There are many rumors about me, and your father spent enough time at my table eating my food." She leaned in close to Silas. "What did you hear?"

At that, John Peale, her husband, seemed to wake up. He smiled and turned to speak to Silas, although he didn't get up from his chair.

"Did you hear she'd been in prison, boy?"

Silas shook his head.

"She was, you know," said her daughter.

"Did you hear that she owns an ivory horn from a sea cow and that she stirs her cauldron with it to raise storms?" Mr. Peale asked again.

"Also true," said Joan Peale, and laughed.

"Or that she can speak a dozen languages?"

"Now that's a lie!" shouted Mother Peale. "Seven and no more."

Silas smiled. He liked the Peales enormously and already felt like a part of the family, even though he'd been in the store only a few minutes. These were the kind of people he always knew he'd like but never met in Saltsbridge. People with interests. People with pasts.

"Silas," asked Mother Peale, "since you're here, would you mind taking a few things back with you to your uncle's?"

"Sure," he said, but Mother Peale saw by his face he took no joy in being at his uncle's and wasn't keen to go back to that house quite yet.

She brought out a large box of assorted candies, and a bag with some bottles in it. They clinked together as she lifted the bag to the top of the counter and pushed it toward Silas. Looking at the candy, she said, "I guess your uncle must be glad you're there."

"I suppose."

"Well, Uncle Umber is sure filling up the candy bowls for company."

"Maybe," said Silas, but then, thinking about it, he added, "He must be eating it all himself, because I haven't seen any candy bowls in that house."

At the mention of Uncle Umber, some people in the back of the store began whispering. Joan Peale said loudly, "Okay, Silas Umber, here is your uncle's order. I've got it all right here." She raised her hand slightly as if to stall the talk.

"Don't forget the gin!" someone yelled from the back.

And before Joan could holler back there to shut up, someone else shouted, "Uncle Umber don't drink."

"All right then!" said Joan loudly.

The man who helped with stock said, "Umber's got company. Who the hell do you think is eating all that damned candy he orders? Just put an extra bottle of gin and some more scotch in the box with the candy, and I'll take it all over. Save us a trip when he sends for more hooch tomorrow."

"No need for that, Will Garner," Joan said, as she gestured with her head and shoulders toward Silas. "Amos's son is staying at the Umber place. See? Here he is. You don't mind taking this stuff back with you, do you, Silas? Your uncle will appreciate you bringing it home. I'm afraid he doesn't much care for coming here."

Someone in the store said, "Proud. Charles Umber's always been that way, even when Mr. Bowe fired him."

Joan Peale turned to glare at the crowd, but it was too late. Silas had heard everything, and everyone around him looked embarrassed.

Silas looked down at the boxes, saw all that alcohol, and knew then that his mother would not improve here in Lichport, and worse, that his uncle not only approved of her drinking, but seemed to be encouraging her to continue. *Why?* Silas would have thought this was one thing on which he and his uncle might agree. Uncle was orderly, precise. When his mother drank, she was sloppy, slovenly, her words rough and inconsiderate as they tumbled out of her mouth without thought. There must be another reason his uncle didn't mind his mother being drunk all the time—

"Why don't I walk with you back to your uncle's house and let Will get back to stocking the shelves?" Joan swept Silas out the door, as she pulled a little wagon with the boxes of candy and the bag of gin behind them.

Once they were walking, she asked, "You doin' all right since coming here? I can't imagine how it must be coming back to Lichport, your dad missing and all. And living in that house—"

"I'm okay," Silas replied. "A little lonely, maybe. I've got a lot of time to myself. I used to think that's what I wanted, but now, well, I have a lot of time to think, that's for sure. Maybe too much. I guess I'd like to know more about the town. More about my dad and how he spent his time here. I'd sure like to know if anyone here knows anything about what happened to him."

Joan paused, as if choosing her next words very carefully. "Silas, if I knew anything about what happened to your dad, I would have told you the minute I laid eyes on you. Fact is, no one knows. Some got their ideas, but no one has ever liked your uncle much, so he's an easy target for suspicion. There are folk you could ask, maybe after you get to know the town a little better—" She seemed to think better of saying more along those lines and instead asked, "Silas Umber, did you know you once had kin all over this town? Do you know where your mom was born?"

"Where?" asked Silas.

Just before they turned left down Coach Street, Joan Peale pointed past Beacon Hill and to the left and said, "You see those dark trees past the hill?"

"Yeah."

"On the other side of those trees is Fort Street, and it was there your mother was born."

"On Fort Street?"

"Oh yes. If it were daytime, you might be able to see the chimney of the house a little above the trees. And at the end of the street are the gates to the Arvale estate, where most of your folk once lived, long, long ago. Yes, Fort was a very grand street once. Richest folks in town lived there. Only people of quality. Do you know much about your mother's people?"

They turned onto Prince Street.

"Only that they had money, and didn't think much of people who didn't."

Joan Peale laughed. "That's true enough. They were an old Lichport family. Gone now, almost every one of them. They were quite the party-givers, back in the day. They liked rich company and showing their belongings and pretty daughters to advantage. So when the town turned downward, they were one of the first families to pick up and go. Funny how you and your mom are living here now. I'll bet you could even live in that house if you wanted to. I'll bet it was left to your mother. Of course, now that she's living with your uncle, she'd have no need of it."

"I asked her about whether or not she had a house here. But she told me her family's house burned down, and that was one of the reasons they all left for Boston and New York," Silas said, as he wondered whether this was another of his mother's many lies about to be revealed.

"Well, you can see it for yourself sometime; the house is still there. People used to leave flowers on the porch. On some of the porches of the other houses, too. But no one has visited Fort Street in a long time, I think."

"Why would people leave flowers on the porches?"

Joan merely said, "You should ask your mother." With that, she put her arm around Silas's shoulder and walked him back to Temple Street.

"Ah!" Uncle exclaimed when Silas came in with the items from the store. "He leaves a man of the house, but comes home as the help! How endearing. Silas, do run those things back to the kitchen, won't you? But you may leave the candy on the steps, and I'll take it upstairs later."

Then his mother chimed in.

"So you went to the store? At this hour?"

"I met the Peales, and Joan Peale walked me back. She told me about Fort Street."

Dolores Umber was up out of her chair with surprising speed for a woman who'd been drinking all evening.

Uncle spoke quickly, to defuse the coming storm. "Oh yes, not such a nice neighborhood now. All those abandoned houses."

"Then why do people leave flowers on the porches?" Silas asked.

His mother's face went absolutely pale. She asked, "You didn't go into any of those houses, did you?"

"Are there flowers? Still? How queer," Uncle interjected. "People have such strange customs even in these enlightened times. Still, how quaint, no? Flowers for those who have passed on, yet remain fixed . . . in the memory."

"No, I didn't go in. Joan just pointed out the street to me. But why wouldn't they leave flowers on the *graves* of dead people? Why on the porch of a house?" Silas asked. He sensed that he was close to something his mother definitely didn't want him to know about.

"Obligation . . . ," Dolores muttered as she dropped back into her chair and tipped the contents of her nearly full glass down her throat. She promptly poured herself another.

Uncle cleared this throat and said, "It's nothing, Silas, just one of our strange, enduring Lichport traditions. Some old practice, I believe. Some of the families here brought their odd beliefs with them from across the sea and held tight to them. We've always been a little . . . different here, my boy. In any event, the flowers are just a curious way to say 'farewell' to the past. That's all it really is when you get right down it."

"Why would anyone say 'farewell' to a house?" Silas pressed. "I mean, what's the point of—"

Uncle interrupted and said, through slightly clenched teeth, "As I said, strange folk, hereabouts. Even in these modern times you may still observe, on our fair streets, the most remarkable eccentrics and vagabonds."

Dolores spoke up again, her eyes closed and her lips pulled tight.

"On and on and bloody on! Doesn't anything in this miserable town ever end?"

CHAPTER 19

OBLIGATIONS

DOLORES HADN'T WORN HER PEARLS in a very long time, certainly not since leaving Lichport a year after her son was born. Her mother had given her the strand of luminous little moons, just as her grandmother and her great-grandmother had done, from mother to daughter right down the line. She had been obliged to wear them on "State Occasions," on those days when the entire clan gathered together en masse: weddings, funerals, holidays, and the dreaded *visitations*.

She woke early and put on her best dress, the black taffeta with a deep V collar that she'd once thought looked very fine on her and still showed off the pearls. She put on shoes with proper heels, then looked at herself in the long mirror. She didn't smile, but she was pleased with what she saw. Of course, she reminded herself, this was not a social call. A drink would help. She was tempted, but told herself she could have a double the minute she got back to the house. *Keep your head about you. Keep your head high. Walk over there and come back and it's done.*

Since the first moment she'd set foot back in Lichport, Dolores could hear her mother's voice, waking and sleeping, every moment, a constant harangue in that high, slow whine about her obligations to the family.

"Dolores? Dearest heart? I don't care what you *think* about any of this. It's what you *do* that matters. Think what you like, but you will keep up appearances and remember your obligations. He is still family, Dolores, whether you like it or not. If you are in Lichport, you will pay a call at that house, without fail. Visitations are an *obligation*."

She couldn't bear the lecture any longer and knew there was only one way to get that voice to be quiet. So Dolores was going to Fort Street, to the house where she was born.

Before going to bed, Silas stood outside on the front porch to get some air, and, looking to the corner, saw that Bea was there. He walked down Temple to meet her. She smiled as he approached, and as Silas got next to her, she began walking too. Neither of them spoke. Bea drew even closer to his side, though she did not touch him. They walked in silence, pleased to be in each other's company, making a complete circuit of the block, up Fairwell, around Prince, down Highland Street along the cemetery fence, and back onto Temple, arriving again in front of Uncle's house. Silas looked up, hearing a door close somewhere inside the house, and when he looked back, Bea was back at the corner, where he'd first seen her. She waved at him and vanished up Fairwell Street. He smiled to himself and went back inside and up to bed.

Silas woke up early the next morning from the most vivid dream he could ever recall having.

He was standing in a high-ceilinged hall, before a long carved table set with silver, and in the hundreds of chairs around the table, Silas's kin were seated, rows and rows of all those from whom Silas was descended. He could feel that immediately. These were relatives and ancestors. Living and dead both. Hundreds gathered together to eat, each in clothing from their own time and land. The walls were hung with faded crewelwork tapestries, complicated stitched depictions of cities, towns, and great ancient houses, and with that curious insight that attends the dreamer, Silas knew these were the places where his relations had once lived or lived still. The largest tapestry, hung behind him, showed the most bizarre house Silas had ever seen, a great manor with centuries of additions, towers, and long-galleried wings stretching off, back and farther back in the forced perspective of the weaving, almost more city than house. Above the main door of the house on the tapestry was stitched, small but legible, the word A R V A L E.

Around the edges of the hall, and standing in the doorways and porticos, darker forms from even earlier times stood, barely visible now and nameless, remembered only as vague shapes sharing common blood.

Silas knew the names of only a few, his closest and most recent relations. His mother was there, seated a few chairs down, his uncle by her side.

"This is not my chair . . . ," she said, but Uncle ignored her and set upon his food, pecking and tearing at it like a vulture. Sitting in his uncle's lap was a child wrapped in cloth and hooded, its features hidden. The child reached out a hand toward the food, but Uncle pushed it away saying, "Patience, little man." At the far end of the table, some people with ruffled collars raised their glasses to Silas and laughed loudly, delighting themselves in so great a company, all joyfully carousing together. His grandfather was sitting next to him and kept filling his glass, so that wine poured over the cup's lip and down onto the table. His grandfather took no notice of the spilling wine: "The dark drink of oblivion brings little comfort in this house. So, it's wine or nothing for me!"

Directly across from Silas was an empty high-backed chair, and each time his eyes fell on that ebony throne, he began to stammer at those around him, although they ignored his questions and concern. What is this? Silas shouted, pointing at the chair. Who is coming? Who sits there? Some of the people down the table laughed knowingly, but no one would answer his questions. Fear rose in him, because he was sure that his father should be sitting there, yet even here, among the dead, his father was missing, and no one else in the great chamber seemed to notice Amos's absence.

Silas continued to yell, Who sits here? Who is coming? *but no one heard him, and far down along the table, someone stood on his chair and, ignoring him, called for music.*

Silas woke up from this dream angry, frightened, and frustrated. Had his father been in the dream, but hidden, one of the dark forms in the doorways? Was he coming? Had he left? Or was he gone, and neither the dead nor the living noticed or cared? All the ancestors and relatives had chairs appointed to them, so why was this chair—his father's, he assumed—empty? His mother and uncle were there too, so this was a family gathering; the living and the dead were present, so *where was his dad?*

Silas squirmed in the sheets twisted around his legs. He disentangled himself and tried to fall back asleep, but it was well into the morning and he was too aggravated by the dream's mysteries to do so. He dressed and went downstairs to the parlor. He was thinking he might go out and explore the Temple Cemetery to the west of the house, the one he'd passed last night while walking with Bea. His mother came down the stairs, and Silas could overhear some of her conversation with Uncle in the breakfast room. His mother sounded impatient, Uncle condescending, and at the end of the conversation came a word Silas didn't like.

"No. No. I am not going *into* the house."

"But Dolores, really! It is an anachronism. Totemism at its worst. I really can't believe—"

"I trust you will not mind if I take some flower cuttings from the side garden?"

"As you wish," Uncle said, and chuckled. "Please convey my best wishes to the Fort Street zombies."

"I would prefer it if you did not use that word."

"Of course, Dolores. They're not zombies, but really, are you sure—"

Before Uncle could finish, his mother was out the door, leaving the house for the first time since coming to Lichport.

A few moments later, when Uncle returned to his work upstairs, Silas quietly followed his mother out of the house.

CHAPTER 20

THE YOUNG AND THE RESTLESS

HE FOLLOWED HIS MOTHER as she made her way up Fairwell Street. She was still well in view and hadn't seen him behind her. As he walked, that word "zombies" stuck in Silas's mind and seemed to open an unpleasant door in his memory that had long been closed.

Silas paused, remembering the first time he'd seen a zombie movie and how it had scared the hell out him. He was ten years old and couldn't sleep, so he'd snuck back downstairs to watch TV. It was a black-and-white movie, and as the picture came into focus, there it was, shambling across the screen.

At first Silas thought it was supposed to be funny, the way the zombie walked drunkenly this way and that, never in a straight line. But then there were others, some pulling themselves from their graves with their mouths open and eyes rolled back like hungry infants, and they made awful moans as if the soil from their graves was rasping in their throats.

That was when he got scared. So scared he couldn't move, even to turn off the TV. He was terrified and fascinated both, but too scared to call for his dad, or even turn his head away, because he knew if he did, he would see one of those corpses with its rotten head cocked to one side staring at him through the window.

Amos had heard the noise and came downstairs. He took one

look at the screen and another at his son's face and quickly turned the TV off.

"So what was that movie about?"

"Monsters . . . ," said Silas, who couldn't stop looking at the now blank screen, eyes wide and unblinking as though they'd been taped open.

His dad turned Silas's shoulders so he and his son were looking at each other and said to him, "What kind of monsters, Little Bird?"

"Dead ones. Really scary dead ones. Corpses. Dead bodies coming alive and eating people."

"Silas, that's not what that movie was about. That's what was in it, what you see, and it's not too nice, I know, but those terrible images are about something else."

Silas looked at his dad questioningly, as his fear began to fall away a little at the calm certainty he heard in his dad's voice.

"It's about living people forgetting their kin. More and more, people bury their dead, but then they forget about them, almost like they weren't family anymore just because they died. Every now and again, those living folks get to feeling bad about how they don't even know where all their kin are buried. Then one of them writes a book or a movie about zombies. Dead folk who come back angry. It's just people feeling a little guilty. That's all those movies are about. Zombies are just reminders that someone has been forgotten by their kin."

"But they eat brains . . ." Silas said, still unsettled.

"Of course they do. That's the part that should have been remembering them."

Even though he felt better after talking with his dad, Silas was still frightened by what he'd seen. He didn't think about zombies all the time, but they stayed close to the surface of his fears, and he sometimes thought about them when his dad told stories about the funeral business, although he never said anything because he liked his dad's stories about his work and didn't want him to stop sharing them. When zombies would sit up unexpectedly in his thoughts, Silas would try to force them out of his mind right away. Sometimes he was successful, but not always.

As he grew older, he began to think his fear of them might have been related to how much he wanted to believe his dad could protect him from anything. If his dad was a mortician, then it was his work that prepared the dead for actually being dead. As a mortician, Amos was supposed to make sure the dead weren't moving anymore, even made sure their mouths were stitched closed. Those zombies in the movie suggested to Silas that maybe his father missed things sometimes—that maybe he didn't always pay attention to his work, that some of the corpses he got ready for burying maybe weren't really ready but his dad just hadn't noticed. His dad had important work to do. Silas knew his dad wasn't perfect; his mother told him that all the time. But if his dad didn't do his work perfectly, every time, then some people wouldn't be ready for death, wouldn't be ready to be dead, and maybe they'd come back angry. And now that he wasn't sure what his father did for a living, maybe that meant Amos hadn't been right about everything after all.

After a hesitant step, Silas ran to catch up with his mother.

A wet, chill wind was blowing into town from the sea as Silas turned the corner onto Fort Street. He was worried about what he might find there. Far down the street, he could just see his mom coming through a gate and its overgrown hedge, her brief visit at the house apparently already concluded. Her hands were empty now; the flowers she'd been carrying were gone. Silas backed into some bushes so she wouldn't see him. As she passed by, he saw she was ashen-faced and walking much more briskly now than when she'd left Uncle's house.

Nervous and breathing hard, Silas was suddenly overwhelmed by the scent of wisteria, despite the bare green vines he had seen a moment ago. Halfway down the block, he could just make out the roof of the house, which rose above the gate through which he'd seen his mother emerge. As Silas stared, he thought he saw a pillar of fire rise from the roof and lick at the sky with a blue-hued flame, but when he looked down and back up again, he saw only the overgrown chimney, the vision merely a play of light from the sliver of blue sky against the incoming clouds.

The wisteria smell was overpowering, and that rich perfume reminded Silas of funerals, because when his grandfather died, everyone had sent flowers. When Silas had entered his grand-father's house on the day of the funeral, he was nearly knocked down by the smell of roses, lilies, tuberoses, stock, heliotrope, irises, lavender, and bowls of wisteria flowers. His dad had told him this was the old way of Lichport, which still clung to the tra-dition of scented flowers, used to mask the smell of the corpse during the wake. . . .

Enough. That was enough. He was making himself nervous.

The pavement was broken everywhere, and weeds tall as bushes had grown up through the cracks. The property on his left was enclosed by an enormous thicket of briar roses, their blooms long since blown. Among the thorns, buried like bones in the high green bushes, there was a gate. The heavy vines had long since wound through every part of it, including the bars, which ren-dered the gate unopenable. Through gaps in the bars, Silas could see a small portion of the front garden. Like everything else on Fort Street, it was wild—a sort of wilderness of high self-seeded shrubs and randomly growing trees laid over a lost world. Near the steps of the house, there was a small patch that had been cleared, and in it, Silas saw something that caught both his attention and his breath.

There was what appeared to be a woman kneeling in the small clearing. Silas thought she might be a mannequin or some kind of absurd scarecrow, because she wasn't moving. The figure wore a broad straw hat, very tattered at the edges and dirty, with weeds springing up from where the crown met the brim. Bees were swarming all around her limbs, setting down in groups on her exposed and discolored hands and neck, yet she didn't brush them away or flinch. She wore a floral dress, much stained, especially over the arms and down the front, and moss grew from the fabric around the hem where it touched the ground. Silas wondered how long ago the figure had been put up in the yard, and by whom? Kids messing around? Someone's idea of art?

Silas leaned forward and put his face right up against the gate to get a better look. *Did she just move?* Silas thought he saw the figure bend slightly, very slowly. *Wait. There!* It haltingly reached its hand forward, slowly and almost imperceptibly, toward a small bunch of weeds on the ground in front of it. Not sure what to do, but knowing it was rude to stand and stare, Silas said, "Good morning, ma'am."

He waited for an answer, but none came. The woman, who had just taken a full minute to wrap her hand around the weed, stopped moving and was still again. She said nothing, but her head tilted slightly backward, toward Silas, although her face remained hidden behind her ruined hat. Then her arm jerked slightly and her body rocked back, and there was the weed pulled free from the ground, clutched in her brown hand.

"Okay, well, good day to you, ma'am," Silas said, wondering who she was and how many people actually still lived on this street he thought had been abandoned long ago.

The plots were very large, and there were only four or five houses on each side of the street, separated by what might have once been formal lawns but were now fields of weeds as tall as summer corn. Far down at the end of the street, he could make out a high wall and great gates, each bearing an ornate letter *A*. *For Arvale*, Silas thought, just as Joan Peale had said. Beyond the gate, low clouds hid in shadow, then revealed the highest chimneys, spires, and towers. Again and again they quickly flashed in the brief light, as if they couldn't decide whether or not they wanted to be seen. A great familiarity was rising in his blood and drew him toward the end of the street, but when he arrived in front of the gate where he'd seen his mother emerge, he stopped, unable to wonder about anything other than why his mother had come here.

Silas turned to look at the front of the house of his mother's family. He found he could barely see it from the sidewalk; like the other houses on Fort Street, it was surrounded by a vast hedge, high and dense. Visible above the greening roof, the chimney was almost completely enveloped by ropey vines of wisteria and green ivy that held its color against the coming of winter.

The gate to the front yard stood open, but torn bits of foliage lay about it, probably from where his mother had opened the gate, perhaps the first time it had been opened in many years.

As he made his way through the hedge, Silas could now see much more of the mansion. It was an enormous place, a house people had added to over many years as the family swelled. There was an eighteenth-century central structure, with three stories and five dormers that emerged from the top floor. The windows were high and wide, and the front door was set into the house's brick facing and framed with ornamental pillars that supported a curved classical arch over the door. Two wings emerged from the sides of the house, perhaps built in the early nineteenth century, but Silas wasn't sure because they were made with bricks that matched the earlier architecture. It appeared that at some later date, a large open porch had been added to the front of the home.

As Silas pushed his way into the yard, he followed the same rough path his mother had just used. He had to break some low branches off some of the many small conifers that had been planted there, and push through an array of weeds and overgrown shrubs to reach the front of the house. He mounted the stairs slowly, worried that the rotten wood might give way under his weight. He looked up and back over his shoulder repeatedly, a response to the unmistakable feeling that he was being watched, maybe by something hiding in the weeds. Or maybe his mother had seen him and had doubled back.

Silas looked back over the yard one more time but saw no one, so he walked up onto the porch. It was covered with dirty plastic flowers, bottles, many old vases that might have contained something sweet at one time because they were filled with dead ants, and small abandoned beehives that floated in murky green water. Potted plants, mostly dead ivy, were stacked up near the boarded-over front door; a few had fallen over and sent their roots down through the rotten floorboards of the porch, so they were now thriving and crawling their way over the brickwork that covered the front of the house. One vase by the door stood bright, brimming with the fresh-cut flowers his mother had brought.

Like most of the wood on the exterior of the house, the boards over the front door were dry and partially rotted, so it took Silas only a few minutes to pull them loose. His mother had not gone into the house, unless she'd done so by another way. He thought it strange that the front door would be unlocked. Why bother boarding up a house when you hadn't even bothered to lock the front door?

Silas opened the door and stretched his head inside to listen and sniff the air. No noise at all. He guessed the roof was sound because the interior, so far as he could tell, seemed well preserved, although everything was covered in dust. There wasn't much of a moldy smell, either, so there probably weren't any broken pipes or major leaks.

He walked inside and stood at the center of the entry hall. From there, he turned left and entered a long octagonal room with a marble fireplace on one wall. The windows, bookcases, and ornamental shelves were all flanked by flat, decorative columns that extended only a few inches from the walls. Portions of the walls had been embellished with detailed paintings of Roman urns filled with flowers. The wood floors were piled high with books and magazines, some with dates as recent as fifteen years ago. An enormous bed stood at the center of the room, surrounded by many chairs, which all faced the bed. It seemed as though, at one time, lots of people had been sitting there together, like an audience in a theater, as they looked on the bed's occupant. The bed was long since empty, and its embroidered bedclothes hung in tatters from the canopy. It might have been the weight of them, and perhaps the work of moths, that had put tears and holes in the once-rich fabric.

A tapping sound from the far end of the room startled him. A sparrow was sitting on the ledge of one of the windows, striking the glass with its beak. It must have flown in, maybe coming down the chimney. The little bird was beating its beak on the window, and as Silas approached, it became frantic, as it turned over and over and flapped its wings madly. He tried to open the window, but it had been sealed shut, and he didn't feel comfortable breaking the glass. The bird fell off the ledge onto the floor, then leapt awkwardly into the air, flying from the room into the hallway.

Silas turned back toward the entry hall to see if he could find the bird when another noise caught his attention. From the upper floor he heard a hollow scraping on the floorboards, as if a chair was being shifted perhaps. He didn't move, hardly breathed, but heard nothing else.

As Silas walked back into the entrance hall, he could smell turpentine or pitch. To his right, long stairs rose to the upper floors, and, his curiosity stronger than his fear, he began to walk up, careful to stay close to the wall in case any of the stairs proved weak. The turpentine smell grew stronger as he approached the second floor. He crossed the landing, and before him stood a very wide, closed door that would, Silas assumed, lead to a larger room that overlooked the front yard and Fort Street. In front of the door, several more dried-out ivy plants in ornate porcelain vases had been left on the floor.

Quietly Silas walked to the door and turned its tarnished handle. The door swung open silently into a room flooded with light from the large windows facing the street, and for an instant, Silas couldn't see through the brightness. The smell of turpentine burned in his nostrils, dizzying him.

As his eyes grew accustomed to the light, Silas instantly froze in the doorway, seeing what looked to be a corpse positioned upright in a chair by the window. His eyes quickly flashed about the room, but he couldn't focus on anything except the body in the chair. It was clothed in a stained dark suit, a long morning coat, and a loose cravat. There were several large, sealed Chinese vases near the corpse, and the smell of honey and pitch were even more pervasive in the room than they had been on the upper landing.

Without moving from the doorway, Silas saw that the corpse

was not rotten but desiccated, like the dried meats that graced his uncle's dinner table. And it was swollen in places, its arms seeming especially strong, with thick, long nails on each finger of its large hands. Its skin was discolored, very dark in patches, almost black on the neck and bottom of the jaw and about the wrists and lower portion of the hands.

Silas had just begun to shift his attention to the room when very slowly, almost mechanically, the corpse turned its upper torso and raised its arm to point at Silas in the doorway. He felt his heart jump. With a slightly jerky motion, as if its head had previously been stuck looking forward out the window, the corpse continued to turn its head toward its guest and opened its mouth; opening and closing it several times, as if it were testing the muscles, preparing them to speak.

Silas looked on, wide-eyed. It was just like the night he'd watched the zombie film on TV. He couldn't run or speak or move or think of what to do other than not to blink for fear the corpse would—in that split second—rise out of its chair and take a step toward him.

The corpse made a long, low hiss, an exhalation of breath from windpipes long sealed, now opening again to air. The voice, as it emerged, was somber and deep, but beneath it was a strange sound, a kind of rattling in its chest, as though the walls of its lungs were desperately clapping to get attention. Slowly, again and again, it drew breath into itself, and Silas could see its chest rise and fall. Then it spoke.

"Name?" it rasped.

Silas couldn't make his mouth work.

Then, slower and louder, as if it thought Silas hadn't heard it or perhaps spoke another language, it said, "What . . . is . . . your . . . name?"

Fear had a hold on Silas, and he was breathing so fast he thought if he didn't start running, he would pass out, but his legs would not obey him, so he stood there, fear-frozen just outside the door, staring and panting, the corpse's question ringing in his ears. After a moment of trying to control his breathing, Silas managed to whisper his name so softly he could barely hear himself say it.

The corpse made a throat-clearing sound and began to speak with more clarity and not quite as slowly. Its tone was refined, well polished if a bit rusty around the edges, bearing the confidence of one who was used to being obeyed.

"'Silas' is not a Lichport name. I don't recall any Silases in Lichport. What were your grandparents' names? On what street did they reside?"

Silas opened his mouth, but no words came.

"Well?" the corpse demanded.

"Um—," Silas tried to form the words. "Silas is my first name, sir. My last name is Umber." His voice cracked as he spoke.

Was the corpse smiling now? Was the tanned skin of its face stretching into a grin?

"Now that is a name I know. We're kin, child! Come closer! Your mother's father's father invites you in!"

Silas looked about the room as he entered, calmed only somewhat by the corpse's hoarse but kindly and familiar tone. The rooms downstairs had once been well-appointed, but this was a room in which someone with money had spent a lot of time. Even with the dry rot and falling plaster, Silas could see that it had once been very fine. The room was wide and high-ceilinged and had perhaps been the house's best bedroom, or maybe a family gathering place away from the busier ground floor. Some of the walls had been painted with verdigris foliage, and edges of the ceilings were adorned with carved moldings. Moth-eaten dark velvet curtains hung, most still drawn back from the windows, the rest mimicking the starry night sky with the light shining through their many holes. There were mahogany chairs placed about the room, and like the chamber downstairs, many books had been piled about on small tables. Tarnished silver urns adorned both ends of the marble mantel.

Silas looked back at the corpse of his great-grandfather in its large, leather upholstered chair, mustered up enough courage, and said, "Sir? May I ask . . . when did you—I mean, what are you—Sorry! I mean, are you . . . are you . . . dead?"

"You are suggesting I am dead?" The corpse raised his arm and pointed at Silas in mock recrimination. "Yet here we are speaking to each other. I would suggest, then, that I am not dead, although I admit, I have looked better."

Silas looked at the animated corpse, its tight skin pulled thin over the skull, the finger bone pushing through the leather flesh of the hands, the vacant corpse-stare.

"Then, well, why aren't, I mean . . . how do you . . ." Silas stammered toward a question but couldn't find one that didn't seem rude.

"It's a joke, child! Of course I'm dead. Don't I look dead?"

"Well, I would say yes, you do look a little . . . dead," Silas answered, aware of how ridiculous he must sound.

"Indeed I do look 'a little dead,' and that is because I am, in fact, deceased. Oh, you should have seen folks when I died but kept going about my business. I was not the first person in town to do that, not even the first on this street, but it always takes people by surprise. People assume that after a funeral, you will be quiet, that the dead will rest in peace. I am afraid I may have disappointed them in that regard. At first, some people just kept bringing casseroles, like the wake had never ended. They were clearly unsure of the protocol when a person just up and says 'no' to death. Still, for a while, they accommodated my . . . eccentricities. See that album over there?" The corpse pointed. "Please, feel free."

A photo album rested on a small table near his great-grandfather, thick with captured moments out of the family's past. Most were in black and white; a few near the end were in color.

"I think, for a time, it was even considered fashionable when the old pater stuck around. It seemed to bespeak a certain nobility. I must say, I am inclined to agree. So at first, when the heads of some of better households remained beyond their allotted hour, our families obliged us, as you can see."

In the photographs, Silas saw a bizarre collection of images. The usual sorts of pictures taken at family gatherings—Christmas, Easter, even the old Lichport holidays like Revolution Day—but in all of them, there was the corpse with the family posed around him. A Revolution Day summer party: a family picnicking in their yard, striped hats with stars, sitting on blankets, and next to the blanket, a chair with a smiling corpse dressed in a dark suit. Children made faces behind its back. Just another member of the family. In many of the photographs, the corpse's eyes were open and so was his mouth, clearly caught by the camera in mid-sentence. People seemed to be pleased enough at his presence, although at every holiday gathering, Silas noticed, there was one little girl in the pictures who always looked upset when she was set to pose next to the corpse. In several of the pictures, she was crying and reaching out in the opposite direction of the corpse to someone standing just out of frame.

"For a long time, we just continued as we always had, but

then, and who knows why, our families seemed less and less inclined to care for their ancestors. Perhaps our presence bothered the children, or maybe they wanted to get on with their own lives, who can say? Some just boarded us up inside our houses. Others began their separations more delicately with the tomb houses. You'll see them behind certain of the homes on this street. Elaborate stone tombs, built to be miniatures of the main houses. The family would just take their dead but slow-departing beloved and move them in with all their favorite belongings, and if lucky, the old corpse might be let out for one or two holidays a year, maybe his birthday."

Silas was looking at the photos near the end of the album. The scared little girl was now a young woman, and he could see by her face, by her frown, that she was his mother. The last pictures seemed to chronicle the family packing, preparing to move out of the house in which Silas was now standing. Several images showed people hugging the corpse, saying their good-byes, and always in the background, there was his mother, standing as far away from her grandfather as she could.

As if he knew what Silas was looking at, his great-grandfather said, "Can you imagine? Your family leaving you in your house to rot? Just one day telling you, 'We're moving on, You have everything you need, Gran? Dad, you gonna be okay?' And then they board up the front door and never come back. There is very little dignity left in you when your kin turn their backs while you can still see them go. To be fair, some just moved camp. Over to the new houses on the south side of town, facing the water; or they built large homes on Prince Street or Garden. Some would come back every now and then, for birthdays, you know. Most just left town. Those never came back.

"After the families left, other people began to come. Strangers mostly. Rather like pilgrims. They'd come to touch the hand of a corpse. That's so old-timey, don't you think? Used to be believed, so I learned, that to touch the hand of a corpse brought good luck and could heal many afflictions. People used to come once or twice a week. I should have hung out a sign and charged a fee.

"And let me assure you, my boy, this is not by any means a Lichport-only phenomenon, though, generally speaking, it happens only in the best families. What do you think all those royal mummies are in Egypt? I'll bet they started out just like me. Made a little fortune all their own, nice things around them, a fine home. Who wants to up and leave all that behind after you spend a lifetime winning it from the world? I'll bet you a hundred dollars some of those 'mummies' locked up in their tombs or in museums could speak if they wanted to. Bet they are still dreaming away, even now, in their bodies. Wouldn't knowing *that* wake people up to their obligations!"

"Obligations to what?" Silas asked. "What do you mean? If someone's dead, what else are people supposed to do for them?"

"I mean: Families don't die, Silas. I mean: We have obligations to our kin, to our ancestors, whether they are with us bodily to remind us or not. We don't just stop at our skin. We go way back. Every one of us. I have had a bit of time to think about this, and the new fashion for abandoning ancestors troubles me, even though I'm not really part of the world anymore and, obviously, can't really be objective. Silas, a question?"

"Certainly."

"Have you ever seen anyone like me before today?"

"No, sir. I most certainly have not."

"What do you make of this?" The corpse gestured to himself. "You seem to have inherited the brains from our side of the family, and goodness knows your father is a learned man regarding such arcane matters. Have you come across this sort of thing much in your literary adventures? Or has your father spoken of it to you? 'Restless,' we're sometimes called, but the word 'Restless' has never sat well with me, and I'd like to know what else people in my particular situation might have been called."

"I think," said Silas, hoping this would be taken the right way, "I think you are what used to be called a *revenant*."

"That's not some kind of zombie, is it? I am mortified by such indelicate associations."

"No. No. Not at all. A revenant is just a person who's died, but who hangs around for a while, that's all. I think there are other names in other places. I read about these things in ancient Greece called the *ataphoi*, and it just means people not buried in their ancestral tombs."

"Were *they* dangerous?"

"I think so," Silas admitted, self-conscious now for mentioning it.

"Perhaps revenant is more appropriate then."

"Yeah, those are more like people—well, they are people, some nice, some not so nice, but they just won't lie down when they die."

"Yes, that sounds right."

Silas was utterly riveted watching and hearing his great-grandfather speak, but he couldn't help thinking, as he looked at the corpse, wouldn't death be better than what he saw before him? Continuation, yes, but in this way? He had to ask:

"I can see how it would be very lonely . . . are you happy like this? Happy to continue in this way for as long as it lasts? Other than the family not coming around anymore, is there anything that troubles you? Does it, well, does it hurt?"

"No, it doesn't hurt, but there are some problems, I've found.

For one thing, I don't sleep anymore. That's the only thing that troubles me, really. It's all one long day now. Drowsy dreaming and wide-eyed awake, one and the same. I look out the window some days and see my children come up the street toward the house, toward my steps, though they've both been gone for a while now. Other days, I see folks I don't recognize coming and going so much faster than before, so I know days have passed, passed me right by because I am not moving. Not really."

"And my vision and hearing have changed. Seeing is different now. When I focus on something, there is a sort of shift, and it's like I'm both here and there, subject and object, all at once. I see something, but can very keenly see and feel myself seeing it. Maybe that's death encroaching, the moment—for me, a long one—where one distinct being becomes part of everything it's ever known, everything it's seen, smelled, experienced. Also, I don't get around much anymore, and I used to enjoy a walk after supper. Sometimes I hear things. Voices. And I know they are not from anything around me in this world. I think that's because I have one foot here and another there, so I can hear things in both."

All the fear had left him, and Silas's heart had grown very tender toward the old man. He was nodding in understanding all the while as his great-grandfather spoke to him.

"I know what you mean," Silas said. "I have trouble sleeping sometimes too, these days. And when I do sleep, I have strange dreams."

"About your father?" his great-grandfather asked.

Silas nodded at the directness and accuracy of his great-grandfather's question. "Why do you ask that?"

"Because no one comes here unless they're looking for something, because the dead sometimes visit the living in dreams, and because we're family, and so I can hear a little of your heart and can tell that an absence has broken it."

"Yes, I've been dreaming of him a lot lately, although in one particular dream, everyone was there but him. I can't stop thinking about him, because I don't know where he is."

"Your father came here on several occasions, you know. He would sometimes stop here on those rare occasions when he'd be called up to the great house at the end of the street, the old Umber place, though he wouldn't say much about his business there, and I've never been farther than Arvale's front gate. Amos always had the most interesting questions, and he was extremely polite and gracious. Most of those flowers on the porches of this street were put there by your father. I think I was a help to him, but again, that was long ago."

"Have you seen my dad recently? He disappeared last year and no one's seen him. Maybe you have, or know something about where I might find him?"

"In that time he has not come here, Silas. At least I don't think I've seen him. Hard to say anymore because minutes, hours, and days don't mean the same to me as they used to. I can see some things far off, but it's mostly my own kin I watch, coming and going about their business. When I see them, it's a long way away and always through a mist. But if you like, I can try to catch sight of him, though I can't promise anything will come of it. I can't see things just because I want to, and sometimes it's like staring into a sky without stars. If you want me to look *away*, to look for your dad, you'll have to help me, because he's not a blood relation to me. Would you like me to try?"

"Yes, sir. Please. I'd be very grateful."

"Then why don't you sit down next to me. It may be easier if I hold your hand, since your father's blood is in you and not me . . ." His great-grandfather paused and looked down at Silas. "May I ask you something?"

"Of course," Silas replied.

"You are kin, my great-grandson, and I am glad to try and help you, but I wonder if it wouldn't be too much to ask for something in return?"

"If I can do something for you, I will."

"No one comes here anymore, Silas. Everyone is gone, and no one comes back. I understand. They want to get on with their lives. And no one wants to be reminded of the inevitability of death every day by a corpse sitting with them at the dinner table. Still, a visit every now and then would please me very much. Every now and again, I would like a little news of the world. Some gossip."

Silas smiled at his great-grandfather, and the corpse's face became just slightly more taut and seemed to be smiling back. A bargain had been struck.

Silas extended his arm, and his great-grandfather slowly took his hand.

It was a very strange sensation, Silas found, holding hands with a corpse. His great-grandfather's skin was very dry, but a little waxy on the surface, like a candle. It still had just a bit of suppleness left in it, which explained how he could still move. Silas felt the nails right away. They were long and sharp at the end because some had broken off, or had been broken off, when they got too long. On his middle finger, his great-grandfather wore an ancient-looking gold ring, set with an enormous blue sapphire. Silas's eyes were captured by the stone's pale light until he felt the corpse's grip close in on his own hand. It was not painful, but it was very strong, and Silas knew that if he had wanted to pull away, he very likely would not have been able to do it. Already, even as he continued to speak, a change was coming over his ancestor: The color of his eyes had dissolved, turning first to spheres like clear quartz, then becoming milk-white. His mouth stretched open, and the words seemed to come from deep within his torso, like they were spoken at the bottom of a well, no longer formed by his dry lips, tongue, and whatever was left of his vocal cords. His voice came up in a low, hollow rasp and yet seemed to fill the whole of Silas's hearing.

"Silas, you may ask me questions. I'll try to answer. I don't know what I'll say when this starts, so prepare yourself. This is just the damnedest thing," said his great-grandfather, and with that, the corpse went completely rigid, as though he had been poured full of cement. Silas looked down at his hand, held firmly in the corpse's stonelike grip, and then up at the corpse's face, and when he began to speak, it was not in the voice of a moment ago— familiar, familial—but something else, far older, far stranger, the combined voices of every ancestor with whom Silas shared blood speaking in chorus.

"You stand in the house of the long line, the full glass, and the word of welcome. Yet the ebony chair is empty. The chair of the Janus . . . who shall take this perilous seat? Where is the wanderer? Where is the lost one? Who—"

"Yes!" Silas cried out, interrupting. "That was in my dream!"

"—shall sit in the accustomed place of his kin? The hall is full, yet one is absent. The chair of ebony is empty still. Bestir! Bestir! Why do you wait? The Road of Virgil stands open! The Orphic strain pulls at the soul's strings and draws the listener toward the abyss! You ask for words, but I shall say no more!"

"Wait, please, I—I don't understand. . . ."

"In the hall are those bound by blood, bound by the pact. You seek your father but cannot see him. And all the while, the ebony chair is empty! Who shall hold the threshold when the Door Doom comes? I have given you words, but I shall say no more."

"Do you mean my father is there in the hall? Why can't I see him? Is the hall this town? Lichport? Why isn't he there, in the empty black chair, in the place across from me? Is he still here in Lichport?"

"He is where he has always been. The ebony chair waits for another in the hall of Arvale, though you cannot see the matter aright. Enough, I shall sink down!"

"Wait! Please! Can you just tell me where to find him?"

"Long is the son's way, and it is fraught with darkness. Those who see absence know only longing. The sun sinks down into the sea. The dog howls from the cave of bones. The earth roars at the sin of Cain. The ship of souls lies at anchor, waiting. Those who are lost shall be doomed to wander. Only those who know their own place may seek the place of another. The ebony chair awaits its owner. Look behind you to find what you seek. Take up the mask of Janus and your work begins! You must look behind to see ahead. Before you stands the ebony chair and the dark hall. Seek not to see your father in that hallowed seat, for it is thine own. . . . Now I sink down. . . ."

And with those words the corpse closed its eyes, and its head rolled to one side and did not move for many moments.

Softly, Silas leaned over closer to his great-grandfather and said. "Are you okay?"

The mouth of the corpse began to move, opening and closing again like an automaton, before speaking.

"I am all right, just not entirely myself for a moment. Was I able to help you?"

Silas felt embarrassed, because he was sure there was something his ancestor had said that would be helpful, but he would have to think about it and try to untangle the threads of what he'd heard.

"Yes, I think so," Silas said.

Perhaps sensing Silas's confusion, the corpse said, "Give it some thought. An oracle can be a damned obscure thing. I am sorry I couldn't be clearer, but this kind of thing goes its own way, and I have no power over it once it starts."

"I'll try to see what I can make of it."

"I will think about it too. There may be some other folk here in Lichport, or close to Lichport . . . I'll try to remember. There are three women who I think knew your father. By rights, you may inquire of them, though they may not be easy to find. I expect their old house still stands at Coach and Silk, but wait a bit. Be here more. Maybe you know someone who can show you around. See more of the town, and you will have an easier time finding folk who may help you. I suspect when the ladies who dwell in that mansion are ready to see you, that's when you'll be able to see them. *Wait for the light.* . . ." But his great-grandfather's voice was getting thin, and he said, "I don't think I have it in me to say much more just at present. Perhaps we could talk about that another time? I will have to rest now for several days."

Silas thought maybe his great-grandfather was holding something back, maybe just trying to ensure that Silas would come back and visit again, although he could see his ancestor did indeed look tired: His head hung forward, shoulders slumped, and his arms hung limply from his shoulders. Whatever force it was that animated his body, it had clearly been exhausted.

Before Silas turned to go, he said "Great-grandfather, thank you so much for your help. I have very much enjoyed my time with you."

"That is very kind of you to say, Silas."

Silas began to turn away, but then looked back at his great-grandfather.

"Sir, I don't mean to be disrespectful, but wouldn't you like to rest . . . finally? Be done with it all?"

His great-grandfather turned his head in a slow, graceful, tired arc toward the window, and the light played across the stretched skin of his face, showing its translucence.

"Child, if I wanted to go to bed, I'd have been set under the dirt a long time ago. I am waiting."

"May I ask, for what?"

"To see what happens!"

"What happens? To what?"

"Any old damn thing. To the town. To me. For the stars to fall. Who knows how long this trick might last? So, my wise great-grandson, to the offer of sympathetic immolation—or whatever you may have had in mind—may I gratefully decline?" The corpse paused. "But Silas? You come back and visit me, won't you? Besides, this is your house now."

"My house?"

The corpse's hand was rising slowly, pointing at a table covered in documents near the wall.

"Well, I know your mother doesn't want this house—couldn't even bring herself to come inside, aye, I know she was here—so that makes it yours. If you hand me that stack of papers over there, and a pen, I'll change the will."

Silas watched as his great-grandfather slowly turned the pages of his many-paged will, struck through several lines, and carefully wrote in Silas's name.

"There now, it's all yours, Silas. What's left of it. And all you have to do is pay the occasional visit."

"I would have come anyway," Silas said sincerely.

"I know. And that makes it especially nice to give you a little something."

His great-grandfather was still writing, now on a small, stained piece of paper he had removed from a pocket inside his jacket. At the bottom of some barely legible lines, he made his signature. Folding the paper up, he handed it to Silas and said, "Is your father's friend Mrs. Bowe still residing in Lichport? Yes? Then please deliver this to her. She'll know what to do with it."

Silas took the paper and put it in his pocket, resting his other hand on the corpse's shoulder. He was eager to come back and hear more, and in the meantime, maybe his great-grandfather would think of something or see something that might help him find his dad.

The visit to his convivial ancestor's house left him feeling unsettled now about when it was that life actually ended and death began. Before meeting his great-grandfather, it had all seemed more cut-and-dried. Death might be a sort of memory loss, when people or spirits forget who they were in life. Silas was also not especially comforted by his relative's version of life everlasting. As he closed the door behind him and took the wooden steps two at a time down into the overgrown front garden, he could not quite decide whether the Restless had conquered time or been trapped by it, making limbos of their own undying flesh. As he closed the gate behind him, he caught his finger on a thorn. He stood looking at the drop of blood on his fingertip for several moments before briefly putting it in his mouth and making his way home. At least he knew he might investigate a little farther afield about his dad, and he even had an address, a place to begin. And as for someone to show him something more of the town, as his great-grandfather had suggested, Silas was hoping Bea might oblige.

He went to see Mrs. Bowe. He had the paper to deliver to her from his great-grandfather, and he wanted a little more time to think before going back to Temple Street. As he entered his house, with his own key, Mrs. Bowe called from the other side, inviting him over.

"And where have we been today?" She asked from the dining room, as she set a sphere of crystal back on a shelf.

"Fort Street."

"Really? Well, I trust you saw to your obligations?" she said with a small smile.

"You seem to know a lot about my family, Mrs. Bowe."

"Yes—" But then the smile left her face. "Formally, professionally, Silas, I don't approve of that sort of thing. The dead should not be encouraged to linger. But the Restless here in Lichport keep to themselves, and those are their houses, so they can go on living in them if they like, I suppose."

Silas was still having trouble accepting that everyone in town knew about these matters, about living corpses in the houses. He meant no disrespect to his great-grandfather, but what kind of a town was this?

Remembering the note, Silas handed Mrs. Bowe the paper his great-grandfather had asked him to deliver.

"He wanted me to give you this," said Silas.

Mrs. Bowe paused before extending her hand to take the note from him. Her eyes became small as she opened the paper and read its contents. "I see . . . I see. All right. I will make arrangements. Silas, you are about to become a man of means. . . . Your great-grandfather has made you a very generous gift."

Not wanting to press her about the note's particulars, and not sure how he felt about taking money from someone he'd only just met, even family, Silas changed the subject. "My great-grandfather told me that there might be some other people in town I could ask about my dad, but he was too tired to go into much detail. Do you have any idea whom he might have meant? He mentioned three women and described the house where they might be found . . . maybe that tall house on Coach and Silk, is that the place he meant?"

Mrs. Bowe's face tightened, but then she raised an eyebrow as a shadow of fear crossed her face.

"The three . . . ," she said under her breath.

"Who?"

"No one," replied Mrs. Bowe, sitting down. "That house is mostly empty, though it is true that your father has certainly visited it. It's a very old house with some remarkable architectural features. Your father used to say that in some houses, and I'm sure he meant in the *features* of some houses, there are things much older than the town. Elements brought from elsewhere, other lands. Antiques and architectural ornaments, that's all. We have some very remarkable homes here," she said, her back straight, her face now expressionless.

"But Silas, surely this will keep? I can't imagine why your great-grandfather thought this was important just now. It's not safe to go wandering through these old abandoned houses. Here," she said, walking toward the bookshelf, "if you're so interested in that old house, I am sure we can find you a book or two about the architectural history of Lichport. Wouldn't that be interesting?"

CHAPTER 21

THE NARROWS

Silas awoke barely an hour after going to bed. Despite Uncle's lecture on the virtues of hard mattresses and how they induce "light, healthful sleep," Silas was finding it more and more difficult to rest in the house on Temple Street.

The hard mattress wasn't helped by the fact that the house did nothing but make noise. Like its master, the house itself was restless. Branches scratched against the windows. Heating pipes banged suddenly and the floorboards creaked, even when no one was walking on them. And the knocking. It could begin at any time and might continue for up to a half hour before it stopped. The first time Silas heard it he thought something upstairs was being struck repeatedly, the sound of something hard hitting something soft. Sometimes it sounded like stomping, over and over and over, on the walls and floor. Uncle always explained away the noise: the pipes, or rodents in the walls, but Silas didn't believe him. He hadn't lived there very long, but he already knew most of Uncle's tells. When Uncle laughed, he was lying. When Uncle changed the subject, he was lying. When Uncle tried to sound like he was siding with Silas instead of Dolores, he was lying. So where was all the noise coming from, and why did Uncle keep lying about it?

Since following his mother down Fort Street, Silas felt differently about the large houses he saw and the large house he was currently occupying. Now there were too many closed doors for his liking. Too many unexplained noises.

So when Silas awoke in the dark of his room and heard the sounds coming from the north wing, he tensed. Uncle was awake too. The thought of Uncle wandering around the house while he and his mother slept made Silas feel nauseated. He imagined Uncle standing outside the door to his room, or his mother's, while they slept . . . listening, maybe even opening the door a bit, staring as the hall light sliced across closed eyes. Looking at their bodies like the subjects of his photographs. Just the thought of it threw a chill up and down Silas's back.

He sat silently in the dark, barely breathing, hardly moving. But then he thought of the town waiting just beyond the porch: *I am not a prisoner in this house. If I want to take a walk in the middle of the night, what are they going to do? Lock me in my room?*

He got up and dressed himself normally, as though it were morning, with no attempt to be quiet anymore. Again, his great-grandfather's words were close to him: "See something more of the town." He pulled on his jacket and shoes, and before leaving the room, he got a flashlight from his backpack, because although most of the streetlights seemed to be lit, he knew some certain of the lanes were darker than others. He turned on the hall light and walked confidently down the stairs, across the entrance hall, out of the house, and into the street. *See?* he told himself. *Not a prisoner.* And as he walked, he began to hum to himself.

At dusk Lichport held its breath, but by midnight, the town had begun to talk to itself.

Silas could hear faint voices way down by the docks where a ship might have arrived, the sound of night birds calling out their sharp evening laments away over the marshes, and music, the high, long whine of a violin, from somewhere down toward the sea. From the south, perhaps from within the wide expanse of Newfield Cemetery, dogs were barking. Now, at midnight, Lichport was awake and almost lively. He walked north.

Silas looked at the Umber family plot across from him, hoping beyond reason that he'd see Bea waiting. The rusted arch stood empty, framing nothing but the air. *Of course she's not here,* he told himself. *What would any girl be doing out alone in the middle of the night?* But the other noises rose up to greet him, and Silas followed the distant tune of the violin, away toward the sea and the wharf and the Narrows.

Both his mom and Uncle had told Silas to "keep clear of the Narrows."

The Narrows was the "lower" portion of Lichport, which crawled right up and out from the sea in crooked lanes and turning alleys. "Full of low-class people," Uncle said. "Shopkeeps and criminals," his mother added, telling him that "people have gone missing down there." But the Peales lived in the Narrows, and that was all Silas needed to know about it.

The Narrows were not hard to find, for most of the east/west running streets drained into the Narrows and then down into the sea. He returned to Temple Street and walked west, then walked up Coach for a couple of blocks, looked down Lower Street, and could see that it quickly plunged downward very steeply. After a foot or two of cracked pavement, the street bubbled up into a river of old polished cobblestones that ran down through all the lanes and alleys of the Narrows.

The Narrows was another world compared to "higher Lichport," as Uncle called it, far more ancient, yet its old houses still stood proudly, cemented in place by years of salt air and dampness. It wasn't difficult to see how the streets of the Narrows got their names. Some lanes were so thin that if you stretched out your arms, you could touch two doors on opposite sides at once. On most streets down there, the houses leaned so precipitously in toward the street that they actually met at the top and formed an arch that blocked out the sky. Where the sky did show through, Silas could see that thick, black clouds had rolled in off the sea, and the air was wet with the promise of rain.

Some of the "cottages," as Uncle called them, had their windows open, and people were cooking late dinners for night visitors. On the air Silas could smell roasting meats, and plenty of fish, and boiled cabbage. The main streets had lit lamps, although many of the side lanes and alleys were dark, or only dimly illuminated by lanterns hung beside a cottage's front door. Unlike the upper part of town, the Narrows were truly alive at night. Voices flew up and down the slate-clad streets, bounced off the walls, and faded as they ran farther and farther from their sources. Silas glanced down a dark lane and saw two people in long coats lock their door and raise lanterns in front of them before they walked off down an even darker passage to whoever awaited their company in the small hours before dawn.

Silas wasn't sure what time it was, or how long he'd been wandering in the maze of the Narrows, but it didn't trouble him; there was a well-worn homeliness about this part of Lichport he found welcoming. Eventually, he'd arrive at the docks, or he'd begin walking uphill and would soon find his way back to the upper portion of town. But he didn't want to do either. He liked these streets, so old and unchanged, and alive. So different from the affluent neglect of "higher" Lichport. He was absolutely sure his father had walked these same lanes many times, and as he wandered them now himself, he felt somehow closer to his father.

Silas's reverie was interrupted by a terrible, low wail. Just ahead, from the mouth of an ancient-looking alley, someone was in pain. The long, low cry was carried by a breeze that smelled like wet stone and damp earth, and cold and rotting things.

Not a woman, Silas thought, and not a very young child. But it was hard to tell because the sound had gotten very soft, as though made through a blanket or a wall or from under the ground. His mom's murky warnings rose up fast in his mind. *Murders. Muggings. Criminals.* Maybe someone had been robbed, or stabbed? He was about to run when he heard the cry again, louder this time. Someone was definitely in agony.

He stepped toward the sound and into the mouth of the alley-way. The air was very cold, and Silas knew immediately that the sun never penetrated this alley or fell on its green stones. He took another step. Two. He moved slowly because he didn't want to give up the option of turning and running away if necessary. With each step, he could feel his feet slipping on the mold-damp cobbles, but he pushed forward, still unable to see the source of the sound, which now seemed to be coming out of the very walls of the buildings around him. No lights were lit in any of the windows.

The alley turned slightly to the right, so Silas crossed to the left side to see around the turn more easily in case something lay in wait. His nerves were starting to get the better of him, so he began to quicken his pace. The ghostly cry rose in Silas's ears, and he thought he must be very close now to its source. He checked the covered doorways and peered down side alleys but saw nothing.

Then suddenly he froze. Before him was a small cottage, very old, its windows dark and unrevealing. The lamplight from the street flowed strangely across the ancient, rippled glass. Silas blinked several times but then was sure of what he saw.

The house appeared to be more brightly lit than the other buildings around it, and its pale glow made the rest of the alley seem less substantial. Despite the cloud cover and the deep hour of night, the stones of the cottage's walls seemed cold-lit by a moon that had swung too close to the Earth.

Silas was transfixed by the cottage door, drawn to it like an insect to a deadly flame. The strange crying had stopped. Somewhere near him he heard a voice say, "A room for the night . . . a room for a traveler," followed by an odd, knowing laugh. Then the awful moaning, like some wounded animal's last cry, rose again both behind and before him. The icy sound grew louder and more shrill until Silas could not move. His limbs became cold and still as steel. Now the cry was in him, running like a fever through his frame, and Silas mouthed words that were not his own: *I am your son, I am nobody, I am your son, I am nobody . . .* , and every part of him froze up as he felt the possessive truth of the words that pooled in his mouth. Those words became his beginning and ending, and that was all. The long cry became his name, *"Nobody. Nobody,"* and the light of the door and the end of everything he once knew hung there on his stilling breath.

CHAPTER 22

NIGHT VISITING

Friends and neighbors started arriving after ten o'clock, a little earlier than usual. Most evenings, people didn't begin their night visiting until nearly midnight, but everyone was worried these days, with the fog as thick as it was, churning up from godforsaken deeps and rolling in sooner and sooner each night. Mrs. Kern was usually among the first of the night visitors, yet no one had seen her that evening, so Mother Peale just stole out to be sure all was well. Nothing to fret over, as it turned out. Mrs. Kern had put in a long day's work mending nets and had gone early to bed without letting anyone know. All as it should be.

On Mother Peale's way back home, she saw something that gave her pause. Three crows perched on the crooked spine of the old Banks place, which stood abandoned at the entrance to Dogge Alley where it emerged at Silk Street. Just three crows, cawing at one another high above the cobbles. But everything meant something, as her mother used to tell her, and Mother Peale would give a reading to anything she saw that struck her as strange. And this did.

Out from the entrance to Dogge Alley, the air blew cold, and she took this as another bad sign, so she turned down the lane, although it was her strong preference to leave this place to itself whenever possible. She had walked only a dozen paces into the alley when the cold of the stones rose up into her. A few yards in front of her, a young man stood stock-still, his face blue and frightened. *Silas Umber!*

She could tell at once. Imagine walking the Dogge at night! Anyone with Lichport blood in him should have more sense. Let alone an Umber! Well, raise a child in Saltsbridge and this is what comes of it. Not to mention it had been threatening to rain all day, and here he was taking a stroll in the middle of the murky night. Well, Mother Peale could forgive him that, for wasn't she out herself on such an evening?

Silas was staring at a portion of the wall that belonged to a small ruined cottage and did not hear the approaching sound of her feet on the cobbles, nor the sound of her stick on the stones, nor her breathing, which had become very fast and loud as it drew the sides of her nostrils in and out rapidly.

"Silas Umber!" she said very loudly with command in her voice, as one would speak to a child about to touch an exposed flame. "Silas Umber! Do you hear me, boy?"

Silas did not move. She could see his hands were trembling. She bent down and picked up a small pebble and threw it at him. It struck him on the cheek and the sting brought his eyes shut, and then he looked up. His eyes were wide and fearful, and he began to turn slowly, as if he were building up the courage to walk toward her.

"Silas, do not move! There is something between us, child, something terrible sad. Stay where you are please, Master Umber. It'll pass in a moment. Oh, oh," she said, her hand fluttering over her chest, "you don't want to come close to such sadness as this . . ." Her voice began to break, and a distant look came down over her like a veil. "I am nobody's son. . . . ," she murmured below her breath.

"Ma'am?"

She moved her hand over her heart again, but this time as if brushing something away. She hummed a child's tune and put words to it, forcing herself to smile as the words came: "*Good night, sleep tight, wake up bright, in morning light, to do what's right, with all your might . . .*"

Silas began to smile a little at this too, not quite sure what she was saying but responding more to the sound of it, the singsong sound of her motherly voice. "What did you say?"

"Nothing. Just a little ditty to start our going home." The smile left her face as she strode to Silas's side and took him by the arm firmly, almost roughly, and drew him away, down and out of the alley. As they were about to emerge onto another lane, she looked back over her shoulder and said clearly and without embarrassment, "Power of heaven and power of God I have over thee. Power of heaven and God over thee." The old woman's face flushed, and she looked at Silas again.

"It has passed. Come with me now. Right now!"

And with that, she pulled Silas along with her out into the lamp-lit street that rose away from the sea and would soon lead them to her door.

Silas had to walk fast to keep up with her. "Who was that?" he said, as though they had only just met a neighbor in the street whose name he had suddenly forgotten.

"The Sorrowsman," Mother Peale said, then paused and asked him softly, "What did you see, child?"

Silas became suddenly confused at the question. "I didn't, I mean . . . there was something there, a sound, someone was crying. I think . . . I am supposed to do something." Silas walked so slowly that he nearly brought them both to a halt. "I can remember . . . may we just stop for a second?"

"No, no. Let it go for now." She pulled him along even more

quickly but was excited to hear a hint of the father in the boy. *You will indeed have to do something*, she thought, but said to Silas, "You don't need to think about such things yet. Thinkin' on them brings them close in, or takes you out to them . . . either way, let it be until you're ready. That back there is stuck, and if you think too long on it, you'll get stuck too. Lost and stuck. Some folk are just lost, don't know where they are, or how to move on. But we know where we're going, don't we?"

"I guess so . . . ," said Silas, still hazy, but then admitted, "No, actually, I don't. Where are we going?"

"Home, boy! We are going home."

Mother Peale led him up the turns of Stepcote Lane, which rose from the wharf, the steepest but widest street of the Narrows. Now that she had slowed her pace, she began to talk more freely, a lightness coming into her voice, despite the subject.

"Some places ain't at all safe after dark, even for an Umber. It's not often seen, the thing that walks in the alley, and why it's walking so strong now, well, I might be able to guess with that rare ship coming in on the mist. Even with its rarity, we in the Narrows give Dogge Alley a wide berth by night, though during the day, skip up it or down it without a care in the world."

"But more importantly, Master Umber"—she leaned in close, speaking very softly—"you must know that we are for you, and for you taking up the Undertaking. Most of the folk of the Narrows knew your father as a good man. I thought of him like my own son. You will always be welcome here in the Narrows, and among my kin most especially. I knew your father, Silas. And I know *you*." She said this last part with an especial emphasis, and she put a long finger up against the side of her nose and tapped the end of her nose twice, and Silas understood immediately that she was familiar with aspects of his father's life that he was only beginning to guess at.

"I don't have your father's book learning, but I know something of this town and the things that have happened here, and more than a little about all the folk of the Narrows, living and otherwise. You come to me with any trouble, Silas. Any trouble, you hear?"

"I understand," Silas replied gratefully but full of confusion. Still, he was glad to know someone who knew things about his dad and didn't go pale at the thought of being asked. Despite his experience in Dogge Alley, it felt good, walking arm in arm with Mother Peale, over the cobbled streets past some of the oldest houses and cottages he'd ever seen. The mist-strewn Narrows wound itself around him like a bandage, and for the first time since coming to Lichport, Silas felt protected.

"Mother Peale, I don't want to appear like I don't appreciate his, um, hospitality, but I don't much like my uncle's house. I think he may have had something to do with my father's disappearance. I don't know. There are things in that house, and my uncle is . . ." He found himself grasping at words, unsure of the implication of what he might say, but sure that there were so many things just wrong about his uncle and that house. "There are locked rooms and such strange noises. I was thinking about calling the police in Kingsport, maybe speaking to someone there about my dad. I think that's where the investigator came from when my dad disappeared."

"Silas, hear me now. No one in Kingsport cares about some Lichporter going missing. People come and go here all the time, and no one takes any notice. We are an island unto ourselves, and always have been. More importantly, we take care of our own. Good or bad, we settle our own accounts. You understand me?

We don't bring the outside in here. Never. You keep your eyes open and be wary around your uncle. And if there's any need for justice, well, you have friends here who will stand behind you. But I'll tell you this, the sooner you take up where your father left off, the better it'll be for all of us."

It was raining, the whole wet darkness of the night pouring down on Lichport. Silas and Mother Peale made their way through it, up and up the lane, moving from one overhang to another. But the rain refused to merely fall. It spilled like marbles through the lanes of the Narrows, rolling this way and that, seeming at times to splash up from the wet cobbles. Even with the rain, Silas wanted to stop and ask Mother Peale a hundred questions, but suddenly she let go of his arm and called out, "Hey there, the house!" and just ahead, a door of worm-riddled, salt-crusted wood opened before them, golden light falling out of the house and into the wet streets like broken rays of the sun on the sea at dusk.

The house was low and gabled, perhaps three hundred years old, and Silas had to stoop just slightly as he stepped across the threshold. The door opened into a room with many exposed beams that ran across the ceiling and descended vertically into the walls. These were very thick and dark, smooth with the patina of time and wax, and the paneling on the walls was a kind of satiny, lustrous grayish brown, toned by the smoke of hundreds of years of hearth fires.

"Come in, boy! Come in," the old woman said. "Take a glass with me by the fire and warm yourself. A bad night, yes? A bad night to be wandering." She addressed the others in the room: "And look who I've found, roaming our dark and lonely lanes!" At once, everyone looked up, and after only the shortest pause, began whispering excitedly, worriedly, frantically. Caught in their many stares, Silas held his place by the door; only his eyes moved about the room.

The house's compact exterior gave no hint of how very large it actually was. The wide main room, which also served as the kitchen and dining room, looked like a museum; there was very little of anything modern to be seen. There was a phone and a radio, but these sat on a chest that might have dated to the sixteenth or seventeenth century. Any modern objects just seemed to dissolve into the ancientness of the walls and furnishings. The room looked as it must have hundreds of years ago. Around the hearth hung iron implements, hooks and long-handled spoons, tongs, pots of all sizes, brooms, skewers, bellows, and bed warmers, and there were dozens of other objects that Silas couldn't identify. Small lanterns hung from the ceiling beams, their jeweled panes casting angles of light in every direction. There were several large wooden hutches against the walls, with shelves full of pewter plates, cups, and pitchers of all sizes. This was a house that was accustomed to company. A long trestle table ran down the center of the room, and most of the chairs were filled by Narrows folk, some eating sooty potatoes that looked to have just come out of the fire, some drinking, all talking and whispering to one another. Silas imagined that he looked on an eternal scene, an evening caught in time that had played itself out over and over, unchanging, through hundreds of years.

He wondered if an old house like this might be haunted. How would he be able to tell? The more Silas saw of Lichport, the more he began to believe the world of the dead *is* our world. Or something that lurks alongside it, like the shadows cast from the common objects all around us. The dead are dark reflections of the familiar, Silas thought, insubstantial, but present and visible from the proper angle. Or maybe a ghost was only a thing that endures, like the furnishings of this room, like the chairs, or table; a little worse for wear, but still here because someone cherished it, or because it was made of such hardy stuff that time couldn't wear it down fast enough.

"Don't stand out so, Silas! Come in! Come in! Be at home here, by our fire. Leave the night out where it lies and look for no better nor stranger company!" Mother Peale said merrily as she gently clutched Silas's arm and drew him farther into the room toward the fire and into the heart of the gathering.

From their clothes, it was clear everyone here looked out to the sea for a living and not to high town or any other landward direction. These were working people, and they wore work clothes that hadn't changed much in the last century.

A young woman reached out her hand to him and said, "Please take a place by the fire, Master Umber. Warm yourself."

"Give him a stool, and let him take his ease, there, next to my man," said Mother Peale, "and bring him hots to guzzle and chew." She pointed to an unoccupied spot close by the fire, next to her husband, old Mr. Peale, whom Silas recognized from the market. Although close to the fire, Mr. Peale's skin was ashen, and he didn't take any notice of Silas sitting down next to him.

"There, now!" said Mother Peale smiling broadly. "And how many times have I seen your own father sitting just there, on that very stool, hard fast by my fire? The sight of you there, Silas, in your father's place, now that warms my heart and no mistake. And don't you take no worry of my quiet husband. He's had a bad time of it this week and is weary. I've told him to take to the blankets, but he'll have none of it. 'Not ready for bed,' he says! Now where's that grub and grog?"

From a doorway somewhere toward the back of the room, kitchen noises could be heard, and in short order, a steaming bowl of chowder filled with shellfish, clams, and potatoes was handed to him. Mother Peale's daughter Joan was there and came quickly to Silas's side to put a warm mug in his hand. Silas thanked her. He set the mug down on the table and dug into his stew. His encounter in the alley had given him a powerful appetite.

Now that ceremonial matters—warmth and welcome—had been attended to, folk began to talk among themselves, and the reactions to Silas's arrival seemed to run in several directions at once. Most appeared glad to see him, while others looked fretful. Some just continued on with their discussion as if Silas Umber walking into the house happened every night and didn't warrant such a fuss. "Have I interrupted a party?" Silas asked.

Folks looked confused. Mother Peale shuffled over to Silas and put her hand on his shoulder. "No, no. No party. Just a little evening's gathering. We have 'em most nights." Then she laughed knowingly. "Why, in the Narrows, we're up until all hours! Don't folks in high town do any night visiting?"

"Oh, *course* they do!" added Joan. "Only, none of 'em remember to leave their houses. Just sit around all night waiting on company, but each of 'em too afeard to go past their own doors after dark." More laughter rose up to the rafters.

A somber voice spoke up from the corner.

"It's no laughing matter. I don't see nothing here to laugh about! The boy's father gone and the mist ship coming and all. There's nothing I see to give a smile to—"

"James Voss," someone cried out, "settle yourself! There's no need to worry this young man on account of our troubles."

"Our troubles *is* his troubles. Every last one!" James Voss replied sharply. "And besides, there's lost and then there's *lost*. Everyone knows that. Forgive my directness, Master Umber, but though your dad loved this town, he had the wanderlust on him sure. And before him? There weren't an Umber in ages who kept to his proper business. Yes, even your father, bless him, wasn't afeared of wandering from his right place. I mean, taking his family to Saltsbridge!" James Voss raised his voice and gestured out to the room. "And every person in this room knows who put the wanderlust on him!"

"Oh, James," said Mother Peale, still laughing through her rising annoyance, "there's no reason to read your own troubles in other folks' faces! Just because your dear wife Mary prefers you at home, close to her own loving bosom, where she can keep a good watch on you!"

And at that, the room broke out in shouts, knowing smiles, and cries of "James Voss, James Voss, never shall roam! Run along, Jimmy! Your wife calls you home!"

The room unraveled into all manner of talk. People introduced themselves to Silas, and offered their concern, comfort, and best wishes for his family during this trying time. Some delicately, almost idly, raised the topic of his father's work, and Silas suspected people were eager to know if he would be continuing to serve in his father's office, although no one would offer very much information on what precisely that work entailed. Silas had been making a circuit of the room, but then drifted back toward the fire and pondered what it might mean to go into the "family business." Suddenly Mr. Peale sprang to his feet and began to shout, his eyes wild, fevered sweat flying from his brow.

"Get that bell ringin'! Ship's comin' in and no mistake! Ready your souls, for when she sails, she takes on new crew, and they don't ever come off that ship again. You all know my meanin'! Them's that board that ship don't ever come back and don't go nowhere else neither. No way off . . . no way off . . . just black deep below and black deep above and ropes of mist about your throat like anchor chains!"

Everyone in the room went silent and stared at Mr. Peale. Mother Peale went to her husband and whispered something in his ear, and he quieted. She stroked his brow, and he became drowsy and slid back down into his chair, his eyes half-closed.

"Nothing we didn't already know, right?" she said to the room. "The mist ship's come before, in your fathers' and mothers' time, and here we still are, so be easy, friends. Be easy. We'll ride this bad weather out!"

Folks moved themselves into small groups, talking in low voices, all speculating as to whom the mist ship might be coming for.

"Let's not borrow trouble," Mother Peale said. "We'll all know more than we'd wish to know soon enough."

She looked down at her husband, who was asleep now in his chair. Mr. Peale's breathing was shallow, and Silas could see he wasn't well. Mrs. Peale left him in his chair and went to the other side of the fire to where Silas sat with his brow furrowed and fretful.

Mrs. Peale leaned in close to Silas and whispered, "One foot in each world now. Light and shadow are becoming one to him. That's how I know he's close. Some dying folk are like that. They open their eyes, and instead of seeing what you can see right in front of you, their eyes shine with the light of another land entirely, a land behind and beside the land of the living. You can tell when you look at him, can't you, Silas Umber?"

Silas nodded.

Mrs. Peale took Silas's hand in hers.

"Is there something, child, you want to ask me?"

"Is he gone? Is my dad gone? Is that ship Mr. Peale talked about coming for my dad? He's dead, right? And no one wants to tell me that something's coming for him?"

"What kind of thoughts are these? Silas, no, child. Pay my husband no heed when he's in one of his fits. Don't let the troubles of others take hold of you so."

She stroked Silas's hand, brushing his questions and worries aside. She looked up toward the ceiling and tried to smile and distract him.

"I remember, young sir, your last visit to town. That was for your grandfather's funeral. Oh, we were all sad not to get a longer look at you then, but I understood. Your father and mother didn't quite see eye to eye on more than a few things . . . but who knows the truth between husbands and wives, eh?"

"Did you go to the funeral, then?" asked Silas.

"I most certainly did, though I noticed you didn't stay too long. I expect your mother didn't care to be around your grandfather's house while his funeral was going on and his corpse lay in the parlor. She never did cotton to custom, even though her family is one of the oldest in town."

"Do all funerals in Lichport have the deceased laid out in their own homes and not in the church or a mortuary chapel?"

"We keep the dead in our homes as well as our hearts when their time comes. Only right. That's how it's always been done here. Used to be done just like that and more often in other places as well, but people have just decided they'd rather not be too close to the dead, even their own kin. Even during those last final moments, when a little kindness can make all the difference, people now give up their duty, their sacred duty, to strangers, having their funerals and visitations in 'mortuary chapels.' Makes no sense to me. Give me Peller over preacher any day!" A loud assent rose up from the guests, who'd been shamelessly eavesdropping. Some even raised their glasses.

"And here's to our new Undertaker!" someone called out, raising his glass to Silas.

Confused and red-faced with embarrassment, Silas tried to convince himself he'd misheard the toast. He raised his glass and said, "To my dad," and everyone raised their glasses, and some hung their heads in respect, and some folk looked out the windows, and one man opened the front door as if they expected Amos Umber to walk right in at the sound of his son's words. There was only dark and quiet out in the lane, except for the sound of the rain that splashed down the gutter in the middle of the street, nothing more.

Silas could feel Mother Peale and the others looking hard at him. Folks were expecting him to continue his father's work despite it being obvious that he knew nearly nothing about it. But Silas knew now that Amos was important to the people here, and that meant he was important too. If nothing else, here were people who cared about what had happened to his father and cared about what would happen to him.

"Peller over preacher, you said. What does that mean exactly?" Silas asked, hoping to learn a little more about his dad's work.

"Yes," Mother Peale said to Silas and the room, "well, don't get me wrong; a preacher is a fine thing, but at some times more than others. Silas, did you know that here in Lichport, we don't even have a preacher anymore?" Silas looked up her, his face a waiting question mark.

"For one thing, the preacher, the last one, and it's been some time since there was one, never could do anything lasting about *Them*. I think it's because he didn't believe in what he was doing. Sure he wanted to be helpful to folk, but in a way that made sense to him. Not in the old way. Not in *our* way."

"So someone would come to him. 'Father,' they'd say, 'we have a problem. Can't sleep at night for the noise. Pale folk walking through the house. Voices in the night. Things missing and moved. Important things, personal things. Lost. Stolen.' And the vicar would see the wild look in their eyes, put there by worry and lack of sleep, and he would say, 'Why don't I come home with you and let's see if I can't put some of your worries to bed.' Back he'd walk with them, from the church where they'd sought him out, all the way, even to the Narrows, if Narrows folk they were. And when he got them home, he'd play like he believed them. Believed every word of their concern. 'Of course I see them,' he'd say, like he was talking to a child. 'Yes. Just there, by the cupboard, two sailors, yes, just as you said. And what? Upstairs? Yes. I heard it too. Voices. Who could it be? Of course. I'll be just behind you,' he'd say. Up they'd go, and there! On the landing! A young girl weeping and crying, her eyes closed, her face white as flour. 'I see her,' he'd say to comfort them. 'She is so very pale, just as you've said. And how sad she looks,' he'd add, feigning it all. Then he'd ask the folk of the house what they'd like done. 'You would like the visitors, the pale young people, to leave this house? I am here to help,' he'd say.

"So out would come his book, and he would start talking to the air, pretending to talk to Them, but into the air his words would go and no further. 'Out you go now,' he'd say a little louder than usual. Now the curious part is this. He was a priest. So his words had some power, even if he didn't know it or care. So those pale folk, they'd hear him all right, and would, to a degree, obey. They'd hear his words: 'These good people would like you to leave this house,' he'd tell them. 'So let's go! Out!' And he'd herd them, like they were animals, through the rooms and into the hall, waving his arms like brooms brushing cobwebs all the while. Then he'd have the person who invited him hold wide the front door, and he'd sweep all the pale folk out into the street and help close the door behind them. And that would be that.

"Back to the church he'd go, feeling pretty smug. And, truth to tell, things might be all right for a night or even two. But sure as I am speaking to you now, any neighbor who sat up by a window would see Them. The pale folk. Sadder, or angrier, than ever. See them at the doors and windows and walls of that house, trying all night to get back in. And eventually, whether by crossing the threshold because the power in the vicar's words ebbed, or by coming back in through the walls, seeping through like a persistent damp, they'd get back to where they started, and it would all be worse than before, and no one but the Undertaker could get 'em settled. Ask anyone what they'd prefer: priest or Peller? I bet there's not a one who wouldn't ask for the Peller, for the Undertaker. For your father, who is dearly missed."

Perhaps to keep the conversation from returning to anyone's views on his obligations, Mother Peale put her arms around Silas, her shawl like wings to shield him from the curious room. Her breath smelled like fresh bread, and she said to him, "You come to me anytime, my son. Come here anytime. . . ."

It was a long while before the laughter died down and folks started to drift away from the fire and toward their homes. Joan Peale and her husband, who both lived above the store, offered to walk Silas home, which they gladly did even though it took them closer to the center of uptown than they liked to go at night.

When her last guest left, Mother Peale began to extinguish the oil lamps and candles about the room, until only a single taper burned by the hearth next to her high-backed rocking chair. Then, with a strong and loving arm, she helped her husband up the stairs and to his bed. His eyes were closed even as he sat on the side of his bed, even before his feet were off the floor. She laid him out, and pulled the covers up over him, and turned off the little electric light on the bedside table. She left the room and closed the door quietly behind her. *The company is good for him*, she thought. *He'll sleep well tonight*.

Mother Peale returned downstairs and was neither shocked nor frightened when she looked across the room to see the pale little girl who sat on the stool by the fire, just by the foot of her chair. The girl was looking into the glowing red embers of the hearth, but their light seemed to bend around her body, for the small child's face remained white as the risen moon.

Mother Peale crossed the room and took her accustomed place in her chair. The small girl looked at her, and the old woman welcomed the child into her lap. Immediately, the child put her head on her mother's chest and closed her eyes. Mother Peale began to sing softly—"*Hush-a-bye, little one, aye, aye, hush-a-bye, little one, aye*"—while she rested her heels on a stone of the hearth and pushed her chair back and forth, while she rocked the poor child, her first, dead now these fifty-four years.

SILAS STOOD UNDER HIS WROUGHT-IRON NAME at the gates of the Umber family cemetery. He had been whistling for a moment when he saw Bea coming down Fairwell Street. She was skipping, her feet hardly touching the pavement, moving in and out of the pools of light cast on the ground by the streetlamps. They had met for short walks several times before, always finding each other, seemingly by accident. Strange but also nice, Silas thought, that now if he thought about her, conjured up her face in his imagination, more often than not when he went outside he'd find her waiting for him. But it happened too often and felt too good to be a coincidence, and Silas knew it. Was she stalking him? He hoped so.

"How did you know I needed someone to show me around?" Silas asked, smiling but surprised at how quickly Bea crossed the distance between them.

"Well, it's very easy to get lost around here, especially if you're new in town."

"I'm only sort of new—I was born here. But thanks. That's very kind of you," he said, leaning toward her.

"I know," Bea said. "Believe me, I'm not this nice to everybody."

Silas looked at her face, so pale, as if the sun hardly ever touched it. He wanted to touch her check, but leaned a little closer instead. "I'll consider myself lucky then."

"Oh, you have no idea," Bea said, as she began to skip away, just out of reach. Without pausing, Silas followed her through the gate and away from his family's bone houses.

"I was thinking, Silas. I could, if you want, show you some *places*," she said, drawing out the last word as if it might mean something more than a mere walk around the block. Silas wanted to see more of Lichport, and he wanted to see it in Bea's company.

He grinned, then replied in mock surprise, "Why, that's *remarkable*! I was just thinking the *very* same thing! What kind of sights do you think I should see?"

"I like the places that people mostly leave alone. Quiet places. Well, mostly quiet. Silas, our little town is so old, and such a lot of awful things have happened here. Would you like to see where some *things* happened? I'll be your guide. Your very own special guide. It'll be fun. I can show you a house on Morton Street where you can still see the bloodstains on the wooden floor of the abandoned house. No one even tried to get them out after the body was spirited away from the murder scene!"

"I'm not sure I want to see too many places like that."

"Okay, I can show you others, if you like, quieter places. Places I *really* like."

"All right," he said uneasily. He wanted to trust her, even though something in the strange light of her eyes and the odd coincidence of their mutual attraction to the gothic told him to go slow. But she wasn't like other girls. He could see that already.

"Show me your places."

She looked at his feet with a grin that went from ear to ear.

Silas tried to smile too. "I'll bet we like lots of the same things," he said, trying to assure himself that this game was okay.

"I bet you're right. So how about I show you where most folks in town have gone?"

"You mean Saltsbridge? Kingsport? Just how far are we walking tonight?"

"No, no. Not them. I don't know anything about the ones who fled, the ones who left by the broad road. They go their own way and hardly ever come back."

"But I came back," Silas said, cocking his head knowingly to the side, as if his only plan all along had been to come back to Lichport so he could take this walk with Bea.

"Yes, you did. And that makes you something of a rarity," said Bea, playing along. "But I mean everyone who *stayed* here. Would you like to see where they've all gone? The dead, I mean?"

Silas felt his heart beat faster.

Bea had his full attention.

"There are so many places. All the old folk of Lichport, dreaming away under their sheets of soil." She laughed at that. "Would you like to see the plots? The cemeteries are what Lichport is best known for. Know the cemeteries, know the town; that's how it is here. For oh so long now, people have died here, and they did it so well, folks from away wanted to come here to rest too. Lichport is famous for its 'Restful Soil.' Come on, you might see someone familiar."

There was something knowing in her tone that made him uncomfortable, and he wasn't sure where things were headed, but he couldn't look away from her. He followed her with his eyes, and her eyes called him on.

She began to skip backward, never looking away from him, leading him down Fairwell Street.

"Oh! Wait a sec," Silas said, suddenly realizing which way they were going. "I'd—I'd rather not go near Temple Street if it can helped. I've . . . seen enough of it."

"I understand," Bea replied with concern. "We'll go down

Prince Street. It will take us past some interesting places and still get us where we're going, eventually."

"And where *are* we going, Miss Bea?"

"Here and there . . . ," she said, still skipping lightly on the pavement, smiling to hear him say her name. "Here and there."

And so it went.

As fall turned the trees to flame, Silas and Bea met most nights for the next two weeks to continue their grand tour, a welcome distraction from the tedium and growing discomfort of life at Uncle's.

There were so many places to see. Many nights found Silas and Bea strolling among the stones, weaving their way through the town's greater and smaller necropolises. He lost track of how many they visited as the town's groves of the dead began to merge in his mind into one vast cemetery, the innumerable graves and tombs separated only occasionally by the homes and streets of the living. It was as though the town had carved itself from an enormous funereal forest that had always been there, as though all the dead of the world had always been brought to this plantation of Lichport by the sea.

There were only a few streets in town they didn't explore. Silas had no desire to return to Temple Street, even though it boasted the long-abandoned and historically remarkable ancient burial grounds of the brothers of the temple. Silas also made a practice of avoiding Garden Street where the gallows once stood atop the little rise in the middle of the park. The worn, square stone that had served as its base was still visible. Mrs. Bowe had told him the name of the street had been changed, many years since, because no one wanted to remember it had long been called Gallows Street after the punishments that used to be carried out there.

They often visited favored cemeteries repeatedly. *Their places*, Bea called them. However, delighted and a little dizzy to be in her company, Silas would sometimes forget where he was—one carved stone flowing into another, making a river of names—until a particular monument came into view.

Silas loved the mausoleums of the founding owners of the American West India Company, which were strewn with sky-piercing minarets and once golden domes. High arched doors emulated the palaces and the grand tombs of Mughal India. Now small bushes and weeds had taken root in the rotten leaves caught where the domes met the columns, spoiling the once perfect arcs of the roofs. Even the green foliage added a sense of loss. How long, Silas wondered, until their roots would pull apart the stones?

At dusk, Silas liked to visit the plot that Bea had shown him behind a large ruined home on the town's southeast side. It contained a tomb built in the fashion of a temple dedicated to Artemis. Graying columns still stood, holding the angled roof aloft, not a single one fallen. Within each column, Bea told him before they walked on, a body was entombed, standing to better meet the Day of Judgment when it came.

Their walks often brought them to the massive gates of Newfield, the vast cemetery that sprawled at the town's south side. High walls with Gothic finials and decorative towers curved around the outside of the cemetery and gave it the appearance of a medieval city.

"You like the lion?" asked Bea, who enjoyed watching Silas enjoy something.

"Very much," he said, running his eyes over the massive bronze animal that guarded the cemetery's main entrance. "We're friends already. I've come here to sit and think a couple of times, you know, just to get out of the house." He put his hand on the enormous paw. "The bronze is always warm. I guess the sun must heat it during the day enough so that it stays warm at night. Anyway, it's nice to sit on." He climbed up and over the leg into the open area between the paws and the chest, in one of two rounded corners where the leg met the body, and settled comfortably and familiarly into the curve. He stretched out there, feeling the warmth of the bronze rise up and into his back. It felt like the sun was shining beneath him. Looking over, he saw that Bea had taken a similar position on the other side. They were very close to each other, their legs almost touching. The two of them lay there, two portions of light against the dark, time-worn bronze, arms folded behind their heads, as they looked away down the long avenue that led from the cemetery back into Lichport. Bea began humming.

"I like that tune," said Silas.

She laughed coyly. "I know you do."

"Will you sing it for me?" Silas said, flirting a bit.

She said nothing, but as she sang, she added his name here and there, as though the song had always been sung about them.

> O the summertime is coming
> And the trees are sweetly blooming
> And the wild mountain thyme
> Grows around the blooming heather.
> Will you go, Silas, go?
> And we'll all go together
> To pluck wild mountain thyme
> All around the blooming heather
> Will you go, Silas, go?
>
> I will build my love a bower
> By yon pure crystal fountain

And on it I will pile
all the flowers of the mountain
Will you go, Silas, go?

If my true love he were gone
I would surely find another
Where the wild mountain thyme
Grows around the blooming heather.
Will you go, Silas, go?

As the words of the song trailed off into a hum, Silas sat up, leaned on his arm, and looked at Bea's face. Her eyes were closed and her body was still while she sang. As she hummed the tune, the sound seemed to come from some other place, a time far away from this moment under the quickly sinking sun. Silas couldn't speak—did not wish to speak—because he feared that if he started, he would tell her something stupid and fawning about how much he liked her. She was different. Beautiful and different. She never talked about modern things, or anything outside of Lichport. And sometimes her words fell very softly on his ears, as though they were from a long way off and carried to him on the wind. But his heart beat quicker when they were together despite all—despite the distance between them, despite being from very different parts of Lichport, and despite the fact that every minute he spent with her made him feel guilty because it drew him away from trying to find out anything about his dad. But she acted on him like a spell, and in their moments together it was just the two of them and nothing else.

Bea had opened her eyes and was looking back at Silas. She smiled and said his name, drawing him deeper into their moment together, under the rising stars of evening.

"You know," said Bea, "there's a real lion inside this statue."

Silas sat up a bit, still a little dreamy, as he looked up at the lion's head that loomed above him.

"Really? Inside the sculpture?"

"Yes. And it was your great-great-grandfather on your father's side who put it there."

"You're kidding, right?"

"Not at all. This statue is a sort of tomb. Well over a hundred years ago, a ship wrecked on the reef during a storm. The ship was carrying animals for the zoo in Kingsport. A storm at sea had damaged the ship, and they were coming to port here instead of Kingsport for repairs because the ship was in some distress. But the mooncussers heard of the ship, and thinking there might be valuable cargo out of Africa or India, they went out and lit their false light and tricked the ship onto the reef."

"Mooncussers?" Silas asked. "That's a word I don't think I've heard."

Bea looked away briefly. "It's an old Lichport word. A word some of the sea folk in town know because it was used by their ancestors. Mooncussers were just thieves, men who swore at the moon when it shone bright because the moon is a blessed beacon to ships near these coasts. Their business, generally carried out on dark nights, was to make ships think they were being led to safe harbor by the lighthouse lamp. But in fact, the light was false and often led ships and their crew to their deaths. Then the mooncussers would wait on the shore for whatever cargo washed up from the wreck."

"That's horrible!" Silas said. "What kind of person would do that?"

"My brothers," Bea replied, as she drew into herself. "It wasn't so uncommon. It's sort of an awful tradition among the coast towns. Always has been."

"Oh, I'm sorry," Silas said. But he couldn't help wondering how such things were still practiced, even in a town as odd as Lichport.

"No. It's okay. I didn't get along very well with my family."

"Yeah," Silas said hesitantly, not wanting to let the rest of his life bleed into his time with Bea. "Neither do I."

"Well," Bea continued, "seeing that false light and hoping for safe harbor, the ship turned too soon and hit the reef. The townsfolk came down to the quay to see the ship and its rare cargo come in, but the ship broke apart. Soon after you could hear the screaming of the sailors and the strange, awful sounds of the animals dying in the water or thrown onto the rocks. That was a terrible night. It seemed that neither man nor animal could survive the wreck. But the lion did. It managed to swim to shore. When the 'cussers came down to await their spoils on the tide, the lion had recovered enough to kill one of them in the cove. It was your great-great-grandfather who caught the lion. He had a cage built for it and kept it. Loved it like a child of his own. And I believe the lion lived for many years. When it died, your great-great-grandfather commissioned this statue. It came in pieces all the way from London on the biggest two ships you ever saw. He had the body of the lion preserved and placed inside, and then the sculpture was assembled, and here it still stands."

Bea started to climb down from the paw, but Silas didn't move for many moments. He thought about that dark hidden chamber of bronze somewhere deep within the statue, where the lion slept.

The moon was up, and small lights had begun to appear among the tombs and mausoleums of the cemetery. Unnerved a little by their mysterious glow, Silas asked Bea if tramps lived in any of the buildings.

"Maybe. Lots of folks live here. I guess there could be tramps.

Sometimes there are night markets in the center of the avenues. People come with things to trade. Old things. Strange things. Lost things. It's not easy to find what you want in the world, but sometimes, every now and again, someone has just what you're looking for and then . . . then everything might change."

"I'm not sure I understand what you mean."

"Well," Bea continued, "have you ever lost something? A toy? A watch? A ring? Someone you love? All those things have to go somewhere, right? Now some people, when they lose something, they feel sad about it for a bit, but then they move on, they forget about it. Other people, though . . . they make a place in their heart for that thing—whatever it was—and they can't let it go, and the loss of it eats at 'em day after day and eventually, they can't get any rest at all. Those are the ones who come to the night markets. Looking for just that one thing that will make them feel whole again. Would you like to go and look? Have you lost something?" She was being coy now, but below her soft, playful words there were teeth.

"Haven't you ever lost something?" Bea went on. "C'mon! Maybe we'll find it. What are you looking *for*, Silas?"

Silas didn't answer, although his mind held fast to the image of his father's face. It felt like she was leading him on, like she knew something about him, and he didn't like this new game of hers.

More and more lights appeared. Many of them could now be seen brightening a long row of tombs fashioned in the Egyptian style. Tall columns, fluted and shaped like closed lotus flowers, stood idle, the roofs they once held up having long since fallen in, leaving open to the sky a lengthy gallery of ornate, open doorways. The thresholds were flanked by statues of the jackal-headed god Anubis and opened into small tombs with hieroglyphic walls, or to stairs leading down to the catacombs. Some of the doorways now seemed to glow as if inside them, down within some lower chamber, torches had been lit.

Then, in the distance and down that shadow-strewn avenue of obelisks and sphinxes, Silas could hear voices rise and begin to wander in the air.

He grew more and more scared. Maybe it was the way the light swayed on the overgrown walls of the tombs. The idea of a market of lost things unnerved him. What would he find there? There was only one thing he was looking for, and he knew it wasn't waiting over there with whatever was hiding inside the tombs. This was not for him, and he told himself that instead of finding something he wanted, it was more likely that something he didn't want would find him. His usually adventurous nature had completely dissolved.

"I want to go home," he said, and started, without warning, to walk back toward the gate—leaving Bea, who was rapt watching the rising lights of the Newfield night market, to catch up with him.

They passed through the gates and quickly left the bronze lion behind them to cool in the night. Silas and Bea walked back up Fairwell Street. By the time they reached the corner of Temple, Silas noticed Bea was shaking from the cold. He reached out to put his arm around her, but she stepped away, beyond his reach.

"You don't like this street either, do you?" he asked her, looking west toward Uncle's house.

"No. I don't like it down there at all, Silas," she said, and even as they passed the street where Silas and his mother resided, Bea tilted and turned her head toward her rising shoulder, as if something had crawled inside her ear and she was trying to shake it out.

"Me either," Silas said, noticing her discomfort. "I live down there, you know, but I am thinking of leaving."

"I wish you would. I don't like that street. There are things in the houses there . . . things that are not happy to be where they are."

Silas asked her to tell him what she meant, what she'd heard, but Bea had gotten very quiet, and when they reached the gates of the Umber cemetery, she smiled at him and glanced up at the name on the arch. Silas looked too, but when he turned back, Bea was gone and he was alone again, looking through the gate at the tombs of his silent ancestors.

CHAPTER 24

FORTUNE, MY FOE

THE HEAVY AIR IN SILAS'S ROOM SMELLED LIKE STALE CANDY.

Tired from exploring with Bea, Silas had fallen asleep easily. Now, in the middle of the night, he was awakened by the sound of raspy breathing just above his face. He lay absolutely still, sure that someone was standing over him. The room was dark, but the blackness above him felt somehow deeper. He knew it was not Uncle in the room with him, or his mother—the breathing was so irregular that Silas thought the person must be ill. He could feel himself being looked at, and the room felt smaller, closed in about him as if someone had pushed the walls in about the bed. He waited several moments for the breathing above him to stop, or for the sound of footsteps leaving the room. But the breathing continued, along with an awful sound of air desperately being sucked through a constricted throat, as if someone was trying to draw breath through a straw filled with thick jam.

Outside his room, from the north wing, he could hear his uncle singing, the words drifting down the hall and onto the landing, wandering here and there into the other rooms, under doors, through the vents, winding their way about the shadow-strewn upper floor of the house.

Fortune, my foe, why dost thou frown on me?
And will thy favors never better be?

Wilt thou, I say, forever breed my pain?
And wilt thou not restore my joys again?

In vain I sigh, in vain I wail and weep,
In vain my eyes refrain from quiet sleep;
In vain I shed my tears both night and day;
In vain my love my sorrows do bewray. . . .

As the song continued, his uncle's voice rose in volume and in pitch, yet through the words, the awful raspy breathing continued. Silas knew it was no dream, knew he was awake, but he was afraid to open his eyes. The sound of broken breathing was coming and going in time with the words of his uncle's song, one word in, the other out, faster and faster, just above his face. . . .

Ah, silly Soul art thou so sore afraid?
Mourn not, my dear, nor be not so dismayed.
Fortune cannot, with all her power and skill,
Enforce my heart to think thee any ill.

Whoever stood above him was in some kind of distress. *Why is he in my room?* Fear ran through Silas like a current, for he imagined that in the dark, with him, was his father's walking corpse, escaped from some hidden basement or walled-up room of the house where Uncle had hidden it.

Look, he told himself. *Just look. Count to three, then open your eyes*. Then he just opened them without counting. For the briefest instant, he saw a face looking down on him. It was not his father, but he would never in his life forget that face. The eyes were far apart and slightly misaligned, and although it was hard to tell in the dark room, the head's shape seemed unbalanced, larger on one side than the other. Silas's own eyes were wide open in amazement, and very quickly and without thought, he drew in breath to yell. But before he could make any noise at all, the face was gone and the breathing sound with it. Just before it vanished, that terrible face had smiled, the edges of its contorted mouth drawing up just slightly at the corners. And when Silas threw his hands up to push it away from him, he felt nothing; whoever it was had dissolved into the thick, oppressive darkness of the room.

Silas swiftly reached over to the bedside table and turned on the lamp. The light revealed . . . nothing. There was nobody else in the room with him. The door was closed. No one had left. He knew absolutely that he wasn't dreaming and that he had been lying there wide awake, listening to the raspy breathing, the air warm with the smell of sweets.

Away in the north wing, Uncle's singing continued and sounded slurry and confused. Maybe Uncle had taken a glass with Dolores earlier that evening. Silas got up from bed and dressed. It wasn't hard to guess where the singing was coming from—Uncle was in his Camera Obscura. More words stumbled down the hall of the gallery, rolling along the walls and floors.

> Live thou in bliss, and banish death to Hell;
> All careful thoughts see thou from thee expel:
> As thou dost wish, thy love agrees to be.
> For proof thereof, behold, I come to thee.

Silas crept through his uncle's bedroom and then on through the study, which was piled high with books and some of the fossils and other specimens his uncle had at some point brought from downstairs.

He could hear Uncle speaking very clearly in the Camera Obscura. For the first time since Silas's arrival in the house, the door to the room had been left open slightly, its great bronze locks unset. Silas got up close to the door, but stayed away from the gap; he could hear Uncle's voice, as he spoke to someone in the room.

"By my hands you shall know the perfection kept from you in life. As you were—bound to this mortal flesh—how many more years could you have possibly known? Twenty? Thirty? And I never would have let them take you from me. Never. Now you shall live forever, and we will see so much more of each other. We can at last be a proper family, a peaceable family. No dark box for you at your day's end. *In claritas* shall you remain, forever. Do you see? No more corruption, for now, Death trembles at the sight of you."

His uncle was now chanting more than singing, rocking his head from side to side, his voice becoming a crescendo as he pounded his foot in time with the song. Every time his foot struck the floor, the shelves in the outer room shivered, rattling the bottles displayed along their lengths. When he peeked through the gap, he could see that as Uncle pitched his voice around the Camera, he stood upon a small ladder, gently holding the hand of a limp arm and seemed to be speaking to it. Silas could see that Uncle's eyes were wild, circled in distress and sorrow and madness. Uncle pressed the lifeless hand to his face but looked through the cracked door right at Silas and just went on singing. . . .

> Die not in fear, nor live in discontent;
> Be thou not slain where blood was never meant;
> Revive again: to faint thou hast no need.
> The less afraid, the better thou shalt speed.

Silas couldn't see whose hand it was, but fear set every nerve in his body on fire. At his first step away from the doorway, the whole house shook, as if it was filled with a giant heart trying to beat its way out from inside the walls.

The pounding noise appeared to wake Uncle from his macabre reverie, and as he seemed to realize that the always locked door was open, he dropped the arm and, nearly falling coming down the ladder, shot to the doorway. Pulling the door shut Silas could hear him fumble with the mechanisms of the bronze locks while the door shivered with frantic vibration.

As he moved backward, his eyes still on the door, Silas tripped on a stack of books and fell over. He did not stop moving, and when he hit the floor, he began crawling toward the door leading away from that awful room. At the threshold, Silas pulled himself up and ran. Uncle began yelling now at something inside the Camera Obscura, and Silas could still hear him through the closed door.

"Not yet! You must remain. I will bring him here. I will bring him back, then you won't want to leave, will you? No, no! Then you will be content to remain, won't you? No more trying to leave . . ."

But Silas had heard and seen enough. Back in his room, he was sick with fear at the thought that Uncle had been talking to his father. But that couldn't be. How could his father, or part of his father, be in this house? He would know. Somehow, he would just know. He couldn't think. He could only run. Something horrible was happening in this house, and he must get out. *Coward! Coward!* said his eyes as they watched his hands furiously packing clothes in suitcases, a few books on top. Quickly and quietly he carried his suitcases down the back stairs and went into the yard to the carriage house, where Uncle had insisted Silas's boxes of books and other belongings should remain until they could find "a more suitable place" for his "former life."

Silas found a wheelbarrow and stacked it full of boxes of his books. With a couple of his belts, he tied the suitcases to each other like saddle bags and put them over the top of the boxes. Their weight helped hold everything down. Not the most stable mode of transport, but he had no other choice, and he desperately wanted not to have to return to Uncle's house tomorrow, if ever.

As he came around the side of the house, Silas heard a sound above him, like a coin being tapped on one of the windows of the second floor of the north wing. When he looked up, he could see only the dark glass panes set in their heavy frames. There was a glint of light from one of the windows, but when Silas blinked to look again, he saw nothing. Worried his uncle might follow him into the yard, he quickly brought the wheelbarrow around the front of the house and turned his back to Temple Street.

He rolled the awkward wagon of his possessions up Fairwell. Who could he go to? Which of the several people he barely knew could he impose on to put him up? He thought of Mother Peale, but her husband was probably dying, and she had enough on her plate without Amos Umber's homeless son showing up in the middle of the night. He thought about his great-grandfather's house, and he knew he'd be welcome. But the idea of the long walk down Fort Street, in the dark, past the overgrown gardens, past the ruins of the other houses and their *occupants* . . . it put a knot of fear in his stomach, and he abandoned the idea. Maybe in the morning, in the light, he'd make his way there.

The street was empty, but as he went past various houses and the large, untended shrubs and bushes in front of them, he heard things rustling in the undergrowth. The wheel on the wheelbarrow was coming loose, and Silas started to panic, as he imagined having to sleep in some doorway, or in one of the rat-infested, abandoned, and boarded-up houses. Best to just keep walking then. He went up Main, then back along Garden until he was panting and anxious, unsure of where to go next. He kept walking along Garden and turned up Coach Street, hoping some-one or someplace would stand out. He wondered how late it was now and what time the sun would rise.

He looked in every direction and saw nothing to welcome him. Fear danced in his stomach, and his childhood was all around him: standing alone in front of the class, looking down the rows of other children and watching them avert their eyes. *Go away!* their faces all said. *Don't sit near me. There's no place for you. We don't want you here!*

As he approached the corner of Coach and Main, he began to change his mind and considered heading for the Narrows. He remembered his great-grandfather's words: *Be with those you can trust.* Then, around his neck, he felt the long-idle key to his father's house given to him by Mrs. Bowe burning where it lay against his chest. He walked more quickly, until he came to the edge of Mrs. Bowe's property, where he could see the sunflowers lit by the moon as they rose up around the Bowe family crypt at the garden's corner. He took out the key on the chain from where it hung next to the pendant of Janus that his father had given him, and leaving the wheelbarrow briefly on the sidewalk, he walked up the steps to his father's house and put his key in the lock.

This is your house, Mrs. Bowe had told him.

Silas was usually uncomfortable taking people at their word. But tonight he had neither the heart nor the inclination to doubt her.

SILAS TURNED HIS KEY IN THE LOCK. He paused for a moment at the threshold of the partially opened front door, one foot in, one out. His skin was hot from pushing the wheelbarrow, but a breeze rose up that cooled him and blew leaves about the porch, past his feet, and into the foyer of his father's house.

When he looked into the entrance hall, he could see that everything was quiet, undisturbed, perhaps just as his father had left it, nothing changed since Mrs. Bowe had given Silas the key. Back outside, the wind was quickly picking up, and cold gusts slowly pulled the trees one way, then another. Waves of leaves rolled down the street, only to be whipped back by the growing wind as it changed directions.

Silas crossed the threshold and entered into his father's— his—house. He was home, and he could feel it in every breath as the dusty air filled his lungs. Tiny bits of death, he thought, tiny particles of the past, now part of him, part of the rising and falling of his breath. Nothing in the house had been cleaned in years. So here was his father, lying like an invisible film over everything. Particles in space, in the house, on everything in it, settling again now that he'd closed the door; settling over Silas's outstretched hand, falling on his skin, sinking in. In that small way if no other, Silas was partially reunited with his father. Now the house was *their* place.

From her bedroom in the adjoining house, Mrs. Bowe heard the door on Amos's side open and knew Silas had come home. She wanted to go to him, to welcome him, to hold him, because she knew if he was here, then there had been trouble back at his uncle's house. *Let be*, she told herself. *Leave him for the night. Morning is soon enough for welcomes.*

When Silas awoke early the next morning, he was still tired. He fetched the boxes he'd left in the front hall the night before and brought the books into his father's study through the large pocket doors, which he had opened all the way.

A familiar voice called to him.

"I'm surprised those old doors opened that far! Your father usually liked them closed. When he was in his study, I think he liked to feel closed off from the rest of the world. How much nicer this is. It lets so much more light into the study." The smile on her face became concern as Mrs. Bowe asked, "Would you like to tell me about last night, Silas?"

"Not really," he said, but as Mrs. Bowe crossed the distance between them, he began rambling, as bits of detail began to fall out of him like shards of glass from a broken window. Before he knew it, he had blurted out most of what he'd seen and heard at Uncle's, focusing much of his attention on describing the door to the Camera Obscura. And then, without pausing to catch his breath, Silas asked, "What do you think my uncle keeps in that room?"

Mrs. Bowe put her hands on his to stop him from talking, and said, "Don't go back there, Silas. Leave that house be. Never go to that room again. Never. Just stay away from that house!"

"But what about my mom?"

"That's her choice to be there," Mrs. Bowe said with a hard edge to her voice. "She's never made good decisions for herself, not even as a child. Besides, she does more harm to herself than your uncle is likely to do to her. If she wants to be in that black house, well, you just leave her to it. But you keep away from there now you're out of it. You hear me, child! I don't know what Charles Umber has locked away in that room, but it's nothing that will bring anyone any good, I can assure you of that!" Mrs. Bowe was flustered and nervous now herself, and tiny pearls of perspiration were forming on her brow.

She drew in a long, deliberate breath to mark the end of one subject and the beginning of another, dabbed her forehead with a handkerchief she drew deftly from her sleeve, and asked, "Shall we take a turn about the houses? I see you have brought some books with you. May I assume you are here to stay then?"

"Yes and yes." He answered both her questions at once.

Mrs. Bowe showed Silas the lower rooms of her house first, the dining room with its many portraits of the women of her family, and near the front of the house, the small office where her father had once conducted the business of the mortuary emporium, the door leading to the mortuary proper, and stairs leading down to where bodies had once been prepared.

"Did my dad work here with your father?"

"Did he what?"

"Work here, in the mortuary, with your father?"

"I don't think I understand you, Silas. Are you under the impression your father was a mortician?"

Confused, Silas replied quietly, "Yeah. My uncle told me he wasn't, but he didn't elaborate, and I didn't believe him anyway—"

"I knew it! That's your mother's handiwork. . . . She wouldn't have wanted Amos to tell you anything." Her face flushed with anger. "Your father was an Undertaker, Silas."

"So he was a mortician. Undertaker is the same thing as a mortician. Aren't they the same thing?"

"Not in this town," she said. "Morticians prepare the body of the deceased for burial. And that's important work, don't mistake me. In some places, they help the family come to terms with the departure of the deceased, and in some places, they organize the customs that surround the burial. But here in Lichport, a mortician only prepares the physical body for burial, and in my father's case, makes available the funereal trappings. Coffins, coaches, mourning clothes, postmortem portraiture, death masks, carriage plumes, mutes, and the like. Before my grandfather's time, the family would prepare the body themselves, as had always been done. And when my father died, people went back to that practice, for the most part. Those who remained in Lichport, that is. I have long suspected people only came to my father for that work out of respect for my mother. But the older families and the families that came here from afar to bury their dead have long appreciated the elaborate funeral processionals, and the men of my family have long supplied those trappings. Those have always been needed. Still, our fathers' work was not unconnected."

Silas could barely take it all in.

"Mutes, did you say?"

"Yes. The presence of mutes at funerals is a very ancient custom," Mrs. Bowe said matter-of-factly. "There were once several families of mutes in Lichport, who made their livings just attending funerals. One of the families still remains."

Of course, thought Silas. *Families of mutes.* When Mrs. Bowe said it, it felt completely commonplace.

"Mrs. Bowe, everything you tell me is strange and familiar both. I can't explain why it feels that way. It's like I've lived here all my life, though I've never really been here, and I've known that some of what my father was telling me all my life was a lie. Well, not a lie, but a story I would one day get to understand, even the parts that I now know weren't really true. I know I was born here and lived here for a very short time as a baby, before my parents moved. But I'm sure I don't remember anything from that time. It's like when I look around this house. Everything seems new and old to me at once."

"The memories you're having aren't the photograph kind of memories we have when we recall something we did on a particular day. These are blood memories. What I am telling you speaks to your blood. You know these things to be true because your ancestors knew them to be true. You are remembering things, *deep things*, that's all. And it's nothing to be afraid of," said Mrs. Bowe, smiling kindly.

They had walked through her home and back into his house and had returned to his father's study. Silas liked being in here. The walls had a way of drawing him in, with all the warm wood paneling and the books stacked to the ceiling and the paintings of the sea; some with the ships of past centuries sailing, their sails high and full of wind; others just of the sea itself in its various moods, blue water, green water, gray and black under the moon. Silas felt peaceful there, and closer to his father than he'd felt in a long time, maybe even closer than before he disappeared because in this room, his father had been allowed to be himself.

The room was filled with things his mother would never have tolerated in the Saltsbridge house. The study was stacked with what his mother would have called "crap." Crap, and "trouble things." She told him once that "trouble things" were any object that had to be picked up when cleaning, things that gathered dust and made a room look cluttered. But Silas had made a careful study of what his mother did and didn't like, and came to have a deeper understanding of what "trouble things" really meant to her. They were any item that reminded her of something else. Anything that had meaning beyond its immediate function. A kitchen knife was fine. A knife with an inscription and a story was a trouble thing. A throw-away-when-finished paperback novel was fine, so long as it was actually thrown away. A book that made you think about yourself too much, or revealed something of the past: trouble. She had a bit of a double standard. Her rich heirloom furnishings were always acceptable, perhaps because they were about her family's prestige and its position in the world. But anything, *anything* Amos or Silas brought into the house other than food and clothes was almost certain to get the evil eye.

But here, in his house, everything was welcome. Anything that took his father's interest, or inspired him, or formed a portion of his work; all had been given sanctuary. The room was lined with bookshelves that spilled their contents onto the floor, where more books were stacked unevenly.

On one wall, a map of the town hung barely visible beneath the numerous newspaper cuttings that had been taped or pinned to it. Amos's handwriting seemed to be on everything: map, scraps, articles, notes. His dad loved music, and there were shelves filled with sheet music and old records. On a small wooden music stand near the desk was the sheet music of a lullaby, and Silas read the words, the slow descending tune flooding into his mind like a rushing tide. His dad had sung him this song when he was young, but Silas hadn't remembered it in a long time.

> Hush-a-bye, little ones, aye, aye;
> Hush-a-bye, little ones, aye.

The night birds are singing,
The bells are ringing
And it's time for you now to fly,
Little birds,
It's time for you now to fly.

Fly with me, fly with me, aye, aye;
Fly with me, little birds, aye;
Your mothers are waiting,
For ages awaiting
Little birds to their waiting arms fly!

Silas sat down at the desk and took out his father's pocket watch, running his thumb around the smooth silver dome of the skull. He didn't care to know the time, it just felt good to hold it and hear it softly ticking in his hand. He had begun humming the tune of the lullaby without even realizing it. Thoughts of Uncle's house and his mother and worries of what next began to quiet below the tune of the song and the ticking of the watch.

Here, in this room, even the sharp edge of his dad's absence softened, lulling him, leaving him numb but temporarily happy in the company of his father's possessions. Part of Silas knew this was only an illusion of happiness, but for a moment, the bigger part of him didn't care. He was sitting at his father's desk, and in his hand was his father's pocket watch. All around him were his father's things. He leaned back in the chair and closed his eyes, breathing in deeply.

Mrs. Bowe quietly left Silas to his reverie. As she walked back down the corridor connecting his house and hers, she thought, *This is too much for a young man, too much change at once, and all of it bad. Oh, Amos! You've told him so little. Left it to me, eh? Left it all to me? Well, so be it. I'll do what I can for him. But Amos, I will try to keep him from the worst of what you've left him. Holy Mother, I will!*

Mrs. Bowe opened the door at her end of the corridor and gently closed it after her. And for the first time since Amos had disappeared, she didn't lock it.

CHAPTER 26

NIGHT MUSIC

Music played again next door, softly drifting through the walls, under the door, and was now taking a turn about the lower rooms of Silas's house, distracting him.

He was sitting at his father's desk, writing down some thoughts in a small empty diary he'd found in the drawer. On the desktop was an old nib pen, worn, smooth-handled—obviously a favorite of his father. The ink bottle was still mostly full, so he began using his dad's pen to write. At first he found it awkward, stopping, dipping the pen, tapping it on the lip of the bottle to remove the excess ink, then returning to the paper. But as he did this over and over, he warmed to the ritual of it, and the pauses took on a rhythm. Think. Write. Pause. Think. Write. Pause. Over and over and even the scratching sound of the pen on the rough paper he used became musical.

But then the other music started, and everything fell out of tune.

Too distracted now to write, he put the end of the pen into a glass of water to clean the nib. He swirled it around and around, and the ink still on the pen began to spiral in darkening clouds. He took the pen out and watched how the ink revealed invisible currents and eddies in the once clear water. He wondered if the air around him was also filled with invisible things, imperceptible patterns, invisible spirits moving alongside him, stirred up by every little movement and action like the layers of dust in the house when he walked by.

But again, his thoughts were interrupted by the soft, intruding tune.

He'd been at his father's house for over a week, and every night it was the same. Just after eleven o'clock the music would start, and he could hear it, coming down the corridor between houses, through the walls. Sometimes the words of the song would rise up loud enough that he could hear them, too. It might begin with "Sentimental Journey." But the second song—sometimes played over and over—was always "Love's Old Sweet Song." When it began, that was when the dancing started.

> Once in the dear dead days beyond recall,
> When on the world the mists began to fall,
> Out of the dreams that rose in happy throng
> Low to our hearts love sang an old sweet song;
> And in the dusk where fell the firelight gleam,
> Softly it wove itself into our dream . . .

If he listened closely, he could hear slow feet moving about the floor and the boards creaking all along the length of the room. The words from last night's dance still turned in his head. . . .

> Even today we hear love's song of yore,
> Deep in our hearts it dwells forevermore.
> Footsteps may falter, weary grow the way,
> Still we can hear it at the close of day.
> So till the end, when life's dim shadows fall,
> Love will be found the sweetest song of all . . .

Every night, music and the sound of dancing. None of this seemed to fit with his image of Mrs. Bowe, although he hadn't known her very long. As far as Silas knew, no one else ever visited

Mrs. Bowe at the house, and he'd never heard anyone even knock on her door after dark. *So who was she dancing with so late at night?* He didn't like eavesdropping. *None of my business*, he thought. But the whole affair unsettled him, and he longed to find out what was going on.

Mrs. Bowe didn't lock the door on her side of the corridor between their houses now, and she had told Silas that he was always welcome to come through. But the idea of walking into Mrs. Bowe's house so late felt like an intrusion, even though he couldn't imagine her having a private life. She never left the house except to work in the garden. His mind made up, Silas walked toward the door, slowly turned the knob, and pushed it open halfway. The music got louder, and he could smell candles burning. He took one careful step at a time, trying to be quiet. He passed the service porch, then walked more quickly as he came through to her kitchen. Standing where he'd eaten breakfast every day that week, he could hear the music was coming from the front entrance hall, or maybe the parlor.

He continued, barely breathing, into the dining room and came to a stop in the doorway that led into the front hall. There the air turned suddenly cold, and without thinking he pulled the collar up on his jacket as though there were a wind blowing inside the house.

Silas wondered if she was maybe a little crazy, mad in that quaint way old women who live alone sometimes are. She didn't own any cats, so Silas had never thought so before, but what he saw before him made him rethink his first impression. There was Mrs. Bowe, and she was dancing across the polished wood floors of her entry hall. She went round and round in a circle, her arms up at odd angles, as if holding on to something. *A lonely eccentric*, Silas thought. *Just a little off from spending so much time by herself. There's nothing wrong with dancing with yourself. Nothing wrong with it at all.* But the cold air was unusual, since her house was always so warm, and the way she held her arms, and the smile on her face . . . as though someone else was dancing with her. That thought scared him. He knew he'd interrupted something very personal and very strange.

There was something else in the room. Silas could feel it as a kind of heaviness in his stomach and limbs. The full shame of his intrusion tightened his chest and he wanted nothing more than to leave, but his nerves had gotten the best of him, and he couldn't seem to remember how to take a step backward.

Cold air and fear had him now. He couldn't look away as Mrs. Bowe circled the room, and he couldn't think of anything to do but put his hands in his pockets, perhaps to warm them, perhaps to feel less exposed. His hand was glad to find the distraction of his father's silver watch. He turned it over and over nervously in his hand, more and more quickly, like a frightened priest or a nun running their fingers over a rosary in frantic meditation. He made little circles with his thumb around and around the smooth top of the silver skull until suddenly the catch opened, and the jaw of the skull dropped, exposing the dial. His thumb pressed in fast to explore the new surface, pushed against the dial, and stopped the hands of the clock.

Everything in the room changed as a mist rose from between the floorboards.

It felt to Silas like the world had been turned upside down. Or like he was riding a high-speed elevator that was arriving at its floor and his stomach was a few seconds behind his head. It felt as though there was no longer any gravity, and he didn't know if he was floating or falling. He could not speak, could not open his mouth. The stars had stopped turning. The earth and all about him were still, and nausea rose up in him and flooded his guts.

He could not move, and his limbs felt as though they had been poured full of cement.

Then things tilted, just slightly, and the room grew brighter and the cold air fell away from him. Each candle in the room became a beacon, and he squinted at their light. The gray mist that had washed the room a moment ago was gone; indeed the details of the room were so flooded with light that all he could see with any clarity was Mrs. Bowe dancing with a tall man who looked directly at her and at nothing else in the room.

Silas recognized the dancing man from all the pictures in her house. There could be no mistaking him, although he seemed younger than he was in the most recent pictures Mrs. Bowe had shown him. This was her lover, dead since the war. Even without the photos, Silas could tell by the way Mrs. Bowe looked at him that she loved him, and that her love for him had not lessened in the many years since his death.

And in that instant, Silas realized he was looking at a ghost.

He'd seen a shadow of his grandfather at his long-ago funeral, but the difference between what a child remembers and what a man sees can be shocking. There was a ghost dancing in the room before him, and he could see it plainly. Silas clenched his eyes shut and then opened them. The ghost remained. Not an illusion or a trick of the light. A spirit of the dead was present in the room, and as Silas stared at it, unable to look away, he felt the walls crumble around the world he knew. Here was something he could see with his eyes. Not an odd noise, or the memory of a bad dream hanging in the air upon waking. The ghost not only moved through the room, his presence filled it and acted on someone else Silas could see, on another living person. Now he knew the stories he'd read were true, and the thought of an invisible world existing alongside his own both thrilled and terrified him. And somewhere, buried away deep inside him, a hidden chamber of his heart opened. Silas felt an odd hopefulness, because even if his father *was* dead, he might still be found.

But the fluid dance of Mrs. Bowe and the ghost was intoxicating to watch, even though it pushed goose bumps up through his skin. Silas was lost in their dance. He was getting very cold, but he hardly noticed. He could not look away. Nothing moved. The world held its breath as they held each other and slowly waltzed around the living room.

As they continued to turn about the room arm in arm, Mrs. Bowe was looking only at her man's face, as if nothing else in the world existed. But then the ghost's head snapped back to look over his shoulder at Silas, keeping his eyes on him, a fixed point, although the ghost continued to move about the room to the music. Then, looking again on his beloved, the ghost brought their dance to a halt and slowly raised his hand, pointing to the doorway where Silas stood frozen to the spot, his mouth slightly gaping, his breath shallow and frantic.

Silas couldn't run, couldn't step away from the doorway. It was as though he'd been struck with lightning. Panic filled his body as the ghost held him in its gaze, not looking away even for an instant. Something rose in Silas's throat, and although he desperately wanted not to moan or make any noise in fear, he wasn't sure he could stop himself. He clenched his jaw against it, but when he felt Mrs. Bowe's hand on his shoulder, he quieted and felt the fear slip away from him a little. He released the watch and took his empty hand from his pocket, and the ghost was gone. There appeared to be only Mrs. Bowe and himself in the room. The music had stopped. But as he took Mrs. Bowe's hand and walked toward the parlor, the ghost appeared again before him.

"Come into the parlor, Silas," said Mrs. Bowe very kindly as she gently tugged at Silas's sleeve. "Come in and meet my man."

Silas walked slowly into the parlor as Mrs. Bowe went to the crystal decanter of brandy on the table. The ghost continued to look right at him but didn't speak, and despite the chill of the room, Silas's brow was hot as an ember.

The ghost reached out his hand to Silas, who didn't know what to do, couldn't think. He tried to speak, but fear held the words in his throat and he only coughed roughly, staring. The ghost smiled and turned back to Mrs. Bowe, with a last intent look at her face before he faded from the now warming air and took his leave of the living.

CHAPTER 27

INNER WORKINGS

MRS. BOWE SAT IN HER FAVORITE CHAIR. She looked tired, but her face was glowing.

"It's late, and I am used to being alone after my little reveries," she said, raising the brandy glass to her lips. "Give me a moment to compose myself, and I'll meet you in your father's study and tell you a little something before I go to bed."

Silas was sitting at his father's desk when Mrs. Bowe came in and pulled the heavy velvet curtains closed before she took a chair by the window. She waited for Silas to speak.

"May I . . . I mean . . . was that your boyfriend?" he asked gently.

"He is the husband of my heart, although we were never married."

"How long has he been dead?"

"Oh, a long time now. But 'dead' sounds so unkind, so impersonal, and *they* don't like to be reminded about it; besides, he's still here, so why bother upsetting ourselves with details? But now I shall ask you a question. It seems you have discovered something about one of your father's artifacts, yes?"

"I'm not sure what happened. One moment you were alone in the room, and the next, he was there. I mean not there, really, but *present*, I guess."

"I can tell you exactly what happened. You held the watch in your hand, and then you prevented the dial from moving. Nothing more."

Silas slowly took out the watch and set it on the table in between them, then he looked up at Mrs. Bowe, waiting.

"I think it's best if I don't speculate too much, but I will tell you what I know. I think Amos left the watch behind for a reason on the night he disappeared, and now you have it, and I think that is in accord with his wishes, though I would strongly have preferred it had your father told you of these matters himself. Still, I always found him a man of remarkable foresight."

"A man of such 'remarkable foresight' might still be around," Silas said a little coldly.

"True enough." said Mrs. Bowe, as she picked up the watch.

She examined it closely. It drew the eye and no mistake. Mrs. Bowe could feel the gravity of such things, the weight bestowed by age and meticulous, precise, almost ritualistic craftsmanship.

"I had seen it before," Silas said. "My dad showed it to me back in Saltsbridge."

"Really?" she said, surprised. "I thought he never carried it out of Lichport, but maybe his work took him farther afield than I knew. I shouldn't doubt that it was so, thinking about it now. Doesn't matter. He could do with it as he pleased. It was his absolutely. And now it's yours."

Silas picked up the watch and looked at its inscription, trying to read it aloud, stumbling a bit on the Latin: "*Vita Fugit Ut Hora.*"

Mrs. Bowe translated, "Life flies away, as does the hour."

"Mrs. Bowe? Before . . . when I saw you . . . you could see . . . your friend, couldn't you?"

"Yes."

"And the watch allowed me to see him too?"

"At first, yes."

"So the watch lets you see the dead." He knew this now. It wasn't a question.

"It does. But it is not consistent and may show you much more than ghosts."

"But you don't have one, do you?"

"No," she said, slightly confused at first by his question, but then, when she realized what he wanted to know, she added, "I don't need such a device to see my man. More to the point, he very much wants to be seen by me. Sometimes the dead wish to appear to the living, and if they are able, they will show themselves, just as my man appeared to you again after you put the watch away.

"I love him very much, and he loves me. If the heart is true, death may have no power over love. And when the desires of both the dead and the living are in accord, a bond of adamant exists, and neither death nor time can come between them. That is what I believe. The death watch, for that is what it's called, is another matter entirely. It lets you see things that are lost to the eyes of the living. And it lets you see them whether they want to be seen or not. It is an intrusion. As it was tonight. But for your father's work, perhaps for yours, it is a necessary intrusion, for you cannot help that which you cannot find."

Silas looked down, a little embarrassed, but his eyes were quickly drawn back to the death watch, the curve of the skull, the bend of light across the silver, the miniature elegance of the jawline.

Mrs. Bowe gave him a thin but sincere smile and continued.

"You should not put too much faith in objects, Silas, nor invest too much belief in their small portions of power, although I can see you are fascinated with it, now that you know something of what it can do. Things can go missing, get lost, lose their shine . . . and then where will you be having relied on them? Better to invest in your own wits and God-given talents, and those bonds that exist between people. To be sure, that watch is very special. And with it you may see many things. But not everything may wish to be seen, and more often than not, what you can see *may then see you*. So have a care. The death watch is a sad token, I think."

"How do you mean?" asked Silas.

"Because it merely confirms the dead's own pitiable state, merely shows with more clarity how a spirit is trapped in a moment out of time. Timeless. Endless. No way forward. No way back. However, some good has come of your father using it on occasion, so perhaps it's for the best. I think your father found that the more he used it, the less he had need of it, if you take my meaning. It was something he took no joy in, for all its oddness. I respect such things, respect their power, but in the end I put more faith in a sympathetic heart than a pocket watch."

Silas knew there was truth in her words but wanted to use it again, wanted to walk out the door and see every corner of the town with the ghost-eyes that the death watch bestowed, no matter what Mrs. Bowe said. Silas knew that if his father had left it behind, it was because he wanted Silas to have and to use it. Maybe he was supposed to use it to help him find his father, alive or dead? Silas could feel Mrs. Bowe watching him stare at the death watch. He looked up and asked her, "Is this the only one?"

"Your father thought there were others, although I don't know if he ever held one. There were some early treatises written about them. You may find them somewhere here in this library, or find notes derived from them in your father's writings. Here," she said, looking through a small stack of old printed pamphlets and odd orphaned pages of long-lost books in a folder atop the desk, "your father collected information on the death watch, though most of what he found was speculative and I don't believe told him much more than he learned by using it."

She handed Silas a piece of old paper. It was a page from an early book, maybe sixteenth century, judging by the image and the typeface. On the front was an engraving of the death watch. The mouth of the skull was slightly open, and the mechanism could be seen. Below it was a printed caption: "An accurate facsimile of the Hadean Clock, or Death Watch, an infernal machine, rendered from the actual artifact." In the margins around the image were handwritten notes relating to the watch. The small, broken annotations were penned in a good, clear hand, although the ink had faded somewhat with age, so Silas brought the page close to his face to read them.

> The dead reveal little of themselves,
> but may be compelled.
>
> Running water may confound the
> watch's properties, as streams and
> rivers remind the holder of the
> fleeting nature of time.
>
> When time stands contemn'd,
> you may not know what shall be
> reveeled, for every place where
> man hath been bears the mark of
> his passage that endureth, but most
> subtle. Lykeways, Mysthomes,
> Lands of Shadow, and the Dead
> themselves be ever about us and
> onlie Time prevents owre findinge
> them.

And below those, a note in Amos's modern, crabbed handwriting:

Stilled hand shows the other side . . . the other worlds. Colors fade from the familiar and those things that move, or flow, or breathe, gray in the sight. The past of a place, or the appearance of the ghost, may rise in high relief against the background of the present. Old light emerges in the vision, and long, unnatural shadows are thrown from familiar objects, as if two sources of light exist at once. Objects are caught between these light sources, one from the present, one from the past. In this way, the workings of the death watch are not so different from the workings of the memory. In fond recollection, the dim past rises up in all its golden glory, and the present fades away. And here is the watch's most obvious danger: Those who live too much in the past may come to share perdition with the dead, who are themselves lost to the present.

Mrs. Bowe extended her hand, and Silas put the death watch into it. She ran her thumb over the dome of the skull, warming the silver.

"Your father rarely used it anymore I think, so facile had he become at perceiving the dead. For a time I wondered if there was any power in the watch at all . . . if it wasn't all in the beholder. But once, being curious, I tried it."

"What did you see?"

"I would prefer not to speak of it."

"Mrs. Bowe, forgive me, you seem to know a lot about these things, yet you never seem very comfortable talking about any of them. But I don't really have anyone else to turn to . . . I hope that my questions don't offend you."

"I am very comfortable talking about them. I am just a little uneasy discussing them with *you*. That pendant you wear tells me it was your father's choice to let you into this world, despite his present absence. His choice. Not mine. Yet now, I'm the one left to fill in all the blanks. I loved your father as my dearest friend and I will abide by his wishes, but I am desperate that nothing ill should befall you. It is hard for me to see how I can reconcile his wishes for you and my own desire to keep you safe. I want to help you, so I will try to see a way through this hedge. Give me a little time, Silas. I think you will find, eventually, that I am up to the task.

"As I said, the work of our families shares a frontier. Your father and I worked together in the past to bring the bereaved what comfort we could. It was my honor to work with him. Your father was a man of sense, and he knew how to look through the records of the past and find things that might be of use to people. We shared that. A love of the old ways. I suspect you do too. And he was a good talker. People liked him, and so they told him things that are not often spoken of anymore in society. He wrote it all down, as you know."

Silas looked at her with eyebrows raised, waiting for details. If he'd had a tail, it would have been wagging furiously.

"Ah. I see. Did your father never show you any of his writings? Or any volume containing the writing of your ancestors pertaining to these matters?"

"No. Never." Silas was practically panting. "Are there any?"

"Indeed there are, and this is how we shall proceed: We shall let your father's own words and the words of others like him educate you. That is the way."

She looked away from Silas and cast her eyes about the room, deep in thought. Very suddenly, she got up and paced the length of the study, until she stopped with purpose in front of one of the shelves higher and deeper than the others.

Silas's heart was beating hard in his chest.

On the shelf sat what looked to be a large rectangular object, wrapped in a piece of old woven rug. She reached for it, but paused and instead asked Silas to get it down. "It's an old, heavy thing, and I wouldn't want to drop it. Yes, bring it down with your own hands. Your father was the last person to touch this book. From father to son it passes now. Blessed mother, guide their hands—"

When Silas brought it to the desk, Mrs. Bowe nodded him on to indicate that he should unwrap it from its shroud. It was an enormous book. More than a book, it was an ark, stuffed with hundreds of pieces of paper, pages of other books stuck and stitched into it all through its length. Its covers were large, leather-bound boards, and it looked to be over a foot thick.

"This book was part of your father's work. It has been held by all the Undertakers of Lichport, all of whom were Umbers, so this, too, must come to you. It has not always passed from father to son, but I believe it is best when it is so. However, it is not yours. It belongs to the town. I would have thought you might have seen this, but perhaps your mother didn't want such things about. Amos was given this book when he took the job of Undertaker. I know because I was the one who handed it to him. It is my job as . . . as town crier, if you like, to make sure the ledger gets from one Undertaker to another. Once, long ago, I read that three generations of Umbers came and went before an Undertaker took up the ledger. That was a bad time for dead and living both. So, people will be eager that you continue down the path of your father, whether you wish it or not. I must say, you are the youngest person to ever hold this volume, and that makes me uneasy. And, unless I've missed something, you have not formally accepted the position of Undertaker of Lichport. With your father not here to advise us, well, we'll just let things unfold as they must. You have stopped the hands of the death watch and looked kindly on the dead—let that betoken an auspicious beginning."

"But—stopping the watch was an accident."

"Honest error may play prologue to wonders. I shall pray that it is so."

They looked at each other as a strange understanding passed between them; then Silas slowly opened the book. It smelled like his dad. Old. Dusty. Ink and the mystery of ancient things crumbling between the pages. His eyes were wide as headlamps.

"Here are the names," said Mrs. Bowe, pointing at the first pages, "all the names of the dead going back to the town's founding. Of course, curious as your father was, he added a great deal to the book. I know from talking with him that he used the book as a sort of scrapbook of anything he could find about the town, about the lore of the dead, anything he thought would help him in his work. The entries go back a long way. I know that. In adding to it, he took part in a conversation with other Undertakers going back hundreds of years. What will you say to them, Silas Umber, young as you are?"

Silas didn't answer.

The book was open, and every page spoke his name in the creak of bindings and the raspy turning of thick pages.

As was her way when Silas's attention was about to become lost in something, Mrs. Bowe quietly left the room. Silas hardly noticed that she was gone, his eyes seeing only the book in front of him. He pulled out the chair—Amos's blazer hanging from the back—and sat down at his father's desk.

His hands shook as he turned the pages. His first thought was of spells. Did the book record rituals? Incantations? He had read enough folklore to know such things existed, and the thought of his father being master of such arts excited him, because he would have liked to have such secret wisdom, some portion of knowledge larger than himself, something he could control and use. Secrets that would work *for him*, instead of the usual kind, which just made him feel small and left out.

He flipped rapidly through the pages. Dozens of small pieces of paper and parchment blew out of the book and onto the floor. Silas realized with a sinking feeling that these had been bookmarks of some sort, perhaps marking the pages his father returned to again and again. Whatever they had once marked, those favored pages were now lost until Silas could find them again on his own.

He closed the book and began again at the beginning.

Silas slowly opened the cover first. There on the flyleaf had been pasted in an old engraving on a piece of heavy paper. The imagery was Roman, although the engraving was probably from the seventeenth century. The central image depicted a tall figure enthroned before a tomb with its door half-open. The seated male had two bearded faces adorning its head, one that looked toward the tomb, the other that looked in the opposite direction, down a road leading from the door of the tomb and off into the hills. In the hand facing the tomb, the figure held out an elaborate key. Below the printed image were words written in thick ink by an early hand:

> *Hail, Lorde of Gates! Hail to He who sees All Worlds and Watches at the Thresholde. Hail, Lorde of Vaults and Mystpaths! Hail, Janus, Father of the Undertaking and Maker of Wayes. Be thy roades e'er blessed!*

And below this were some letters he could not read. Some in Greek. Others looked like quickly written Egyptian hieroglyphs, but he wasn't sure. On the back of this page had been inscribed a list of phrases. Many of these Silas could make out, as they were written in only slightly faded ink in bold capital block Roman letters. It looked like a handwritten table of contents, but none of the entries had corresponding page numbers. Silas could make out

THE PATHE OF VIRGIL
ACTS OF DISSOLUTION
EXTREME UNCTION
YE DARKE CALL
RITES OF JANUARIE
WATER OF LETHE
DOOR DOOM

But as he continued to turn the pages, the handwriting became a real problem. Much of it seemed unreadable. Although it was mostly in English—many entries appeared to be translations from older works—it was still like trying to listen to someone with a very thick accent. Silas could see a few words clearly, but they were quickly crowded out by the words he couldn't read. The first few pages were the easiest, perhaps because their subject was clear and meant to be read by anyone.

Announcements. The first thing Silas noticed was that whatever the book had *become*, it had *begun* as a ledger of the town's dead, recording their birth and death dates. The earliest date of death was recorded for Robert Careborn, who died at age fifty-three in 1625. Some of the entries, many in fact, had the word "PAX" written next to them in the margin. A few were noted "LOST" or "WANDERING." Some were recorded as "MALEFIC." Others as "RECURRENT." The handwriting in the margins was in a variety of styles, indicating that numerous authors had commented on one another's inscriptions.

After the death of Agnes Farnham in 1761, only the names of Umbers were recorded. Silas assumed that at that point, the public death ledger was carried on in another book, and this enormous volume had come into the possession of the Undertakers of his family. He followed the long list of names, most of them unknown to him, most of the older ones clearly from the Bible: "Jonathan, Abel, Sadoc, Enoch, Joram, Jonas, Abram, Solomon, Uriah, Caleb." A few of the names had a small drawing of the double head of Janus next to them, Silas assumed at first because they were Undertakers.

When he got to the end of the list, he saw that it halted a few inches above the bottom of the page. The last complete entry was "William Umber," and the date of his funeral ten years ago was in his dad's handwriting. Below that, the page was empty except for a final incomplete entry: "Amos Umber" with a Janus head drawn beside it that had been crossed out, followed by his dad's birth date and a blank line for the death date to be inscribed.

Silas paused, then ran a finger over his father's name and continued reading.

After the entries of the dead, very little in the ledger was sequential. Silas turned page after page. Most of the handwriting was unreadable. Several pages contained only newspaper cuttings. These, at least, were easy to read. Most were clippings that had been pasted into the ledger, stories about accidents, murders, and terrible deaths that someone thought might be related to or result in ghostly activity. The headlines were terrible:

AVENGING PREACHER—FIRST FATHER AND THEN SON SHOT
WHILE ATTENDING TO THE DEAD

GIRL GUILTY OF MURDER—SEVENTEEN-YEAR-OLD CONVICTED
OF POISONING NUMEROUS PEOPLE

DIED BESIDE HIS GOLD—AN OLD MAN SEIZED BY DEATH WHILE
GLOATING OVER HIS HOARDED WEALTH

DOWN IN THE CABIN, DEAD—A LITTLE BOY'S NIGHT
WITH HIS FATHER'S CORPSE, AND THE BABY AND HIS SISTER—
HIS COLD AND DREARY VIGIL

A VITRIOL FIEND'S WORK

KILLED INSTEAD OF CURED—AN OLD MAN, TO CURE THE GRIPPE, CUT
ARTERY BY MISTAKE—GIRL DIES OF BLOOD LOSS—
HE DIES FROM THE SHOCK

But the other pages were largely mysteries. Page after page of foreign lines and curves. Silas tried to pay attention, but his eyes began to blur and hurt.

He looked up from the ledger, and his surroundings slowly came back into focus. The room was cold. He looked around and thought about laying a fire on the hearth, but as it was close at hand, he pulled his dad's coat off the back of the chair and held it up for a moment. It was a little big for him, especially through the shoulders. It still smelled like his dad. He pulled the jacket on and then crossed his arms in front of him, imagining his father was hugging him, one of those long, been-away-for-a-few-days-and-missed-you hugs that always made Silas instantly forgive his father's many absences.

Blinking a few times to resharpen his sight, he looked down at the ledger again, slowly and passively, almost as if he wasn't trying to read it. Letters seemed to rise to his eyes. He could begin to see each handwriting style, each word, as its own accent. Now a sentence seemed clear, then a paragraph. Now a whole page became plain reading. Voices rose from the pages as though the book itself now spoke to him.

Then he saw clearly what the book contained: many long quotes from even more ancient books and records, diagrams, and spells to bind the dead. To release a soul, to protect and banish. There was much poetry, or portions of poems containing lines an Undertaker had probably once thought illuminating in some way.

He saw that toward the end of the book, there were lots of pages in his father's handwriting. Some mentioned the watch, others were broken entries and brief comments.

"What you see can also see you," his father wrote in a margin. And below it, even more cryptically, "We are who we were."

As Silas continued to read for the next few days, he returned often to the back portions of the text, not just for fragments of lore and instructional notes, but because reading those entries in his father's hand made it feel like his father was coming into clearer focus too, like Silas was holding up to the light parts of his dad's strange and rapidly deepening work and world.

The problem was, his father recorded information all through the book, as did its other contributors, taking every opportunity to add to, elaborate on, or refute what previous Undertakers had recorded. This made some pages read like overheard arguments. Even so, reading those words breathed life into their writers—his father and all the others who had written these lines and left them just for Silas to find and read. His people were speaking to him.

The closer he looked, the more ages of the town, the more voices and hands rose up to greet and confound him. Not all the voices were kind. Some recorded terrible things, awful happenings with equally frightening resolutions. He could see that the book was more than a ledger. It was chronicle, journal, and spell tome, utterly occult even in its most common account. It was about the dead and what they can do and where they reside and how they may be dealt with, controlled, banished, and brought to peace. Many lifetimes of records spilled from the pages before him. There was no index. Some texts ended abruptly, as though pages had been removed. Some parts of the book wouldn't lie flat because extra pages and portions of other manuscripts had been glued or stitched in. Some texts had been written over, or hastily added in the margin; others had been amended by the taping in of related works. He could see that someone, perhaps his father, had taped in some bookmarks with labels such as

"Bindings," "Banishing," and "RE old district Restless," but none seemed entirely consistent, or made a whole work of any topic. So Silas concluded that reading the ledger would be much like his relationship with his father: deep but hieroglyphic, rich but full of secrets, half-truths, mysteries, and fragments.

He opened the ledger somewhere in the middle and began reading again. He decided this was how he would continue to read the book, since it was impossible to examine it in any kind of order. He would simply open it and look for any text he could read.

He read day and night, pausing only to eat what Mrs. Bowe brought him. The fresh eyes of morning, Silas found, were best for the nearly illegible texts that had eluded him the night before. But he preferred night reading, because that was when the voices came. As he read, always by candlelight, he would begin to be able to make out voices that seemed to read along with him. He didn't know what to make of this and was afraid to use the death watch in his house for fear of seeing something that would make him feel uncomfortable there. He simply imagined that these were the voices of his ancestors and the other folk who had added to the ledger over the years. *Not so strange a thing*, he thought, *for when we read, don't we summon the past into the present? Hold out our hand and invite an author to sit with us for a time?* Although he sat by himself as he read, he never once felt alone while doing so, and because of that, he read from the ledger almost constantly, letting the book's marvelous distraction dim, for a time, the candles of his other cares.

CHAPTER 28

BORROWED TIME

SILAS HAD BEEN LIVING IN HIS FATHER'S HOUSE for almost two weeks. In that time, he'd scarcely left the place, spending almost all of his days and nights poring over the Undertaker's ledger. He'd sleep briefly in his chair, or on the sofa in the study, but on waking, would continue reading.

He was studying a translation of an obscure Egyptian text relating to the soul leaving its tomb to travel abroad, when he looked up to rest his eyes and saw through the window that Uncle stood on the sidewalk and was staring up at the porch. For an instant Silas panicked, but he quickly suppressed the fear that Uncle could bring him back to Temple Street by force. Silas was home. He was not a child to be fetched or taken anywhere he did not wish to go. Here, he was the man of the house.

Silas opened his front door and called down to the street, "May I help you?"

Uncle looked startled, as though he had been caught in the act of doing something, but gazed up at Silas from the pavement and said, "I believe you have borrowed my wheelbarrow."

"You came here for your wheelbarrow?"

"Yes. They'll have need of it in the garden."

Silas was sure he'd never seen a single gardener anywhere on Temple Street, and the back of Uncle's property was a wilderness, so he knew Uncle's visit was an excuse to confirm his location.

"Of course," said Silas. "I appreciate the loan." He rolled the wheelbarrow awkwardly down the front steps and put it down roughly on the sidewalk by Uncle. "I'm sure you have a lot of heavy things to move around the house. I do hope I haven't inconvenienced you."

Uncle refused to take the bait, saying instead, "Silas, your mother and I both wonder when you plan on returning home. A night or two out among friends is a fine thing, of course, but we are a family now and you should be with us."

Silas replied very calmly, "I'm not sure about that. I have work to do sorting through my father's things, and I'm not sure how long that will take, so I think, for the time being, it's best if I stay here." Silas could see his uncle was clearly upset by this, but kept his composure as he shielded his eyes from the sun's glare.

"I understand your desire to pick over your father's leavings, really I do. Very understandable, though there's no reason we couldn't have all his things brought back to the carriage house for you to peruse at leisure. I could even help you—"

Silas put up his hand. The thought of it all sickened him: going back to Temple Street, moving his dad's things, his uncle touching them.

"No, no, Uncle. Everything is fine the way it is. Please give my mother my best wishes and tell her I will visit her soon." Without waiting for a reply, Silas took the stairs two at a time, walked into his house, and closed the door behind him.

When he entered Mrs. Bowe's kitchen for lunch, he saw the table had already been set, spread with fresh fruit, cheese, and bread. Mrs. Bowe raised an eyebrow when she saw him come in and asked, "What was all that chatter on the sidewalk?"

"My uncle came for the return of his wheelbarrow."

The color ran from Mrs. Bowe's face, the blush of her cheek

turning to chalk at the mention of Charles Umber.

"He came here? Oh, Silas, he's not in the house?"

"No, no. I didn't even let him on the porch."

She calmed a bit, the color returning to her face. "Good. Silas, I don't ever want him in the house, not even in the garden, though I don't suspect he'd ever step foot in there. . . ."

"Don't worry," he assured her. "I don't want him here either."

Silas could see he had distressed her, so he changed the subject and asked Mrs. Bowe about her ghost-man. He'd been feeling guilty about not seeing Bea since he'd come here, and it was no coincidence that he was more than curious about Mrs. Bowe's relationship with her dead boyfriend. And while he'd been too wrapped up in the ledger to think of much else, he had dreamed of Bea several times since seeing her last, and secret love was of interest to him, whatever the circumstances.

"When you met, did you know right away you loved him? Was it love at first sight, I mean?"

"Very much so."

"But you never got married? Didn't your family want you to marry him?"

"No, because everyone in my family understood that I would never marry because of my particular calling. Of course, that did not mean I couldn't have a male friend. As you know, he was very special to me, and still is."

"Your father didn't want you to marry? Didn't fathers used to insist on stuff like that?"

"It was not his decision. It was mine and my mother's, and we decided that I should not wed, as is sometimes the custom among certain of the women in my family who are born with . . . particular gifts. In the Bowe family, it is the women who have the say over such matters; indeed, it's our name the family bears. The men whom Bowe women marry either take the name Bowe, or keep their own, as it suits them, but Bowe women do not take other names. Not ever. Perhaps this was for reasons of maternal pride. More likely, people didn't want Bowe women hiding behind the names of others. They wanted to know who we were and where we were. Sadly, my mother died early, and perhaps in his grief, or because he began to change his mind about holding to custom, there was a brief time after my mother's death when my father's judgment became clouded by worries of what would become of his business. So he began to hint—just hint, mind you—that I might marry, for the family's sake, despite his knowing that it would be a break with custom and the promise I'd made to my mother. There was someone he thought promising for a while, a young man, the photographer who worked with him. This was the photographer who would take pictures of the bodies, for the families to remember their beloved dead. It was quiet work, and he was a quiet man. He took beautiful, somber pictures, but there was something about him I didn't like, even then. And in any event, I would never break with custom. So, I told my father, and this young photographer, to put the possibility of marriage from their minds."

Silas immediately knew who the photographer was, and he desperately wanted to ask her what she meant about her "particular gifts," but he didn't want to risk Mrs. Bowe getting offended, or reticent, or embarrassed, so he kept silent and listened as she continued.

"My father and I argued about it for a long time, several months. He would go quiet about the proposal and then suddenly bring it up again. But always I told him there was no love there and besides, he knew my mind, and my mother's, about my never marrying: A Bowe woman, such as myself, does not marry. I didn't have to elaborate, although honestly, by that time, with all his simpering and long looks, I didn't even want to be in the same room with the photographer."

"It worked out okay, though, right? I mean, no one forced you to take a husband, so it turned out okay. You just waited them out, and your father and the photographer eventually got tired of asking?"

"It was even easier than that, though there was some unpleasantness."

"What happened?" Silas asked, moving forward in his chair.

"The man who asked for my hand, the photographer—but of course by now you have figured out this is your uncle I am speaking about—he was . . . *let go* by my father."

"Fired?"

"*Let go*. My father simply said he would no longer be in need of his services. He paid him a full two months' wages, and that was dear money in those days because the town had long begun to go bad, folks moving away and fewer and fewer coming here to bury their dead. Nearly all the shipping had stopped and moved to the larger ports south and north of us. Even the overland import of Asian funereal vessels from the western coasts had begun to slow. I mean, we had money. Savings and investments left to us by relatives. This is a large house, but we built it and own it outright. I just mean to say, that was very kind of my father to give him so much after what he did."

"You don't want to tell me what he did, do you?"

"Well, Silas, he is, after all, your kin, and I—" She paused. "Perhaps, just for tonight, we should leave the past alone, just leave it. I won't lie, your father did not think much of him either, but it's not my place to dig up the awful past, particularly since he and your mother apparently have an *understanding*."

"I have already drawn my own conclusions about my uncle, and I don't like or trust him," Silas said firmly. "I think he probably had something to do with my father's disappearance, though I can't prove it yet. There is nothing you could tell me about him that would surprise me, and I doubt there is anything you could tell me that would make me enjoy his company any less."

Those words hung on the air for several moments before Mrs. Bowe began to speak again. Her brow was pressed into creases of concern, and she looked at Silas hard before she began.

"Silas, I am so happy you're here, happy to have the chance to know you. I loved your father so. Still love him, wherever he is. But I prayed you would never come here because of what I know about your uncle."

Silas could see she was becoming increasingly nervous and upset, and he put his hand on top of hers. She gasped slightly, breathing in deeply and slowly, trying to regain her composure.

"All right then, all right," she said, drawing in as much air as she could, calming herself. "Your uncle is a dark man, a man of dark thoughts and dark deeds. That's what I know. Most of the folk in this town will not receive him. The people of the Narrows have threatened him with bodily harm should he come among them any farther than the Peales's shop."

"What did he do to offend them?"

"He married one of them."

"But his wife left him. At least that's what he says."

"Yes. That is what he says. Whether you or anyone else believed him then or believe him now is another matter. She's gone, and that's all anyone knows for sure. And I know he had something to do with her very sudden absence."

"Do you believe that, or do you *know* it?"

"I find it hard to accept that she would have left Lichport

without so much as a good-bye to her kin. Leave your uncle? That I'd believe, for she was unhappy to have married him within the year. But go in the middle of the night to heaven knows where and never a word since to anyone in her own family? That I will never believe. When Narrows folk take their leave, they die in their beds, or at sea, and in no other way. And when they are "lost" at sea, they are never truly lost. Even then, word comes. Some news always arrives—the corpse will wash back up on our shore, or some sign will appear on the sea or be brought here by the tide bringing word that one of our own has gone below. Narrows folk don't get *lost*. And they always send word . . . if they can."

Silas's chair had become uncomfortable, and he couldn't settle. He stood up and paced the floor. People lost. Lost. His father lost and his uncle right there, at the center again. And of all the ideas now set swimming in his mind, chief among them was the image of his mother sitting in that house, with *him*. He was glad to be gone from there, but he found little cheer in it because his mother was still there, and it was becoming clear that his search for his father would take him back to his uncle's house.

Why would the mortician fire Uncle? What kind of thing could a photographer do that was so wrong? Silas could see clearly in his mind some of the photographs from his uncle's album. Faces that appeared to sleep, and yet were not asleep. He turned the pages in his memory. The dead boy leaning awkwardly against his young sisters. Living husbands holding their dead wives. Mourning mothers holding still infants in their arms.

Suddenly one picture flashed into his mind, eclipsing all the others. The ivory-white hand. The picture that had brought on that awful, brooding quiet in his uncle. The hand. Silas knew the trouble must have something to do with the photograph of the hand.

Mrs. Bowe looked at him questioningly, but then looked away as though she did not wish to hear what he might say. Silas reached out and put a hand on her arm, and spoke as softly and gently as he could.

"The reason your father let my uncle go, was it over a picture of a lady's hand?"

"Oh, heavens!" she exclaimed, louder than she'd meant to. "Have you seen such a thing? Has he kept it after all this time? Then my father was right."

"He kept everything. He has albums of photos. He's very proud of them. By the look of his house, I don't think he's ever thrown anything away."

Mrs. Bowe retrieved a handkerchief from her sleeve and gently drew it across her brow, which was glistening slightly in the low light.

"Why would he keep such a thing, I ask you?" she said very suddenly. "Yes. It was the hand. I expect it seems such a little thing on the surface. I mean, it's just a photograph. Seeing such a picture, you might even think it was taken by mistake as the corpse was being arranged."

"No," Silas said gravely. "You can tell how careful he was when he took it. It's a pretty special picture. I couldn't stop looking at it."

"Awful, is what it is, when you think about it even for a moment! He just covered over the face of that kind, dear woman as if she didn't exist. Covered her face all up and drew the hand away from her side and lay it on the dark cloth for *contrast*. Contrast! I'll never forget that picture. I saw it on my father's desk. Just a picture of a hand. But why do such a thing? You see, Silas, the folks who'd come to have a picture taken of the body of their dearly beloved, that is an act of love. Good photographs were expensive, and sometimes death came fast, so they might not have a recent picture of the dead to remember them by. Often, it was parents bringing children. The child died and the parents would want a picture with them. One last moment together before they put their own flesh and blood, and all those hopes, down into a bed of clay.

"My father felt this was a holy thing, helping folks in those moments, helping them to remember their loved ones. He was proud to have the services of a good photographer who wasn't troubled by taking pictures of the dead. It was always traditional here in Lichport, but in other towns, death portraits had gone out of fashion. That's why so many folks would come here. Because we valued, still *do* value, the old ways."

"So he took a picture of her hand?" Silas said, trying to bring her back to the story she had started.

"Yes, he did. And that picture had nothing to do with any kind of loving remembrance. He thought something was special about that woman's hand, and he wanted a picture for himself. No one in the family asked him to take that picture. Who would? Knowing her, and the kind of woman she was and what she had done for her children . . . putting her other arm into the ground *with them*."

Silas only nodded, remembering the little things his uncle had told him about the woman, about the loss of her arm, but his mind was swimming now. His uncle was a man who took things that didn't belong to him, a person who didn't care about the wishes of others.

"My uncle is a man, I think, who is proud of his trophies," Silas suggested.

"That is precisely what he wanted," said Mrs. Bowe quickly,

as though they were of one mind on the matter. "A trophy. Something only for himself. Something to look at when he was alone. Well, she wasn't his to take. She wasn't an object. She was a person and deserved respect, alive or not. My father saw that picture and got quiet and then got terribly angry. He went to his desk, got the money, and sent your uncle from this house. Needless to say, marriage between your uncle and myself was never mentioned again. But every day for the rest of his life, whenever my father looked at me, there was an apology written on his face. How the thought of me marrying such a man haunted him."

"What did the rest of my family make of this business?" Silas asked.

"Your grandfather came to call, of course, wondering why his son had been sent away. I've never been sure what my father told your grandfather, but whatever it was, he obviously wasn't surprised by it, and he never asked my father about it again, though they remained friends. I think your grandfather pitied your uncle. Maybe that's why he left him the house and the money like he did. Or maybe your uncle just worked on him until he signed everything over to him. Don't know. I know this much, though: Your father was left right out of the will, and that was your uncle's doing, one way or another."

She was breathing hard again, worked up as if everything was happening in the very moment of the story being told. She turned her head toward the window, where the dark glass reflected them both now that the sun had set.

"I thought my father destroyed the picture, but it's clear now your uncle kept copies of all the pictures he took. I am sorry to hear that, very sorry. I hate to think of him looking at those people. Running his fingers over their faces." She looked back from the window and closed her eyes for a moment, then smiled very weakly.

"Well, it was not long after that incident that I met my man. My father made no objection, although I know he wished we would have married and had children. And when my man died in the war over the sea, I wore black as any widow would, and no one said anything against it."

Silas could see Mrs. Bowe was tired and feeling uneasy, as though she felt she had said too much. Maybe it was just the mention of his uncle's name that brought some portion of him into her life again, into her home from which he had so long ago been banished. But there was so much she knew. So much more Silas wanted to know, but already he was feeling protective of her and didn't want to do anything that would upset her further. It was clear she was always going to be of two minds about sharing troubled family histories with him. Maybe about everything. He knew Mrs. Bowe felt responsible for bringing him into Amos's world, but the more they talked, Silas was also pretty sure she felt guilty about whatever she told him.

Her fighting days were over, he could see that. That was why she didn't leave the house. She was safer inside with her memories to protect her. She had done a lot for him already. She'd made a home for him and had given him the key to his father's world, and he loved her for it. So no more questions if he could help it; he would have to keep Mrs. Bowe out of it.

Silas knew then that he had to keep looking for his father, and he knew, from what Mrs. Bowe told him, that part of his search might take him back toward Uncle's house on Temple Street. What he needed most was some perspective on his father's work and a better understanding of the town, and the parts of the town where that work took place.

LEDGER

There are also hells beneath hells. Some hells communicate with others by passages, and more by exhalations . . .

—COPIED BY JONAS UMBER FROM *HEAVEN AND HELL*, BY EMANUEL SWEDENBORG, 1757

CHAPTER 29

CAMERA OBSCURA

THE ROOM WAS FAR COLDER than the air outside, and steam rose off Uncle's face as he entered his Camera Obscura, still sweating from his walk home with the wheelbarrow. As he set the complicated locks on the door behind him, he could see his breath in the broken reflection on the ornate metal lock plates. He locked this door to keep the room's occupant in and also out of habit. But since Silas had left, there was no one else in the house who might disturb his private work in the Camera. Most days found Dolores numb before noon and lounging in the parlor or "retiring" in her room. Since Silas had left, the mood in the Camera had become angry and agitated, far more so than before. The room's occupant knew Silas was gone, and the air bristled as Uncle entered by himself. When he walked in the room, the hair rose on the back of his neck, and he could feel the cold anger filling the chamber with an acrid, metallic smell. His brow furrowed in disappointment as he lit a candle.

His plans had begun to fray about the edges. He knew it, and his own aggravation wasn't helping. Uncle had hoped Silas would come back to the house. He had hoped this wouldn't be difficult to accomplish. Indeed, Dolores was doing most of the work for him. Uncle assumed her slipping health would inspire her son to come back to her side. Let her slip. Then Silas would come back to play the dutiful son.

From the middle of the chamber, Uncle could feel eyes watching him.

He spoke into the air of the room, trying to invoke a feeling of confidence and calm.

"I can see why you long to be near him. Despite his upbringing, there is something very remarkable about our Silas. Perhaps it is his sympathy. Or his independence. You admire that. And he knows you're here, doesn't he? He can feel your distress. He sees what a person has inside. That kind of perception is admirable. It can only come from pain. He has been hurt. You have been hurt. That is the kind of bond you can't just conjure into existence. But we shall make a home for him, won't we? Right here with you. In the bosom of his family. In the very house where his father was born. What symmetry."

Uncle pulled a chair up to the glass, settling in for a chat.

"You would like to have your kin closer to you? Yes. I now see what is best. You want Silas close to you. . . . Yes, that will remedy all, but it will take a little time. He must come of his own accord. At least at first. Now he is in that *other house*, and it will be hard to get him out.

"Time. Always time. I know. I know you are lonely.

"Perhaps there is something I can do to fill the gap until Silas returns. Perhaps there is someone who can share your discomfort and bring you some ease, someone who might calm your shattered nerves. Someone to mother you a bit until our larger plan ripens.

"Will you abide? Just a little longer? For me? If I bring you something nice?"

The candle blew out, leaving him in the acrid darkness of the Camera, and Uncle said with a tired sigh, "How kind of you to indulge me."

CHAPTER 30

BEACON

SINCE SEEING THE GHOST of Mrs. Bowe's man, Silas almost never put down the death watch. If it wasn't in his hand, it was close by, in his pocket, or on the table in front of him, where he could always see it, although he was careful not to stop its hands. He wanted to use it, but felt doing so for mere curiosity would be somehow . . . inappropriate. It was a tool, not a toy. And knowing now what it could do, he was also frightened by it even as it exerted a pull on his imagination. No matter where he was—in his house, walking through the town—he wondered what the death watch might show him should he choose to use it. Maybe there was a way to use it to help him find his dad. His great-grandfather had told Silas to see more of the town if he wanted to find out more about his father.

There was no straight path to the top of Beacon Hill, so Silas picked his way among the crowded gravestones that jutted up like crooked teeth from the mossy, flesh-fed earth. He tried not to walk on the graves, but it was hard to tell exactly where they were. Very few of the tombstones were aligned or faced the same way. Most leaned in various disjointed angles. Some had fallen forward, their names now pressed into the ground. Others reclined as if looking up at the sky, waiting for something to happen. Silas walked around the hill, his motion upward slow as spaces between the gravestones appeared infrequently. Simply climbing over any of the monuments only to hasten his ascent was unthinkable, and besides, there were the names.

Everywhere he looked, the names of the dead were inscribed about him. Fisher. Barnaby. Kettle. Ransom. Hariot . . . He could almost make a song of the inscriptions—a song leading right back to the earliest days of the town's founding. Silas noticed that as he went higher on the hill, the names seemed stranger, more old-world, harder to read, and he realized that the ancient townsfolk began by burying their dead at the hilltop, and slowly made their way down with the passing generations. It seemed only right the oldest townsfolk should have the best view. Mounting the top of the hill, Silas could see why the first Lichporters chose to bury their dead here: Out a bit, past the ragged edges of the Narrows' slate-roofed tenements and low gabled houses, the sea ran wide and far, flowing over shoal and deep water, streaming back across the horizon to where the first settlers had started from. From the hilltop, the ancient dead could look over their town and remember their distant, ancestral homelands, all at once. Surely, with such a view, the dead rested well here.

The names. In other cemeteries, the stones were mute, but here they spoke to something deep inside Silas. These were his people. He could feel the sense of belonging in his feet. The earth of the hill warmed him, rose into him from below the ground, welcomed him home.

As he gazed out, Silas could see the roofs of the old pretentious nineteenth-century mansions on Coach Street rising high over the Narrows and looking down on them just as the rich folk had looked down on the poorer fishing families of the Narrows long ago. To the west, he could easily spot the spire of the near-abandoned church and some of the higher buildings in "new" town. To the south, tall trees in the park and the streets of the better neighborhoods blocked his uncle's house from view, and Silas thought that was just as well. Farther to the south, he could see the flat green expanse of Newfield, the town's other cemetery, created about a hundred years ago when Beacon Hill was too full to push even a finger into the corpse-filled ground.

Questions came to him. In a cemetery such as this, where the town's dead were stacked below the earth, generation after generation, did the spirits of the dead congregate? Did ghosts keep close to their graves? Mrs. Bowe, he imagined, might say that you just know when things are peaceful with the dead of a given place because you feel at ease, nothing "pushing down" on you, when you're standing there. And Silas did feel at ease. Beacon Hill was about the quietest place he had ever stood. A breeze gently pushed some leaves about the monuments, but there was hardly any other noise at all. *Here*, he thought, *the death watch might reveal something more of the town*. Maybe the ghosts of his own kin were about. Maybe they would help him or show him something that might lead him to his dad.

Silas took the watch from his pocket, and as the metal warmed in his hand he could feel the mechanism inside it softly whirring and ticking like a baby's rapid heartbeat. That small, sure pulse, the push and pull, as though the coursing of time and blood were the same. He pushed his thumb down hard on the watch's hands, quickly drawing in breath. The force of the watch's inner workings pushed against his finger, but the dial had stopped. Instinctively, Silas shut his eyes. With the exhale, he opened them.

A mist rose from the sea and sent long tendrils winding up the lanes of the Narrows, slowly crawling into the higher parts of Lichport. On and on the mist came, lapping at the base of Beacon Hill like little waves. But as the mist drew closer, Silas could see shapes moving within it and rising from it. White, frayed forms, a procession of people made from smoke. He could see them now on every street of the town. Weaving in and out of buildings and streets, many of the forms looked up at the hill, quickly made their way toward it and reaching the bottom, began to rise up the slope toward Silas.

At the bottom of the hill, Silas saw Bea, although there was something odd about her. It was hard to tell from so far away. Did she look older? Her clothes were different. He'd never noticed them before. Had she always dressed like this? She wore a long, old-fashioned dress that flowed around her feet in the mist. It looked like she was crying, and something that appeared to be fish but must have been silvery bugs or moths were swimming and circling in the air around her.

Other gray forms continued up the hill toward Silas. When they came within about a hundred feet of him, the wraiths stopped, hanging on the air, as if waiting for him to say something. He couldn't speak, and the ghosts raised their arms toward him, palms outstretched, and all around him Silas could hear the sounds of pleading and the most pitiful cries.

Unable to move or speak, Silas stood frozen, watching the spirits continue their ascent, passing without pause though tombstones and trees, some crying, some shouting—a river of the dead flowing upward toward him.

Just behind Silas, a voice called out, and he dropped the watch. The ghost-forms and flowing mist instantly blew away from the hillside as though caught by a great wind, even though the air was utterly still.

The voice said very clearly, "Master Umber! It is very kind of you to visit the dead, and you are always welcome on the Beacon, but too much time among the stones may not be the best place for you, just now. May I show you the way home?"

Silas picked up the death watch and hid it in his pocket, as he tried to recover his composure. "Oh, I know the way. I'm okay, thanks." He turned around and saw a tall, thin man wearing a long, tight-fitting black coat and a wide-brimmed hat.

"Of course, of course. It is a short walk back the way you've come. I suspect you are looking for your father, but he is not presently among my flock," said the sexton, gesturing to the gray stones of the hill.

Silas looked out over the herd of tombstones, then smiled and turned to thank the man, but he was gone already, probably making his own way down the other side of Beacon Hill toward the small cottages leading to the river. When Silas looked at the bottom of the hill, he saw with disappointment that Bea was gone too, vanished with the mist. But now he wondered, had she been waiting for him, or merely pausing there on her way from one place to another?

When Silas returned home, Mrs. Bowe had dinner waiting. The table was set with two bowls, fresh bread and butter, and a large pot of soup set on an iron trivet. Steam rose toward the light that hung over the table.

"See anything interesting on your walk?" asked Mrs. Bowe as she ladled soup into Silas's bowl.

"Nothing much."

Mrs. Bowe nodded at the lie, handed him the bread, and said nothing.

CHAPTER 31

LEAVING

DESPITE THE FEARFUL VISION at the Beacon, Silas continued to use the death watch. The sound of its ticking attracted him, and he told himself that if his father had left it to him, it must be okay to use it. Just once in a while. Not every day. He would trust his intuition, and maybe whatever the death watch showed him would lead somewhere.

More often than not, with its hand depressed, the death watch showed Silas things that he was at a loss to define, although these mysteries were themselves enticing. Each new vision was an invitation to use the watch again, just for a minute, just to see what else might be present. He told himself he was looking for "clues."

He saw forms that moved across the earth that were not ghosts yet seemed spectral in the way they rose up out of the ground into the landscape and then faded or fell away. With the watch, Silas could see red, lately fallen leaves that were blowing on the wind suddenly become something more than leaves. At the edges of the path along the river, the leaves swirled and rose into vaguely human shapes. Silas wondered what they were; he queried the air, but the shapes had no voice and seemed to have no mind and so paid him no heed.

With the watch hands held, the leaves rose up, turned in the air, and drew themselves up and together into arms, legs, the suggestion of head and torso. The more Silas watched them, the more he was convinced they were not ghosts at all, but only memories. Like the leaves themselves, dry reminders of the passing years.

At first the image of the walking leaf forms was unsettling, but as Silas watched them he began to notice they never went very far. One would "walk" a ways, perhaps a few steps, perhaps a hundred yards at most, and then fall back to earth, its leaves quickly scattered. Others would spin upward in the wind and move as one form in another direction, then dissolve into the brown rotting leaf horde, cast down and indolent again on the grass.

After seeing the leaf-wraiths several times, Silas gave them little thought, even when he began to see them without using the watch. People had always walked along the river, as they went here and there, and that long line of folk left small impressions of themselves on the ground. Year after year, the earth bore their weight, carried their stride, remembered the passage of all the faceless wanderers—memories held by the land. Nothing more.

When he walked home, the leaves would eddy behind him. Silas thought that the worlds of the dead and the worlds of the living—or, rather, the past and the present—were not as far apart as he'd once thought. Fascinating as they were, such visions were only distractions and brought him little comfort, for the death watch had yet to show him anything that might bring him closer to his father.

And if the spirit will not be banished, nor
brought to Peace by other means, and causeth
the consternation of its kin or their needless
demise, or would be in anywise revenged upon
the undeserved livinge, let sucke a spirit be bound
and sealed in iron or some other sturdy vessel of
metal and cast then into some divers deep pit
or into the sea. Learned authors and venerable
undertakers will attest that the bottom of the
Red Sea, most favoured for such rites, is full
littered with such unruly souls and their small
caskets.

—COPIED OUT FROM THE RECOLLECTIONS OF FATHER
GALDING, VICAR, ST. MICHAEL'S PARISH, 1794

They are prisons. As the tin corrodes over time, a sliver of light may enter the cell and begin to rouse its prisoner, who has waited, perhaps for centuries, for liberation. Though, by that time, most often the spirit is much degraded. There may be little memory left to it beyond its pains and ever-increasing wrath. So, at last, when it escapes or is released, as eventually it always is, it is drawn home with a near-mindless pull, caring only to spend its fury upon once familiar things, those people that may only remind it of its innumerable and irretrievable losses.

—Undated marginalia in the hand of Amos Umber

CHAPTER 32

SMALL SPACES

IN HIS FATHER'S HOUSE, there were many small rooms along the back of the upper hall. Silas slept downstairs, in a room that might have once been a private study. He preferred the ground floor. He didn't like the view that could be seen from many of the upstairs bedrooms. When he looked south from the windows on the upper story, he could see across the top of Mrs. Bowe's garden into the park that grew wild over the back of her gate. In that garden was a small clearing, in the middle of which was a little rise where the gallows stone stood. On that stone the wooden gallows had been erected for hangings long ago. And on the other side of the park was a depression of earth surrounded by high, dark trees. Mrs. Bowe had told Silas this was once colloquially called "the hole," and it was the common burial place of those executed criminals. He had been tempted several times to use the death watch to see the spirits that attended on those spots, but something always held back his hand. He knew, just plain knew, that whatever lingered in the park didn't want to be seen, and he was more than sure he didn't want anything that haunted the gallows stone seeing him.

So he favored the view from downstairs. But at night, when he couldn't sleep and the upstairs windows were turned to mirrors and afforded only reflection, Silas sometimes walked the upper gallery and explored the rooms until he got tired.

He'd had another dream about Bea. Although it took him close to Uncle's house, he had waited for her on several nights, only to be disappointed. Maybe she'd left town for a while. In his dreams lately, she appeared often, skipping ahead of him, singing, calling him along, laughing, until they reached the edge of the millpond and her face began to change and sharpen, lit by the dream's unnatural light. Then Silas would hear the sound of water splashing, and he'd wake up, confused and frustrated, unable to get back to sleep.

Six doors down on the right side of the hall, Silas found a very small room, almost a closet, with a desk and a chair, and all the walls lined with closely packed shelves on which were tins, old iron boxes, and bottles of every size and description, all tightly sealed. There were also some very old-looking small metal caskets, one of them rather ornate with tarnished silver filigree work that covered its rusted surface. On the floor of the little room several concentric circles were inscribed, and the same geometric images were carved into the surface of the desk, only in miniature.

Somewhere in the ledger Silas had read that in the past, restless spirits who could not be brought to peace by any other means would be banished into containers like these and sealed up, there to remain until time, corrosion, or both released them. Looking at the shelves brought Uncle's cupboards to mind, filled to brimming with preserved foods. A feast of things held over past their allotted time. And now here, shelf after shelf of ghosts, tinned and preserved like jellied meats or bottled like the tomatoes of a hundred summers ago. A collection of unfinished business. A pantry of souls.

Next to the desk, there was a box that had in it several tins whose seals had been broken, that were pierced with holes or had the lids pried away, rust falling off them. Who had trapped their occupants and why? And why did his father bring them here? A sense of obligation, perhaps. Silas wondered for a moment why his father hadn't merely opened them all at once and been done with it. But, as he looked closely at some of the tins and boxes, he saw how very meticulously some had been sealed—wrapped with innumerable layers of cord or wire, not that it would have made them any more secure or held the soldered lids on any tighter, but it might have been a comfort to whoever had sealed the spirit inside . . . the sure feeling of winding cord about and about and about the tin, binding its contents, an act of will as much as metalwork.

The more Silas thought about it, the more likely it seemed that the contents of most of these containers would have been troublesome. He thought the circles on the floor and desk might have been a kind of protective magic, additional safeguards his father had invoked before he opened a tin, in case its contents proved dangerous. Tentatively, Silas reached out to one of the shelves and carefully brought down a red metal can that read, PRINCE ALBERT LONG-BURNING PIPE AND CIGARETTE TOBACCO. The top of the can had been sealed with lead, and then it appeared to have been dipped in wax as well. A tag had been tied to the can with the inscription

HOME OF JOHN D./ 1932/ANON./SPIR.MALEDICTUS/3 DECEASED PRIOR TO CONTAINMENT.

Very gently, Silas held the can in both his hands and felt it begin to hum, as though it was filled with bees. His mind went back to his uncle's cupboards again, to all the tins forgotten at the pantry's back—things gone sour in the fullness of time. Potted meat turned at last to putrid soup. Looking at the tin in his hands, the carefully wrought seal along its edges could be interpreted to read, "Leave me be. You don't want what I got locked up in me!"

But the longer Silas looked at it, the more the tin also eerily suggested, "I have a secret, open me and find out!" As he shook off the voices in his mind, he realized why his father kept such things here. Anyone else who found one might have easily assumed there was a coin or some valuable inside, and without thinking, pried it open only to discover some gibbering thing, angry at its many years kept in so small a space. It made Silas feel claustrophobic even thinking about anger like that being so confined. He gently put the tin back on the shelf.

He couldn't help wondering if something in this room might be related to his dad's disappearance. Some vengeful ghost attacking the first person it saw after it was released? Silas didn't like thinking about even having such objects in the house. Some of them were rusted and might at any moment be about to let go of their contents like some spectral jack-in-the-box. What should he do with them? He didn't know their histories and so couldn't risk opening one, and the thought of throwing them away, or sinking them into water somewhere, the sea or maybe the millpond, seemed very wrong, like condemning someone without knowing their crime, or even their name. He left the room, went downstairs and found the ring of keys to the inside doors, came back upstairs, and locked the room from the outside.

Silas was startled by a sudden sharp hissing sound outside the window in the room next door. He'd heard that noise before outside several of the upstairs windows, so it must have been coming from a lower portion of the roof covered by one of the eaves. Some animal, he guessed.

He walked softly across the room and looked out the window, but saw nothing. But after his experience in the tin-room next door, he felt skittery. He went back downstairs again, this time to fetch the death watch from his coat pocket and pick up a flashlight.

He opened the window as wide as he could and climbed out onto the roof. He shone the flashlight into the overhang where one section of the roof hung out over another to form a small cave. Within was a weather-worn nest of pale sticks that he could see now were actually small bones. He heard the low hiss as before, although it grew louder the closer he came to the bones. He drew out the watch on its silver chain and opened the skull to get at the dial. The moment he pressed his thumb on the hand to halt its progress, the hiss exploded into the air right in front of his face, as though the sound had been flung at him. There below the eaves, half-edged in shadow even with the flashlight pointing at it, was a large raccoon, its head low to the shingles, crouched among its bones, hissing and chittering madly at Silas, who nearly fell backward off the roof when it appeared. Silas quickly released the watch's mechanism, then looked once more at the nest of dried and exposed bones before crawling back into the house, shaken and cold.

Before he'd released the death watch's hand, he had seen a light in the distance beyond the rooftops. Past Mrs. Bowe's garden, past the park, on the other side of Coach Street, past the woods along the marsh, the spires and columned chimneys of a tall house glowed with an incandescent light, but when he put the watch away, the light slowly faded. Silas wasn't able to go back to sleep, but lay in bed turning over in his mind what he'd seen. The bones, the strange light, and what either might portend.

The next morning he returned to the roof, gathered up the bones, and brought them to the backyard to bury them, near the compost heap in Mrs. Bowe's garden where all the scraps from the kitchen were thrown. Silas placed some of the choicest bits from last night's dinner into the small grave before covering the bones with earth. Just to be sure, that night he went to the roof to try the death watch once more. In the distance, he saw the light again, brighter tonight, as though a star had been hung on the distant house's weathervane. When he looked away from the light, he saw that the space below the eave was empty and quiet. *Good*, thought Silas. *Good*. As he'd been burying the bones earlier that morning, he'd thought that up until recently, he might have kept the skull and displayed it on a shelf. *No*, he thought, *let it all go back to the ground. Just let it go.*

Now, again unable to sleep, he walked the upstairs gallery and wondered: If even a small space on his roof held a ghost— let alone the cemetery—what about all the empty buildings in the town? The deserted lanes and cottages? The lonely streets lined with great houses, overgrown and abandoned? Were they all homes to the dead? Did "ghost" simply mean "forgotten," or "thrown away"? Was a ghost present everyplace something was left behind, or abandoned, or undone, or an unspoken word had fled the world? And if a ghost was remembered or acknowledged, did it just leave? Or did it stay stuck to that place, waiting for something else to happen? Could a ghost forget itself? Forget who it was and where it was? Was it the Undertaker's job to remember those ghosts who'd forgotten themselves?

Through one of the bedroom windows, through the reflection of the room he stood in, Silas saw the light from the house on Coach Street, bright as a beacon on a lighthouse, and remembered that his great-grandfather had told him to watch for a light, that there was a house where there might be someone who could help him. Silas stared out the window until the light began to fade in the approaching dawn, then went downstairs and quickly dressed. It was early, and he left the house with the death watch in his pocket before Mrs. Bowe could call him for breakfast.

In life, a person will come and go from many homes. We may leave a house, a town, a room, but that does not mean those places leave us. Once entered, we never entirely depart the homes we make for ourselves in the world. They follow us, like shadows, until we come upon them again, waiting for us in the mist.

—FROM *THE SOUL'S HABITATION* BY JONATHAN UMBER, 1789

CHAPTER 33

IN STITCHES

SILAS STOOD BEFORE A HOUSE at the corner of Coach and Silk Streets. There was no question this was the house of the people his great-grandfather had mentioned, the place Mrs. Bowe didn't want to say much about. He also found it marked on his father's map of the town, circled in ink with a small "3" written next to it enigmatically. He might have continued the search at home, to look for a reference in the Undertaker's ledger, but minutes and hours felt like stones in his stomach, and if there was something in this building that might point him toward any news of his father, he wanted to find it. Besides, hadn't this place "called" out to him?

He had been standing in front of the house for ten minutes, in hopes that someone might see him and come outside. He didn't like the idea of just walking into houses anymore, even one that was so clearly abandoned. The front door hung at an angle, and most of the windows on the bottom floor were broken, their glass hanging like fangs in their frames. Thick vines of ivy grew up the house, and their leaves gave it a shaggy look that blurred all the straight angles of the walls. The house had a Georgian roof, a Colonial window, a nineteenth-century door knocker. Like so many of the larger houses in town, it was a veritable patchwork of architectural details from its long history. Yet behind the walls, or under them, in the odd conjunctions of certain of its angles, Silas could sense something older than the structure; the hidden lines of an ancient floor plan far, far older than the building he could see, older even than the town.

The door nearly fell from its hinges when Silas tried to get past it and into the house. The main room was very large; the farther walls of the room and the ceiling were hung with shadows and couldn't be seen clearly from the entrance. All around the entry hall and the front room were many chairs of different styles. There were also old carved pews, set at random angles, that gave the room the look of a waiting room, or some kind of derelict bus station. Many pieces of furniture and some statuary, all from different periods, were thrown about the room as if left here by the furious tide from some long ago tempest.

A beam of sunlight came in through a broken window and fell on the staircase with inviting brightness, and Silas decided to explore the upper floors.

The stairs wound upward in a wide circle and were much longer than he expected. Silas became increasingly tired as he ascended the stairs, sure he'd climbed much higher than the roof of the house, yet the next floor was still some ways off. The stairs finally brought him through the high ceiling of the lower floor and to a landing that formed the entrance to an enormous chamber with tall ceilings that followed the various peaks of the roof. Perhaps as a result of the strange angles of the many supporting beams, the room looked far larger than the third story of the house he'd seen from the outside. The room was empty except for three spinning wheels gathered around a vast hearth at its center. Across his vision, gray forms gathered, and Silas knew he was not alone. He brought the death watch from his pocket and set his thumb against the dial, but as he began to apply pressure to the mechanism, a woman's chiding voice came from the far side of the room.

"You don't need to use that, you know. Very rude, I call it. We are pleased to receive you, Silas Umber."

Startled and embarrassed, Silas returned the death watch to his pocket. At once the room changed. It was now a large, plain wooden chamber across whose heights spanned large, curved pale beams that gave the impression of standing inside a whale. From the many beams hung weavings and knittings and knotworks, a vast loose tapestry, with various parts of the room holding different scenes. Most were small and quite intricate, more like pictorial tattings than weavings. All were detailed, even exquisite, the work of careful hands unhurried by time. Looking closely at the hangings all about him, Silas could begin to discern their subjects: buildings, streets, avenues, cottages, some of them vaguely familiar.

When he looked up, three women stood in the center of the room. They appeared to be in their thirties, yet their gray eyes bespoke a greater age. They wore very long dresses and aprons of rough cloth, with sleeves rolled back along their lengths, exposing white skin and long hands tipped with delicate fingers sharp as spindles.

"You approve, then, of our work?"

Silas was rapt as he looked over the room and over all the details of the enormous web of weavings, but said quietly, distractedly, "It's very fine . . . all the details . . . extraordinary. But may I ask, what is it all?"

"Misthomes," said the first of the three.

"Obsessions, stations of habit, fixations, traps," said the second in a singsong voice.

"The places in between," said the third. "The shadowlands."

"Do you mean, like limbo?" Silas asked, confused.

"If you like, though that sounds far too singular, and falls very short of the mark," said the third of the three.

The charged air of the room, the resonance of their voices, and the extraordinary nature of the tapestry all told Silas he was in the presence of Mystery, so with great reverence in his voice, he asked, "Will you tell me what it is you have made here?"

The first smiled and spoke again, and when she did, the voices of the other two seemed woven in somehow with her voice, giving her speech a choral quality.

"Silas, stir your mind! Here is the whole town and its long history stretched out before you. Many scenes are here, woven in pale silk and knitted in sturdy wool. Look close and see the first suicide on Prince Street marked in red tatting. And there is embroidered a teahouse where some souls sit and drink and long for home. And here, the Theater of Love Confounded set forth in widow-worthy lace, where many passionate but foolish souls have tarried too long in the third act. Attend, attend!"

He didn't know where to begin. Each stitch seemed to have a story, and the weaving as a whole, its complexities and possibilities, left him unable to form a question. There were too many emblems hanging in the air before him to decipher any single one.

The ladies stood patiently, waiting for him to recover. All Silas could think of was to ask them about themselves.

"Ladies," he said hesitantly, "may I ask how you came to do this work?"

"Reading the work *through* its author, eh? How unfashionable!" said the first, then added, "He wants our life story!"

"Get an advance before you tell him anything!" said the second, laughing.

"It is a tale worthy of the telling," said the third, more soberly.

"But truly," said the third, her voice going low, "it is the most common story in the world. Girls gone bad."

"I'd like to hear it. I think our threads have tangled for a reason," Silas said.

"I like him already," said the second of the three, perhaps acknowledging Silas's polite choice of metaphor.

"Very well," spoke the first. "Here is something of our latest ending. . . ."

The women seemed to speak with one voice, although clearly only one was speaking at a time. As they spoke, the second of the three began working her long needles very quickly, and Silas could see a figure made of thread the exact same color of his clothes, standing in a room stitched in pale wool, and the figures of three women standing before the first, dark knots for their heads and frayed threads for their tall bodies. Around him, as he watched the second at her work, their voices rose together. Silas found it a very strange sensation, to see and hear people talk when their mouths didn't appear to move, so after a moment, he closed his eyes and listened.

We three have been friends for many years, sisters almost, meeting in this very room. Or rather, a room on this spot, for this building is far newer than we are and the old house was long ago destroyed, yet we remain here among the shadows of what was.

We had no love of church, neither of making supper after. So much fuss. Each Sunday was like a curse. We couldn't bear it. So we formed a little Sewing Circle. That was in the year 1692. A long time ago. We made blankets for the sick and poor of Lichport. So at the beginning, we were not censured for our behavior. We were modern women, even then, and had business to attend to!

But we were married off young, and our husbands, like most then, were men of the sea. Gone for long stretches, making their living upon the whale's road, and that suited us, though it was dangerous work. Many sailors did not come home—though ours always did—and we'd make shrouds when needed. And since our men were so often gone, we met more often, and that people didn't care for. It was thought then that we should be about our housewifely business. But our own company suited us best, and when our husbands came home and heard harsh words from the old men of Lichport, well, they had some harsh words for us. Blows, too. Remember the time. Those who were different were a problem. We had become a problem. We were talked about. Our men stayed home from the sea to school us in good behavior . . . but we are not, by our natures, conventional.

For a time, we obeyed, if only to avoid the beatings. And we waited. And the call of the sea came upon them and they set out, convinced we would abide by their word and make them proud before our neighbors. To church, to church! they said. Keep the Sabbath and keep the home! Instead, the evening after their ship had sailed, we went to the cliffs and stirred the sea into a fury with words. A broom and a cauldron and the right charm were all it took back then. Round and round we stirred the water and the sea complied, became a tempest, and the bottom of the sea sang out to their ship and drew it down and down beneath the waves . . . and so went their ship and all our troubles—well, some of them. But someone had seen us. To be fair, we must have stood out that evening: three women standing hooded at the cliff edge . . . what must people have thought! But we were ever bold and unapologetic, even at the day of our hanging. And for using spellcraft to contrive the death of our tiresome menfolk, death was prescribed as the cure for our modernism. They called us The Devil's Mistresses. Absurd. We'd never even met him.

Well, a little time later our bodies were cut down from the gallows and buried away from the church, which pleased us, frankly. And a little time after that, we met again. So habitual had the meetings of our Sewing Circle become that they did not end, even in death. And here we are, still at our work, though it has expanded somewhat, and we now know better what we are and what our work betokens.

They were all three pointing at parts of the web with their long fingers, inviting Silas to look more closely. Some threads of the web trailed down through the floorboards, up the chimney, out the window.

"Where do they all lead?" Silas asked, fascinated, his eyes moving this way and that along the lines.

"Oh, child! We don't know where all the threads go. We don't leave this place very often. But we do know that the misthomes of Lichport, some of them, are connected to other places where the dead share similar histories. These places are not only for one place and one time. People have been dying since the beginning, and so there are many roads through the mist. Some are still used. Some are just waiting to be used again. Others have been long forgotten but are still there when the light is right, or when someone remembers it, or when someone dies in a rare and particular manner. Some of these paths are even shared with roads of the living. Once a road has been used to carry a corpse, even roads that are used every day by the living, it is always 'lych' from that day forward. Forever and always a lychway shall belong to the dead, in some measure. That is law."

Silas craned his head to look at the web hanging in the air above him, then looked again in each direction, where long, thin threads connected portions of the weaving in different parts of the room. It was beginning to make some sense, the way certain parts of the tapestry tied one place to another, like paths or roads.

"Is it a map, then?" Silas asked.

"Perhaps, Silas Umber, you begin to read what is written here. All deaths are connected because all people are connected. However distant, our lives are linked by ancestral threads, faint though they may be," One said.

"Clever. Clever," said the second of the three. "Like the father."

Silas felt all the muscles of his neck go taut, and he broke out in a sweat.

"Did my father come here very often?" he asked in a low, tense voice.

"Not if he could help it." The third laughed. "I think we made him uncomfortable."

Silas could see why. He could feel their strength, their age. While he couldn't yet perceive the expansive role these three women played, he could sense that they knew far more than they said, which made him think they were something more and far stranger than mere ghosts. They also seemed to like the attention, which made Silas uneasy, as though no matter what he asked them, they would tell him only a portion of what they knew, to keep his interest, perhaps, to keep him coming back. This did not inspire trust. But if his dad had come here to speak with them, there must have been a reason for it.

As if reading Silas's mind, the first said, "Oh, when he came to us, your father loved to look upon the tapestry. He would come and just stare, studying it for hours and hours. Sometimes he would write something down in his great book. But most often, he would come and just wander the lines and lanes, the streets and stitches with his eyes, following one thread to where it met another, as though he was looking for someone, which I suspect he often was."

"Did my father see the tapestry as I am seeing it now?"

"Oh!" said the second again. "He *is* a clever boy. Cleverer than the father, I warrant, and maybe braver too, wouldn't that be helpful? That is a very perceptive question, Silas Umber. *Very*."

The first of the three spoke again.

"The tapestry changes all the time, though some roads and places appear again and again. Sometimes, a place that has been appearing for centuries vanishes very suddenly. Your father might have known why. The comings and goings of individual features are not our concern. We weave what we see, and when the vision fails, we stop and start somewhere else. So you will see some elements as your father saw them. Others, well, your father would have benefited from your insight, I have no doubt. Besides, he is only one man, with his own particular ways of seeing the world, and he lacked your wounds, I think, and those must be a considerable boon to you. Pain grants *such* perspective. I can guess your life has not been easy. Be proud of your scars, for they most certainly affect what you're seeing now. Like you, your father had desires and fears of his own, and those affected how he saw the dead and how he saw things in this room. But there is something else you'd like to ask us, I think."

Silas shifted his weight from one foot to another. Out of politeness and perhaps fascination with the tapestry, he had waited to ask them about his dad. He didn't know what the protocol was for interrogating people like the three women before him. But hearing her query, Silas's own question came flying out: "Have you seen him? Is he here in Lichport? Is he dead? Did my uncle have something to do with his disappearance? Will I see him again? Has he been here recently?"

"Enough!" said the third. "In the old days, you'd have been allowed only one question."

"Yes . . . ," recalled the first, and then said, looking rapturous, "One question and then the gift. Oh . . . the gift . . . But that was long ago, and we needn't stand on ceremony with one whose family is so well known to us. Why, we are nearly family ourselves."

"Silas," the second began, "if your father is alive, we can be of little help to you. And if he's dead, well, it is still a complicated affair. Your father wandered through so many spheres, who can say where death might have taken him or where it might hold him? Numerous lychpaths cross through Lichport, and though there are many signs of him in the skeins and threads, we cannot be sure when such evidences appeared or what they betoken, although we stitched them ourselves. Not all signs are for our eyes. Also, your father walked very often among the dead and their habitations, so his paths are shot through with their threads to such a degree that it is hard to untangle them. So he may be alive, or deceased, or lost somewhere in between, and we likely could discern little difference."

"Perhaps," the first of the three mused idly, "you've been looking in the wrong Lichport. . . ."

"Please tell me how to find him," Silas begged, the desperation growing in him.

In response to the longing in his voice, the three came to stand before Silas and leaned over him like mothers about a wounded child.

The second said, "You must look among those who have also lost something. Those are the folk who may, *may*, be able to help you. Such ghosts can also be the most dangerous, the ones most likely to be unable even to acknowledge your presence. But there may be a chance—"

"Where would you send him then?" asked the third.

"To the marshes. To the Bowers of the Night Herons. To the nests. To the mothers of the lost. He has lost something. He should go to them, although it is unlikely they will see him or speak with him."

"Slim odds, I give that path—but the farther he walks, the farther he may yet be able to walk . . . 'way leads onto way' as they say . . . ," said the first.

"Yet there is a resonance. Their threads will easily twine

together, no matter what follows the first knot. Here are complementary colors. It could be a beautiful scene, eventually," said the second.

"Please!" Silas insisted, frustration flooding through him. "Tell me!"

"I will do more than that. I will take you to them." And the second of the three stood close to him, drew her long shawl about her, and extended her hand to Silas, although he was unable to take it. "In the old days, no one set first foot upon a lychway alone, and he should not walk there by himself," she said to the others. Then she turned back to Silas.

"Child, will you come with me, though very likely nothing, or something much worse than nothing, may come of it?"

"Yes. Yes, I will."

"At the very least, you shall have set foot to the dark road appointed for you, and that is a beginning."

"Oh! This is rare! Our dear sister is to play Virgil to the Undertaker. That *is* putting the cart before the horse," said the third of the three.

"Most rare!" said the first. "Safe travels then! And Silas?"

"Yes, ma'am?"

"Please see you don't keep her out too late, now. We have so much work yet to do."

The first of the three looked out the window, to watch Silas and their sister make their way back up the road and toward the marsh. When they faded from sight, the first and the third could not stop thinking about the boy. The boy and the father. The father lost. The first felt the mist rise in her mind, and her eyes rolled back. She crossed the room by intuition, picked up her small, bone-white shuttle, and moved to a neglected corner away from the other. She worked very quickly, and soon an image began to form from the threads she worked so carefully—a small house or square room made all of knots, far along a thread, very distant from the other places on the tapestry.

"What have you there?" asked the third of the three.

"Too soon to tell . . . ," whispered the first. "Too soon to tell."

"And this one here? Closer in?" the second asked, as she pointed to a house with dark windows, all embroidered with somber silks of gray and brown and black.

"I do not want to look too closely," replied the first. "There is madness there, and the resident is not in full knowledge of its estate. Oh. Anger and terror both. And betrayal."

"Surely there is something you can tell, something you can see?"

The stitches became more rapid, but more repetitive, and the first said, dreamily, "There is a cradle, a vessel . . . the signature of entrapment and containment . . . and look, a bee preserved in honey-colored threads. Very curious." Deep within the stitches the outline of a cradle could be discerned, and below it in the tapestry, links of stitches hung as chains. And above them, a single bee heavily embroidered in gold.

"No more!" said the first, quickly jerking her head up away from the stitches. "I can hear it crying. A terrible song stirs the air. I will not look again upon this place. If you wish to know more, we must ask the boy."

"Silas? Why?" questioned the third.

"Because he has come very close to it. Because this place cries out for him. Because the threshold to this awful Shadowland," said the first, pointing again at her bit of stitching, now covered in thick, uneven loops, "is in his uncle's house."

LEDGER

In 1672 Jeremiah Abury was lost among the marshes when in his fourth year of life. While his mother, a good woman of this town, slept upon the warmth of a summer's afternoon, Jeremiah wandered from their house, taking himself up the very middle of the road. From that day he was never again seen in Lichport. The next year, the great birds began to congregate in the trees overlooking the marsh. Night birds and herons. And come the eveningtide they could be heard, their long plaintive cries sounding from high up in those high branches. There were only a few at first, but each time the soul bell in town rang out for a child who died, or a mother who did not survive her birth time, another bird came and made its nest here.

—FROM THE LICHPORT CROW, BEING A COMPENDIUM OF
REMARKABLE TRAGEDIES OF OUR OWN FAIR TOWN

In the northern counties, rocking the cradle toom, or empty, is considered most ominous. For then it may be assumed that another occupant eagerly awaits the place of the first and may bring about its demise. It is further held that rocking a toom cradle and hearing the hollow creaking it makes shall call the wandering souls of lost children to it. We pray such may find comfort where e'er they be.

—FROM THE PAMPHLET "A BRIEF AND TRUE ACCOUNT
OF PORTENTOUS CUSTOMS" BY SAMUEL UMBER,
UNDERTAKER GENERAL, LICHPORT

In Rama a voice was heard
Weeping and in lamentation and great mourning,
Rachel crying for her children
And would not be comforted
Because they were no more.
   —JEREMIAH 31:15

CHAPTER 34

BOWERS OF THE NIGHT HERONS

THE MARSH IS CLOSE. *Do you have your timepiece with you? Good.*

We are nearly there.

Silas Umber, prepare yourself.

Few among the living can bear losses such as these. And those who do endure them, or die from them, come here to wait.

When traveling among the salt marshes, it is best not to walk alone. Many things are lost among the tall reeds and brackish waters, and the folk who look for them are often single-minded in their search, unwilling to show kindness to others. Focus. Come in company or do not venture here. Everyone knows the wisdom of this. Nearly there.

Always it is the same. The mothers of loss nest outside of town. Maybe north, maybe south, maybe both. Walk out of any town, and if you walk far enough, you will find a place such as this one. Always isolated. Always with a grim history. Loss calling out to loss down the ages.

Your father came here only once. And he would never speak of it, though the bowers weighed heavily upon his mind. Amos said only that some places needed time, and you could do nothing for them until that time had passed. Well, some kinds of pain a parent cannot bear to look upon. To lose a child. And now you have lost your father . . . and though your father lost a father, it is not the same, is it, Silas? You will see them. You will look upon what haunts this place. You will see what your father could not.

Before people ever came to Lichport, the marsh was here. And when people did come, they realized very quickly that it was not a place for idle wandering. People got lost here. Folks who couldn't be around others sometimes camped at the edges, but never for very long. Your people were among the first, and their ancient estate still stands, still casts its shadow upon the marsh where it comes closer to the sea. Who can say what brought them here? Something in the air, perhaps.

Indeed. Silas Umber, look up.

High in the branches is where they've built their nests. Each nest empty, as you see. But on the edge of each, there are the night herons, waiting, always waiting. On most nights, even in town, you can hear their cries of longing take wing across the marshes. Never are those calls answered. Such is their estate. You are surprised at how large the nests are. The branches come from very far away. Some were found floating on the surface of the sea. Others plucked from ruined houses, perhaps where some of their living days were endured. Others from places where they've picked among the hedges and tall grasses, looking, always looking, never finding.

Where are their nestlings, you ask? Lost. Some at birth. Some later in life. A few who dwell here never had children, only longed for them all the days of their sad lives. No matter, for a hole in the heart is hard to heal. The heart wants what it wants, and a lost child is a terrible thing, a door closed forever.

No. No. The children do not come here. They are in other places, other shadowlands. Always on the margins, never able to find their own way home. Never able to find their way here where loving arms await them.

There is yet more to see here, if you would like. Ask them what you will. Yes. Use the death watch and tell me what you see. I suspect you and I may not see this place in quite the same way. . . .

Most of the dark-winged herons, their underbellies glowing white, were perched on the edges of their nests. Others flew in widening circles over the marsh, and made their short throaty calls that fell echoing, searching, among the reeds.

Silas brought out the death watch and stopped its hand.

He could still hear their cries, but the sound had become longer, stretched into wails, long questions drawn across the air with a knife. And where once the birds and their nests stood in his sight, now great platforms of interwoven branches spread across the upper limbs of the trees, and, pulled through the branches, stitching them together, were bits of rotten fabric, children's blankets long ago grown threadbare, torn by the winds. On the platforms women sat in high-backed chairs, their faces thin and drawn, the tattered crepe of their mourning gowns hanging down from the trees like Spanish moss. Before each of them was a cradle, empty and hollow, lying on its side.

Silas opened his mouth to say something, but several of the women began to wail and cry above him. Another, who had been walking in circles around and around the base of her tree, altered her arc and walked close to Silas and reached out her arm in a pleading angle. Unable to look on her face, racked as it was with the pain of loss, Silas closed his eyes. Then, against his skin, he felt the brush of a wing, and in that instant whatever he might have said or asked flew from his mind.

Evening was approaching. Silas stood gaping, trying to speak, trying to recall his question. There was something he wanted to ask, but he couldn't remember what it was, and after a few more minutes at the edge of the marshes, under those ancient, empty bowers, among the weeping mothers of the lost, he couldn't remember why he'd even come here. His eyes welled up with tears, became red and salted as though the marsh water had been drawn up into his body and mixed with his blood.

A voice that seemed familiar said, "Why do you stare so among the shadows of the lost? Come away, Silas Umber, let us linger here no longer. . . ."

Someone stood next to him, speaking, but he could neither remember who she was nor turn to look at her. He could hear her singing softly then, something, a little childish rhyme, and he could just make out the words that floated up to join the spilling moon rising over the salt marshes. . . .

> Once I saw a little bird
> Come hop, hop, hop;
> So I cried, "Little bird,
> Will you stop, stop, stop?"
> And was going to the window
> To say, "How do you do?"

But he shook his little tail,
And far away he flew.

The song had ended, or was about to begin again, and flocks of night herons took up their accustomed cries. Silas couldn't listen anymore, couldn't remember why he'd come, and he felt, suddenly and very strongly, that he must leave this place. He turned away from the marsh, away from the lady who'd brought him, and without another word, as though she wasn't there, he walked home, his heart even emptier than before.

Mrs. Bowe had placed a candle in the window.

It was that kind of night. Wandering folk moving, everyone agitated and nervous, both the living and the dead. "Holy Mother, see them home. All to their hearth sides this night, and every night, and all. Bring him home," she prayed at the window.

Silas was out on some business. She used to leave a candle in the window some nights for his father. *A little light to lead you home*, she'd say. And except for once, it had always worked.

But now she could hear someone walking along the sidewalk. Someone with wet shoes. *Oh*, she thought, *oh! If he's gone to the millpond again!* She considered herself a peaceful woman, but she would give Silas more than a piece of her mind if he had gone to that place.

She threw open the doors, ready to give him harsh words, but when she saw his face, with all the color gone out of it and his breathing so labored, she gathered him up into her arms as she had done before and brought him inside and over to the large wingback chair by the fireplace.

As she put more wood on the fire, she said, "This is becoming a habit," and she stooped to pull the wet boots off his feet as he lay his head back. "At least your father's good boots are not going to waste," she told him with a smile as she tried to make light of it.

Mrs. Bowe lifted the boots to put them by the fire to dry. She knew from the look of them that he'd been to the marshes; she could feel the drag and suck of the mud on them, the pull of deep places, and the tearlike droplets that still clung to them. The brackish water glistened in the firelight.

"The marshes are the loveliest place, I think, *by daylight*. I used to walk there very often when I was young. I would take the longest walks along the marsh edge, sometimes even wandering a little ways into the interior, though it was always so boggy. Still, it was a very fine place for bird-watching."

Silas looked up at her.

"They are still with you, you know. A part of them, all about you, pulling the sadness up out of your bones. I can feel it coming off you now, like water from those boots. That's how it is with the dead sometimes, Silas. Your losses, their losses, become the same . . . this is the real danger of the road you're now traveling down."

Mrs. Bowe put her hand on his chest and felt the pendant that she knew his father had given him. "Silas, you must be of two minds. Look things straight on, but keep your own wits about you. If you look at the dead for too long, you become like them. Do you understand me? Keep one eye on them, and one on the road home. Always."

But even as she spoke, he drifted off to sleep.

I might as well have been married, she thought, *for all the men who come home late to me expecting to be put to bed and then fed breakfast.*

She went to the window and pinched out the candle.

LEDGER

Death be not proud, though some have called thee
Mighty and dreadfull, for, thou art not so,
For, those, whom thou think'st, thou dost overthrow,
Die not, poore death, nor yet canst thou kill me. . . .
—John Donne, "Death Be Not Proud"

THOUGH DONNE SPOKE OF DEATH'S
BEING THWARTED BY THAT HEAVENLY
ETERNITY OF THE SOUL PRAYED FOR BY
SOME, YET HIS WORDS COME CLOSE
TO THE MARK IN MATTERS PERHAPS
RELATED TO THE UNDERTAKING. FOR THE
RESTLESS DO NOT DIE, IT SEEMS, BUT
EVADE DEATH BY SIMPLY CONTINUING. THE
EARLIEST CASES IN LICHPORT HAVE NOT
BEEN SUFFICIENTLY DOCUMENTED, SO I
WILL BEGIN BY VISITING SOME OF THE
HOMES ON FORT STREET FOR EVIDENCE.
THIS IS, PERHAPS, BEYOND THE PALE
OF MY CALLING, AND YET . . . AND
YET, I THINK WITH SOME THE CORPSE
MAY ITSELF BECOME A KIND OF LIMBO—
A TOO-FAMILIAR TRAP THAT HALTS
THE SOUL'S PROGRESS AND KEEPS
THE SPIRIT EARTHBOUND BEYOND ONE'S
ALLOTTED TIME—AND SO IF I CAN
ASSIST THEM TO ACHIEVE A

PEACEFUL, NATURAL PASSAGE, I MUST. THE OTHER ROAD FOR THEM, AS IS PRACTICED BEYOND THE GATES OF ARVALE, IS TERRIBLE INDEED. BUT THEY ARE A FASCINATION, I MUST ADMIT, FOR THE RESTLESS ARE PRIVY TO SUCH SIGHTS AS THE LIVING MAY NEVER KNOW. . . .

—Notes concerning the Restless written by Amos Umber.

AND I SHALL RULE OVER MY HABITATION ON EARTH AND SHALL IN DEATH WEAR THE CROWN OF THE TWO LANDS, AND SHALL REMAIN IN WHATSOEVER FORM I CHOOSE AND SHALL FLOURISH EVEN AS I FLOURISHED IN LIFE, AND MY HOMESTEAD SHALL BE AMONG THE EVER-LIVING CEDARS. I HAVE OPENED THE WAY UP TO ETERNITY. MAY MY COFFIN BE MY OWN UNDYING FORM. LET NOT THE DOOR TO THE LAND OF THE LIVING BE SHUT TO ME THOUGH I AM DEAD.

—A spell or prayer from the ancient Egyptian *Coffin Text of Aaru the Scribe*, translated by Amos Umber

CHAPTER 35

REACHING OUT

SILAS STOOD NEXT TO THE CORPSE, HOLDING ITS HAND.

He leaned over and put his other arm around his great-grandfather's body, hugging him tenderly, not minding that the embrace left small smudges of preserving pitch and honey on the front of his jacket.

"You're as good as your word, son!" his great-grandfather said, his mouth moving slowly around the sentence.

"I like to keep my promises," Silas replied, smiling. "Besides, I was wondering about a few things, and I thought of all the people I know in Lichport, you would be least likely to be . . . troubled by being asked."

"Happy to oblige and very happy for the company. What would you like to know about the gray legions? I presume you're not here to talk about the weather?"

Silas raised an eyebrow in surprise and appreciation at his great-grandfather's directness.

"How many kinds of dead folks are there? I assume that like every person, every ghost is unique, right?"

Slowly, almost imperceptibly, the old man nodded, then cocked his head to one side and squinted slightly, looking closely at Silas's face.

"So, you intend to follow in your father's footsteps and take up the family business, eh? I can't say I'm surprised. You have more of an Umber look about you. But let's hope you've inherited some of my good sense to temper the rest."

Silas said nothing, admitted nothing. He could not say the words. He could not admit out loud that he had made a formal decision, but he knew, and knew more certainly with each passing hour, that he had already set off down a path from which there would be no returning. Silas only inclined his head slightly in confirmation. "For the moment, let's just call my questions academic in nature."

"So be it, but I am not the expert your father was. He was a scholar of the first order and learned things that few if any folk now living ever did. His studies probed deep into the abyss, far into the lore of the dead. I have none of his book learning. I can only tell you what I've seen and what I've heard. Oh, yes, I can hear *them*, even sitting here. A person in my state hears everything. The past is a chatty companion, I can tell you. But as for ghosts, your hunch is correct: There are as many kinds of ghosts as there are people who've died. You really can't count on any consistency at all. Some exist side by side with other ghosts who are like them. Lots of dead folks wandering around battlefields, for instance, or in old buildings. Some know where they are, some don't. Some want to be there. Some don't."

"So can the dead choose for themselves whether or not they remain among the living? Are they bound in some way?"

The corpse's head moved to one side and looked up slightly. "I trust you do mean to be ironic, asking me such a question?" his great-grandfather asked, beginning to make a sound that might have been laughter. "No, no," he said. "I know you are sincere, so let me answer you in kind. It seems to me there is no absolute answer, Silas. Some of the dead are fascinated by their own condition, or enjoy what they think of as the freedom of it. An existence with no more obligations. Sometimes ghosts of that sort group together, just as in life. There are places in this town where this has been happening for a very long time, just old folks gathering, never really moving on, just enjoying one another's company, one fine evening going on and on, only dawn never comes to break up the party.

"Other ghosts are stuck, but in a different way. Like the line of a song playing over and over in your head. They're supposed to forget their lives, move on, but they can't or won't. Most of these types don't even know they're dead, or don't want to face the idea of death, can't admit to themselves it's just plain over. Those are the ones you may be able to help. Give 'em a little push out the door. Remind them they've got places to be. Remind them to put down whatever is troubling them and get on with getting on.

"Others prefer to wait around because maybe they're afraid of what's next. Maybe they have some particular business they're waiting to see to its end. Maybe they just like where they are, or where they were. These are usually pretty clever. They're working the system, and they know it. This type you may find in very old places of gathering, very old houses, too. Some even get along with the living. Oh, yes. One long party for some, as I said, but in the end, I suspect, someone will have to pay the bill.

"Some of the ghosts that huddle together in groups do so because they share a common experience. Only usually this experience is something not so nice, and it's the pain of it that holds them close to the world of the living. And, since they share common pain or trouble, they sort of stick to one another, these spirits do, get bound together somewhere in a kind of limbo. Ghosts like that can be a very big problem. Very hard to settle them because you can't pull 'em apart. Their shared grief or fear makes them strong, sets their feet in concrete, and gives them wills of iron. What's worse: All that pain together can pull you in, make you start forgetting who you are, where you are. It can draw up old memories that you'd rather not think about. So where the dead gather together, or are bound to a particular place for any reason, you be careful!"

Silas was hanging on every word. Everything his great-grandfather said, he knew, was an important key to who his dad was and how he lived, and who he lived with, so to speak. "What kinds of ghosts do we have here in Lichport?" he asked a little hesitantly.

"All of them. Every kind you could imagine and plenty of things you would never want to meet. This is an old town, and it's had more than its share of awfulness. Good times too, to be sure, but, well, things have happened here that have left terrible stains on both the living and dead." The old man reached out to where Silas sat next to him and brushed his dry fingers over the small stains on Silas's jacket before continuing.

"Silas, this is your town now, your home, and I'm glad you're staying, but you are walking down a dark road. From what I can tell about that vision last time you were here and from your questions, I am worried now that as much as he lived to help folks, well, your father may have come to a bad end. You're thinking about his disappearance and how to find him, and you're thinking about his work. Silas, I must tell you that more and more I feel these things are inseparable."

Silas sat, his breath catching in his throat. His eyes began to burn, and he put his arm up, pressing it to his face over his eyes.

His great-grandfather took Silas's hand and said, "From where I sit, I can't be sure of anything, and I'm not saying he's dead or alive. I don't know. I'm just saying that if anyone can find Amos, it's you, and you'll do it through seeing the world with your father's eyes. Your father spent his life helping folks, and that kind of work grants a person, I suspect, a lot of perspective. You might want to consider taking on a little work to fill your days. You never know, you might encounter someone or something who can point you in the direction of your dad."

"Do you mean I should continue in my father's work? The work he was actually doing before he disappeared? I wouldn't know where to even begin. I've read some of his writings, and I'm beginning to understand something of the nature of my father's calling, but I don't know much about *how* he did it, or *where* exactly he left off."

"Oh, I don't think he 'left off' at any one point. His work was always ongoing. For one thing, there are so many dead. And some come and go frequently, perhaps only appearing on certain days. Others are gone for a long time and then come back for who knows why and then need to be attended to again. So there's no lack of starting places, if that's what you mean. But truly, if you open the door, the work will find you. The kinds of things your father saw, well, there may have been a reason they stood out to him particularly. In this, the living and dead share something in common. Every person, and every spirit, sees the world in its own individual way. Though all our paths cross many, many times, in life and death, to some degree, Silas, we each inhabit our own world. You must find the work that is trying to find you. Ask yourself: What would my father do? And where can I do the most good?"

His great-grandfather was looking at his own hand, ancient-seeming, dark but almost translucent as he turned it over slowly in a beam of light coming through the curtains. When the light struck the sapphire in his ring, a blue flame seemed to dance on his hand. Without looking up, he added, "Perhaps you can recall a portion of the world that has already reached out to you for a little help?"

"I can't think of anything that needs my help—"

"I mean," said the corpse, moving its hand out of the light and into shadow, "what parts of town unsettle *you*? I mean, really, Silas! There are a few streets in this town I wouldn't walk down on a bet, and I'm already dead! Where do you feel the most uncomfortable, the most scared? There may be a reason why they bother you or why whatever dwells in such a place has sought to frighten you." His great-grandfather added wryly, "Surely, Silas, not all the streets you've visited in Lichport are as nice as this one."

Away down deep in the Narrows, Dogge Alley winds its odd, dark way between the more optimistically named Silk Street and Pearl Lane. The abandoned cottages and little leaning houses on the Dogge are certainly very old, even by Lichport standards, and have been the location of so many unspeakable acts, that it may surprise the reader to learn that the respectable women of Lichport have made it the object of especial study.

In the last century, the women of Lichport's Ladies' Historical Auxiliary, whose job it was to find and exhaustively report on the merits of all the town's "Ancientest Muniments and Most Curious of Architectural Achievements," could not leave it off their register. Yes, even those venerable dames, who wore lace on weekdays, dared to descend the dim lanes of the Narrows to make their full and sober judgments of Lichport's antiquities. However, those ladies, who strained to find the worth of even the smallest piece of carved molding if it was more than twenty years old, and even if it lay within a less-than-fashionable part of town; yes, even they pronounced this lane of cottages in the Narrows "intriguing but not quite quaint," and "very noisy and somewhat nerve-racking due to an unfortunate reflective quality of the slate and cobbles resulting in startling noises that quite distract from any architectural interests."

It must be noted as a testament to their dedication to all matters historical that they generously included the cottages of Dogge Alley on their hallowed register because, surely, it was the oldest part of the Narrows, and of course, the oldest of anything must always be noted. They never inquired of the Narrows folk why most of the cottages on this particular alley were long ago abandoned, and why one in particular still stands in such a sad state of ruination. Neither do they mention why no folk of the Narrows will enter that ruined cottage. I am sorry to report that neither may I enlighten the curious reader in regards to these eldritch curiosities. We must merely assume that the dear simple folk of this ancient street have long since moved on to more modern and hygienic premises in one of the northern ports. Bless them.

—From *Town and Down: A Traveler's Handbook to the Neighborhood Environs as Well as the Funereal Monuments of Old Lichport* by Samuel Oddtern, 1892

Tacitus says the Gauls accounted the noontide ghost to be the most terrible of all apparitions. Hence, the Church still retains its midday prayer to hold at bay the powers of those spirits strong enough to walk abroad in bright sunlight. The Gauls further conjectured that what we take for the heat of the noon sun is, in fact, the fiery breath of such ghosts falling on us. I cannot give credence to speculations about their "fiery breath" but attest to the awful power and nasty disposition of spirits who choose, or are forced, to walk the world by day or may appear during any hour of their choosing. Such appearances are usually evidence of a very terrible and unresolved burden on them that must be settled with all speed by the Undertaker. From my experiences, it is at midnight, and not noon, when such ghosts should be feared most.

—Marginalia of Amos Umber, 21 June 1973

CHAPTER 36

DOGGE ALLEY

SILAS WALKED FAST TOWARD DOGGE ALLEY. He pulled his father's jacket close about him and held the death watch in his hand, thrust deep into the front jacket pocket. He was walking quickly because if he stopped to think about what he was doing, he'd turn around and go back home.

A few hours earlier, after leaving his great-grandfather's house, Silas had stopped home briefly to eat lunch. Maybe because she saw something in his face that spoke of trouble, Mrs. Bowe had asked him pointedly where he was going. Silas ignored her question and asked instead what was for dinner that night. Mrs. Bowe only stared at him, waiting. Silas didn't want to upset her by his silent avoidance of the subject, so he hesitantly told Mrs. Bowe of his plan. He could tell by her look she wasn't any too pleased.

"What exactly is it you think you're going to do down there?"

"I'm going to try to help, I guess. I want to help. Besides, maybe I can find out something about my dad."

"From whom, for goodness' sake?"

Silas didn't answer.

"Well?" asked Mrs. Bowe.

"I'd like to help the people down there in the Narrows. They've been very kind to me. I know they don't like that place, and Mother Peale told me Dogge Alley has gotten worse. The ghost saw me, looked right at me, so maybe I can do something for it like my dad would have. It's been there a long time, so it might have seen my father. Maybe I can help the ghost, and then I could ask it for help."

"So you think that whatever it is that's been haunting that alley has just been sitting around all these years waiting to help you with your problem? Oh, Silas, really!"

"What I mean to say is, I want to continue my dad's work. I want to help."

"I don't think you really know the implication of what you're saying"—she paused to consider—"but maybe that's for the best. Aren't you scared at all?"

"Yeah. I'm scared of what happened last time, what little I can remember of it. And what might happen this time if no one comes to help me. I don't want to end up like my dad, lost somewhere and alone. I mean, I want to be like him, just not in that way, and the only thing I can think of to do is this. I can't just sit here every day drinking tea."

Mrs. Bowe blinked at the comment clearly directed at her, but slowly swallowed her tea and went on.

"We don't know what's happened to your father, so don't borrow trouble. And I think you're not quite understanding what an Undertaker's obligations are to the dead. I wish your father were here to talk with you about this, because there is so much I don't know about his work. Still, I think he might have told you that you must learn to see death as something more than loss, more than absence, more than silence or a cold room or a bad dream, or a dragon that needs to be slain. You must learn to make mourning into memory and understand that memory is the dead's chiefest problem. For once a person takes leave of his life, they become so much more a part of ours. In death, they come to be in our keeping, so to speak. They find their rest *within* us. Thus, in remembrance, we are never alone and neither are they. It's only when the rites of remembrance aren't kept up, or are ignored, or can't be met for some reason that things go bad; when people die in secret, or by violence, or they leave important things undone. And that's where maybe you can be of some help, although I don't know if your wistful heart will be help or hindrance. Your father would have had other words for you, but here are mine: Keep the dead and their needs foremost in your mind. Foremost. Forget about what you want to happen and remain focused on what needs to be done in order to bring peace to the dead. A ghost is a puzzle in pieces, and you must be patient in trying to put things into place. Be polite. Ask questions, but let it speak. Silas, hear me: Let the dead speak their *peace*. Let it speak its Peace."

"I understand," Silas said, almost waving away her words, "but I still want to ask it about my dad. It's been there a long time, and Mother Peale said my dad spent a lot of time in the Narrows. Whatever's there might know something."

Mrs. Bowe furrowed her brow and looked hard at him.

"I suspect whatever is waiting for you in the Narrows will be not an 'it' but a person, and I advise you to remember that. I might also suggest you focus on what *they* need, Silas. Even the dead deserve a little consideration . . . a little kindness," she said, putting down her teacup and leaving the room.

Silas tried to put his conversation with Mrs. Bowe behind him and steel his nerves for whatever was waiting in the alley.

He wasn't worried about being able to find the ghost, because he had met it before, and he knew from Mother Peale that it had been heard at all hours, even at noon, since folks began to feel the arrival of the mist ship. He also knew from Mother Peale that it was pernicious and that it was very old.

Again, Silas came to Dogge Alley from Silk Street. He did not wait to get far down the alley, but instead stilled the hand of the death watch even before he stepped onto the cobbles of the Dogge. This was a mistake, because the Narrows is so ancient a place, its lanes are filled with the dead at most times. So the moment Silas stopped the watch's hand, the dead were all around him, wandering this way and that on their business. In front of what might have once been her home, a young woman stood in a doorway, her arms larded in blood. Two doors down, three young men ran across the street and through the wall on the opposite side where there had once been another lane, now long blocked by newer houses. Silas was staring at the throng, when as one, the river of ghosts turned their heads toward him. Startled, he let go the watch dial.

Now the street appeared empty, though Silas's fear had been sharpened to a fine edge.

As he stepped into Dogge Alley, a doleful cry went up, rising from the stones as if one huge, wounded body was buried under the long length of the street and every step a person took on the alley caused it pain. Silas continued to the cottage Mother Peale had pointed out to him. The same cottage where he'd had so much trouble before.

Focus on what you've come to see, he told himself.

He pushed his thumb onto the death watch's dial. It stopped moving, and for an instant, the world went absolutely silent, all the familiar sounds of the Narrows, of the living, getting thinner and thinner, dying on the air.

Silas slowly raised his head to look at the street and staggered back in terror at what he saw. The ghost of the alley was directly in front of him, its mouth stretched wide and screaming. It was as though a radio had been turned on when the volume had been all the way up when last turned off. Silas fell backward, but on rising found his perspective tilted out of all proportion as the alley seemed to draw away from him, the walls of its buildings becoming the stones and boulders emerging from the earth in a long valley. He could see other folk, or the gray shapes of folk, wandering in the half-light of the valley, each isolated and alone though they stood close by their fellow spirits. None could see another in that valley where every ghost cast a shadow as long as its last lonely breath. Within the complicated angles of those shadows, Silas and the ghost stood staring at each other.

The ghost was terrible in appearance. The top of its skull was smashed in, from what must have been its death wound. Mist poured forth from the side of its head, as though it was bleeding smoke. Roots crawled through its form, clung to the surface of its body, pierced its skin as though it were a clod of earth caught in the roots of a great tree.

Silas stood staring at the ghost, unable to look away, and felt his limbs go numb. He tried to rationalize away the terrible sight and told himself that the ghost didn't mean to appear as it did. The ghost couldn't help it. This was how it looked because this was the moment that had become its reality. As Silas tried to reason out the ghost's appearance—the meaning of the crushed head, the roots—his arms and legs began to move freely again, but his chest started to ache and he clutched at it, not in pain but in pity.

Silas looked on the ghost's shattered face. He watched the bloody mud coursing over its form, the stream of tears flowing in rivulets down its body and pooling in the air before its heart, and he felt such sorrow for it. And something more than pity rose up inside him too, as he began to think of the worst thing his heart had ever known: that long night his dad didn't come home, the long nights that followed, living all those days . . . alive, but feeling like something was rotting inside him. What if he had died during that time? Looking at the ghost before him, Silas knew exactly what would have befallen him. There was the ghost, changed into a reflection of its own loss. Broken. Stopped in the moment of its death. No other moment for it after, ever.

The more Silas examined the ghost's appearance, the harder it was to stop thinking about the ghost's body, rotting somewhere. And then, increasingly, about himself and his own pain. His thoughts began to blur at their edges.

The ghost backed away from him, screaming still, and walked to the base of a tree a few yards away. There it thrust its hands into the earth, raised its mouth skyward, and roared until Silas thought he would go mad at the sound reverberating in his skull.

Silas tried to think of questions to ask it, to try to help, but as he spoke, the valley darkened and black water rose against the roots of the land.

"Are you okay? How can I help? What happened?" One question after another, and none of them seemed to have any effect on the ghost, who had begun to fade around its edges, and perhaps, feeling itself fading, began to cry piteously.

"Where are we now? What is this place? How did you come here?" continued Silas, hardly noticing the ghost's increasing distress. Above the valley, great black birds flew against the dim carnelian sun.

Then, very suddenly, the ghost began to shriek loudly, and words became woven with its wail. "Nobody I am nobody I am no body . . ."

Silas froze, fear rising high in him again, and he stopped talking, but wondered frantically: *What if this were my father's ghost?*

And though the thought put a stark, cold chill in his blood, he pursued it. *What would I say to my father, right now, if this was his own ghost?* Without meaning to, his eyes began to well with tears. He said to the ghost simply, "What has happened here?" And then he sat down in front of the ghost, waiting, crying softly as he looked at it.

And though it did not appear to open its mouth, thin words rose like ribbons of smoke in the air, and Silas could just hear them before they unravelled into silence.

"It is lost in the earth. It has no mother. No father. It is no one's son. It is unclaimed. It is nowhere to be found, comes from nowhere has never been when it came home there was no door no welcome no food no fire only blood from blood only blood from blood blood from a mother's hand blood from a father's hand it is no home where once was home nothing there no mother no father it cannot be seen a mother put it back in the womb deep root bed now it is lost Their son is lost it is no one's son it is lost to them by them no body . . ."

"Wait, wait!" clamored Silas. "It's too fast, I don't follow you."

Silas ran the ghost's words over and over in his mind. *Lost to them by them.* The riddle was not complex, but it suggested awful events. *Blood from blood . . . blood from a mother's hand . . . a father's hand.*

Silas stood up, and holding his hands in front of him, he moved them slowly up and down, as if telling the ghost to wait. Then, with deep sympathy and insuppressible fascination, he asked, "Did your parents kill you?"

The ghost hung in the air, still as a figure in a photograph. Features began to emerge from the mud of its face, the mouth first among them.

Silas went on, encouraged at what seemed like progress, but again, he gave the ghost no chance to respond, pressing it with incessant questions. "That's what happened, isn't it? Someone in your family killed you? Right?"

But the ghost only went on repeating itself, over and over, with almost no alteration to the stream of words flowing from it, and soon, its face was running again with dark mud, most of its features reburied in the slurry.

Silas felt his face reddening in increasing aggravation. He was partially angry at himself. There might be another way to ask, and he didn't know what it was. Or maybe the ghost was afraid to admit what had happened to it. Maybe there needed to be more of an exchange. If Silas spoke to it about something else first, maybe it might speak more about itself. What to ask it? Maybe the ghost knew something about his dad. It had been in the alley a long time, maybe it would be easier for it to talk about something unrelated to its own misery. Silas thought this might be worth a try and said, "You know, I've lost a parent. My dad disappeared, and I haven't seen him in over a year. Maybe you've seen him. His name was Amos Umber. My dad. Missing. Have. You. Seen. Him?"

The ghost's form began to shake and the space on its face where its mouth might have been tore open. A shriek flew from it, piercing the air. "Where are the bones?" it howled pitifully. "Where are no one's bones?"

Silas was stunned by the ghost's sirenlike cry. His eardrums were close to bursting. The scream cut through his flesh, his blood became ice, and the bones of his body felt like they were cracking from the sound. He opened his mouth and, unable to stop himself, began to scream as well.

The ghost went silent.

Silas's scream fell back into his throat, and he stood for a moment, unable to think or move. His ears pulsed with pain. He couldn't see for the fear that now began boiling over into anger.

He blamed the ghost for not wanting to be helped, and he began to think of other people he knew who never listened to reason, like his mom, and so consigned themselves to needless suffering.

He began yelling, not stopping to think about what he was saying, just yelling and letting all the bile out of the bag.

"You're dead, you know! Cold! Over! You are yesterday and never again, so give it up, will you? Hello? Can. You. Hear. Me?"

The moment those words left him, Silas could see the ghost cracking at the edges of its form, like mud drying and crumbling. He immediately regretted his selfishness. *Think!* Silas told himself. *Just shut up and ask it again. Don't talk. Listen.*

"Sir, I am sorry. I spoke first and should have allowed you a turn to speak. Please tell me, why are you here? Why are you so troubled? Please say the words yourself." And because he'd read an account in the ledger where such phrases were traditional, Silas added, "In God's name, please speak."

And so the ghost began.

The Lonesome Valley was growing lighter, as though true morning was coming to it for the first time. The long, solitary shadows seemed to shorten, the lightening world adding solidity to the ghost's form.

"He went away, across the sea."

The ghost stopped, as if remembering something, and then began again.

"*I* went away, across the sea, to seek my fortune. And fortune I found, though it was many years of hardship and toil before that happened, and so I sent no word home, for fear of shame. But years later, I found myself more fortunate, and with my rich earnings I sailed for home again. When I arrived in Lichport, it was too late to put my heavy bag of gold in the bank, for it was almost night when my ship arrived. So I made for home, happy to be bringing such good fortune home to my ma and pa. When I arrived at the cottage, I hardly knew it, roof falling in, a broken window. And I knew then that my parents had fallen on very hard times indeed. All the better a homecoming it would be, for I would pour gold into both their hands. I knocked on the door and when my ma opened it, how careworn she looked. She stared at me as though it were the first time she'd ever laid eyes on me. My pa, too. I had grown a beard and looked only a poor, wretched traveler. Here's good luck, I thought. The laugh's on them! I asked for lodging for the night, and tomorrow, I thought, I will surprise them indeed: their own son returned home and they not able to even recognize him!

"They must have seen my bag, or heard the chink of gold within it, for so poor had they become, so destitute and miserable from holding in their hearts the thought of their son, lost over the sea, that they conspired and while I slept . . . while I slept . . ."

The ghost paused in his tale, and his whole frame seemed to run red, as though he was standing beneath a gutter spout and the sky was raining blood.

Silas looked at the ghost. He did not speak, did not look away. After a few moments, the ghost continued.

"They murdered their son while he slept. Their own son. They murdered *me* while I slept because they had become so poor. Because I had been gone so long and had been no help to them."

The ghost could now be very clearly seen. Silas saw a young man standing before him, perhaps in his late twenties, his face and head covered over with the wild tangle of beard and hair long from sea travel.

"May I see them?" the ghost asked Silas.

"I don't know." Silas was unsure what the ghost meant. Was

the ghost asking to see his bones? His parents' bones? "I don't know what happens now. You are still here, so I think there is still something to do. May I ask you your name, please?"

"I was Roger Arliss in life."

"Mr. Arliss, may I ask you one more thing?"

The ghost nodded.

"What became of your body? Where did your parents bury your body?"

The ghost's form shivered in the air, but he pointed to a tree a little ways off from where he and Silas were standing. Silas drew his hands from his pockets and released the dial of the watch. The valley faded from view, and because good words had passed between them, Silas found he could still see the ghost, who continued to point at the small, thick tree that could be seen through the window of the cottage. A dim sun had risen. Night had passed.

"Mr. Arliss, I think you would like to be buried next to your parents. Is that so?"

The ghost wept at those words, and Silas continued.

"I know your name. I have seen the name Arliss among the graves on Beacon Hill. If I can restore you to them, I will. Mr. Arliss, may I have your permission to move your bones?"

Still crying, the ghost nodded his head slowly up and down.

Silas went into the little overgrown yard behind the house and found the rusted head of an old hoe. He began to dig in the soil at the base of the tree the ghost had pointed out to him. It was late morning when he found the bones a few feet down in a shallow grave. Silas brought the bones out into the air, unwinding some from the roots that had held them during the many years, they had been hidden in the earth. With a piece of yellowed moth-eaten lace curtain from the cottage, he wrapped the bones of Roger Arliss and carried them away.

Silas took Silk Street along the waterfront and then climbed the footpath up to Beacon Hill cemetery. He couldn't quite remember where he had seen the Arliss graves, though he knew they were old and closer to the top of the hill than the bottom, so he walked in a tight spiral, slowly working his way up the hill. By the time Silas had found the graves of Roger's parents, Elias and Judith Arliss, on the Beacon, it was late in the afternoon. He set the parcel of bones down on the earth between his parents' graves.

"Master Umber," said a familiar voice behind him, "how nice to see you again. What brings you back to our hill of peace, may I ask?" Without turning, Silas knew it was the voice of the sexton.

"Good afternoon, sir. I am here on business, I'm afraid."

"Yes. I can see that you are. You have your father's look about you."

"I wonder if you can help me. I need—" Silas began, but the sexton gently interrupted him.

"If you return to the hollow oak at the bottom of the hill, you will find that your father kept a spade hidden within the trunk for, I believe, such a purpose as yours. Bless you and bless your ways, Master Umber. You are as fine a man as your father."

Silas had knelt to unwrap the bones, and when they were set out on the lace with the late-day sun on them, he rose and turned to shake the sexton's hand, but found him gone, already around the bend of the hill, and only his shadow trailing behind him. Silas walked down to the tree and there, inside the trunk, he found the spade waiting. He lifted it from the tree, feeling the polished handle, the blade indented from years of digging through rough earth and small stones. He wondered how many times, for how many graves, his father had used this spade. *No different*, Silas thought. *I am no different from him now, for we are in the same business. I am about to dig a grave for a ghost with my father's spade.* And as strange as the thought might have seemed, there, on the Beacon, it felt the most natural thing in the world.

With the spade in hand he climbed the hill again, and between the two Arliss graves, he dug a hole perhaps four feet down. He dug until he found the other bones. He wanted to put Roger Arliss truly among his kin. Though the earth was loamy and soft, it was much harder work than he'd imagined, and by the time the hole was deep enough, Silas's back and arms were sorer than they'd ever been and the day was nearly spent. Into the hole he set each bone, one at a time. Then over the bones he laid the piece of lace and, taking up the spade once more, covered everything up with earth. The world was going quiet at the coming of twilight. The birds had stopped calling from the trees of the hill. Silas stood by the graves in that silence for many moments.

When he looked up, the sun was very low, and the edges of the sea were burning with the last embers of the dying day. In a moment that light would be extinguished by the falling night, and the surface of the water would be still and dark.

He wondered if his father had some formula or ritual words for moments such as this. In the ledger, many of the words he'd seen seemed stiff, formulaic and formal. His gaze hovered on the two names cut deep into their shared tombstone, and with his finger, he traced the letters of the son's name on the stone next to those of his parents. Then he spoke their three names out loud into the evening air—the father, the mother, the son—and then said, simply and very tenderly, "Rest in peace."

And they did.

Silas looked down, opening and closing his aching palms, and despite all the dirt pressed deep into his skin, he could just trace the lines of his father's hands in his own.

CHAPTER 37

MIST SHIP

As SILAS DESCENDED THE BEACON, he found the town flooded with fog.

Instead of going home, he walked back into the Narrows, though he could hardly see ten feet in any direction. He wanted to walk and revel a bit in his success. With the fog came a sharpening of his other senses, and soon he heard sounds he'd hardly ever noticed before: the soft rasp of shoes on stones, the lap of the water against the pier posts—higher pitched than the low flop of wave on sand—the whip of a flag atop a mast, bells from buoys and bells from ships, a world of common music heard only when listening particularly, or when a heavy mist made the world blind.

Silas found Mother Peale waiting near the water. She had been standing and "having a listen" as she called it, waiting for something. Silas came up next to her and looked out in the direction of the water.

"There is peace now on the Dogge," he said.

"Truly?" she said with real surprise in her voice.

"Yes," said Silas. "I think Roger Arliss is at peace now. I feel that he is. Walk on the Dogge and see."

"In time. Sometimes, after a bad stint, a place needs to be on its own for a while, to resettle, if you take my meaning. I am impressed that you could do what your father couldn't. Your father tried many times, but that ghost would never speak to him. But not everyone can see the same thing, even when they are both looking right at it." She went quiet for a moment, but then added, "Or maybe you and that ghost have something in common." Before she could explain, or Silas could question her, she said in a whisper, "Do you hear that? A quiet sea. Slack tide. Not coming in, not going out. Just a moment in between. Maybe that's what it's like for *them*. Not here. Not there. Nowhere. Tide'll be coming in in a moment. But for the lost ones, the tide never changes. It just goes on and on, never an end to the pause, until, well, I guess until something changes. Like now. Things are changing here. You can feel that, I know."

"What do you think it is that's causing the change? What's making people so nervous?"

"Some say it's you being here. I agree." And she smiled at him. "Others say things haven't been right since your dad disappeared. Lots of folks think things have been wrong for a long time. Maybe that's true too. Some say it's because the mist ship is coming. Because even now it's making its way into port. Nights like this herald hard days ahead. But there's no mystery to it. Every hundred years it comes. 'Everything to its hour,' as my mother would say, 'everything to its appointed hour.' A hundred years. That's the bargain. One hundred years between visits, but sure as anything, when the years run up to a clean century, there it will be. That ship has always run regular," she insisted. "It's predictable, like the holy days coming and going, each to its own quarter. . . . All Souls', and Yuletide, and Midsummer, round and round and back again."

"I have read something about ghost ships in my father's writings, about ships that become prisons for the dead, wandering on and on until the world's end, occasionally coming to harbor to take on crew, or to revenge great wrongs done to their captains. Where are they when they're not visible to the living? The old sources do not say," Silas said.

"No tellin' . . . but every hundred years, in it comes and it won't leave until it's had its due," said Mother Peale. She looked away from Silas and pulled her hands under her shawl. She began to walk along the harbor, and he followed her.

Silas thought she knew more than she told, that she was holding something back. Maybe she thought this was likely to scare him. Yet if the ship came only once every hundred years, anything anyone knew about it could only be speculation, stories handed down. How frightened did she think he'd be by a legend?

As if in answer to his unspoken questions, Mother Peale said, "It's a bad business, Silas, I don't mind telling you. Very bad. Bad folk are on that ship, and it brings only the worst sort aboard. No one knows who it'll take until they're took, and that's what makes everyone so edgy. One thing for sure. No one wants to sail on that ship, for once you're aboard, you don't never come off it."

Silas and Mother Peale were approaching the last wharf, near where Downe Street emerged at the seaside, before turning back up into the Narrows to make their way to the Peales' house, Silas hoped, for supper. Suddenly, Mother Peale grabbed Silas's arm.

"Listen!"

"I don't hear anything."

"Then stop trying to hear 'anything' and listen."

Silas shook his head. No remarkable sound found its way to his ears.

"Do you trust me, Silas Umber?"

"Yes, ma'am. I truly do."

"Then hold my hand and use that watch your father most surely left to you."

Silas wasn't surprised that she knew about it, and it was obvious from what he'd told her about the settling of matters at the Arliss cottage that he had at least begun to consider going about business as his father did. So without hesitation, he took Mother Peale's left hand in his and held it. With his right hand, he brought the hand of the death watch to a stop. Immediately Mother Peale's hand clutched his like cold iron.

"There! Now don't tell me you don't hear that, boy!" She was peering into the mist as though her eyes might burn a hole right through the very air. "It's far out still, but, ah! The voices!"

And rolling in with the fog came the words. Strange and strangled as though screamed from underwater. Subdued, resolved, hollow, drowned. The voices were distressed and full of fear. Then, like waves, the voices rushed up and broke near Silas and Mother Peale, drawing thin as a whine until the cries sank into the sand and were gone, before the next wave of sorrow rolled in from that ship that yet lay beyond any mortal sight.

Mother Peale was looking at Silas with her eyes wide and questioning.

"I can hear it. Oh, God. I can hear it," he said, and as the voices churned in the dark water, Silas's mind became a whirlpool of worry, wondering whom the ship was coming for, frantic that it might be—*Enough!* he told himself. He couldn't even think it. It could be anyone. Even someone he now knew in Lichport. For didn't everyone have secret parts and shadows? How well did he know anyone here, really?

"How long until it comes to harbor here?" Silas asked in a near whisper.

"Soon," was all Mother Peale said, and her hand lay cold and still in his.

CHAPTER 38

CAMERA OBSCURA

IT HAD BEEN A LONG NIGHT IN THE CAMERA, and Uncle's tenant was troubled. The preceding week had been no better. Lights had been unexpectedly going out in the upper floors. Blasts of cold air tore angrily through the north gallery. The knocking and banging noises had continued unabated between the floors and behind the walls. And in the few moments of sleep Uncle could find, he found only dreams he prayed to forget.

Uncle could now admit that his original plan had almost completely fallen apart. His dream of a whole, right family living under his roof, well, he would have to apply himself more earnestly now. Silas leaving the house had made matters much worse, far more difficult, in fact, than he could have anticipated. Rising waves of anger permeated the whole house like smoke from a blocked chimney fire. The Camera had become a chamber of constant aggravation. Uncle blamed Silas for this change in the house's mood. His nephew's presence in the house had had a surprising and much appreciated effect on the occupant of the Camera. A calming influence. That temporary peace was now ruined. Uncle still hoped Silas could be brought peaceably back to the house, though he suspected that such an event might only happen if it was carefully arranged. It would take time, and as things stood, more immediate action was required. Waiting was accomplishing nothing.

The book of photographs he and Silas had looked at together was still open on the table just outside the Camera, and every time Uncle stared at it, he could recall more and more about her life, her sacrifice, about that woman and her arm who, in death, had gotten him fired all those years ago. Ironic, he thought, that it was Silas who reminded him of her.

Despite dying at the age of ninety-two, and despite the early loss of her arm—that loss necessitating her remaining hand having to do twice the work in her later years—how young she had looked at her funeral, he remembered, and how remarkable that hand had been. She had labored in joy for her large family every day of her life. Yes, her remaining hand should have been creased and worn. When he had seen the photo again with Silas, Uncle had immediately remembered the story of the arm this woman had buried with her dead children. In his mind, he could see her arm resting within its box among the bones of her offspring, a comfort to them still. What a heart she must have had to think of putting her arm, lost to infection, into an early grave. He understood immediately. It would hold them in death. Serve her as though it were still attached to her. It would hold her children and keep them safe against the long, long night of the grave. He understood her mind. And like her, he had something that needed comforting. Something that needed to be held and watched and mothered.

Uncle held her closer to his face so he could see the details of the arm in the low light, and he recalled how moved he'd been by her appearance on the day of her funeral. There was something pure about her, something incorruptible even then, especially her hand. *Let the hand stand for all*, he had thought when he took the photo all those years ago. That was why he'd covered her face. He was drawn to her corpse. He remembered how he wanted to comfort her, in death . . . how softly he spoke to the family. "Let us draw her favorite shawl about her, to keep her warm, her family's love to work against the cold." Her kin liked that. In that way, the missing arm she'd buried with her children would not disturb the appearance of the corpse. He pushed cotton into a long glove and set it in place of her already buried arm, in case anyone should touch the shawl; all would seem right and whole. He wanted her to look her best.

He looked again at the photo of the woman's remaining hand lying across her body. He was admiring his work now, noticing again how he'd arranged the lighting to make the skin glow like alabaster. He said to the photo, to her incorruptible portrait, "Now I know why I have kept you all this time."

He had paid homage back then to her life, her mothering, her perfection. Now he would pay her another honor.

And then, at last, even her name had come back to him across the chasm of years: Mary Bishop.

Her name was Mary Bishop.

Uncle's mind began to prowl in several directions at once. Could Mary Bishop be a possible solution for his problem in the Camera? Could something as simple as a mother's love console the Camera's occupant? That arm—surely it must have brought such peace to those cold children of hers. Such comfort. A mother's love was what was needed. The calming presence of a mother's love. Where the father and son had failed or fled, let the mother— one far better than the first—bring peace.

There were ways he knew to call and bind the spirits of the dead. Certain rites. Prayers more Babylon than Bethlehem. He knew already he would get no sleep that night. He took the relevant books down from the shelves and quickly found what he was looking for. He was spoiled for choices. A world longing for congress with the dead had recorded numerous methods of bringing them back. From every nation of the ancient world, here were words and acts to bring the living face-to-face with the deceased. Charms to make the dead speak. Spells to make them serve. Rites to make them reveal secrets taken with them to their graves. His hands were starting to tremble with anticipation. He had made a ritual of slowly looking through the vellum manuscripts and early bound books, had taken no wine, had bathed before searching through their pages. He was grateful that so many other people, driven by need and want, had turned to these practical philosophies to see their way through their mighty problems. He had pored over his books, leather-bound heresies from his brothers in Arte, and had found readily enough the text he needed. Actually, there were many versions of what was known as the Dark Call, that dangerous rite by which the dead are forcibly called back to earth, back into the limbo of their bones. Such practices were held accursed by the church, hated by the dead, and despised by all ethical philosophers, but what did moral folk know of his dilemma? *Let those who live with my burdens judge my actions*, he thought.

To enact the Dark Call, articles associated with the deceased or "mummiae" were required and considered most efficacious: bones or body parts. Such mummiae were to be collected by plundering the graves of the dead. So he could see his course plainly now. To the grave. To the box among the bones. He needed the arm. Of course, any part of her would do, but in his mind, he wanted only the arm of comfort. The arm of the mother.

Though it wouldn't deter him from his path, the idea of plundering her grave began to let worry leak into the corners of his mind. It would involve leaving the house, and because the occupant of the Camera was being very difficult, he didn't like the idea of going out, unsure of what it might do in his absence. Still, he knew where she was buried and wouldn't need to be gone for long. He knew just where to find the headstone, with its extraordinary carving of the arm, and he hadn't seen a car enter Newfield Cemetery in many months. Dolores could be locked in her room . . . she spent most evenings half-unconscious anyway. He would go at night when he could be assured of privacy. There would be the unpleasant work of unearthing the grave and actually removing the arm from the remains. Unpleasant, though he had no fear of corpses per se; it was just that even the thought of smelling something rotten turned his stomach. Not to mention, there were often wild dogs that roamed Newfield Cemetery after dark, and they scared him because those animals didn't appear to fear anything themselves. How their frequent baying at night set his teeth on edge.

But he made himself smile at this. *What have I to fear?* he thought. *We are all just dogs digging for our bones.*

Alas for those poor souls, enslaved by thieves, who bring forth their resting bones from the earth. For no peace have the dead when one holds in bond even a portion of their remains. Yet, if avenged or honored by those hallowed rites yet known, such a spirit may rise up as a terrible and mighty soul.

—From the *Codex of Klytaimnestra*, translated from the Greek by Jonas Umber

CHAPTER 39

DARK CALL

THOUGH UNCLE HEARD THEIR BAYING in the distance, from their hiding places among the tombs and mausoleums, he encountered no dogs.

The soil was heavy but soft from the recent rains. It took him two hours to dig down to Mary Bishop's casket, buried on top of the twin coffins of her children. Removing the lid, which crumbled when he pulled at its edges, he saw the remains of Mary Bishop's fallen chest. The coffin was rotten right through, and this was a boon because the body was mostly bones now. The smell was merely mold and earth and not the rotting stench that would have so distressed him. Uncle pushed the bones aside and dug a little further until he found the small box among the bones of the twins. Removing the lid, he gazed on its contents with fascination and wonder. Unlike the body, the arm in the box was almost perfectly preserved. Was this the curious action of the illness that had taken her arm in life? The surface of the arm was shiny and very smooth and gave off an odd scent that seemed almost floral.

"Truly, madam," he said, still panting from digging up the grave, turning the arm over in his hands like a holy relic, "you are one of God's anointed."

He put the arm back in its small casket, and setting it on the edge of the grave, pulled himself out. He shoveled the earth back in and laid the sod back on top. The once flat earth over her grave was now a little hump. He hoped no one would notice before it had a chance to settle. But who would come to see it? Most of the people who had kin in Newfield buried them here to forget about them. And where were those survivors now? Off and abroad on their adventures, just as the dead of Newfield were on theirs, making their remarkable, though common, progress through loam and time into nothingness.

And even if someone did notice the grave had been despoiled, what of it? This was hardly the first grave to be plundered in Lichport.

Mary Bishop?
Mary Bishop!

Someone was calling her name.

The voice was unfamiliar, but incessant, and she followed it like the tolling bell of a buoy through the mist.

When she saw the light, she stopped, but on and on the voice called her, drawing her closer and closer.

She emerged from the mist in a small, well-lit chamber, and the light hurt her eyes.

Welcome, the voice said. And, *You are bound to this place and to these, your remains.*

A weight came upon her, and it seemed she could draw no breath. It felt like hands were upon her throat and her chest and shoulders all at once, crushing the wind from her, yet she could not swoon, did not expire, but could feel the awful constriction like the tightening of a knot.

She knew that she was dead, and had been for some time now,

though she did not know where she was, or what had become of her. She knew she hadn't come home, because home smelled like biscuits and here, no smell she loved welcomed her.

Fear rose up in her, and she screamed. Something else in the room screamed too, and she could feel the pain in its cry.

She looked down at her body and saw that a blackish and burning light, like embers, glowed at one of her elbows and no arm was there. She was dressed in a garment colored by the earth, yet barely perceptible, swirling colors of mud and leaf mold in varying states of decay, but thin as a wisp. If she could scream, she could speak.

"Where are my children?" she asked. "Where are my remains?"

The features of the room began to fill themselves in and become solid in her sight.

The stern voice of her conjuror came again:

"'Who knows the fate of his bones, or how often he is to be buried? Who hath the oracle of his ashes, or whither they are to be scattered?'"

A man stood before her next to a large, olive-shaped globe of glass in which a form was suspended in translucent gold. He was holding an arm, her arm, and he smiled amiably, as though he was welcoming a guest into his parlor on a Sunday. But there was something in his tone that made quote into curse, and she screamed again in chorus with the form that floated in the enormous glass ampoule.

The man spoke again as he put the last knots in a piece of cord he had wrapped tightly about her arm. He said merely, "Here you are, and here be you bound." And in his words were an acid truth that she could feel burning through her form.

Uncle set the arm at the foot of the massive vessel. He looked through the glass and past its contents and could see that there was now something else in the room. He could not see the ghost, but as he finished the Dark Call, the air seemed to divide and the floor of the Camera was awash with mist. There was a faint shadow rising against the inside wall of the room, and a ringing in his ears began that—he guessed—was the sound of the ghost's screaming.

But Uncle only smiled again, covered his ears, and raised his own voice.

"But here is a child, changed through time to be sure, but no less a child in need of a mother's love." He pushed the arm closer to the foot of the glass.

Something else in the room gibbered familiarly.

And then Uncle heard her voice again, though in his mind or in his ears he did not know. The sound was very low, like the hiss of a leaking gas line.

"This poor creature is not mine."

"Of course he is," said Uncle flatly. "At least, he is now."

"No."

He took up her arm once more and bound to it a flat stone of gray slate with more cord. He reached up and over the lip of the vessel, placing the bundle on the surface of the thick liquid and watched as it slowly, very slowly, made its way down to the bottom of the glass. "Madam," he said with all formality, "welcome home."

A pitiful shriek rose up again and filled the room as Mary Bishop's shadow on the wall turned golden and her arm sank to the bottom of the honey-filled vessel, coming to rest against the preserved thing that was kept within it. Uncle did not know if the whole house could hear her awful crying, but he could remain in that room no longer. As he unlocked the door of the Camera to leave, the roar briefly subsided, revealing only the small sound of something tapping softly. Tapping, tapping, against its prison of glass.

◆ ◆ ◆

Later that night, Mary Bishop slipped into Uncle's all-too-rare sleep, waiting for him around every corner of his dream, flying up at him with wings of fire in place of her arms, screaming so that the world shook and trembled behind his eyes. Every night after stealing her arm from its resting place, the dreams would come again. Some by night, some by day, but whenever Uncle closed his eyes, she was there, waiting for him.

If Uncle was lucky, the sound of banging on the walls and floor of the Camera might wake him from those nightmares. Finally, between the continuing noises in the Camera and the new dilemma of the screaming and terrible apparition in his dreams, he stopped sleeping completely. Then he knew what madness was, and soon he could not easily remember even his own name.

After seven nights, he knew this arrangement was impossible and decided to release her. He admitted to himself what he had perhaps known from the beginning: It must be kin. Only blood kin could bring peace to his house.

Using an iron from the fireplace in the gallery, he fished the arm out from the vessel and severed the cords that bound it. He had no intention of going back to Newfield to rebury the arm, and indeed, the dogs had been howling and barking every night since his last visit. Instead he walked to the edge of his property and threw it over the gate, over the narrow street, and into the wild briars of the long-abandoned Temple Cemetery—his accustomed dumping ground—speaking only a few words of parting when he heard the arm land among the foliage:

"Mary Bishop, I release you. Rest there and come never again to my house. Trouble me no more. . . ."

But she neither heard nor heeded his words.

Her ghost had already risen from the brambles in the form of a great, dark bird and was flying silently toward the salt marsh and the Bowers of the Night Herons.

CHAPTER 40

NOT EASY

Uncle was on his knees, sweeping broken glass onto a piece of newspaper, when another jar crashed to the floor. He jerked himself upright, all the muscles of his upper body and face pulling taut as piano wires.

"Enough!" he shouted, but then deliberately calmed his voice. "There have been mistakes. I know you are angry."

Uncle had spent much of the afternoon locked inside his innermost workroom, the Camera Obscura. He had been speaking for much of that time, his voice rising and falling, pausing, and continuing as if in conversation. "I will make it right. I will bring peace again to this house. You have waited so long. I know. I know you are lonely here. I will bring him back for you. Silas. Your kin. The blood must be present and the same. Again and again I failed to see the simple elegance, the symmetry, but you knew, didn't you?"

He looked at the shelf near the boarded-up window, allowing his eyes to pass briefly over the reminders of his several previous attempts at reconciliation: the box of his wife's hairbrushes and nail parings; the parchment scroll; family photographs—one of his brother Amos, another with the hooded child standing in the doorway of a nursery; his own photograph of Mary Bishop's arm.

"Let blood be kept by blood. That way is best. I see that now. No more relics. Let the child come home again. Let kin keep kin. This is the path of resonance and of sympathy. I will bring him back to this house. For you. Because when you are together, here, there shall be peace without ending. You would like that, wouldn't you?" Uncle leaned over so he could see the eyes, and be seen by them.

"No need to speak. I know now what you require, what is needed." He rested his hand on the top of an open crate of bottles containing an amber liquid. He slid the box over so he could get all the shards of glass that had scattered under the table.

"Almost done. Ah, there. You see? Everything clean. Everything accounted for."

He gently lifted a bottle from the crate, and as he went to place it on the shelf, it slipped from his shaking hand and hit the floor with a pop, sending glass and a pool of slow-spreading golden ooze across the floor. The room seemed to inhale suddenly, holding its breath.

"Sorry," he said in a voice that seemed soothing but had sharp serrations along its edge. "I know such noises are awful to you."

Uncle paused and waited to see if anything else was going to happen. He looked at the other glass jars in the room. A few of the smaller containers moved very slightly, shook, clinking briefly against their neighbors on the shelf, but a moment later all was quiet again.

He looked down toward the floor, still shaken.

"I know you do not care to be kept in this manner. No. No," he said, his head jerking this way and that as if trying to hear some small, distant sound. Uncle's voice strained with sympathy and impatience. "I am not hiding you." At those words the dim light in the room seemed to sharpen, crystallize, light and shadow becoming more distinct at their edges, while the air grew heavy, like someone breathing under a blanket.

Uncle ground his teeth together, then locked his jaw as though he was waiting to be hit.

"I am protecting you. You know this." He paused again, listening before going on. He spoke more quickly, in a lower tone.

"This is your place, *your* home. Our home. We were both born here. You are safe here. This will not change. We have always been here. We always will be here. You must trust me a little longer. We are family and shall endure through the years as family. No other way can insure eternity."

Uncle was tired. He could hear movements downstairs. Dolores was awake. He began to turn out some of the lights in the room. He would go down and meet her for a drink in the parlor. He smoothed back his disheveled hair.

"Rest now. Soon all shall be well. All shall be well." He was almost singing these words. "I shall bring the child home again. Your very own. All for you as it should be. Patience. Rest."

He bent over slightly and looked closely into the large vessel. He could see the soaking hair was standing up now in the viscous golden liquid, like once waving kelp now frozen in place. He climbed the small ladder next to the glass, then reached down and moved his hand through the thick syrup, passing it gently along the top of the head, brow to back, again and again, smoothing the hair into place, though he knew it wouldn't stay. After a few moments, he drew back his wet, sweet hand and climbing down, wiped it back and forth on his apron for many minutes.

"Better, yes? Be easy. Please."

A crack in the boards covering the window allowed a single line of late daylight into the chamber. Motes of dust moved back and forth quickly, swirling as they rose and fell through the revealing beam like tiny glowing flies. *Will nothing here be settled?* he thought angrily. *Easy. Be easy.* He quickly tried to calm the rising pitch of his thoughts.

Enough for today. Failure after failure.

It was nearly dinnertime. He removed the stained apron, hung it on its hook, and looked once more at the room. His eyes nervously swept the entire space, making sure everything was as it should be. He still felt uneasy. He would have porridge for dinner, or bread, to soak up the acid and anxiety from his delicate stomach. He put out the last light, drew back the inner bolt, and left the room through its only door, locking it again behind him. At the sound of the outer locks sliding into place, something in the room exhaled and loosened its grip on the stilling air.

The spirit, as it enters into the Other World, is immediately recognized by its friends and acquaintances, for spirits recognize a person, not merely by his face and speech, but also by the sphere of his life as they draw near it. When anyone in the Other Life thinks of another, he thinks of his face . . . and when he does this the other becomes present, as if he had been sent for or summoned.

—From "Certain Useful Notes and Translations from Swedenborg's *Heaven and Hell*," copied out by Jonas Umber

CHAPTER 41

TOGETHER

IN SILAS'S MIND, all the time he spent with Bea melted into one long evening of looking at the sea and stars, of looking at her and hearing her words, her voice surrounding him like a song. Silas loved the distraction Bea provided because when he was alone, all he could think about was how he didn't know what to do next about his dad. When he was with her, he could think of nothing but her; she worked on him like a spell.

Now he was alone again, trying to hold off the coming day. He lay in bed, awake but with his eyes closed, thinking about the night, about Bea; little moments, strung together like jewels, were turning over and over in his mind, growing brighter in remembrance.

She loved the footpath by the river, and at night, the sound of the rushing water was soft music running alongside their conversation.

"Will you ever leave Lichport, Silas?"

"I don't know. I don't have any plans to leave here. Where would I go?"

"Will you promise me, Silas? Promise me that you'll never leave."

"I'll try," he said tenderly.

"Try not to leave, or only try to promise?" she asked, looking away at the sky.

"I'll try," he said again. When he looked at her face lit by the pale moon, he thought his heart would break for the way it glowed, her perfect features, so familiar, limned in pearl and opal light. "You are beautiful . . . ," he whispered.

And Bea looked back at him, the light slipping from her face, and said with a voice he could barely hear, "You always say that, my darling."

Another night, they walked far north of the Narrows, around the bay and out to the lighthouse. The surface of the sea was embroidered with stars, for the moon was nowhere to be seen. Bea had asked him about his family, and Silas had said he wasn't sure what to tell her. He had hoped she might have known his dad, and sometimes she looked as though she was about say something when Silas mentioned him. But she never did. So he asked her about her family, and to his surprise, she avoided family questions too, and asked him another question instead.

"Don't you want to kiss me, Silas?"

"I—Yes, I do. Very much." Silas thought about leaning over, but stopped. Then, without thinking, he did it; inclined his head toward her with his eyes closed. But nothing happened. When he opened his eyes, she was standing several feet away by the lighthouse. He got up and walked toward her, hurt and embarrassed.

"Not yet, Silas."

"Okay. It's fine. I just—"

"We can't. I think you know that. Not yet."

He looked away from her and down at the sea throwing itself against the rocks far below them.

"There is a great lantern up there," Bea said, drawing his attention back, gesturing to the top of the lighthouse.

"Oh, yes?" Silas answered, trying to refocus on her voice.

"Think of all the ships it's called home from the sea . . . think of all the people it's saved. Sometimes on certain nights I think I can see a light up there on the tower. Isn't that odd? No one's been in the lighthouse for years and years, but I'm sure I've seen it. Little lights are good luck, you know. Lights seen over water are good luck. They'll always lead you home."

"Really? I think I've read something different—," Silas started to say.

"Maybe," Bea replied sharply. "I guess it depends what you want to believe."

"And didn't you tell me that sometimes people lit fires to make ships crash on the rocks? How can you tell which lights are dangerous and which ones lead you home?"

Bea smiled at him thinly but didn't say another word as they left the lighthouse with the rising dawn. The sky was burning as the sun rose over the water, and its early fire hung at the edges of the world and in Silas's tired eyes. They silently parted company by the fence at the bottom of Beacon Hill. Silas returned home feeling confused and heartsick. As he entered the house, his father's belongings seemed to glow in the early morning light like a reminder. He knew he had to keep looking for his father, had to keep trying to learn *how* to look.

Exhausted, Silas made his way to bed. Sleep came quickly, but it cast him on the rocks of troubled dreams.

Only certain of the dead truly pose a danger to the living. Those who die by violence, or before their appointed hour, those executed for no just cause, those dying in youth upon the battlefield, and, of course, the drowned.

Once, in a villa rented by my family in Athens, a very wretched and most terrible ghost appeared to us, shackled upon its feet and wrists, water pouring from its mouth at every moment like a grotesque spigot. It would often wake a member of the household, putting its hand about their throats to wake them. Or it would stand before me, screaming, always in some small hour of the night, bidding me to follow it to the inner courtyard, whereupon it would then swiftly vanish. My wife and family bid us leave the place. Instead I had the courtyard dug up and lo! There was the ruin of an ancient well, long since covered over. The bottom of the

well was drained and a skeleton found,
shackled in the same manner as the ghost.
At my insistence (and expense), a
public funeral was held, and never again
did the ghost appear or trouble the house in
any manner.

—from the lost account of Athenodorus, found and translated from the Greek by Jonas Umber in the year 1792

CHAPTER 42

LETTING GO

Mrs. Bowe stood by the mausoleum in her garden, listening. The bees had been bringing her news of Silas's rambles about town. She had looked into her mother's crystal and discerned that he was not alone on many of his walks. She knew, now, who he'd been spending his time with. Although she could see no more than a shadow moving beside the boy as he walked, she knew it was the drowned girl. She had come free of the millpond again.

Mrs. Bowe told herself it was none of her business.

But of course it was her business.

She knew Amos would not want Silas going to the millpond or consorting with anything that resided there. She knew that as sure as she knew her own name. Amos had confided in her that there was something about the millpond that gave him nightmares, and Mrs. Bowe suspected that the drowned girl had played at least a small role in his many excuses for moving to Saltsbridge with his infant son and wife.

"Just give it a wide berth, particularly as the year turns," Amos had told her. "It is a critical place for children at all times, and for young men especially."

She didn't want to worry the boy, and maybe everything for the moment was fine. He certainly seemed happier lately, if not a little distracted, but she didn't want him going near the millpond again. She knew something about the place. She knew about his father's experience with the ghost there and how it had followed him and how it disappeared during his father's courtship. She knew how Amos had seen the spirit looking at him once through a window as he stood over Silas's cradle. Mrs. Bowe feared that anything she told Silas would only make him even more curious. And clearly, the girl from the water had already appeared to him many times. No. In this instance, action needed to be taken, but discreetly. She didn't want to upset the boy, after all.

Mrs. Bowe waited until after dinner to bring up the matter with Silas. She only knew what the bees told her and what she'd been able to spy within the crystal. But those were more than enough, and the bees were never wrong. She'd been raised right, though. No confrontation. Just a little story before bedtime. She crossed the passage between their houses and called to him from the doorway.

"I'm here, in the study," Silas called back.

She went to him there. "I thought I might share a little tale with you."

"I'm a little old for bedtime stories, don't you think, Mrs. Bowe?" Silas asked, looking up from his reading.

"Then call it a cautionary tale, if you prefer. Now, are you sitting comfortably? Then let's begin. . . ."

This all happened long ago, right here in Lichport.

There was a boy, a handsome, charming lad from an old family. He was sure of himself, sure of what he wanted, and when he fell in love he gave everything he had, though the girl he loved was not like his people. She was lovely, but wild, a thing of the woods and meadows. She hardly spoke, so he gave her his song. He played her music of his own making. He sang her honeyed words, and his sweet voice made the world grow still about them. He gave her his heart. But for all this, his bright days with her would end too soon in shadow. Though their kin knew nothing of their love, for they hid it, the lovers soon announced their engagement and came very quickly to their wedding day.

No one was surprised that things went bad fast. There was u pall over the whole business, folks said. And it was true. Even the torches at the wedding dinner sputtered and hissed and would not light. Some thought this an ill omen, but such folk spoke their concerns softly, for who wants to hear of dire portents just as a bride and groom's hands begin to intertwine? So, to the music of whispers and prognostications of the worst kind, they made their vows and tied the knot.

Well, he was a high-born fellow, graceful, descended from good stock. Maybe that's why he loved her. Because she was so very different from him. She was wild, and no one knew who her family was. He loved her wild heart. And he never complained at how often she would take to walking along among the trees at the edges of the marshes, for that windswept place spoke to her and she heard a kind of music on the salt-sweet air that no one else could hear. And though folk spoke ill of her for doing so, often she would go to the marshes alone. There, she could be just another creature of the wild among the other wild things. Folks knew no good would come of it, and no good did.

One day, as she wandered and her husband waited for his supper, a serpent of the marsh crept close to her on the path, and when her small foot trod upon it, it bit her on the ankle just as long ago a serpent's poison bit hard the heart of Eve in the garden. Now such poison is as quick and strong as love, and soon she was overcome and so she fell, her last breath stirring the dust of the earth from which man must take his daily bread.

That is where her husband found her, just there by the marshes, and that is where his heart fell all to pieces. But he thought highly of himself. So highly that he would have things his own way or not at all. What's mine is mine, he said, and was resolved to take her back, to bring her back.

And there the tale goes right to hell, for under the earth he goes to fetch back his love, despite knowing what we all know: Some roads must lead away from home and do not, cannot, ever again return. Not ever. He was clever. Too clever. He knew just where to take up the mist path to that dark land. And because his love for her burned strongly still in his chest, he needed no map to follow on that dim and turning road, but walked his way right to the doors of Hell.

How long he walked he did not know, but when he found the high hall of the dead, he did not hesitate. He took her hand in his and led her away. But the King of the Dead, the Lord of Hell, could not be got around, for this was before the Revolution, and a king's word still held sway in the colonies. Strong are the gates of his land, and no one may enter or depart them without his leave. Still, he released them both, saying only, "Go, but do not look back."

Such is the Devil's way. Let the rope out easy and slow, easy and slow.

Up and ever up that youth walked, and though he could no longer feel her hand in his, and though he could not hear her breath and though she said nothing, on and on he walked, feeling as sure of himself as any man in his predicament could. Walking still in the mist, when he could see the trees before him glow in the light of the sun, he spoke her name, just once. But she says nothing. Makes no answer. So he thinks he's lost her, you see? Lost her somewhere along the way, so he turns to look, and well, that was it. He really did lose her then and for what? A little impatience.

That sweet girl's face hung before him on the air for the space of a breath, but then, oh then, it just fell away from him and back down into the earth and sank to that other place, where he would never see it again so long as he lived.

"Is that always how the story ends?" Silas asked earnestly, almost desperately, twisting in his chair.

"Yes, if things run their right way. Yes. That is how it *must* end. Because, in case you failed to notice"—Mrs. Bowe's voice dropped—"she was d-e-a-d."

"But what if things ran another way?"

Mrs. Bowe didn't like the direction this was taking. But she didn't want to lie to him, not outright. *What would Amos want me to tell him?* she asked herself. She knew in her heart that eventually, Amos would have told the boy everything, but not yet. Not yet.

"Stories wander around, go from one land to another, sometimes parts change."

Silas leaned forward in his chair.

"There is another version. It ends a little different. But it's stranger, that story, and I don't rightly understand all of it. It's a song, and it came across the sea, and it's in books. There's no mystery about where it came from. The mystery is what it says. But it's late, Silas, and I can't go fetching up old songs at this hour."

"But how does that one end? How is it different from the Orpheus story you told me?"

Of course he'd know, she thought.

"Yes. Orpheus. But in this other version, this folk version, he is called Orfeo. And when Orfeo goes to the King of the Dead to get his girl back, he plays music for the dead, and they all think so highly of it, their king asks Orfeo what he wants to be paid for his marvelous song. Orfeo asks for his lady back, and the king tells him to take her and go home."

"Doesn't he look back? Doesn't he lose her?"

"I don't believe he does. The song ends with Orfeo going home and becoming king."

"I like that ending better," Silas said.

"I will have to disagree with you," Mrs. Bowe said softly, now regretting bringing up the other version of the story.

"Why?" asked Silas, his voice rising. "It's much better that way. Orfeo gets the girl he loves, and they go home and live together, and what's wrong with that?"

"Because it is unnatural. Those who go to the halls of the dead do not return, and if they do, it is only because they may be of use to the King of the Dead. But it is getting late and you've had your story, young man. So enough. We can argue about ballads over breakfast. To bed, with us both."

"I'm not tired," Silas said. "I'll stay up a bit longer. Good night, Mrs. Bowe."

"Suit yourself."

But as she turned to go, Silas spoke again.

"What if just part of the story is true? What if love can conquer death?"

"You mean like me and my man?"

"No, I was thinking of something more . . . I'm not sure . . . forgive me . . . something more *real*. Like when Orfeo brings back his girl."

Mrs. Bowe went absolutely white and knew she had made a mistake. She should have left the matter well alone. She also knew she would now have to intervene. It had already gone far enough.

"Silas, really!" she exclaimed, wide-eyed. "Just how in the world do you intend to find that out exactly?"

"It's just a question. . . ."

"Well, some questions lead to trouble, and that's no lie!" She tried to regain her composure, smoothed the front of her dress as if brushing off crumbs. "Silas, they don't come back, dear. They may linger like a long shadow before twilight, but they do not return. At least, not in any way you'd want to get close to. Leave it be, now."

Mrs. Bowe walked across the passage back into her own

house, her hands shaking. It was already becoming clear the boy was going the way of the father. That was expected, and she was proud of him, in a way and to a point. What she didn't like was how quickly he seemed fascinated by that road on which there were few turns and no returning. She'd let it go too far.

Resolve rose up her, and if she didn't stop to overthink things, she might be able to see it through and help him. Striding more confidently now, she went to the tomb in her garden and spoke to the hive. In an instant, the bees were swarming toward the millpond, then flying low over the murky surface, carrying water back through the window of Mrs. Bowe's parlor and depositing it, droplet by droplet, on her mother's crystal. She touched the water with her finger, spread it across the surface of the stone, and softly spoke words into the air as a veil within the crystal parted. "Drink. Drink. Drink, Lonesome Water. Sink down. Go low, child. Cold One, go low. Go back to the murk place and attend your bones. When you see him again, then you will sink down. . . ."

The bees hummed in circles about her head.

"I know," she said, "but it may hold her long enough."

She intoned sharply, finally: "When they are together next, let the waters take hold of her again. He may look upon her once more. Then, let night descend. Then, let the waters take her and winter lock her in her bones." Her voice blended in the air with the sound of the bees, and the water on the surface of the crystal turned to ice.

Between the hours is where they reside, just under the minutes by which we count out our days. They are always there, wait- ing, out of time, and when the sands are still at the bottom of the hourglass, we may take hands with them.

—Marginalia of Richard Umber, recorded 18 September 1836

CHAPTER 43

ADMISSION

SILAS HADN'T SEEN BEA for a couple of days. It seemed that when he was thinking about his father, or his work, she was less likely to appear, as though she knew that she wasn't at the front of his thoughts, and was jealous about the time he spent thinking about anything other than her. She seemed to feel him thinking about her, and when he wasn't, she stayed away until he did.

But Silas was thinking about her. He couldn't help it.

Bea was distracting him in every way, more in her absence than her presence. Thoughts of Bea drew him away, even in sleep, from focusing on his work, further and further from finding his dad. It wasn't only her strangeness. Silas needed someone who *wanted* to be with him, and she did.

Despite all the time they'd spent together over the past weeks, he still didn't know much about her, but he had figured out a few things. He could almost admit to himself the kind of girl she was. Not merely different. Something more. When he was with her, it felt like there was nothing else in the world. When they were apart, he was filled with guilt for all the other things he had allowed himself to forget. But then all he wanted was more time with her, and so it went in his mind, around and around.

At the top of the stairs leading from the street to his front door, there was a spot where the paint was worn thin and the gray wood showed through. Silas liked to sit there and imagine his dad sitting and thinking, watching the street or the sky. And that was what Silas was doing. Sitting on the front stairs, thinking about Beatrice. Clouds were passing quickly above him, high and fast, sailing shadows down the street and to the west. Every few seconds, a beam of sun darted through the clouds and probed the ground like a searchlight.

He'd been there since early morning. He'd had another Bea dream and wasn't able to get back to sleep. He'd begun to fret, turning the problem of his distraction over in his mind. Silas knew, somewhere in his gut, that he should stay away from her. Even his dreams about her were beautiful but dark, always framed in coldness and shadow. He knew she had problems. It wasn't that she was a bad person; he just knew she was probably going to be bad for him. But maybe she was the kind of bad he needed right now. Maybe it was a good bad. Or not. Like how the air seemed to condense when they were close, or the way her skin sometimes looked as if cold water was coursing beneath. No. None of it felt right. But it felt good, for the distraction as much as anything else. He liked the mystery of her. He liked feeling that he might one day be able to figure her out, that one day, he might learn what kind of light she actually was: light-house beacon, or mooncusser's fire.

He liked feeling that it was the two of them. But when they were together, he noticed, the shadows drew in just a little. The world around them darkened. The light wasn't so bright or revealing. All the rough edges of things were rounded down. He liked feeling as though he had a little secret he was keeping from the world, though he was beginning to sense there was something unnatural about their attraction for each other, something dangerous in their desire to be together, in the way she looked at him. Still, Bea was match to the field of dry weeds Silas's heart had become in the time since his dad had disappeared. Their little fire had started fast, and Silas didn't want to worry about what else might catch or who else saw the smoke. When he thought about her, he was warm all over, and it was so nice to feel something, anything, other than scared and abandoned.

The clouds had slowed and gone ashen, swinging low toward the ground. It was going to rain.

He could just go along with it for a while. It was, after all, a learning experience. Like, if you wanted to learn a language, it was best to go and live in that country. And Bea *was* a Lichport girl. Born and raised here, Bea knew so much about the town's dead and living both. He loved seeing the town through her eyes. She was part of Lichport, but also of some other land, an oddly distant place that happened to be right around the corner. Maybe love just felt that way, like a kind of fever dream, making things seem both frighteningly close and unbearably far away all at once.

From the story she'd told him about Orpheus, he assumed Mrs. Bowe knew something about him and Bea and did not approve her. But why bother worrying her with details? Now that he had his own place to live, and was finished with school, he could do as he pleased. How long does a guy have to ask permission for everything he does? His great-grandfather had made a generous gift to him. He was buying his own food when he wasn't eating with Mrs. Bowe or the Peales down in the Narrows. He could live on his own and on his own terms. Okay, he wasn't washing his own clothes, but that was only because Mrs. Bowe insisted on doing it. She derived great pleasure from doing the laundry and found nothing demeaning in it. She said it was something traditional in her family, that her mother and grandmother and back and back were all "washerwomen." He didn't understand what she meant, but whatever. He could pay someone else to help him with housework now if he needed to. The point was, he didn't need anyone's approval or permission for anything anymore.

Silas paused again very briefly, weighing possibilities. "Screw it," was his conclusion. He always thought too much, worried too much. Besides, after the year he'd had, was spending time with someone like Bea really going to make things worse? For once, things weren't quite so awkward. Like with the girl in his homeroom class. She had looked at him sometimes and once, had slipped him her phone number on the corner of a piece of paper. He'd never called her. Wanted to. A hundred times. But every time he thought about it, his mind boiled up with every reason not to do it, every doubt he'd ever had about himself. His mother's comments hadn't helped. She said it was because no decent girl would date a man with hair in his eyes and that he should get a haircut. But Silas had seen pictures of both his parents when they were dating, so he said, "But Dad's hair was over his eyes when you dated him."

"Yes!" his mother spat back. "And look where that's gotten me!"

Silas was sure his hair had not been the problem. Homeroom-girl had given him her phone number despite his hair. She'd told him—when he awkwardly apologized for never calling—that he was "cute, but kinda weird," and that her friends had made fun of her for giving him her number.

"Okay," he'd said, embarrassed. "That's okay."

Most of the girls he had looked at in school wouldn't talk to him at all.

Better to keep Bea a secret. It felt better as a secret. Only the two of them. Only him and Bea. And she was interested in him. Waited for him, sometimes. He even thought he could feel her thinking about him. It was easy spending time with her. They had walked through many of the town's cemeteries together, one after another in no particular order, drifting among the stones,

Bea telling Silas stories of the folk who lay below them.

He might have grown up in Saltsbridge, but that didn't mean he was stupid, or normal. He was his father's son.

He knew she was dead.

Silas wanted to admit that to himself up front. He wanted to be sure he believed it (not so hard, these days) and understood what it meant (much harder). He thought saying it to himself might help, so he did. He said it out loud, but not very loudly: "Your girlfriend is a ghost." He said each word slowly, like part of an equation. A plain fact.

Okay. There it was.

Did they both have to be alive so long as they liked each other and talked to each other? Again, best not to overthink it, he decided. He realized that because she was a ghost, it might make things awkward, but it didn't mean they couldn't have feelings for each other.

What he wondered most about was why she seemed so interested in him. Was it his coming to Lichport that had brought her into the world again? From some of the things she said, it seemed that she had been waiting for him. Just him. Didn't that mean they were connected? If he stopped thinking about her and talking to her, would she even exist? If he chose to forget her, where would that leave her? But, he could now see, when they weren't together, their relationship was a memory too. Just a memory. Same for everyone he knew. Even Mrs. Bowe, whom he'd only just seen this morning. Now: a memory. A figment. Sure, he would see her again, but between one meeting and the next, she was nothing but an ember of the mind, getting colder by the minute. But the instant he thought about her, his memory blew the ember once more to flame.

Rain had started falling lightly.

Yes, thought Silas. *Just like that*. He was beginning to feel his head swim a bit. It all came to this, a glance, a word, a face . . . everyone he knew was, most of the time, merely a recollection. Then a thought fell on him. *Ghosts. Maybe we're all ghosts anyway, just as soon as the moment's passed.*

So what if Bea seemed a little needy and sometimes just stood and stared at him? Who back in Saltsbridge had ever paid him any attention at all? And at least Beatrice talked to him.

Still, guilt nagged at the corner of his mind. He should be looking for his father. He could tell himself that being with Bea was part of his search; in his gut he knew it wasn't, knew it was taking him in another direction entirely. But he just wanted to walk and talk with her, just to be with her.

He rose and walked down to the Umber family cemetery and there she was, waiting, as if they'd had an appointment. As if she knew he'd been thinking about her.

Seeing her there among the tombs of his ancestors—the early light arrayed about her pale skin, the curve where her neck flowed into her shoulders—the line between Silas's obligations and his desires blurred. He willingly took his place at her side.

The Hebrews see that death and dream share a wide frontier. Words for reviving the dead have been widely used rabbinically and in certain of their ancient and accustomed prayers. Their Talmud recommends saying <u>Baruch atah adonai, mechayeh hametim.</u> "Blessed art thou, Lord, reviver of the dead." This is said when greeting a friend after a lapse of twelve months, and upon waking from sleep.

—Anonymous entry, eighteenth century

CHAPTER 44

LAST WORDS

SILAS AND BEA HAD BEEN WALKING together most of the day, and twilight was drawing on. A sickle moon had risen early and already hung low in the late autumn sky. The evenings had grown more cold than crisp and mornings found the leaves rimmed with a hint of frost.

Now they were slowly wandering back toward Silas's house after making their progress through the small cemeteries on the southern side of town: the Lost Ground, whose earth bore the nameless folk who washed up out of the sea, and God's Small Acre, which held the children who'd perished in a smallpox epidemic two hundred years ago. Silas liked this small plot and found it full of tenderness from the living for the dead: tenderness in the smooth corners of the gravestones, where centuries of hands had rested before and after prayers were spoken, tenderness in the slight mounds of earth grown over the graves where flowers and offerings had been left, year after year, thickening the loam. Kindness was especially in the Lost Ground, where the people buried were strangers to Lichport. The townsfolk were hospitable and kind, giving good-quality stone for headstones and adorning them with carvings of dolphins and shells in remembrance of the journeys the deceased had made. Fine, ornate gates were raised to give the plots a feeling of importance and protection. Lacking names, the townsfolk had written brief but charitable descriptions and epitaphs on the stones:

"BY TEMPEST BROUGHT, TO THIS EARTHEN PLOT,
SLEEP YE SAFE, THOUGH YOUR NAME BE FORGOT. "

"BE WELCOME HERE, AND FIND REST, LADY OF THE SEA."

"A WANDERER. MAY HE FIND HIS PATH HOME."

On and on they went. One kindness after another, yet each remaining its own mystery, each stone a fragment of a lost tale.

While Silas was looking at the inscriptions, Bea wasn't talking much. That wasn't like her when they were in a cemetery; she enjoyed telling him the stories of the names they saw, but today she seemed sullen and hardly even looked at him. She had drawn down into herself and didn't even seem to remember who Silas was. He began to worry that she could sense he was having doubts about the two of them.

He stopped walking and turned to look at her. The last light of the setting sun was on them both, and Silas felt hot, though a cold air was coming in off the sea. Bea's expression was distant. She was standing in the light of the approaching dusk, a little dim around the edges. When she turned, she saw Silas looking at her, waiting for her to say something.

"Do you think I'm beautiful, Silas?"

Silas began breathing harder and she brightened, as though every breath he took when looking at her was a gift, a portion of life, given from him to her.

"Do you?" she asked again.

He was turning red. He wanted to tell her how pretty he thought she was, that when he looked at her his eyes were filled with silver light, but he was worried it would come out sounding stupid. So he said, "Yes. You know I do. I tell you that all the time."

"I know you do," she said, mimicking his low tone. "You know, Silas, we could be a lot closer. . . ." She walked up to him and leaned in, the skin of her face luminous and smooth as a pearl.

Silas had thought about this, about "getting closer" to Bea and what it might mean. He realized that one of the things he liked about her was that he could have feelings for her and not worry too much about the future, because, well, she didn't really have one.

"I—I—I don't think I can go any further with you, Bea. I mean, not yet. I don't want to go too fast. We haven't known each other that long, I mean . . ." he stammered, knowing that sounded lame. Wasn't that what the girl usually said?

"We have known each other for a very long time, Silas. Though I guess I'm the only one who can feel that." Her voice trailed off, as though she was thinking about something else now, something further along than where they were standing, what they were saying. Under her white skin, dark ripples began to flow, filling the space around her with damp, cold currents of air.

Silas pulled his jacket's collar up and adjusted his scarf against the increasing chill, the fabric scratching at his neck. Something was now clearly bothering her.

"What's wrong?"

Bea did not answer.

"Bea, please. Tell me what's wrong."

Again she said nothing. She began to sing sweetly, absently as she walked.

Come all ye fair and tender girls that flourish in
    your prime,
Beware, beware! Keep your garden fair
Let no man steal your thyme, your thyme
Let no man steal your thyme.

For when your thyme is past and gone
He'll care no more for you,
And every place where your thyme was waste
He'll spread all over with rue, with rue.
He'll spread all over with rue.

A woman is a branchy tree
And man a clinging vine,
And from her branches, carelessly
He'll take what he can find, can find
He'll take what he can find.

Come all ye fair and tender girls that flourish in
    your prime,
Beware, beware! Keep your garden fair
Let no man steal your thyme, your thyme
Let no man steal your thyme.

Silas thought this was a strange song to sing to someone you
liked. As she finished, there was a challenge in her eyes, and the
smile that usually greeted Silas when she sang to him was nowhere
to be found.

She drew up one corner of her mouth in a half grin and said,
"You like all this, all these reminders of the dead?"

"I do, I guess. I mean, it's part of my life, my dad's life. It's part
of the work some of the people in my family do . . . ," he began,
feeling led on. He kneeled down to pull some dead weeds away
from the base of one of the tombstones.

"You know you can't help them all. By all means, forgive
them for not forgiving themselves, but you Umbers can't solve
all their problems for them. Your dad tried, but now what's
become of him?"

Standing up quickly, Silas whipped his head around to stare back into her face. "What do you know about my father? Bea, tell me!"

She stood silent and defiant, yet her face looked pained.

Silas was angered at the thought she'd been keeping things from him and hurt both by her implications about his family's work and the cruel irony of her comment. He tried to calm himself and answer her accusation. "I never said I was trying to help them all. I will try to do what I can, like my dad would have if he were here. But if you know anything about him, or where he is, you must tell me now. Bea, please."

Bea continued, unmoved by his repeated requests.

"So many were beyond his help. He was so distracted. Like you. You need to focus on what's important." She smiled broadly at him, drawing in close to his face. Her skin was nearly translucent now and blue, as if carved from ice or aquamarine. "I mean, you should spend your time with those who really need you, who really want your attention. Those others? Forget them, let them go. Remember *me*."

"Remember you? From when exactly? We've only known each other a couple of months!" Silas said.

"Silas, we've known each other much longer than that, and you know it."

"No," he said quietly but sharply, "I don't know it."

Silas knew he was missing something. He could feel himself beginning to blush in both embarrassment and renewed anger. He could sense that she knew things about him from a time before he knew anything about her. How long had she known him? His family? What did she know about his dad that she wasn't telling him?

They were walking up Coach Street, approaching Main. As they approached the Bowe family tomb behind its overgrown fence, the wind rose and made dust spirals on the street about their feet, and for the briefest second, Silas thought he smelled a hint of Mrs. Bowe's perfume on the air.

Bea seemed to stumble back away from Silas, as though she'd been pulled, then stood straight again. She tilted her head to one side, raising an eyebrow as if pointing with it toward the fence, and said, "You see that tomb?"

"Yeah," Silas replied.

"You too are about to die," Bea said flatly, but with a strange, breathless giggle at the end.

"What?" Silas asked, shocked and confused. He looked quickly at the street in front of them. Nothing stood out. He looked hard at Bea. "What are you talking about?"

"Sure. You are. Really. I mean, everyone is. Dying is so common. Everyone dies. Are you going to help them all, Silas? Or are you going to spend your time at something that matters? Time flies, Silas Umber. It really does."

He stared at her. Whatever game she was playing, he didn't like it. He was about to demand that she make whatever point she was trying to make, but then he thought again and said quietly, "I—I feel fine, and what I am trying to do does matter."

"If you say so. I believe you," she said with no commitment whatsoever. "Just don't wait too long . . . or what you really want might have moved on. Tell you what, though, just for fun, let's see how long you've got. Okay? Just hold still."

Bea looked at him so hard that Silas thought the stare was going to cut him. His arms went very cold, and goosebumps rose like a rash across his arms and torso. Bea inclined her head toward him and closed her eyes. A breeze was lifting leaves from the ground, but her hair and dress hung motionless.

Finally she said, "I guess you're all right for a while, but only for a while. If not today or tomorrow, next year maybe, or in ten years, or seventy. So hard to tell."

Silas's eyes were wide, and he broke out in a sweat.

"What the hell does that mean? Why would you say that to me?" he demanded, his face forming hard angles about his mouth and eyes.

"Because," she explained, lifting her face to meet his, "I just want you to know how important moments are. All these moments we spend together. They are so dear to me, and they are all we have."

Her skin was taking on a cold green hue, like the weeds at the bottom of a river. The wind continued to rise, and whipped Bea's hair about her face like the thin tails of a scourge.

"That's how you tell me you *like* me?" Silas yelled, the anger rearing up in him. "Well, here's a moment for your scrapbook: I want to go home. Tonight is over!" His voice went low in his throat, becoming a growl. In his head, he felt a door slam shut, and he and Bea were on different sides of it. He regretted his words even as they were coming out of him. The air about them became suddenly freezing cold and full of static. Bea's head hung to the side, as if he'd slapped her with his words. She fell away, into the violence of the wind.

Words were woven all through the turbulent air, and Silas could hear a woman's voice *Drink, drink. Drink, Lonesome Water. Now you will sink down . . . back to your bones . . . down . . . below . . . sink down . . . Now.*

The first stars of evening appeared and were quickly covered by gathering clouds. Bea was already in the distance, dragged away from him by invisible hands. Then, as though a fever had broken, Silas felt desire pour through him. Without thinking, he ran after her. His heart pounded, his body fueled by his fears;

fears temporarily smothered while he and Bea were together, that now flew up into flame from their waiting embers. He couldn't hold on to anything or anyone. If he loved them, they left.

As he ran, he watched, helpless, as she was drawn farther and farther away. He felt broken and couldn't bear the thought of another person vanishing from his life. She was far ahead of him already, the world passing through her easily like water through a sieve, catching on nothing. She was all hue and shade and no substance Silas could feel except with his heart, and her sudden absence had already begun washing the color from his world. Without her, there was only obligation hanging about him like a heavy yoke. What was happening to her? He had spoken awful words, and now she was suffering. Because of him. In his mind he suddenly knew, with the surety of desperation, that if he loved someone, he would eventually drive them away.

"Bea! Wait!" he shouted after her. More clouds had gathered, and rain was coming down in sheets. *Where was she going?* Silas wondered frantically. He knew it would do no good to yell again. He was panting as he ran, his feet slapping against the wet street and then into the mud as he approached the millpond.

Ahead, he could see her. She was standing, motionless, at the pond's edge. She leaned away from it, as if fighting against a force trying to pull her down into the water. As Silas approached, trying to catch his breath, her features sharpened in his sight, then blurred, both in time with his labored breathing. When he breathed out, he could see her more distinctly, as if his breath was filling her form with color, making it more present, more real. She turned to look at him. But before he could catch his breath, or say anything, Bea was pulled backward into the water and drawn quickly below.

There had been no splash, no ripple. Her body slipped beneath the surface without disturbing the dark mirror of the pond. Silas didn't think, didn't pause for a second. He ran to the edge and jumped in after her.

The water was freezing. Silas could see Bea's face in front of him, below, but he was falling fast through the water. As he sank, she smiled. She reached out to him. Her long hair was flowing into his face, and as it moved slowly with the currents of the water, he saw her usually pale eyes lit with cold, bright fire. His mouth filled with water. He tried to scream and drew the water into his lungs. Bea was still there, smiling, her eyes closed as she reached out for him with both hands.

And then he didn't care that he was drowning because, at last, she was touching him. He could feel her hands on him, feel her body moving against his. Her cold embrace lingered on his skin, held his body tightly.

At last, he thought.

At last, her caresses seemed to say.

We are together.

And as she, the water, held him, he grew warmer and his eyes closed and he smiled, forgetting everything but her and how good it felt to finally touch her and feel her touching him. She was there, and he could *feel* her.

Down he fell, with her entwined in currents around him. At the bottom of the pond and in the dim waving light he could see a pile of white stones, and something else, like small branches of pale, sun-bleached wood. *Here is our bed*, he thought as thought left him. Silas closed his eyes and she was there too, waiting in the darkness behind his eyes, and there was nothing else. No family. No sorrow. No mother. No father. Nothing. Just the two of them, together.

But as life began to ebb from him, words rose in his blood out of the sound of his still-beating heart, a strain from a song he hadn't heard since he was a child. It was far off, but the sound kept coming, more and more words, but slowly getting softer as his heart slowed. Broken as they were, he knew they were his father's words, words from long ago . . . but in Mrs. Bowe's voice, trying to wake him, trying to help him.

Fly with me, fly with me . . .
the bells . . .
Little Bird, fly . . .

Then Mrs. Bowe's voice was gone in a swirl of mud at the bottom, and everything was dark. The water held him, no longer a caress. Something was lifting him from the stones at the bottom, and something was pulling him, up or down he could no longer tell. There were other words. Not heart words, but water words. Bea's voice, her tone different now, warming the water. Eddying in spirals. Bea's words were inside him. In his mouth, in his nose, in his eyes. Everywhere in the water were her words:

because I love you . . . live . . . for I am lost I cannot be . . . remember . . . I am sorry . . . live . . . do not look back. remember . . . I am sorry . . . from cold bed I release you . . . in cold bed I will wait . . . Silas . . . come back for me . . .

Silas thrashed his head around to find her, to see her face floating before him in the deep murk, but that was all he had left in him. A second later, consciousness again fled with a trail of bubbles from his mouth, and then he was nearly nothing anymore, no one, just another thing gone cold in the dark.

Then, through the darkness, came the other voice again. Mrs. Bowe. Her tone was sharp as the sun, cutting slashes into the surface of the water.

Little Bird, fly! The voice beamed bright in his mind. Feeling the mossy water in his throat and in his eyes, he kicked out and up from the dark bottom of the pond. When his face broke free from the water, he pulled and pulled with his arms until he felt mud in his hands. He put his face to the shore, and among the reeds, fell again into unconsciousness.

When Silas awoke, his legs were still in the water. As he pulled away, the surface of the pond cracked. The surface had frozen. He dragged himself all the way out and managed to get up on his knees before he threw up. He sat there, freezing cold on the bank of the mill-pond, for he wasn't sure how long. The first time he tried to stand, he fell back to a crouch and vomited again. But the second time he managed to stand up and lean against a tree. He stumbled the short distance back to his house, and as he came down the street, the front door of Mrs. Bowe's house flew open. She came down as far as the front steps to wait for him. He couldn't speak. She came out with a blanket, wrapped it around him, and held him by the shoulders. She brought him up the steps and into the warm house.

Mrs. Bowe was frantic as she got Silas up the steps and half carried him into the parlor where he collapsed on the sofa. She sat by him, singing gently, brushing his brow over and over, until he partly opened his eyes and said, "I heard a song. . . ."

"Just an old song I was singing to you, child."

"But I heard it under the water. . . ."

She stopped him. "Enough talking now, you must rest." And then she whispered, "Holy Mother, forgive me. Holy Mother, let no harm come to him by my hand or any other."

But he was beyond comprehension as he tossed his head from side to side.

"I want to go home."

"Silas, dear, you are home."

"Oh, God . . ." With that, Silas began to cry very softly, folding into himself. "I want to go home, please."

Distress welled up in him like a flood tide.

"What do you mean, Silas? Where do you want to go? Where is home if not here?"

Still crying, he said, "I don't know . . . I don't know what to do anymore—"

"You're exhausted," she said, brushing his brow with her hand. "Morning will bring a new day and a brighter one. But now let's get you to bed. For the moment, dear, that will have to suffice. All the shadows are gone for tonight. Be easy, child. Do you think you can make it to your room if I help you?"

As Mrs. Bowe got Silas into his bed, she tried to smile.

"Good night," she told him. As he closed his eyes, she very softly added, "Oh, Silas. I am so, so sorry. Forgive me."

A few moments later, he was somewhere soft and sinking down again. But he was warm and below the covers, and in the dark of the bedroom, there were no more voices. He fell from himself into sleep, and his name became the name of the night and the silent, distant stars blinking like a million watching eyes.

CHAPTER 45

COMPOSURE

EACH DAY SINCE HE'D NEARLY DROWNED in the millpond, Silas thought less and less about Bea. It had been only a week since then, but each passing day, her image blurred a little more in his mind. Were her eyes blue or green? The harder he tried to remember something about her, the faster she faded, like a dream upon waking. As his memories of her fell away, his other worries sharpened—his parents, his responsibilities, and the clear but comfortless fact that both needed to be attended to as soon as possible.

Still fearful, but more resolved, he decided to pay his mother a visit. As he turned the corner onto Temple Street, his mind said, *It's just a house*, but his gut told him to go back the way he'd come.

It was Mrs. Grey who opened the door when Silas arrived unannounced at Uncle's house. She said "The lamps are lit, Silas," and moved aside to let him in. He could hear his uncle from the second-floor landing.

"Ah! Here he is, without even a note sent round to say he's coming! Silas, I see you've learned Narrows manners. I shall be down to join you and your mother momentarily. You'll find her in her usual place."

As Silas passed Mrs. Grey, she whispered to him, "Be careful, Silas. You can see it in his eyes. The Danger Lamps are lit all the time now. You should keep away from this place." Silas looked around the corner for his mom, but when he looked back to Mrs.

Grey, she had already vanished into the back of the house.

The moment Silas walked into the parlor, his mother began speaking from the chair. Dolores's slumping posture made it look like she had been thrown there. She squinted as she looked up at her son. Her skin had taken on a yellowish hue.

"God, Mom," Silas said, shocked at her appearance.

She took no notice of his concern.

"Are you ready to move back here with me? With us? Your living away from your kin is unnatural. We should all be together here, Si," his mother told him pointedly. Silas could hear his uncle's voice flowing beneath her words; this was his script, not hers. She looked awful. He saw Dolores notice his looking at her and seeing a problem.

"It's the smell of the sea that isn't doing me any good. That rotting smell. Even up in this part of town. Fish and fishermen, crab shells and kelp and garbage floating in on the tide from God knows where. That smell gets into my head is all."

"Then why were you so eager to come back here?"

"You know we had no choice."

"I know, but if you knew it was going to be like this, we could have tried to—I don't know, tried something else."

"It's okay, Silas. I can distract myself. I want lovely things around me. I have that here . . . like where I grew up . . ." Her voice trailed off, but then quickly sparked up again. "Only chance I had to get somewhere *else*, wasn't it? Saltsbridge was no good for us, Si. You know that. We need nice things. You should come back to this house. Not that you ever bothered to say good-bye to me. Well, that's your father all over, isn't it? Just get it into your head to leave without a word and off you go."

Something caught her attention and Dolores lifted her head slightly, sniffing through her nose. "Silas, you smell like the low tide . . . where *have* you been keeping yourself?"

She was talking in circles, and he was letting her get to him, like always. "Why would I come back to this house?" he asked, his voice getting higher as he spoke.

"Where else is there? Not that spinster-haunted pile your father stayed in? Or some poor shack down in the filthy Narrows? That was the rubbish of your father's life. We're meant for better. Doesn't your uncle have enough books for you here?"

Silas had heard his uncle come downstairs and assumed he was standing in the hall, listening and waiting to make an entrance, but as the pitch of the conversation rose, he heard him climb the stairs and return to the second floor.

"Oh dear," Silas said, filling his voice right up to the brim with sarcasm, "now you've scared off the landlord."

"Sure. Have a go at me, or your uncle, the only people in the world who care whether you live or die. Go on and make yourself look stupid. Silas, you don't know anything. I thought it would be better to keep your father's awful life from you. Tried to keep you safe and away from those kinds of people, away from a life filled with ridiculous superstitions and nonsense. I did this, Silas, because I've always known how soft you are. You're the kind of person that other people will always take advantage of. No one can count on a man who's soft on the inside. Believe me, I know! But now I'm thinking it might have been better if I'd let you see a little more of the cruelty of the world, and let you see more of the truth about the kind of man your father was, the *things* that he built his life out of. He was a man of such selfish, wretched, *soft* parts."

Silas rose from his chair. He knew now it was pointless coming to talk with her. No one here would help him. It was all the wrong way around now; he the parent, she the child. He walked to the threshold between the hall and sitting room and stared at his mother.

"What?" she said. *"What?"*

He kept staring, as though he was waiting for her to change into something else. He knew that if he waited her out, she would usually start saying something a little more thoughtful.

"What the Christ are you staring at?"

This time it clearly wasn't working. So Silas spoke again, his voice slow, trying to be reasonable, but behind his teeth was a throat full of quiet, suppressed anger. "I don't think you know me at all. I don't think you've ever been very interested in knowing me. You hated Dad, and now, since he's gone, you hate me instead. And for what? Because I'm like him? Because I care about something other than you? Because I like parts of this town other than Charles Umber's dining room?" That last part rang loud in his head. Yes. He did like being in Lichport. It was strange and full of the oddest people he'd even met, but they were his people, he was realizing. His kind of odd. Both the living and the dead.

"Silas . . . you're my son—," she began to protest, but he interrupted her.

"And that's about as far as it goes, isn't it? I am your son, but what else? We don't have anything else in common, do we? So why should you care? You know, not once in the whole long year after Dad disappeared did you ever ask me how I felt, or what I was feeling. Not once."

She tried to get up, but the liquor swam in her blood, and her torpid limbs pulled her back down onto the chair.

"Silas, hon, it was a hard year for both of us. . . ."

Again, he was at her. "Oh, I don't think it was so very bad for you. You didn't love Dad, so now he's gone, and that's okay with you, right? You got to move out of a house you hated, so that was okay too. You have a few more reasons to sit and drink away the days. Score. Not so bad by my count. What did you lose? Nothing. I mean, what is a lost husband when you wanted him gone anyway?" Silas pulled his coat tighter around him, trying to block the air of the room from touching his skin. Now that he'd started, he was shaking and couldn't stop himself, as if his growing anger was the only thing that could keep him warm.

"Should I tell you how scared I was? Should I tell you how much I worried, how much I still worry, that I might have said or done something that made Dad leave, or that made him feel like not coming home? But then I'd think, maybe something happened to him. Should I tell you how, every night in my mind, I traced over every map I've ever seen, hoping that some point would leap out, some crossroad or lane would stand out from the others and say to me, *He's here, Silas. Your father is here. Come and find him.* And the only place that ever spoke to me was this town. Every street and lane says, *Come and find me.* How do you think it feels to lose the only person who ever loved or understood you? I hear his voice all the time, all around me now, but in my gut, I know I'll never see him again. What am I supposed to do with that? What the hell am I supposed to do with that?"

Dolores looked away. She breathed in deeply and then said, with every thin bit of kindness she could muster, "Honey, your dad is somewhere, we just don't know where that is. And we've done everything we can and can't do any more, so it's time to get on with things. If he's gone somewhere, well, that means he left us, and there's nothing we can do about it. If he's *gone* gone, then he's in heaven." She smiled wanly.

"Do you actually believe that?" Silas responded, surprised at what she was saying.

"Well, Si, no, not really. I don't think I believe in heaven anymore. I mean, I don't know. I believe in the things I can see and touch. I believe in this dress, in this chair, in those candlesticks. I believe we make heaven for ourselves out of what makes us happy. So now, for me, heaven is someplace with nice things, and a full glass, and someone bringing me breakfast on a tray.

"Silas, if you'd just calm down and see things straight on, you might understand. I don't have any money of my own, and that gives me very few choices. You won't like to hear it, but people lose things every day. We've lost a house. It happens to people all the time. I've lost a husband. Commonplace. You've lost a father. Hell, your father lost a father. And to keep going on and on about what you've lost, well, it's unmanly, for one thing. And it's rude, son. It's selfish and rude. This is my home now, and I plan to make the best of it."

Silas couldn't believe what she was saying. She complained about her losses every single day of her life.

"And here's your uncle," she continued, gesturing at the doorway his hurried departure had left empty, "trying to help us despite everything that's fallen out between him and your father over the years. Your uncle would like nothing better than to be like a father to you now, and what do you do? You spit in his face. It's unnatural to throw things back at folks who hold them out to you with both hands. But that's just what you do, you throw it all back. And for what?" Her voice was tightening again, returning to normal, taking back its accustomed edge. "For what? Voices? Memories? Some *nothing* tugging at the corner of your mind because you lost something dear to you? Si, I've lost almost everything dear to me and here I am, still getting on with things."

"Yes," Silas confirmed coldly, "getting on very well. I mean, you've really settled in here, haven't you? And, I see, given my uncle every bit of thanks you can afford by appreciating his gifts to the fullest, the clothes he's bought you, that glass he keeps full to the brim." He was looking not so much at her, but at the rich velvet dress she was wearing. He could feel his face begin to burn as he said, "Actually, Mom, I can't believe you waited a whole year before moving in here. That must have taken a lot of restraint." He was leaning into his words like punches now. He wanted to hurt her, wanted her to know not just what he was thinking but how it felt, too. Under every spoken word flowed wave after wave of implication, and it showed clearly on his face, all the sneers and squints that said, silently, cruelly: A *real* mother would have *felt* her child's pain and done something about it.

Pummeled by Silas's words, not able to get up, Dolores looked like she was going to start screaming at him. But very suddenly, her pointed features fell and her head slumped forward and began bobbing awkwardly; she was crying.

Dolores looked at her son through her tears, moving her head from side to side as though she was trying to see him through rain-splattered glass.

"Just like the day you were born," she mumbled out loud.

"What? What are you talking about?"

"When you were born. I couldn't see your face at first because of the caul. Your father took it off and, Lord, how he cried to see it. I told him to quiet down, that the sound of a man crying was no way to welcome a child into the world. I was just glad to be able to see your face when that thing came off."

Silas was trying to think of something to say to her when he heard, haltingly at first, then louder, the approach of footsteps returning from somewhere deep in the house. A moment later his uncle came up behind him. Quickly assessing the mood of the room, Uncle said, "Silas, that's enough now. Enough." He went to stand behind Dolores, holding her shoulders, keeping her from collapsing entirely. "You can see your mother is not feeling at her best. Perhaps you ought to go now, son."

"Oh," Silas snarled at his uncle, "I was already leaving!"

Silas bristled at the word "son" and was about to start swinging again with his words as he stormed toward the door, but in the moment after loudly pronouncing his departure, a slow banging took up from someplace down the dark throat of the hallway, and up above somewhere, in some deep room upstairs. Like someone pounding a piece of soft wood, or a shoe, or a fist, very angrily against the wall. He and his uncle stopped and stood absolutely still. *Here I am*, the knocking said to Silas. *Come and find me. . . .*

His mind became a thousand moths flying at a single flame—*Dad*. Trapped. Held. Hidden. Imprisoned. Wounded. Lost. All of Silas's suppressed suspicions furiously flooded his mind.

Without warning, he turned away from the nauseating domesticity of his uncle comforting his mother and ran down the hall toward the sound and the stairs. An image of his father bound in some attic had dug its claws into his brain, and he couldn't dislodge it. Locked away. His dad was being held somewhere in this house. *Dad*, Silas thought. *God, Dad.*

"Silas!" his uncle called after him, as if shouting his name would bind him where he stood. But Silas, beyond the grasp of stern words, was already mounting the stairs, two and three at a time. As he reached the upper gallery, the sound of pounding stopped, but he knew exactly where it must have come from. He bolted straight ahead, into the long gallery of the north wing and through the door of his uncle's room.

Silas pushed it open and entered the bedroom. It was hard to see because the large room was lit only by a small lamp on the bedside table. He slowed a bit as he walked across the floor, trying to let his eyes adjust, but most of the room was too dark to make out. Books and papers and empty plates covered the bed. He picked up a piece of a map. It was of Newfield Cemetery and had all the plots numbered. Some had names written on them in his uncle's neat, small handwriting. Uncle had been taking note of where certain people had been buried.

Another small lamp was on in the next room, outlining the doorway with thin vertical and horizontal lines of gold light. Silas opened the door and crossed the threshold. He could see that the workroom had changed somewhat since his last, brief visit. The room was still scattered with his uncle's photographic equipment, but now there were pieces of various projects at different stages, old volumes bookmarked with torn slips of paper, bits of wire for God knows what, several opened boxes of candy, most empty. The amber jewel jars of specimens preserved in golden liquid were still there, but many of the larger jars had been emptied of honey, their specimens now lying shriveled and pale at the bottom of their containers. The last time he saw the room, these things had been lined up neatly on the shelves, everything in its particular place. Now the contents of the room were scattered on the tables and floor, as though someone had been rummaging through them. Drawers were open. On the table where he had sat with Uncle weeks ago, the album of death portraits still lay open to the page of the dead woman's moon-white hand. Next to it now lay old newspaper articles and another map of Newfield Cemetery.

At the far end of the workroom was the locked door of the Camera Obscura. The heavy door was closed tightly like before, bolted with its bronze locks and several others that he could see had been recently added. Silas approached the door, and in the dim light, he could see that the surface of the door had been added to in other ways, scratched since he last looked at it. More of the geometric patterns and strange glyphs had been deeply incised into the door with a sharp tool.

There were footfalls back out on the main landing. Silas could hear his uncle coming off the stairs and moving along the upper gallery now, getting closer.

"Silas?" his uncle queried the second story of the house.

Quickly Silas put his ear to the locked door and listened hard. From somewhere deep in the room, he could just make out a kind of rasping sound. Breathing, or panting, deep in someone's throat. The guttural noise sounded hollow, far away from the door, and in Silas's mind, the dimensions of a large space beyond now began to form. He squatted down, trying to hear anything he could through the tiny slip of a gap under the door. He could see little puffs of dust blowing out from under the door, only to be sucked back under a second later, as if the very room itself was drawing in breath, quickly, expectantly. He thrust his hand into his pocket, opened the death watch, and pressed his thumb to the dial. But instead of looking, he closed his eyes and listened. A rising scream rose out of the boards of the floor, and within that scream was a chorus of noises that crashed into his hearing from some abyss of times long past: small bells ringing and the soft rasp of a rattle, children laughing and an infant crying swirled together into strains of blurry joys and sorrows both. There was yelling . . . one voice trying to control another . . . a fit being thrown . . . chains shaking against a wall and a man . . . his uncle . . . sobbing. Then a voice rose above the other sounds. It was deep and muffled, as if someone was speaking through a cloth held in their mouth. "Saaahhlaasss . . . ," the voice seemed to sob and choke. "Saaaaahhhhlllaaaaassssssss . . . ," and as the exhalation of the word fell away, the room took a sharp breath, and a hand like a vise closed on Silas's right shoulder. Another grabbed the back of his jacket and pulled him up onto his feet, turning him rapidly around. Silas's hand released the watch dial, and the rising cry fell away from him as he looked into his uncle's face. Uncle's skin was red as fire, and his chest heaved like a bellows. Silas could see that Uncle was furious, furious and scared both, but was trying to mask his anger if not his fear.

"What do you think you are doing?" he said, nearly vomiting the words into Silas's face.

Coldly, flatly, though no less shaken, Silas answered, "I think we both know this is not about what *I'm* doing. It's about what *you're* doing."

"Oh? Silas"—Uncle coughed, still catching his breath—"pray tell, just what am I doing? What is it you think I am doing?"

"There's no need to become hysterical." Silas relished seeing his uncle's usual crisp composure wrecked. "But you have done something horrible." Then, pausing between each word, he added, "We both know it. You have committed *unimaginable* acts." In a way, Silas was bluffing. His mind was still reeling from what he'd heard, trying to sort out what it meant, what it might mean. But he could see he had his uncle on the run and so kept on at him, unwilling to let him regain his composure, hoping agitation would lead to revelation.

"We both know you are hiding something, *keeping* something in this room. Keeping *him*!"

Uncle opened his mouth and tried to speak, but no words came. Jumping into the pause, Silas began to scream at him.

"You are a murderer! I am going to the police, and you are going to prison *for murder!*" The words flew out of him. Even as he spat them, he knew he had no evidence, only suspicion and intuition. He didn't actually know whether he was right or not, whether the room held anything more than hidden relics of his uncle's sick, lonely life, but his gut told him that Uncle knew something about his dad, and Silas wanted to hear him say so, or at least see if he could hear the lies working under his uncle's words. "Murderer. Murderer," Silas intoned slow as a spell. "You killed him, didn't you? You always wanted my mother for yourself, so you put my dad out of the picture, right? C'mon, let's go in there together, and you can show me what you're hiding." His bravery rose out of his wild anger, for if he'd stopped to think about it, it was more than likely that if the room did hold his father's corpse, Silas would almost certainly find his own death waiting there for him.

All the red ran out of Uncle's face and he stood there, skin white as the handkerchief in his pocket. He slowly took a breath, trying to compose himself. "Silas, this room belongs to my son. It was his room before he went away"—he coughed—"to school. Before that, it was my studio. It is now, again, my private work-room. The things in it are private. My *private* things. Things of interest only to me, and of course, a few things of my son's, which I know he would not want disturbed."

"You *smell* guilty, you know. Open the door. Just for one second. Open the door and let me see something that might convince me you're not a monster."

"Oh, Silas," Uncle said, breathing so shallowly now that Silas thought he might faint, "I don't think there is anything I could show you or tell you that would convince you I wasn't." Uncle ran his hands down the lapels of his jacket. "And I don't like this game. I will not rise to it. You have set your mind against me despite my only wanting the best for you and your mother."

"You know you want to show me, to be free of whatever you're hiding in there, murderer," Silas taunted him again, and then said, sarcastically, "Where's your humanity?"

"Oh," Uncle said quietly, almost to himself, "somewhere

neither you nor anyone, no, not even I, will ever find it." He was gazing at the floor absently, but then looked up and met Silas's stare with focus, as if he was remembering something. His hands began to tremble, but he continued with increasing calm. "Of course, Silas, if you think so little of me, perhaps you should leave. Leave this house now and don't return until you learn a little gratitude. At such a time, when you are ready to become a part of this family, come back. And then I will gladly give you the key to every room in the house." Uncle brushed the hair back out of his eyes. "But until such a time as you abandon these morbid fantasies and regain your composure and your respect, leave this house, Silas. Go!" This last word wiped the self-assured smugness from Silas's face.

At the word "go," the locked door shuddered and vibrated sharply and briefly on its sturdy hinges. The dust began flowing again back and forth, back and forth under the door, like the breathing of a frightened animal, and the pounding started again just beyond the door. Silas's eyes went wide. In the same moment his uncle's knees went out from under him and he fell to a kneeling position on the floor murmuring, "Squirrels . . . they get inside the walls." *Sure they do*, thought Silas in disbelief. *Someone's in that damn room.* He pulled frantically at the door handle, though he could feel that the locks were too strong for him. He brought both fists down hard on the wood, sending a hollow booming sound through the room on the other side. The pounding stopped. Silence.

"Dad?" Silas yelled, and again, "Dad?"

From the basement to the dome the whole house was still. The only sound Silas could hear was his uncle's soft crying.

Uncle coughed, then spat out, "Your father is not in this house." He said it with such directness, such matter-of-factness, that while the words held briefly on the air, Silas was almost convinced. But then, unable to release his suspicions, he bent down and snarled into his uncle's ear, "You are a monster. And. I. Don't. Believe. You."

Silas left his uncle's house without another word, walking past the entrance to the front parlor where his mother still sat, not moving, just staring into space. Part of him wanted to go to her, hug her, tell her he was sorry for everything that disappointed and hurt her, to take it all on himself and off of her. He wanted to carry her out the front door with him, just get her out of that house where everything bad was made worse. But he knew she wouldn't go. Silas knew she was there because some part of her wanted to be there, among the good furniture and the polished floors and the brother with money. So he walked out the door and slammed it behind him. He crossed the street and stood in the shadows of the trees. Back at Uncle's house, a light went on in a room in one of the upper attics. His uncle, he guessed, going back to work. What was up there? What was Uncle covering up now? Maybe not his dad, he thought as his mind cooled, but *something*.

And then downstairs, there was his mother, so close to whatever his uncle was keeping behind all those locks. Three times Silas started to turn to go home, but when he stopped himself the third time, he went back to Uncle's. He climbed the stairs of the empty porch, lit only by the dim light falling out from the parlor window. Before he knew what he was doing or why, he was moving quietly along the wall until he was standing in front of the parlor window. His pressed his right hand against the cold stone of the house and leaned toward the glass. His left hand was in his coat pocket and the watch was in his hand, his thumb raising and lowering the hinged jaw that covered the watch's dial. Looking in, he could see his mother hadn't left her chair, but her shoulders were shaking now and she was holding her face in her hands.

The light inside the house made the window into a mirror, and Silas had to look through his own face to see his mother. She sat inside his reflection, crying alone in an empty room. He didn't want to feel anything, looking at her, but it felt like there was a stone sitting at the bottom of his stomach. He could see his eyes, reflected in the glass, watching her, and couldn't decide which of the two of them he hated more; her for just sitting there, or himself for leaving her in that house. And then, wondering, he pressed his thumbs against the death watch's ticking hand, stopping the mechanism. He was still looking through the window, but now the light in the room seemed to slant, and figures began to form around his mother, shapes of faded lace and long gowns sewn from shadows, filling the room, leaning in toward her, all of them mimicking her racking sobs in silent pantomime. Most of the faces were blurred, as if streaked with water, rivulets of mourning that flowed in streams down their faces and over their forms. The figures closest to his mother were more distinct, and more familiar. An older woman in a mourning dress with his mother's features reminded Silas of a photo of his grandmother. And next to her, a woman with a similar face, though older, clearly distilled from the same lineage. Maybe many of these spirits were relatives, female relations from his mother's family stretching back who knew how far. Or perhaps these were the Umber women, still bound to the house where they spent their days and nights, quietly ignoring their husbands' strange business, attending only to their private daily griefs.

One of the figures closer to the window and the corner of

the room lacked hands, and the blurred and rounded ends of her arms raised to her face could not stop her tears.

In the middle of the crowd of spirits that wound about her, Silas saw his mother—as through a thin curtain—wipe the last tears from her eyes and begin to compose herself. As she did, the surrounding cloud of gray mourning women began to unweave itself from the room and fall away from her.

Silas could feel his heavy guilt becoming mixed with something else. Was it comfort? Were these women watching over his mother while she remained in this house? What strange and ancient ritual was he watching where, in grief, kin surrounded her, drawn to her by her tears? *Does mourning bring us closer to the dead?* Silas wondered. *It must be so*, he concluded, *that even when we can't see beyond our own grief, we come close to their prison houses.* Drawing his hands from his pockets and letting the clock continue ticking, Silas walked through the front door and went to his mother's side, filled with resolve.

"Let me take you out of here," he whispered.

His mother swept his hand absently from her shoulder.

"Mom, let me just take you for a walk outside somewhere. You can show me the part of town where you grew up. We can talk. Please."

She looked up with anger twisting her face into a snarl. "You keep out of those damn houses, Silas! You hear me? We left for a reason. Your damn father went in 'em, oh, I *know* that he did. Just to gall me. Well, you stay the hell out of them!"

"Mom," Silas said, trying to calm her, "it's okay. I know what's in—" But his words were interrupted by a slow, steady bell ringing over the town.

Raising her head slightly, her eyes still closed, Dolores said through her clenched teeth, "Passing Bell. That'll be for you."

And it shall come to pass that the soul
shalle leave behind its earthly habitations.
How long the soule shall remaine neer the
corpse varieth accordinge to the nature of
the deceased and whether or no the spirit be
bound in somewise to a vessel or to some
especial chambyre or place. Even so, if
it be not so bound, before the spirit goeth
forth upon the Road of Mystes, or Lyche
Waye, it may wander for a time among its
accustomed places and among those persons
who once were and remaineth its kin. If
then the soul riseth up and appeareth in
pleasinge form in the companye of others,
this shall be knowne as the Wake, or
Wakyne, and during that time, the spirit
may disclose very manie things, in speeche
or carefulle gesture, to the living. It shall be
accordinge to the Undertaker in what manner
the soul shalle be Waked, whether through
invitation or command, and whether or no

the Waters of Lethe shall be administered
to the ghost freely, or under compulsion, or
not at alle. In anywise, the Wake provideth
a moste rare moment wherein all earthly
matters of concerne to the spirit or its living
relatives may be rendered resolved and
brought to their moste rightfulle and peaceable
conclusion. Gaudeamus igitur.

—From *The Book of Cerements*

CHAPTER 46

PREPARATIONS

SILAS WALKED HOME SLOWLY from Temple Street. All across Lichport, coming up from the Narrows, the bell rang out its doleful song through the air: *Death, death, death comes . . .* The slow, deep sound was a stark contrast to his own racing thoughts. Silas could almost hear his name in the bell's ringing, calling him to a task he knew next to nothing about. His mother had called it a "Passing Bell." He knew what that was from the ledger, and he knew that what followed the Passing Bell was an important part of the Undertaker's work. But that was his father's job, not his. Yet with every ring, he could hear the town's wish, their unspoken expectation that no matter what had happened to Amos, Silas would step in to fill his father's shoes.

He arrived home and hesitantly walked up the steps of the porch. Mrs. Bowe was sitting in his study, brushing her long hair slowly in time with the bell. For the first time since Silas's arrival, she wore it down. He could see that Mrs. Bowe was lost in her thoughts, and that she was clearly waiting for him. Silas had begun to clear his throat to get her attention when suddenly, the bell stopped ringing.

"God bless the coming and going of all his children," said Mrs. Bowe very softly, looking up, becoming increasingly focused. "Now, we wait. Silas, will you take some tea, or a shot of something to calm you? You should have a little bite to eat, some cheese. I think I have some cold roast beef, shall I make you a sandwich? It will likely be a very long couple of nights." She was speaking as though the two of them had this conversation every day, and her calm was only making him more nervous.

"And you should get *The Book of Cerements*. You will, I believe, find it set into the back cover of the town's death ledger. You may not need it. Your father had a wonderful knack for ritual, and good words often came very naturally to him at such times as they were needed. Perhaps it will be the same with you, but you may feel better just having that text with you."

At his father's desk, Silas opened the Undertaker's ledger and found the small, thin book, more of a pamphlet, set into the thick boards of the inside back cover. It was about five inches high, with a worn, stiff vellum cover. Here was an old thing, perhaps sixteenth century, written, thankfully, in a bold hand in mostly capital Roman letters. Turning the pages carefully, he saw it was filled with prayers and exhortations, words for waking for the dead, prayers of calling and invitation. Words of passage and parting. Like the little book itself, the words were stiff and very old. Some lines were in Latin, and Silas couldn't really imagine his father standing up and reading them, but he could see that there were necessities behind such formulas and phrases, despite their antiquated formality. Here were words that could call the dead back into the company of their kin, and words that blessed the ghost and directed it to depart peaceably. And there were more forceful words—injunctions, banishings, and bindings—should the ghost choose to linger. Beneath the florid, ceremonial language, deals were being struck between the living and dead. *You shall go, but we shall remember you.* These were consensual arrangements. Bargains. From these, Silas began to understand that the Undertaker's job was part therapist, part lawyer, part travel agent, and perhaps, if things went badly, part deportation officer.

He was sure he'd been reading at the book for only a few moments, but when he looked up, there was a tray on the table behind him laden with food, and he heard Mrs. Bowe saying, as she passed back into her house, "I need to get ready. You should find your father's mourning coat in the closet by the door. I've taken it in a bit for you, forgive my presumption. And please, be ready to go at a moment's notice, all right, dear?"

The mourning coat smelled strongly of tobacco and stale beer, not smells he associated with his father. He put it on, pulling his arms slowly through the sleeves, and then waited for whatever was coming next.

Three hours later, as the sun set, there was a knock, first on Mrs. Bowe's front door, then on Silas's. When Silas opened the door, a boy—from one of the Narrows families, Silas recalled—was standing a few steps back dressed in black clothes, a long coat that trailed on the ground behind him, a tattered scarf wound around his neck, and a vest stitched together out of pieces of dark mismatched tapestry. In one hand he held a burning torch, and with the other, he held a letter out to Silas. He pulled his hand back quickly as though he didn't want to touch Silas's hand.

"Thank you," Silas said gravely, while pulling his dad's long coat back up into place on his shoulders. It was still slightly too big on him.

The child said nothing, but gestured at his mouth and shook his head from side to side, indicating that he would not, or could not, speak. He only bowed a little to Silas and then turned to go, walking quickly away down Main Street, carrying cards to other houses in town. Silas watched the boy's torch as it bobbed down the street, getting smaller and smaller, finally turning the corner down Coach Street and vanishing in the gloaming.

The funeral announcement was printed on thick paper and had been made on an old printing press. In bold, ornate letters it announced the passing of John Peale, Mother Peale's husband. At the bottom, in a thin, uneven hand, Mother Peale had written, "Silas, come to us in the accustomed manner. Be welcome as kin in our home. We ask you, Silas Umber, Undertaker and Janus of the Threshold, to watch over us at this time of passage."

A small part of Silas flinched as he read, recoiling slightly at the assumption that he would do his father's job. He would go, because it was the Peales who were asking, but this was by no means a formal acceptance of any permanent position as Undertaker. Yet some secret sleeping part of him began to rouse itself, and despite everyone's assumptions, despite his fear of their expectations, he was excited. He thrust the invitation into the coat's front pocket; there he found a black cravat, which he drew out and wrapped around his throat.

Since the Passing Bell had ceased ringing, a change had come over Mrs. Bowe. Her usually meticulously styled hair, which she wore wound up every day in a tight bun on top of her head, was now brushed out and hung down in long tendrils, spilling over her shoulders, flowing down her back and covering part of her face. There was a restless look about her, especially in her eyes, which seemed small, retreating far back into their sockets. It was as though she was grieving already, seeing the world through a veil, or rather, as though a veil had been drawn aside and she was looking into a place no one else could see.

"I didn't know you were that close with the Peales," Silas said, assuming the changes in Mrs. Bowe's appearance were the trappings of her grief at the death of a friend.

In a low voice, Mrs. Bowe replied, "My appearance has nothing at all to do with my affection for the family. This is a professional visit." She had told Silas a while back that by tradition she had an important role to play at funerals, but she had never elaborated. Silas guessed that it must have something to do with his work. Maybe she'd helped his father prepare in just this way, making sure he had everything he needed, making sure he'd eaten.

Every move Mrs. Bowe now made was deliberate and precise, graceful and fluid—the way she swung her coat about her, a long black robe, much tattered at the hems. She no longer seemed nervous or worried as she often was, and she moved quickly about the house, gathering more things, Silas assumed, for him to take along.

He asked Mrs. Bowe repeatedly if there was anything else he needed to do. *What will be expected of me? How will I know what to say? Where will we go first? How long will I be there?* On and on his questions went until, impatient and stern, Mrs. Bowe turned to him, her face flushed with annoyance.

"Enough. You are as ready as need be. Now, you should begin to think about *them*, not yourself, do you understand? You are an intermediary and have a job to do, but it's the deceased who matters, and his family. Not you. You must keep them and their needs foremost in your mind. This is crucial. Not just for their comfort, but for your safety and the safety of all those attending. Even the kindest person may become confused in the moments following their death, and in the dead, confusion is dangerous. Not to mention, when someone passes from one world to another, the mist rises, a door opens; and so, you must be watchful and aware of everything that is happening around you, for you are the Watcher at the Threshold."

"What does that mean?"

"You will see soon enough. It is something better experienced than explained. Don't worry yourself overmuch. I do not antici-pate any trouble at all tonight, considering the family, but you must be vigilant and focused and ready to act if something goes awry. Watch and listen. You are more than what you think you know. This business moves in your blood. Listen. The world you'll be in tonight is full of spectacle, but you will find, I think, that it is through hearing and not sight that you will perceive the deeper mysteries. Times of passage are far more attuned to the other senses—hearing, smell, touch—for they are more keenly tied to the memory than sight. When we arrive in the world and when we depart it, remember, our eyes are closed."

"What am I listening *for* exactly?"

"No one thing in particular. I am trying to say that the dead manifest and express themselves in more ways than can be merely observed. You must be open to all your senses—but so long as you insist on being centered in your own losses, you may find that difficult."

On one level, Silas knew what she said was true. He had him-self heard and felt the dead in other ways. More and more, even when he wasn't using the death watch, he could feel them around him—a brush on his skin, a word out of time on the air. If he were more focused on such things, and less on what he was looking for, what else might he perceive? Could *looking* for his father actu-ally be hindering him? Could his father be, in some way, standing unseen, behind him even now?

But Mrs. Bowe's tone hurt him. She was a different person suddenly, like she could read his mind and feel the particular nature of his selfish thoughts. It was an invasion. Silas could hear in her voice that when she looked at him, she saw only a child who saw himself at the center of the world, and because that was close to the truth, it burned him a little. Since arriving in Lichport, maybe he had been only considering what was happening to him, how everything felt to him. But what did she expect? He'd lost his dad. Surely she understood how painful that was. Of course she knew. She had been so kind. It was just today, the way she was speaking. Harsher, more direct, like she'd forgotten everything that had happened to him.

But not wanting to argue, and trying to impress her with his maturity, Silas only nodded in agreement at Mrs. Bowe's words, although he could not pretend to understand everything she said to him. He'd remain quiet and try to summon a professional posture. Rise to the occasion. Play the man. He straightened both his back and the knot of his cravat, trying to convince her and himself that he was up to the task. He took *The Book of Cerements* and looked at it again, trying desperately to refocus. On the inside of the back cover, he could make out notes in his father's handwriting, lines of verse and some prose. These were snatches of songs and lines of stories Amos had liked, the kinds of things that might, when read, bring comfort to others. "Bring me my scallop shell of quiet, my staff of faith to walk upon . . . ," one began, and Silas read those particular lines until he memorized them and found, through concentration, some of his fear and anxiety dissolving.

Mrs. Bowe returned. She brought a small leather satchel out of one of the drawers of Amos's desk. She opened it and drew out a vial of crystal half-full of clear liquid, tightly sealed with a deeply engraved silver cap.

"Spill none of this, and don't drink from it. Not ever. Even if you should be dying of thirst. Mother of God, never. This is the drink of oblivion, and it must be offered to the dead, though not all will partake of it. That is their own choice. Long ago, the Undertaker would sit in judgment over the soul of the dead and administer the waters of Lethe according to what they saw. Your father did not hold with that practice and always left the matter up to the deceased, if it was possible to do so."

Mrs. Bowe checked once more to be sure they had everything they'd need, then told Silas matter-of-factly, "We will leave for the Peales's directly." She returned the vial to the satchel and handed the leather bag to Silas, then smoothed his uneven lapels. "It will have to do. Let's make our way."

Silas was surprised by her words. He assumed her role was related to helping him prepare for the wake. He did not think she'd be leaving her house.

Mrs. Bowe seemed to guess his thoughts. "I am sure I told you that I might venture forth for a funeral."

"Oh, so you'll be coming to help me? That's great."

"It's all about you, eh? Again? Silas, as much as I am pleased to walk with you, I am not your guest today. Every funeral must have its Scald Crow." She pulled a large black shawl of homespun wool over her shoulders and drew over it an enormous veil of thin, black, translucent silk. "You will recall my words about the importance of sound at times of transition?"

Silas nodded.

"Well, we both have our jobs to do today, and without me, there can be no funeral. I am the Wailing Woman."

A Report upon the Judgment from
the Synod of 1621 and a report of the
response of many ungodly folk upon its
Implementation:

And the Synod of this yeere adopteth
those regulations laid down by the
Archbishops and Bishops and so
announced that no priest shall attend a
wake or funeral at which female keeners
or wailers cry, scream, disrupt, annoy, and
distract the heart and minds of mourners
from the bosom of their Mother Church.
Any priest or man of Orders who
neglecteth to endeavor to end such
unseemly behavior would be removed
from his parish. And when the word of
the Synod was spread among the people
and when the priests refused to attend
upon such unseemly rites and likewise
refused to attend upon such houses to
deliver Last Rites if wailing was also to
occur in them, then did many ungodly
folk quit this land and take to the sea to

finde some other land lesse Godly and
more accustomed to savageries suche as
these Wailing Women and Peller-Men,
or Undertakers as they are somtyme
called, do contrive to practice.

CHAPTER 47

WAKE

AS SILAS AND MRS. BOWE SILENTLY LEFT the house and walked toward the Narrows, Silas was thinking about the Passing Bell. A few weeks earlier, Mother Peale had pointed it out to him when he'd asked about the odd old chapel built of slate where it hung.

"This building?" Mother Peale answered. "This is our own place, not church, but chapel, and upper-town folk almost never come here. Even when their own church closed its doors, they didn't deign to come down this close to the sea. It's old, Silas, very old, and in its tower is a bell much older than the old church, much older than the town. Oh, yes!" said Mother Peale knowingly. "It's an old thing, all right. Brought here from over the sea, but even then it was old. I can't tell you how old it is, but I can tell you that it was an Umber that brought it here to Lichport. Clever, that Umber was, for those first years were bad ones, and many a soul had to be chimed out of town. It is a soul bell, for it rings out at the passing of a life, rings the soul out of this world and into the next one. That sound, the sound of a bell at death, it's older than any church, that I can tell you. The soul passes and the bell-song rings up to accompany it. Anyway, there are few folks who call for the bell to be rung nowadays, but we Narrows folk keep it, and ring it for them that ask. Many times your father pulled the bell rope, Silas. Will you rise to the occasion, should you be called? Like your father would have, if he were here?"

The bell was silent as Mrs. Bowe and Silas passed the chapel, for death had come and settled in and didn't like to be too much disturbed.

They approached the Peale house, and Silas could hear the wind groaning up from the harbor. Suddenly thoughts of that terrible ship coming to anchor there rekindled his fears, but then the front door of the Peale house was thrown open for them by one of the men of the Narrows, and Silas drew his mind back to what might be waiting for him inside. Though he had met this man before, perhaps on that first night he'd come to the Peale house, the man looked down as Silas and Mrs. Bowe approached, unwilling to meet their eyes.

The corpse of Mr. Peale was wrapped in linen, and a bowl of salt sat atop his chest. Set into the salt, a small beeswax candle burned brightly. Mr. Peale's face was clearly visible, and more peaceful than the last time Silas had seen him. The corpse was lying on a wooden table and below it, flowers stood in numerous vases, their perfume filling the room along with the smell of wax from the many candles on the side tables. The whole room stood in anticipation, waiting for Silas to take his place.

"Stand at the head," Mrs. Bowe whispered to Silas, and went with him.

Despite all the candles, the light in the room seemed dim. All the mirrors had been covered, and black drapes had been put across all the windows, though every window in the house was open.

As Silas stood over the corpse, he could think of nothing but his own father. He knew he should keep his mind on Mr. Peale and his family, but every time he looked at the body stretched out and pale, he saw his dad's face on it, and everything but his own fears flew from his mind. And being close to the harbor added another fear to the others. Out there was the mist ship, waiting. But for whom, he could only guess.

Mrs. Bowe sensed his distraction and grabbed the back of his arm. Her hand was like a vise. "Enough!" she hissed at him. "You are not here for yourself! When you are home you can return to hovering over your own losses, but now turn your mind back to what is before you. Hold the name of the dead in your mind, and do what must be done!"

In the corner of the room stood a man, shifting from foot to foot anxiously. Silas had seen him several times, but always at the edge of his vision—leaning against the wall of a crumbling cottage in the Narrows, or wandering back and forth in front of the Fretful Porpentine Tavern, looking for a handout. "George Bowditch," Mrs. Bowe whispered in Silas's ear, "Sin Eater." George looked at Silas, waiting. At a nudge from Mrs. Bowe, Silas nodded for him to approach the corpse. Someone handed George a loaf of bread, and he passed it over Mr. Peale's body. Over and back, over and back. He was then handed a bowl of beer, and from Mother Peale, a coin. Then, hanging his head, he walked slowly back across the room, his back bent as though he was carrying a great burden. He went out into the street, and as he walked, he ate and drank and made his way home, his stomach filling with the losses and regrets of another man.

Mrs. Bowe looked at Silas expectantly. He knew from *The Book of Cerements* that it was time to call the ghost, to wake the dead. Nervous he'd say something wrong, fearful of what was coming next, and sweating terribly in the warm closeness of the room, Silas bent down to the corpse and whispered into its ear. He could not remember the elaborate Latin formula from the book, and though he held the book tightly in his hand, he didn't want to read something he didn't understand. Instead he spoke plainly and said very quietly into Mr. Peale's pale ear the words that rose up from his mind and heart:

"Mr. Peale, sir? Your kin are all about you. Rouse yourself once more and waken. It is Silas Umber, your friend, who calls you. Fear nothing and come again into the company of your family and friends. You stand at the threshold, and love is before you and behind you. Be with us once more before you take to your road, if that is your wish."

The light in the room began to alter, not brighten or dim, but become more intense, and every object stood in stark contrast against another. Silas looked up, and the ghost of Mr. Peale was rising to stand beside his corpse. A shadow was falling across the body even as the ghost became brighter and more discernible. It was clearly Mr. Peale who stood before Silas, but much altered from the man Silas had known only at the end of his life. The vision of the ghost was charged with vigor. The air around the ghost and throughout the room was warming, and below the kindly aged face, a younger Mr. Peale flushed, rose through the wrinkles, as if all the years of his life were now present within the ghost's handsome transparency. The ghost stood up straight in front of all his family and friends, and seemed to become more solid. In the lines of his body—his straight, proud jaw, his strong arms, his work-hardened hands, the orbs of his eyes, which shone with youth and wisdom both—an entire life could be read.

As if on cue, the members of the Peale family stepped forward toward the ghost. Each gave a brief oration, words filled with love and respect for a father, a husband, a friend. Mother Peale gave no words, but she looked long at her husband's face and he was smiling, and it was enough. She nodded to him and stepped away into the arms of her daughter Joan.

In the presence of his family, the ghost grew brighter until his light filled the room. Then he stepped away from his corpse and wandered forth among the guests, here and there stopping to speak to some particular person, words of parting and affection heard only by the person the ghost was addressing. The ghost made a circuit of the room and then came back to stand in front of his corpse. He looked at Silas, and began to speak, and at once Silas heard such a difference in his voice from the last time he'd chatted with Mr. Peale at the store; it was as if the body's weight and age and sickness had somehow pressed down on the vocal cords. But now, as the ghost spoke to him, it sounded like music, light and moving easily on the air and in his head and heart, the sound of strings and flutes.

"I know you would like to ask me something, Silas Umber. Go on, son."

"It wouldn't be right. This is your time to speak and be with your family."

Then, even more softly and with such care Silas thought his heart would break at hearing the ghost's words, Mr. Peale said, "You want to ask if your father is dead. And I feel you are fretful too about that ship out there that is even now coming into harbor. Perhaps, son, you fear these two things are somehow joined?"

Silas nodded.

"I am sorry, Silas. I don't know who it's come for. But I can tell you this, anyone with a son who loves him as much as you love your dad has no place on a ship like that one out there. About Amos, I fear I can be of little help, though I know in my gut that your father is in some trouble. His was a hard life and no mistake, pulled as he was between this and that. But wherever he is, I know that if anyone can find him and help him, it will be you, son."

Silas began to cry but quickly wiped his face with his sleeve. He nodded at the ghost in wordless thanks. Pulling his coat back into place on his shoulders, he said, "Mr. Peale, I must ask, will you take the water I carry with me?"

"Silas, if it's all the same to you, I think I'll go my own way and keep my wits about me."

Again, Silas nodded.

The ghost looked once more upon his wife, and then at Silas, and finally at Mrs. Bowe, who instantly opened her mouth and began a cry that clutched at the heart of everyone in the room. As the mourners listened to the wail, it became a song, and the words rose slowly on the air, and the ghost grew brighter and brighter with each word until some of the people in the room cast down their eyes. And between the lines of the dirge, her wordless wail would come again and again, . . .

No more, no more, John Peale
Shall sit before our eyes
No more, no more, John Peale
Now is the hour of our good-byes.

No more, no more, John Peale
The wind is on the sea
No more, no more, John Peale
Let the peace upon you be.

No more, no more, John Peale
shall walk the Narrows turning;
No more, no more, no more
Our John is gone, no more returning.

Other voices, some quiet, some loud, joined in with verses of their own, all testaments to the life of a man who had lived well and was well loved. As Silas heard those good words, he prayed that he might live a life worthy of such memorials. He couldn't help but wonder what people might say at his funeral, or at his father's, should it come to pass. He thought that heaven might be no further afield than the hearts of those people who remember us with love. This was what he would strive for. To be remembered well. *In the hearts of others is where we should strive to make our afterlives*, he thought.

Then the company broke apart, people moving quickly and getting food for the tables, bringing barrels of good beer and casks of liquor from where they waited beside the door. Some began singing more riotous songs. By the hearth, some of the men took out dice and began playing, and before Silas knew what was happening, the wake proper was underway.

Although the wake revels went on for two nights and two days—glasses lifted again and again—after a short while, Silas couldn't tell how much time had passed. In one corner of the room, Mrs. Bowe perched on a chair, waiting, speaking to no one. People were sleeping on floors and tables, rising only to begin drinking or carousing again. Occasionally, some portion of the room would brighten, and Silas could see Mr. Peale's ghost smiling over a small crowd of people before fading again into the blur of revelry.

When the appointed hour came, again Mrs. Bowe stood forth.

She stood up from her chair. Men went outside and a few moments later returned with a casket. They put the corpse within it and then stood at the ready around the coffin.

Once again, Mrs. Bowe began wailing and crying. The sound was nearly deafening. Mother Peale drew her hair over her face, stepped in next to Mrs. Bowe, and began wailing too, her mouth wide and the cry coming up from the bottom of her soul. The other women in the room wailed as well. All their voices wound together, and as their conjoined cry went up, everything began vibrating—through all the walls and beams of the house—and the very fabric of the air began to shudder and hum.

Silas closed his eyes. He did not know how much time had passed since the wailing began, for indeed so long as that sound filled the room, time seemed entirely absent. The wail was like nothing else Silas had ever heard, like listening to the first cry of the world at its birth and the turning back of the great darkness. Beginning and ending, all at once. It was the first shrill cry of the babe and the last high-pitched gasp of the dying in one note.

Then the wail subsided in the throats of all the women, and by the door, a boy—the child who'd delivered the funeral announcements—began to play the hornpipe.

Suddenly Mother Peale began to move, shuffling her feet to that queer and ancient tune. She made a dance about her husband's body, jumping after tracing certain of the elder steps, crying, or laughing, tears aplenty. And dancing still, she spoke:

"You came into the world with joy, my love, and I'll send you out the same way." And then she threw her head back and near shrieked with laughter, her knees almost hitting her chin as she leapt about her husband's body, and dancing still, she led the company from the house as the men lifted the coffin from the table. They paused before the door, waiting for Silas to first pass over the threshold before bringing the coffin out into the street to begin the procession to the graveyard on the Beacon, their high burial hill that daily cast its shadow over the Narrows.

Mrs. Bowe followed Silas, wailing again, her veil billowing out in front of her as if smoke was pouring from her mouth into the evening air. Outside, the company was joined by many more of the Narrows folk and other mourners, all in black, long veils, long coats. Many of the mourners carried candles, and the boy with the hornpipe was joined by a group of four mutes—perhaps the family Mrs. Bowe had mentioned to Silas long ago. The four pulled their faces down into contorted masks of sorrow, their eyes flowing with tears, mouthing silent cries.

The procession, with moans and shrieks and every expression of mourning, wound its way up the Beacon. At they approached the grave, Silas saw many of the oldest women of Lichport already there, waiting, perched on the gravestones in some ancient ritual, their veils trailing down onto the upturned soil, their hands dark with earth, torches burning beside them. The pallbearers looked at Silas, who nodded (for it seemed everyone knew very well exactly what was supposed to happen), and without another word, they lowered the coffin into the hungry ground.

The company stood silently about the grave, and all eyes were suddenly on Silas. He reached down and picked up a handful of earth. He held it in his hand for a moment, and then, leaning over, let it fall into the grave on top of the coffin. All the members of Mr. Peale's family did the same, and then everyone in the procession pressed forward, casting handfuls of earth, circling the plot, one after another, until the grave was nearly full. Then suddenly and without warning Silas straightened his back, opened his mouth, and began to sing:

> Give me my scallop shell of quiet,
> My staff of faith to walk upon.
> My scrip of joy, immortal diet,
> My bottle of salvation
> My gown of glory
> Hope's true gauge
> And thus I'll take my pilgrimage.

As he ended his song, the company looked up and spoke again the name of the dead. "John Peale," they cried as one. And in that moment, as they heard their joined voices, as they gazed on the ever-living stars, the darkness in their hearts fell away from them. They knew they would always be together, as neighbors and kin, in this world, and the worlds that followed.

Wind stirred the trees as the mourners began to fall away from the hill toward their homes. Mother Peale came up to Silas and clutched him to her breast, hugging him so hard it pressed the breath right out of him. Then Mrs. Bowe drew back her veil. Silas could see she was exhausted and, taking her hand in his, led her from the Beacon.

The final portion of the funeral proceeded, as was customary, unseen by the living.

Mr. Peale followed at the end of the line of mourners and watched his burial from a distance. Then, for a time, he wandered about the town, making a pilgrim's road of his living memories. At one house in the Narrows, he looked in to see friends sitting about the table, still in their black mourning weeds. Come morning, he was looking out toward the sea from the top of the Beacon. Dark again, he stood by the bedsides of his sleeping children and grand-children, placing his now insubstantial hand, soft as a breath, on their cheeks.

The next midnight found him standing by the spent fire of his own hearth, and there, by the door, was his little girl lost so long ago, waiting for him. His family was asleep upstairs and in their various houses, and he was now eager to be on his way. His little girl waited to walk him to the street outside, where already the mist was rising. She would not go with him, Mr. Peale under-stood—she was waiting for her mama. He walked toward the door, and his child opened it for him. Beyond the door, it was morning again, and in its light, he could see the path that would lead him away, out of Lichport. As Mr. Peale walked down that road, he took his time, thinking he might just take in a few more sights before calling it a day.

THE ADVENTUROUS TRAVELER will find that once proud Lichport is no longer a town you may travel through. You may only go to it or leave from it (which has long been the more usual). In 1924 the Salt Marsh Bridge, part of an ancient highway connecting many of the coastal ports with the north and west, collapsed, killing six people. Six people who, if such accounts are to be believed, still haunt the site of the collapse. Then, in 1931, a large wedge of the cliff above the highway came crashing down, perhaps due to erosion, and destroyed a great portion of the road, tumbling all down into the sea. No plans to restore either the bridge or that fallen portion of the highway were ever even discussed. By that time, most sensible folk considered the town beyond saving. Its shipping has all but collapsed, most of the shops that might appeal to outsiders have long been closed, and if the bereaved or the memorially inclined wish to visit their dead in one of Lichport's numerous cemeteries, well, they shall need to make a pilgrim's progress of it, coming around the long way on the inland road. In and out, both on the same path: long, featureless road running next to the wide, quiet marshes. On that byway, you'll have plenty of time to think about your deeply planted kin and how long it has been since the last time you visited them—the time when you left those cheap silk flowers on their grave. Don't worry. They'll still be there, right where you left them.

—torn from *Gormlette's Guide to Fallen Places*, 2nd edition, 1943

ONE WEEK TO THE DAY AFTER THE FUNERAL of John Peale, Silas was sitting on the porch, reading in the sun, when he saw his uncle coming down the street. Although the sight brought him no pleasure, it didn't surprise him either. Since his last visit to the house on Temple Street, Silas knew it would only be a matter of time before Uncle came calling.

Uncle kept looking over his shoulder and occasionally ducked his head nervously this way or that, as if birds were swooping down on him. How small he looked in the sunshine. Pale, frightened, and exposed. And yet, seeing him like this only worried Silas more: Weak or frightened animals are the most dangerous, the most likely to bite even those who might help them.

As Uncle approached the house, Silas came down to the sidewalk to meet him, determined that his uncle should not even get so far as the porch.

"What excellent timing," Silas lied. "I was just about to stretch my legs. Shall we walk together, Uncle?"

Uncle looked tired from his short walk from home. "Of course, of course," he said, and added, "I am in a bit of a hurry, errands and such. Perhaps we might just stand here for a moment and I'll give you my news?"

"Of course, of course," mimicked Silas, smiling. "Let me guess, you've found my father?"

"No. Silas, I'll be brief. Your mother has agreed to become my wife, mother of my house and all its bachelorish delinquencies."

Silas wasn't amused anymore. He couldn't speak.

"Truly, Silas, every house is like a child, and it needs steady hands to maintain and care for it through the years. The good hands of a mother and father. I have done my best to manage my house, but it needs, I think, a woman's hands to make it a real home."

"And your other wife? She couldn't provide that?"

"Silas, a man makes many mistakes in life. It has taken a long time, much work and painful reflection, but I believe my youthful errors and little sins have been paid for. Forward lies the kingdom of peace. Now that your mother has accepted my offer, I would like your blessing in this, and hope that you may return to help build a life with us."

Uncle's words struck him like a blow. Dizzy from the news, Silas's mind began to throw up scenes from his past, but now his father's face had been cut out and there was Uncle's instead . . . leering down at him in his crib, feeding him from a spoon, clapping in the audience of his fourth-grade accordion recital. The thought of Uncle taking his father's place sickened him. Holding his mother's hand. God. And Uncle's previous wife . . . where was she? Fear and nausea tumbled about his stomach like a ball of snakes. Silas didn't want his uncle to know anything about him anymore. He wanted their worlds to pull apart and never rejoin. There was no way he was telling Uncle anything about his plans to remain in Lichport, to live in his father's house, to continue his father's work. So instead he swallowed hard and said only, "My blessing? Of course. I would like to speak with my mother first, but then I will be so happy to discuss plans with the two of you. You know, though, I am thinking about just moving on, maybe going back to Saltsbridge."

Silas saw the disbelief in Uncle's face, but also the absolute sincerity of his intention. His uncle wanted to marry his mother, and he wanted to know where Silas was. Uncle didn't want Silas getting too far away from "the family."

"Well, certainly, this must be as you wish, but may I tell you something, as your friend? Going back—wherever "back" may be—is seldom a good idea. You can never go back, really, there is only forward. So it must be with you. Your former house in Saltsbridge is gone. Sold to another. All their belongings now fill the rooms where your life once sprawled from wall to wall. Many wise men think to escape their troubles in retreat. Let me assure you, there is no peace to be had in it."

"So wait, you're saying I shouldn't move back into your house?"

"Silas, you are too quick for me. Let me leave you to your thoughts. Come to us soon and we'll conspire."

Uncle began skulking back down the street, but then turned and added with a wan smile, "Your mother misses you, son."

Silas thought of yelling back, *Yes, I'll just bet she does!* but his heart was no longer in sarcasm. Every day he waited for something to happen, for some word of his father to come. He was losing more ground than he was gaining. Waiting and more waiting. He spent his days learning what he could from the ledger and from the things his dad had left behind, but still there had been little progress. And behind the larger worry of his father hung the tapestry of his fears for his mother. It was clearly her intention to stay in that house with Uncle, and Uncle wanted her there. Their seemingly mutual arrangement worried Silas to the bone. He sensed Uncle's interest in his mother had more to do with him than with her. The sight of his mother, sitting in that chair in the parlor, weeping with her face in her hands, haunted Silas now. But he couldn't get her out of that house if she didn't want to leave. If only he could find a way to show her a side of Uncle that would change her high opinion of him.

He needed perspective, the long view, if he was going to find his dad and prevent his mother from doing something stupid and quite possibly dangerous. Silas could see his road must take him back to Uncle's, but not yet. There was another house that needed revisiting first.

He knew with certainty that Uncle was wrong about "going back." To get ahead, sometimes you had to retrace your steps. But suddenly a thought came to him that turned his blood cold: If Uncle planned to marry his mother, Uncle must assume—or worse, *know*—that his dad wasn't coming back. Silas felt his throat go tight, and in his head a chorus of three familiar voices sang out—

Our work goes apace . . . Return, return, return . . .

LEDGER

Plain or straight overcast: This is also worked
from left to right over a single-run thread; to give
the stitch more relief, a round twisted thread
may be laid upon the traced line and covered
with vertical stitches set out close together. . . .

—From a page glued into the ledger taken from
The Encyclopedia of Needlework
by Thérèse de Dillmont, 1884

CHAPTER 49

TANGLED THREADS

Silas entered the high-ceilinged room in the mansion, where the tapestry of misthomes hung, and saw the three women engaged in their work.

They did not turn to welcome him.

Silas was scared of the three women. Not because they were ghosts, but because they were something more than ghosts—old things that continued to weave themselves into the world for reasons he could not yet fathom.

He was hoping for a little perspective. He wanted to look again on their strange tapestry. Maybe, since his last visit, new stitches or scenes had been added. Maybe he'd find a thread that would lead out of the maze his life had become.

The floor was covered in bits of ragged fabrics and broken threads, little heaps of them covering the timeworn wooden planks. There had been many alterations since his last visit. Changes had been made to the map of the lands of the dead. Certain portions had been reworked in brighter or darker threads, perhaps meaning they were becoming more or less present in the world outside. Silas was just beginning to see how truly complex the work of the three women was. Perhaps shade and tone were related to relevance, to whether or not a spirit's limbo was connected in some way with living people. Perhaps the size of the stitching had to do with the number of spirits that occupied it at a given time. This would account for why certain buildings, the oldest, seemed to be overcast in numerous layers of threads.

The tapestry was in a state of flux, shifting as the world outside changed, or as the relationships between the living and dead grew or were forgotten. At many places on the great work, Silas could see whole sections had been picked apart, or enlarged, or reworked with a new color scheme. This was why he'd come back: to see what might have altered. To see the town with new eyes. He hoped beyond hope that something in him or the town or both might have altered sufficiently for him to be able to find an image connected with his father's disappearance. Silas scanned the tapestry frantically as if he expected to see his father's portrait rendered in little stitches on one of the familiar thread-paths. Even as the question formed in his mind, the first of the three walked up to a portion of the work hanging between two beams that supported the roof of the room and, without warning, ripped the stitches from a scene depicting some tall houses high above the meticulous knotwork that had been sewn to represent the Narrows.

"This is sloppy work," said the first of the three. "This will all have to be redone."

She pulled out the broken threads, leaving a bare patch in the tapestry.

"Perhaps not," replied the second. A moment later she began working in the hole with a piece of blood-red linen, roughly binding it down with black cotton thread. "This will hold until we know more. I am hoping to rework the whole scene in gold."

"Too early for gold," said the third with a sigh. "Far too early for gold."

Silas wondered if this was all part of the day's work, a correction. Or were they hiding something from him?

After a few moments, the three ladies all turned to Silas, as if they'd been waiting for him. They said nothing, but gestured invitationally toward the web.

Turning his head to look more carefully about the room, he saw many familiar sites: the marshes had been extended, seemed wider now, and he wondered if this was because he had gone there. At the far end of the weaving, flowers had been sewn in complicated knots all about the houses on Fort Street. Near the marsh, the millpond had been reworked many times in deepening shades of gray-blue silks, the ripples of the water now held fast by tiny stars of white stitches, like ice crystals. Where once he'd seen trees at the edge of the pond, he now saw seven dark human figures looming around the lip of the water. A little stream of footsteps led from the pond toward the town, and this was new too. In front of his house, a small pool of standing water had been embroidered in brown and green silk, and there was another near the Umber cemetery. Looking closely, Silas imagined he could see his own reflection had been delicately worked in.

"Lose something?" the three asked at once.

It unsettled Silas when the three spoke together. It made whatever they were saying feel more like a portent than a comment.

"You know I have—"

"You have been giving some things a lot of attention. We should give you a pair of your own knitting needles! Invite you to join our Sewing Circle!"

"Are these additions about my father?"

"Is that the only person you've lost?" One of the ladies laughed knowingly.

Silas felt embarrassed. He should be keeping his focus on his dad and his dad's work. But the tapestry brought his memories and fears to the front of his mind. Bea had run away, and he had no idea where she was or if he'd see her again. Silas told himself this was for the best as the memories flooded back. He'd nearly died that night, following her into the water. He did not want to go back there. But still, deep in his heart, he knew she was waiting for him.

After looking at the figures in the tapestry for many moments, Silas asked, "What happened there, at the millpond?"

"He doesn't want to know," one said.

"I do. Why don't I?"

"Leave it where it is," said another. "The binding stitches there will not hold long anyway."

"Leave it *be*," said another, and the three laughed at the pun.

"Most are happiest knowing what they know and no more. Besides, love flourishes best in ignorance . . . or in absence."

"I understand that I am amusing you. You're bored here, all by yourselves, and my losses are a source of amusement. That's fine, but don't expect me to laugh along with you. None of this is a game to me," Silas asserted. "I'm asking you to help. Either you will or you won't. Besides," he said, gesturing at the room, "this is all part of my work now, and if someplace in town is not restful, then I *should* know about it. Even if you don't think it concerns me. Keep your secrets if you want to. I'll find out anyway. But then, maybe I won't visit you again, and you three can just sit here listening to the sounds of your own voices and the click of your needles as your spools wind down. I don't expect you have any other visitors, do you?"

"Oh! He's his father's boy and no mistake!" said the second of the three.

"And threats now!" said the first of the three, one side of her face gone black in shadow.

"It's not a threat," Silas said more kindly, hearing a sharpness in their tone that made him uncomfortable. "Neighbors talk with one another, share news. If you don't want to talk with me, then I guess there's no reason for me to come here."

The three ladies drew back into darker corners of the room, working as they spoke. The stitches began to knot and weave as though by themselves, enlivening scenes that came to life as Silas tried to pierce the shadows with his gaze. Behind the weavings, unseen, he heard the voices of the three, still speaking.

"Why did your father leave this town?" asked the first of the three.

"Because my mother couldn't bear her familial obligations any longer," Silas said.

"That answer is astute, but not complete."

"And maybe something was worrying my father, after I was born. That's what I heard."

"Yes. And when that something turned her pale eyes from him to you, he wisely took you elsewhere. Not that she would come for you as a child. Children are of no interest to her. But it is in her nature to be patient. And she has been waiting. Now you have returned—grown so fine and handsome—and those eyes have been upon you again and have drawn you away from your purpose."

"Why was my dad so concerned about her?" Silas asked, knowing now they were talking about Bea. "And what is my purpose?"

"Your father was frightened of her because she can no longer see where her own story begins and ends. Because she cannot discern the passage of time, she is not of one mind about things and doesn't always know that she brings distress and suffering to others, or that those who love her come to no good end. In her present mind, she can only repeat the past, Silas. She cannot change after so long. So she can only bring upon others the fate that was brought upon her."

"And what is that?"

"You understand too little of what you see. You see a pretty face and hear a loving voice. But she is more than that, Silas. Much more. She is cold water and lack of breath. She is emptiness and oblivion. She is the very tide, drawing things to her and pulling them below."

"But she loves me, and I think I—"

"No doubt she does, for otherwise, how could you see her so easily? To love you is her nature. But hers is a love from which no good may come. And your desire for her will lead only to cold, dark places. Already, we see you are concerned by her absence— you want to help her—that is part of the peril. Leave her where she is and continue the work you have begun here."

"If she's in trouble, isn't she part of that work? Did she do something horrible in life? Is that why she's trapped now?"

"Not at all. It is rarely the action itself that binds a person to this fate or that, but how the action is judged and remembered. Really, I shall never know why people let their shame and fear consume them so. She loved a young man. No more than that. But those close to her, her kin, took against her. She appears to be here with you in the moment, but be assured she is of a different time when women, please believe us, were not generally allowed to do what they pleased. She was punished by those she loved, and that makes everything worse. To be killed by your kin is very terrible. There used to be a power that might have been called upon to avenge such wrongs as family spilling the blood of family, but we live now in more 'civilized' times."

"Do not speak the ancient names," said the third of the three.

"I was not going to say them," assured the first of the three. "But I will say that in this country, there is not so much justice as there once was in other lands, and in more ancient times, when such acts might have been avenged by righteous fury."

"Will you tell me what happened to her? I won't be able to think about anything else now. I think it's the least you can do," said Silas.

"Ah, well," said the first of the three, "for your father's sake then. Come to the weaving and look; it is almost all there now in the stitches. As you learn more, the weaving waxes full of sumptuous detail."

Silas walked with the first of the three to where the edge of the millpond had been stitched in small, even knots, from which tall, thin stitches stood as reeds. In the middle of the pond there was a hole, a black place of emptiness in the midst of the image, and a thin veil of watery silk netting lay across it. As Silas watched, the thread-reeds of the pond seemed to wave in a wind as the tapestry shook slightly, and the first of the three began to speak.

In that time, she would look for the white stone.

If they were to meet, her lover from one of the big houses left a small white stone on her windowsill. So, each night, she would look for the stone and see what was to be. She would meet him behind the church, and they would make their way to the little woods that once stood at the edge of the millpond. Upon arriving, she would place the little white stone at the same place on the earth, and before long, a small cairn of white rocks rose up, testament to the frequency and passion of their ardor for each other.

But towns are full of tongues, and it takes only one to start wagging before even the most cherished secret is spoiled. At the tavern, words were said. Intimations. Suggestions. Rumors.

A rock for every embrace, and look how high!

What manner of girl was she?

Count the stones and find out!

And there, to the tavern, her father went to take his daily medicine, for life was hard, even with seven sons.

And there he heard the words about his daughter and her doings. And there his heart was broken.

Go, he says to his seven sons. Go and make it how I feel. Broken. All broken. Break this lover's knot. Go and make it so and do not come back until your father's words hold true. End this shameful thing she's done. And his seven sons hear him, but the first son hears and understands.

So to the pond the brothers go and find there the cairn, and taking many stones from it, they step back into the shadows of the trees and wait.

She comes then—the girl, their sister, some lover's lover—eager and wide-eyed to the millpond. But she sees the cairn has been diminished and wonders why. Some new game of her sweetheart's? She whispers then his name, "Lawrence Umber," but instead of her one true love, seven brothers step from the trees.

Her heart begins to beat so fast, but with fear now, not with passion, for she knows she is discovered.

Just missed him, her brothers say. You have just missed him. Your fine Master Umber departed.

Where has he gone? she asks, trembling.

All they say is: below.

She sees the ripples on the surface of the black water, and she starts weeping and tearing at her hair for the death of her young man.

She is miserable. But her misery rises into anger, and she begins to scream at her brothers. From her knees by the water's edge, she rails at them and will not be silent.

Quiet her, says one.

Shut her mouth, says the youngest to the oldest, and the oldest understands and grabs her face and puts his hand over her mouth, *feeling her hot breath upon his palm. She sets her teeth deep into his flesh, and he cries out. He does not think but seizes her throat and thrusts her face into the water.*

Be quiet. Be quiet. Be quiet, is all he thinks. He hears nothing else but this thought: Silence her for our father's sake. He does not hear his brothers' frightened cries to leave her be, nor the thrashing of her limbs against the water. Nothing. And when he lets her go, after all her shaking stops, she does not move.

What shall we do? the brothers cry, and so the first, all light gone now from his eyes, takes the stones and fills her dress with them, lifting the hem up and, with his belt, securing the rock-filled dress to her waist.

She sinks fast, for she is such a little thing, so lithe and fair. Above her, the moon goes small as she sinks down and down. And when she reaches the bottom, she is alone. No lover's corpse to rest upon. Nothing there but eels and crabs and cold mud.

And now here's truth: Her brothers found her lover, and beat him and drove him from the town to save their family shame, and they told him that if he spoke of their sister to anyone they'd come to kill him sure as dusk ends each day, and that was a promise. And so he fled, ran out into the marshes and toward the woods and away, and lived, though Lawrence Umber was never seen in Lichport again.

But she was not so lucky.

And her story is not over, because sometimes she wakes and rises. When a face pleases her, especially an Umber face, she rises and walks for a time, until she takes him by the hand and joins with him and brings him down with her among the deep water weeds so she will not have to be alone.

As the voice of the first grew quiet, Silas's face was white, all his blood gone heavy and cold, sinking in his limbs. At the knowledge of how close he'd come to death that night at the millpond, his mind began twisting in every direction, coiling around and about itself. Yet part of him knew that she loved him and that in the depths of the millpond, she'd tried to help him. She let him go. He could almost see her face before him, hear her voice, and he knew he cared for her and wanted, truly desired, to help her if he could.

The three ladies could see him becoming uncomfortable. The second of the three spoke.

"Silas, we know this is no easy matter, and there is no right answer about what to do. Your love for her is part of what makes you exceptional. Who but an Umber, who but you particularly could love one such as her? Knowing you have nearly nothing to gain, you love anyway. I believe that is heroic, in its way. But she is a very dangerous someone, Silas. She died desirous of so many things, and very angry, very betrayed by so many. That has confused her and bound her in a state where she cannot see her way out. You know why, I think. What we desire most in life, we shall try to find in death. And right there is the problem for so many souls."

Then the third of the three continued, "Sadly, our ruling passions—our wishes and hopes and desires—are not often in accord with reason or simple goodness. Thus we make our beds in life, and have to lie in them in death. People make such poor decisions and then cannot see a way out of them. Death limits you, believe me. And this is why you must forget her and commit yourself to your path, to your work. Only in that way may you bring peace to those like her. Your father's work, *your* work, helps to mitigate such circumstances, extends a very welcome hand to the dead who need help. But not every spirit can be helped or knows they need it, or even knows that they are dead at all. And such spirits are perilous. The more complicated a person, the more complicated are their deaths. You know those folk you meet? The quiet, simple, good folks one meets often in the daily course of life?"

"Boring, you mean!" said the first.

"Normal," said the third, chiding just a little. "Regular, common people who live unremarkable lives . . . those are the ones who die easy, and when those folk die, they hardly ever get up again. Put 'em in the ground, they stay put and don't trouble anyone again. But those others, those people who are so damn funny, or clever, or mean . . . the ones you always put at the top of your party guest list, the ones who've got their minds made up about something or other, the ones you can't talk out of nothing once they've set their minds on it? Well," she said knowingly, making a sweeping gesture across the whole length of the tapestry from one corner to another, "those are the ones who don't always want to move on. They couldn't let anything go in life. Same in death. They know everything, don't they?" The three laughed loudly together, sharing a private joke.

"Some folks just can't bear to leave it all behind. And you've met one of those, haven't you? The ones who are so stubborn, even their bodies aren't allowed to go to their rest because they've feathered their nests so well," said the first.

"You mean my great-grandfather?"

"Yes. He's one of the good ones. Sometimes the bad ones stay on too. Those are the worst. Though really, you can't blame any of them. Life can be habit-forming, and isn't it always the bad habits that are hardest to break!"

"But those who want things—finery, children, wealth, revenge—desire them so bad they can't rest at night for wanting them. Those are the folks who don't settle," added the second. "One way or another, they want what they want and will see no reason. So when they die, their flesh rots, if they're lucky, but the wanting doesn't. On and on the wanting goes, right past death and into something else."

Silas knew everything they said was true. He needed to think. Every word they said careened into another, and it was becoming harder and harder for him to keep focused. And the little voice was ringing out from the back of his mind, "Come and find me. Find me." Only now, Silas didn't know whether the voice was his father's or Bea's. He turned to go and was almost at the door when the first spoke again, calling after him.

"And Silas, what will you do when what the dead want so desperately is you?"

He waited quietly, unable to answer, unable to leave. Everything had become one to him and he felt, standing there, eyes running across the room from one scene to another, that if he could just bring his mind to bear on one single thing and quiet the rest for even a minute, he might be okay. If he could do that, solve one problem, then everything, his mom, Bea, his future, everything else would begin to sort itself out too. He tried to calm his thoughts, to summon in his heart the one thing he knew he needed more than anything.

He held his father's face in the front of his mind, and in response, the threads and scenes of the tapestry became a blur of color and texture to him. As he watched, some of the scenes stood out in sharp contrast, rising up from the rest, drawing him in. He began pointing at these, buildings and streets of stitches and knots, some looming over the neighboring portions of the tapestry. He pointed to one and then another and asked again and again, trying to piece together the shards of a puzzle, "What is this place? What is it called?"

"Ah!" they exclaimed together. "He has chosen!"

And they told him the names:

The Peony Lantern Teahouse
The Red Parlor
The Yacht Club
The Hall of Twelve Corpses
The Tavern
The Garden of Delights
The Theater of Summer
The Bowers of the Night Herons
The Millpond
The Sunken Mansions

On and on the list went.

Some of these names he thought he recognized from notes in the ledger. Others only felt familiar, like the names of acquaintances met long ago. Some sang in his mind, pulled at his attention like a tide, and those he underlined as he wrote them on a folded piece of paper he'd found in the pocket of his father's jacket. As the ladies spoke the names, Silas noted any clues to their locations he could discern in the tapestry. Some were in the Narrows, others spread throughout the town, overlaid in gauze or transparent silk over buildings and monuments he'd seen many times.

The three said to him, "At last you begin to truly see this town for what it is, for what it has always been. The names we have told you are places wherein the dead congregate and have done so for a long time. Some of these misthomes and shadowlands share their borders with other places. Some, such as the Teahouse, you may find very commodious because it is so ancient in the other countries where it also stands. Beware. Not only Lichport's dead inhabit such realms. All of them were known to your father, who had many times walked within these hostels of the lost, though he knew and visited many others besides."

"Most noble and helpful ladies, how will I find them?" asked Silas with gratitude.

They smiled.

"Most shadowlands and misthomes, or limbos, if you like, may be found to be associated with places you can see without assistance. These are. But your manner of approach will always be crucial. Some may not be entered unless you understand their nature first. Others must be approached in a particular manner, or at sunset, or hungry, or with eyes wet with tears, or while you can hear the sound of the sea, or a child crying. Because of who you are and the death watch you bear, it will be easier for you than most. The names are calls. Hold the names in your mind, and you will find your way through the mist."

"Will I find my father?"

"That's sweet," said the third, "he thinks us oracles—"

But the second of the three interrupted.

"We did not say you'd find him. Only that he has been in these places. Whether he is currently residing in one or another, that is for you to find. But here, let me whisper some needful words into your ear, child. . . ."

She spoke of strange lands and the signs by which they might be found, and Silas tried to remember all he could, but her words were like a dream, and as she drew away from him, his memory made smudges of what she'd told him.

Silas bowed to the three, but as he turned to leave, the first of the three said, "Silas, be careful what you eat on your journey. In some lands, it is fine to sample the fare, especially if you are among beloved friends or kin, but in others . . . well, tasting even the smallest morsel might mean your road home, if you can find one at all, is not so nice."

He nodded in acknowledgment and left the room, walking

quickly from the house of the Sewing Circle, wanting to begin his search before more of what he'd seen and heard slipped away from him.

After Silas had left them, the three ladies whispered in their high, strange room, gathered about the web.

"Wait, wait," said the second, "no need to tear out what was. Stitch over it. Let the past keep its place."

"Whatever was shall be again," said the third.

"Can you see who it comes for?" said the first.

"No. Not yet. But it has only recently arrived. Patience."

And from the steadily working needles of two of the women, blue and green threads poured forth in mighty waves in the air. Then, drawing out a spool of stone-white thread as thin as a hair, the first of the three began to stitch with a needle carved of bone. Here there came the outlines of a ship. The others cast off, and, working now with the same pale thread as the first, began to fill in the gaps: salt-encrusted boards, tall masts, tattered sails that had billowed through storm a thousand times. All in white, but no detail missing. And in the torn sheets of the sails meant to catch the wind, there was now a net of souls. Faces of the damned stitched down in the very fabric of the sails, so that when the ladies' breaths blew across the tapestry, and rippled it like the wind, the faces billowed and distended as though they were screaming or crying.

"It has been a long while since we've worked out such a theme."

"Not long enough!" said the first. "This town is filled with malcontents. Time for them to set sail, I say!"

Then, more seriously, the second said, "Look here at this long thread. Here's a yarn we know—" And indeed, the anchor line stretched away from the ship to another, more familiar, part of the tapestry.

"Perhaps we should tell the boy? Fetch him back," suggested the second.

"Why?" said the first. "You'll ruin all our sport. Besides, he'll know soon enough."

And with that, the three grew silent again, gathering up loose threads, stitching them down where they could.

CHAPTER 50

WE ARE TRAVELERS ALL

SILAS MADE A COFFER IN HIS MIND, and into it he put his uncle, his mother, Bea, his nameless fears, and every other thing he could think of that might keep him from finding his father.

He was going to find his dad. Alive or dead, he needed to know where his dad was and what had become of him, no matter what might be waiting in the mist.

Warm in his father's jacket and a long wool scarf, Silas walked from his house only partly sure where he was going. As he came down Main, heading east toward the water, he wound strong cord around the open death watch, binding the hand of the dial to the face. He didn't knot it, in case he had to remove the cord quickly.

He instantly began to feel the light dizziness he associated with the drawing aside of the veil between the worlds, and already, the town around him had begun to fill with mist. It seeped up from the pavement, winding in gray, snakelike tendrils about his feet, falling in thin rivulets down the walls of the buildings, as if all the structures of the town were boxes filled with fog. Just ahead of him, unchanged in shape but now somehow more alive, Beacon Hill glowed as if on fire. And away to the north and south, from Fort Street and down on Coral, thin columns of blue flames spiraled upward, piercing the low clouds.

From the ladies of the Sewing Circle, he knew the names of the places he was looking for, and he kept those names at the front of his mind, right behind his eyes, and this seemed to keep the others—the ghosts who might be found on every street in Lichport—in the pale half-light of his peripheral vision and away from the path before him. He chose the most familiar place first and made its name into a prayer.

Silas walked and did not stop. Streets rose up before him in confusing composites, familiar in parts, foreign in others, as though the many periods of the town were thin sheets of gauze hung before his eyes and he was looking through all of them at once.

The mist was before him and behind him. As he said the name of the shadowland he was looking for again and again, summoned its image from the tapestry, the brume seemed to abate as though stirred up by his breath, or buffeted by a wind. The mist parted in front of him, revealing some odd angle of the street, or a worn corner of a wall, or a worm-eaten ornament on a carved column, or the small glazed window of an ancient house, or a white quartz cobblestone set among the dark. The signs had always been there, merely unnoticed in the intoxicating flow of time. Silas could see it clearly now: how certain of the strange individual elements of the town, indeed, the world, might form—if seen in just the right way—a map to the land of the dead.

He walked on and farther on. He first went down into the Narrows, for the misthome he sought first lay within its boundaries, close by the sea. Silas noticed the gulls were quiet, and then— as he descended the twisting lanes, arriving at the bay—even the incessant crashing of the waves against the rocks was now absent.

As he walked along the quay toward the tavern, Silas could just hear the voices of the Narrows folk, living people going about their business, unaware of him passing among them. He could not see their faces. On the margins of the lands of the dead, it seemed to Silas, the living could become mere shadows.

As he approached the Fretful Porpentine Tavern at the end of Downe Street by the old wharf, he found it changed from the place he'd seen many times before. He knew the building well enough as a run-down bar where some of the Narrows folk drank, and more than a few transients who'd washed up in Lichport and were unable to find their way out again filled the worn bar stools. At one time, the tavern had been a prominent coaching inn, holding forth at the entrance to town on the ancient coastal highway; now it was little more than another of Lichport's dead ends. Just beyond the edge of the quay, the old highway lay ruined as it approached Lichport, much of it long since fallen into the sea.

The Fretful Porpentine had two doors. One, Silas had seen before. It led to the tavern, where the living drank and met to share news. The second door, which he had never seen, was far older and led—the ladies of the Sewing Circle had told him—to a shadowland of the dead. In truth, they'd said, both doors shared a frame—each leading to a room where the forgotten gathered to forget.

Stepping back, Silas saw the front of the tavern was much larger now as it rose from the mist, and horses stood at a post a little ways away from the door. As he again approached the tavern, those familiar voices behind him fell aside, and he could hear raucous shouts just ahead, coming from inside. The noise rattled the hanging lanterns on their hooks and the glass of the candlelit windows, which cast a jaundiced yellow light out onto the cobbles of the street. Just over the door hung a hand-painted sign he'd never seen before, depicting a porcupine with its quills standing straight up from its back. THE FRETFUL PORPENTINE—TAVERN, INNE, AND TRAVELLER'S EASE was written below the startled animal in bold red letters. As Silas stood looking at the tavern-as-it-was, ghost after ghost flowed past him and into the place. A loud cry of greeting burst through the doorway as each one went in. Silas also noticed, as he crossed the threshold that, while many ghosts were going in, none were coming out.

Silas had seen hastily written notes regarding the limbo of the Tavern in the ledger, but as he tried to recall them, he could no longer discern whether the words that swam in his mind were in the past or present tense . . . the third person or the first. . . .

Just inside the door of the tavern, a sign greets all weary travelers with the words:

Wand'rers, be welcome
Sit down at your ease
Pay with a story
And drinke what ye please!

Here you will always find a lively company, still drinking hard, laughing, cursing, lamenting their losses, and bragging about whatever unspent joys still fill their pockets. Only those who've lost something they don't want to find come here. A wife. A child. A job. A family. A way. If you're missing something and want to forget about it, there is a stool waiting for you just by the door. And there's always something to stay for.

Though always forgotten by dawn, a thousand stories are told each night. Incline your ear.

Just listen to the man with seven sons by the table in the back. He's been here in his cups a long time.

A daughter drowned.

An awful tale. But not unusual, for good girls sometimes come to bad ends. His sons tell him it was their sister and a boy. She went there to meet a boy from one of the big houses. That's what the sons tell their father. The father doesn't look up from his drink, but asks, where is your sister now? Lost, the sons say. That's what they say. Every time.

And the first son, the oldest, looks his father in the eye and nods.

This is not a new story.

Drowned in the millpond, the first says. We were too late, says the fifth son. Gone there to meet a boy. At night. And we were too late. She must have fallen. Fallen. In the dark. But we couldn't help her, says the sixth of the sons. The seventh is silent and looks away from the others.

The father notices the first son's shirt is wet and a little green, just the arms up to the shoulder, as though he's been holding something down under the surface of the water. Another round, says the father, closing his eyes.

And here we go again.

It's the same every night. The family's proud. And she never learns.

Everyone's always losing something. So folks always feel at home. Drink up. Your money's no good here. But everyone must pay. Everyone must put a tale in the till, or who could bear it?

And here's a young man, looking a little lost.

"Get him a drink," someone shouts.

"C'mon," yells another, "let's hear your news from beyond the door!" He doesn't know they are speaking to him. He stands there gaping.

Down from the end of the long, polished bar, someone calls out, "How about a story?" and throws a handful of peanuts that pelt him, rousing his attention.

"Looking for my father," the young man says, startled, and half a hundred heads look up at him.

"You've come to the right place! Plenty of lost fathers here," someone says. A bunch of men with faces like shipwrecks raise their hands, their eyes still guiltily in their cups.

The young man looks. None of them are known to him.

He says again, louder now, "I've lost my father," hoping someone will stand up and meet his gaze, that someone he knows will know him.

His dad, maybe just drinking at one of the back tables, unaware of how long he's been there. Forgetful of how much time has passed, ready to put on his coat and come home.

No one stands up. No one stands out.

But someone shouts, "Not again!"

"Heard it a hundred times!" another hollers, belching his words out from a gut full of beer and ennui. "We've all heard that one before!"

Never raising his voice, the young man asks, "Then do you know how it ends?"

And the whole back room answers as one—the travelers, the wastrels, the lost—all cry out: "No! Do you?"

And the room erupts in laughter as the young traveler takes to his road.

Silas walked on and farther on, and though the Peony Lantern Teahouse had seemed, in the tapestry, to be just around the corner from the tavern, he was walking and walking through the Narrows, all the way back up to what might have been Coach Street, then down the Sloop and along the sea, up Pearl Lane and through a back alley, finally to the place where he knew a ruined building stood in his own time.

Mother Peale had told him that the building had once, at the turn of the century, been owned by a Chinese family, and catered primarily to those folk who had come to Lichport from the west coast by train as laborers, traders, and importers, bringing urns and carvings to be used in funerary rites by wealthy families who found the foreign fashionable at times of death.

Here, within this building, those folk came who longed for a taste of the East. It had been a teahouse but also served as a market, importing familiar items for those far from home, and as a parlor of gossip, where news from faraway families might be obtained. A place to wait for ships or trains that came and went from the other towns and other coasts, bringing news or the arrival of a loved one, or rarely, the beginning of the long journey home.

Mother Peale had showed him a ruin—leaning rooms of skeletal beams; broken benches; an old, abandoned chest in a filthy corner—but before him now, risen in the mist, Silas gasped at what he saw. The sweeping curved roof was tiled and adorned with ornate ceramic dragons. Roosting atop the teahouse and in some of the trees now standing next to it were large nests of cranes that sat patiently, waiting for those who exited the teahouse, although departures seemed to be few and far between. The teahouse stood on carved posts as though it were resting in the water. And indeed, the street below it had become translucent, and under the clear glass cobblestones, Silas could see enormous koi swimming in endless, dreaming spirals.

When the traveler enters the Peony Lantern Teahouse, there is always a place to sit. A bowl of lemons rests on each low table, and your first cup of tea will come quickly, though not always your second.

Lu Yu is the keeper of the Peony Lantern Teahouse, and it is Lu Yu himself who welcomes all who visit. The first cup is always poured for guests from his hands. So as the youth approaches the lacquered threshold of the teahouse, Lu Yu speaks first, joyfully, from within.

"Xiansheng hao ma? Chi fan le ma?" says the keeper of the teahouse.

"I am well, and I have eaten, thank you," says the youth, as he steps within and shakes hands with Lu Yu without hesitation, for here, at the edges of the suburbs of Fengdu, the City of Ghosts, all words are familiar to the ears of a traveler.

Vast as a province, yet cozy as its many private screened rooms, the teahouse is ancient, and in its gathering chambers, the dead eat and drink and wait to be served again. Many have lingered here for a long time, although the dead who pass through the doors of lacquered ebony do not mean to stay. But the teahouse seems familiar to them and reminds them so much of home, so they sit on silk cushions underneath lamps of jade the color of flowers and forget where it was they so desperately wanted to go.

Ah! How delight in sensual pleasures may overcome even the cherished longings of the heart.

They eat. They drink. They savor and listen to the sound of music and recline on the cushions and take familiar comfort in all the trappings of the teahouse, and forget.

Though the food is tempting, the youth does not eat, does not drink. He sees that at some of the tables—when no second cup of tea is served by Lu Yu—the guests look anxious, even embarrassed at having to ask someone else, a stranger, to fill their empty cup.

For some, it is like this. They wait and wait, and eventually begin to pour cup after cup for themselves. This is because they have been forgotten. No children, no grandchildren make offerings to them. No one speaks their names before a shrine. No incense is offered. Their names are not written with a brush onto the scroll of the names of revered ancestors and so, at the teahouse, they must wait to eat and drink, or serve themselves, which many find disgraceful. And because they have wandered so far from home, the ghosts of their children and grandchildren are not here to pour tea for them. These ghosts of the forgotten think: I will leave after a few more cups. But, oh! How excellent are the dumplings! Just one more.

Some visitors to the teahouse stay longer than others. Some are ghosts of those who traveled far in life, those who settled where they found themselves and then seldom thought of home. Yet in old age they began to think once more of lands across the sea, and so longing *entered their hearts. They long for the distant homes and familiar sights their ancestors knew: the green mountains of Wuyuan, the pavilion of Tengwang, the peaks of Jinggangshan, the villages of Xidi and Hongcun, the ancient river houses of Zhujiajiao. But the teahouse is so like the places they once knew, or heard of from parents, and so, why leave? They dream of something so far removed that they no longer know what they long for. Easier to sit and sip and dream. For some, it is easier to imagine a thing than to try to attain it.*

Some will never leave, either because of fear or forgetting. Though you may be a wanderer, living out your days in exile, home is with you always, in blood-song and bone map, and in the echo of your mother's voice as you tell her favorite tale to your children or the children who gather around you in the land of your exile. Home is your most constant companion. When that is forgotten, the doors of lacquered ebony close before you and the land of your ancestors is lost. Then here, in the Peony Lantern Teahouse you shall remain. You may make friends, even meet someone you once knew. If you are kindhearted and pour tea for others, they may repay the favor. Then you may drink, and eat, perhaps, but the joyous cry of your ancestors that might have accompanied your return is a song your ears shall never hear, and the special flavor of the food is diminished, just slightly. So you eat and eat, and hope to regain the savor of your meal.

But be comforted. You will find it is easy to forget what you will never know. And there is music at the Peony Lantern Teahouse, the gu zheng, ruan, pipa, the gourd flute. Listen. One of the flute players is very fine and can imitate the sound of birds.

The more fortunate stop at the teahouse only briefly. For them, the tea tastes robust, the dumplings full of joyous savor. But just one cup. Just one mouthful, then they pass once more through the doors of lacquered ebony to make their way home.

The youth looks upon the lounging ghosts with a heavy heart, for what right has he to trouble them with his own grief, to press them with questions? But there is something about the floral hues of the light, perhaps the music, that makes him long to sit and rest. He passes from table to table, perhaps waiting for an invitation, yet few do more than incline their heads toward him briefly, and most seem not to notice as he walks among them. They only hold their cups up again and again to be filled.

But there, at a table by a window that overlooks the ornamental pond, is an empty seat, and on the bench, a folded robe in pleasing white and gray silk, with a red sash, that the youth is sure would fit him. Lu Yu brings tea to the table, and shakes the youth's hand again, as he helps him take his ease, encouraging him to drink and enjoy the excellent view. But as the youth sits down and lifts his full cup, one ghost looks up at him from the far wall of the room, where music is being played. This ghost looks at the youth as though she has been waiting for him; she holds him with her eyes, and the youth puts down his cup. She stops playing the gu zheng, and rises and gestures to him without words.

He leaves his tea to cool in its cup and rises from the table to ask the ghost the question that had fled his mind when the light of the lamps of the teahouse so enraptured him: "Do you know where he is?"

The girl shakes her head, but beckons the youth to follow her.

Her white gown trails far behind as she walks past him. He can just see at the hems and seams of her dress a flash of bright red silk.

The ghost leads the youth toward the back of the teahouse, where a constellation of staircases rises to upper floors. The ghost walks up the stairs without pausing, never looking to see if the youth is still behind her. She drifts up like rising steam, and as if in a dream, the youth follows.

The two ascend many steps, past many landings and many floors and many screens that lead to many rooms. They come at last to a door, very roughly made of posts, the kind seen by travelers in the coastal *villages, made from the remains of boats when they can no longer be mended. As they pass through, the youth's heart is hopeful that they will arrive at some chamber where he might find the person he seeks, sleeping, or eating quietly, or playing mahjong with old friends. But it is not to be. The room is empty except for a chest and a lantern. Beside him, the ghost is wild-eyed as she points at the chest.*

The youth crosses the room and opens the chest, but finds only clothes, neatly folded, inside. He looks up, but the ghost-girl continues to gesture desperately and the youth pushes his hand deeper into the chest, until his fingers sweep board at the bottom. And there, hidden, he finds strips of folded paper, tightly rolled and wrapped with a piece of torn silk sash.

The ghost weeps then, tears coursing down her face. Her body is rimmed all in expectant flame, and the tears turn quickly to steam on her skin.

"Do you wish me to open this?" the youth asks.

The ghost's mouth opens as if wailing, although she makes no sound.

"Do you want these?" asks the youth, as he holds the papers out to the ghost. She tilts her head back in agony.

The youth looks at the papers and can see characters written on them, and dried flowers are bound up along with the pages. The scroll is warm in his hands, as though it had only a moment ago been clutched tightly in the hand against the heart. Here were love letters, the youth knew. Secret love letters. Unfound, still waiting somewhere beyond the mist. A young man's words for this girl, maybe her words for him. Their private words for each other. Somewhere in the world, these letters sat hidden still, but might, at any moment, be found and read, calling her most cherished secrets from their hiding place back into the circle of the sun.

"Shall I burn them?" says the youth, more sure now of what the ghost wants from him.

While the ghost watches, her tears abating, the youth puts the strips of paper into the iron lantern. As the flames rise inside the lantern, the ghost smiles with an ancient and long-awaited joy. As the letters burn, she falls away to ashes, as though she too had been made of paper. Already her spirit, carried by a crane, is winging to the land of her heart's desire; already her spirit is approaching her lover's village in the province of Songjiang.

When the youth turns and passes again through the posts, he finds himself back in the main room of the teahouse, close to the entrance.

For those who may depart, Lu Yu may walk them to the threshold of the teahouse and speak parting words to them. The youth stands at the threshold and there, he hears these words from the ancient keeper of the teahouse:

> *A thousand mountains*
> *will greet my friend at his departure.*
> *Always, it is the time of spring tea blossoming.*
> *I speak the blessings of spring upon his journey,*
> *whether in early mist or red cloud of evening.*
> *I envy him his lonely travels.*
> *May we meet upon the faraway mountain.*
> *May we share repast by the clear water fountain.*
> *Until then,*
> *light a candle*
> *and strike upon the bell of stone*
> *and remember where your journey began.*

The voice fades, and the mist appears, and the youth takes his leave at twilight from the teahouse that rises like a temple from the suburbs of Fengdu, the City of Ghosts. Because the youth had not eaten, because he'd not tasted even a single cup of tea, he made his way home without passing through the Hall of Twelve Corpses.

As he left the ruin, the broken chest that had once lain on the floor was now burned black, and small embers still glowed on its charred edges. He didn't stop to look closely. He knew the letters that had been hidden within it were ashes now. He walked away and did not look back.

Silas couldn't hear his own footfall, and he didn't know how long he'd been walking or how long he'd been gone. His heart was heavy, and he was ready to go home. He could see now that asking the dead about his father was nearly useless, so burdened were they with their own losses and regrets and distractions. He had no right to press them. It was not enough merely to let them speak. If anything, he should try to bring them comfort, to shorten their suffering. Anything else was selfish, thoughtless, at best redundant. He was also finding it too easy to take on their pain, perhaps because he was more like them than he wanted to admit. Or rather, he had let himself become like them, a wanderer, someone lost in a world he had hewn from his own pain.

He couldn't keep the coffer of distraction at the back of his mind closed. His own past kept flying up around him like moths; old fears back again, the ghosts' problems only serving to remind him of his own. Even the little anxieties that nipped at his heels as a boy were back now as sharp-toothed dogs, following him, barking loudly, drawing more and more attention to themselves. Now, as he looked for his dad, Silas felt like he had as a boy: left behind, alone, forgotten. And he could see, now, his personal feelings made his encounters with the dead and his travels through their lands dangerous and filled with the possibility of entrapment.

He thought he should just go home and forget about the last shadowland he'd planned to visit. He was only going because this place loomed so large on the tapestry and seemed so strongly connected with the seaside and the harbor where his father had spent so much time. Well populated, watching over the ocean, it seemed more likely to be a source of information. But as if thinking made it so, Silas suddenly found himself approaching the Yacht Club, which stood proudly on the rocks overlooking the sea at the southern edge of Lichport, its flags at full mast in the salty wind.

He'd go forward, but he would ask no questions. He would merely greet these ghosts as neighbors and then go home. This was his plan. He was there, so okay, but then, *Enough*, he thought. *It is enough.*

As Silas approached the ornate front of the Yacht Club, gentlemen in midnight blue blazers and white slacks poured from the now open doors toward Silas. Behind them, waiters with trays of drinks were running to keep up.

At the Lichport Yacht Club, there are surprisingly few rules for the aspiring member. Only that you must leave your worries at the door and wear a jacket. Oh, yes, That Sort Of Thing may be all the rage at the other clubs, but not here. But if you wish a bit of gentlemanly company, brandy and cigars and leather chairs, come in and take a pew until Labor Day.

The view is excellent. You can see the wide horizon and all the faces of the sea from the windows, and so the members sit, with their backs to the town, watching the boats sail by, for every day is the Saturday of regatta week. The conversation that moves about the club is respectable, though sometimes it turns boastful, taking on the kind of swaggering tone a man employs when his wife is not there to contradict him in front of company.

"No, no!" say some of the men, their feathers ruffling at the sight of Silas on their porch, the others echoing their sentiments with emphatic

nods. "We'll have none of your kind here! No, none of that rubbish you're peddling, we're staying right where we are!"

"Okay," says Silas, confused. "That's okay with me, really! I'm not peddling anything—"

"Oh, he says that now," scoffs one, "but just wait, he'll be just like the father with his 'time for home,' and 'get ye gones'! Well, we're not having any of it, young man! So you can turn yourself right around. This is private property."

"Wait! You know my father? Have you seen him?"

"Your father is NOT a member of this club. I assure you!"

Feeling a little offended, Silas says, "I'm not here to tell you what to do. I have no intention of telling you to go anywhere. Stay here as long as you like, if that's what you want."

"Just so. Thank you. And, if you don't mind," says one of the men more quietly, in his captain's cap with too much gold braid stitched to its brim, "no need to mention to the wives what's become of us, righty-o?"

"Um—right," says Silas, "but may I ask, what are you hiding from?"

"Hiding!" hollers the captain, his sotto voce gone, "we prefer 'weathering over'! So much quieter here than home. Less chatter, too. More civilized. We spent so many excellent weekends here, some of us just thought we'd stay on, you know, man the helm. A man wants to be the captain of his own ship, and, well, no man can be that at home. So"—orders the captain, mustering his zeal—"you can just move along, Undertaker! We're not leaving."

Silas makes an obligatory scan of the ranks of club members, but sees no familiar faces, nor do any of the ghosts speak up to claim him as kin. It is clear that while nearly everyone knows of his father, no one here knows anything of his whereabouts.

Already resigned to going home, and caring little one way or the other what the men of the club do with their afterlives, Silas raises his hands in mock defeat and hangs his head as he turns to go. But as he *begins to unwind the cord from the death watch, he looks once more on the men of the Yacht Club, who have all turned suddenly and very reverently to the east. The men have moved to stand on the rocks of the breakwater in front of the club, each on his own little island, and they now look out toward Lichport's deep-bottomed harbor. There, Silas can just make out the misty outlines of a ship risen up from the water, its pale, hell-shredded sails billowing in a storm that blows for it alone.*

The men of the Yacht Club raise their drinks in somber reverence to the ship of mists, then drink down the contents of their glasses and throw them to shatter on the rocks, and without another word to the Undertaker, they march back into their club, closing and locking the doors behind them.

As he turned the corner from Coral Street onto Coach, Silas felt, just for an instant, strangely comforted by not finding his father in the shadowlands he'd visited. For one thing, it might mean that his dad was still alive, though that raised many more questions than it answered. Most of those questions circled about his uncle's name like black birds about a copse of trees. And Silas wondered how would it have felt to find his dad just sitting there on a stool in the tavern. Just sitting, glass in his hand, not looking for him, not trying to get home. Just lost like the rest of the ghosts, drunk on their own little miseries, waiting down the years, sharing their stories with strangers, their families so far away it was as though they never were.

Alive or dead, his father was still somewhere, waiting to be found.

The night was clear and fine, and the fixed stars burned with cold light across the sky above Silas as he made his way home to his father's house. Above him, something flashed. He stopped in the middle of the street and saw a star fall, trailing behind it a thin ribbon of fire that faded almost as soon as it flared. Just another traveler, he thought. Just another soul fallen from its sphere. A thing nearly burned out.

Still looking up, Silas felt drawn upward into the pitch of the sky, his stomach turning, because he was standing in the middle of nothing. With every passing moment, the configurations of the constellations were fading. There were no more connections he could see, or remember, or make. He felt his father's face drawing away from him into the dark, his features becoming lost among the invisible lines between the now patternless stars. Where Amos once stood in Silas's mind, now there was only space. Nausea rose up in him, and he felt sure now that there were only two places in town where his father might reside. First, his house, which was full, floor to ceiling, with associations—notes, letters, clothes, books. Objects and reminders that would every day bring him closer to knowing his dad, though not necessarily bring him any closer to finding him. Then there was the other place. His uncle's house, where, Silas increasingly feared, something more of his dad than merely memories lay waiting for him. He started walking quickly up Coach Street, keeping his head down, his eyes only on the road.

CHAPTER 51

RETREAT

AS HE RETURNED HOME from his wanderings among the town's shadowlands, Silas realized that while Lichport had become his home, without his father it was just another limbo to him. Dizzy and nervous from his journey, from the realization that there were, at every turning, worlds within worlds all about him, Silas didn't feel like leaving the familiarity of his father's house. Mrs. Bowe was down the hallway if he needed her, the front door was locked, and everything outside that haunted and confused him was on the other side of that door.

He spent the day reading, wandering from shelf to shelf. First a few lines from one volume caught his attention, then an engraving in another book momentarily drew his eye. After hours of flitting from page to page, Silas needed to stretch his legs. He went upstairs and began opening doors to rooms he hadn't yet gone through with any attention.

He turned the knob to a small room toward the end of the hall and walked in. There were a few old toys in the corners and animals painted on the walls. Silas had opened this door on his first day in the house, but thinking it empty, he'd closed it again and hadn't been back. Now he looked more closely at the room and could see that all the painted animals had faded and the toys were gray with dust and age. He knew this had been his room, long ago, before his family moved away.

When he had first arrived in his father's house, Silas had almost liked the idea of discovering his father's secret life, but slowly he was realizing it was only a secret kept from him. He began to get angry, and quickly the anger turned in on itself and then began to hurt.

He ran to his father's bedroom and frantically began looking through drawers and the pockets of his father's clothes, searching for anything that he might have missed, some clue about his father's disappearance. Some evidence. A note. Anything that could bring his dad closer to his life again or hint at where he'd gone.

Nothing but the pieces of a life left behind suddenly. A pants pocket holding a handkerchief and three quarters in change. A shirt hanging on a closet door with a pen still clipped to the breast pocket. Two dirty undershirts in a pile on the floor by the bed. An unfinished book on the bedside table with a bookmark showing there were seven chapters left to be read.

Silas found keys, perhaps to houses, but there was nothing to tell him where they might fit. He found small notebooks that his father might have carried with him while he worked. The notes were hastily written and nearly illegible. They seemed to be about particular haunted places, small details, circumstances of lives that had come to bad ends; all now anonymous.

Silas found the real estate advertisement for their house in Saltsbridge. This must have been from the days when he was still a baby and his dad was resigned to moving his family out of Lichport. The page had a black-and-white picture of their old house and the layout of the interior rooms with their dimensions. There were numbers and figures scrawled up and down its margins, perhaps mortgage calculations, as well as numerous doodles that made Silas think his dad had had this on his desk for a long time before he told his mother about it and made an offer on the house. Along the bottom of the page was typed "Perfect First Home in Saltsbridge Township!!!" But his father had taken a black felt-tipped pen and struck through most of the letters:

"~~Perfect First Home~~ I~~n~~ S~~altsbridge Township~~!!!"

. . . leaving only the word "P r I S o n."

It felt like someone had hit him square in the chest, and his breath caught in his throat. So that was how his dad thought about the place where he lived with his family. That was why he stayed often here in Lichport. In Saltsbridge he felt tied down, trapped. For the first time Silas allowed himself to consider that maybe his dad wasn't dead or held somewhere against his will, but that he'd just walked away from a life that no longer held any interest for him, away from his son who no longer . . .

Silas dropped the paper back in the open drawer, put his face in his hands, and began to cry. It welled up in him, quietly at first, but then as scenes of the last year ran through his mind, dragging along all his fear and sorrow with them, the sobbing started, big, wracking sobs that he couldn't stop.

Every moment he could think of made it worse. A happy memory of his father, waiting on the porch for him, turned in his stomach like a knife because now he thought he might never see his dad again, and now he thought he finally understood how much his dad hated being in Saltsbridge with his family. Thoughts about his mother living in his uncle's cold house. Seeing himself, alone, walking along the lanes of a town that was crumbling even as he looked on it. The knowledge that the only girl who'd ever liked him was dead and now lost; a figment, a shadow of a shadow.

The sound of his crying had made its way right through the walls. Some moments later there was soft knock at the door that joined the two homes. It took Silas a minute to wipe his eyes and cross the house. When he opened the door, there was Mrs. Bowe. She raised her arms and was hugging him before he could step back. Then he really let go, crying hard into her soft shoulder.

"I know, Silas, I know," she sang. "And that's the worst of it, the part no one ever tells you about."

"What part?" he said, his voice still clenched with grief.

"How it never stops. How the pain of missing people never stops. When you burn your finger in a fire, it hurts, but it only hurts one way because you know what caused the pain and why the pain is there, and you know that it will settle, in a bit. But heart pain has facets, Silas. A thousand different sides, sharp and hard; most of them you don't even know exist, even when you're looking straight at them. When someone leaves, or dies, or doesn't love you in return, well, you may think you know why your heart hurts. But wrapped in there are a hundred kinds of fear all tangled in a knot you can't untie. Nobody wants to be alone. We all fear being left alone, being left behind."

"I don't want to be alone like *them*. I have seen such things, Mrs. Bowe, things that would break a person's heart in two," Silas said.

"I know such things exist. But you must learn to see death as something more than loss, more than absence, more than silence. You must learn to make mourning into memory. For once a person takes leave of his life, that life becomes so much more a part of ours. In death, they come to be in our keeping. The dead find their rest *within* us. Thus, in remembrance, we are never alone. But people forget the power of memory. So we fear death in the deepest place of our very being, because we don't know that memories make us immortal. We focus instead on *being gone* and the awful mystery behind absence.

"Love and death—and those two are very closely bound together—scare us because we can't control them. We fear what we can't control. That fear is really part of what makes us human, but mostly, we're just afraid of the ends of stories we can't foresee. I wish our memories were better."

"I'm not afraid of death." Silas said, the clutching tension in his throat letting go as his tears dried.

"Well, you're the only one who isn't."

"Do you think my dad was scared of death? How could he do his work?"

"Yes. Well, yes, but not like other people. He wasn't afraid of the process of someone dying because, well, what's the point in that? Everyone dies some way or another, eventually. He wasn't afraid of the moment of death, not in most cases, which a lot of folks are, because he'd seen a lot of good deaths, and those lucky folks go easy as you please. Slide right out of the world without pain or grief. He also wasn't afraid of dying himself, at least I don't think so. He'd come close to death a number of times that I know of, and it didn't shake him."

"So he was fearless, huh?"

"No. There were things that scared him terribly. Some I know about, because I was with him when those things rose up close to him. But the thing that scared him most was the thought of something hurting you, the thought of losing you. I know that haunted him. I know that's why he left Lichport. He knew the town was no place for you while you were very young. He knew it had a bad effect on your mother."

"Like everything," Silas threw in, but his heart was no longer in speaking harshly of her. The more he thought about his mother, the more he could see that while they were on different roads, they were each just plain lost. In their life together as a family, maybe for the last ten years, maybe longer, they'd all been living in a kind of perpetual twilight. Not light. Not dark. Not anything. And then when his dad disappeared, the lights went out, and Silas and his mom had been wandering around in the dark looking for a switch. Could he blame her because she hadn't found one either? Each of them had been looking for a way out of their own black midnights, and each of them still had a long way to go until they found some kind of dawn.

"As you please. You know your mother much better than I ever did. But she is your mother and she loves you, even if you don't care for how she shows it, or care for what the weight of her troubles has made of her. Your dad had worries too, but I think he always hoped you could all live here again. The idea of dying somewhere other than Lichport, that scared him. A person likes to think of dying at home."

"Mrs. Bowe, do you think he ran off?"

"No, Silas, I don't. I know he never would leave you like that. He never would."

"Do you think he's dead? Please tell me. You can tell me."

"Silas, I just don't know. You are his son in so many ways— and I know by your eyes you've already seen plenty of this town's strangeness, so I'll tell you this because it's all I am fairly sure of: If he were dead, he would send along word one way or another. Knowing what he knew about the dead and the living and what's between them, and what it's possible to do between one world and the other, well, I can't believe he'd stay quiet unless something was keeping him quiet."

"Then you don't think he's here in Lichport?"

"I didn't say that. I think he may be here, somewhere. I have looked, in my way, and haven't been able to find any trace of him. I know you've spoken with people in town—could no one tell you anything?"

"Nothing that would help me find him, no."

"Not in the last few days?"

Silas shook his head and guessed she had some idea of where he'd been. Maybe a person just looked different after following the dead into their prison houses.

Sitting down, as if asking it wearied her, Mrs. Bowe drew her hands together in her lap and said, "Silas, did you see or hear anything strange at your uncle's?"

"Everything I saw and heard there was strange. Are you saying you think my uncle knows something about my dad? I'm sure he does. I know it. Mrs. Bowe, I'm not asking for facts. I'll settle for intuition. What do you think has happened? What do you think my uncle is capable of?"

Mrs. Bowe got very quiet and drew back into herself, her shoulders slumping forward as if heavy with weight. "I don't know. But there was little love lost between them, and your uncle doesn't seem very distressed by Amos being gone. It's his composure that bothers me. Often it's the sea's calm surface that bespeaks dangerous currents below. I'm not saying I know anything for certain, but your uncle is a man who keeps his secrets close, and it's possible he knows something about your dad's disappearance. Who knows what he may know?"

"I'm not sure I'd describe my uncle as calm. He's like a tight wire all the time."

"Okay, well, maybe I'm just fretful. You spent time in that house, so you know best."

"Mrs. Bowe, I can hear the fear in your voice. I think because you care for me, you don't want to say anything that would make me go back to my uncle's house. But I think my uncle knows *everything* about my dad; what happened to him, where he is. And what's worse, I think my uncle inviting us here was not merely hospitality. He is *doing* something in that house, and he needs my family to be a part of it."

"Maybe, maybe."

Silas watched Mrs. Bowe, the sound of skin making a soft rasping sound as she worried and wrung her hands over and over.

"Your mother is still in that house. And maybe you're like me, fretful. You can't just go accusing people of things. I don't think your uncle should be challenged openly. I think, Silas—and I'm sorry to say it, because I don't want to put any more weight on your shoulders —I think if anyone's going to find your dad, it will be you. I'll help, in what ways I can, you know that. This is your house now. You're safe here and always will be, within these walls."

She drew her shawl around her, put her hand on Silas's shoulder, and told him good night, muttering to herself as she left. Silas closed the door after her and made his way across the hall to his bedroom, hoping that the sobbing, if nothing else, would have tired him out and he'd fall asleep easily now. The house was silent. Even the floorboards had stopped gossiping. It was well past one a.m. and into that portion of evening where things went very quiet, as if the world was waiting for something to happen.

But Silas was tired of living in a world where everyone and everything held its breath.

CHAPTER 52

ANCHOR

MOTHER PEALE ROCKED BY HER FIRE. Silas Umber sat next to her, tapping his foot on the stones of her hearth.

Outside, the night was cold, even for late November. Before dusk a biting wind had risen off the sea and came fast to shore, blowing up the lanes of the Narrows like a quick-running tide, and then rose up, crashing wavelike over the cottages in the midnight lanes, rattling loose slate shingles and blowing smoke in gusts down the chimneys.

Silas was looking at Mother Peale, whose attention was fixed on the embers of the hearth.

"Murk night," she said to the fire.

Though there was no one else in the room, Silas heard a voice say, *Something comes. What is this? What is here?*

Mother Peale said, as if in answer to the air, "The mist ship is at anchor."

Silas wanted to be a part of whatever was happening, so he said, "I can feel it too. I think I've seen it."

On the hearth, the fire leapt up, and Mother Peale turned to look at him, saying, "We all can feel it. I suspect now you could see something more of it if you wanted to."

"Where does it come from?"

"I'm surprised your friend Mrs. Bowe has not told you anything about the mist ship, for it was a Bowe woman who set it sailing on its awful course long ago."

"I think things like that make her nervous," Silas said. "Some of the old stories get her a little upset."

"I see, I see. Perhaps you'd like me to tell you of it? Since you were kind enough to call and keep a widow company?"

"I would, please."

"All right then, since, in a way, this is all your business now." And she began.

"Once and ago there was a sea captain. I will not say his name with things as they are just now." Mother Peale inclined her head toward the harbor. "But he took to visiting one of the Bowe women, a young girl whose mother didn't think very much of this captain, and for good reason. His reputation was a horror in itself, filled with the usual things, more than a hint of piracy and worse. So this mother says no, and no one really knows how the daughter felt about this captain anywise. But this captain, you see, he ain't used to hearing no from anyone, let alone some town woman, so he comes by night and takes this girl from her home and sails off with her. That was terrible, and her mother wept by night and day for the stolen child. But that is not the worst of it, not nearly.

"A fortnight later, the body of her daughter washes up on the beach here. It had not been in the water long, yet was much bruised and battered, and most folks thought she had been beaten to death and thrown in the sea after dying. The girl's mother goes down to the beach, and she looks at her daughter's corpse and knows all—she's wise that way. Puts her hands on the corpse and knows right then everything that's happened, and when she looks up, there, near the horizon, she sees that captain's ship, sailing off after all he's done.

"She waves away her family and neighbors. They leave her there, with her daughter, on the strand. Terrible words she spoke then. Curses and bindings as none should ever speak upon another. And the sky goes dark and the sea churns itself into boiling foam, and she puts the curse of the wave-bound and the water-road on that ship and all aboard it, and that captain most especially. The wander curse, that's what she put on them, and it's a god-awful thing, for it means you may never find rest, never find home. Never."

"What happened then?" Silas asked, sliding his chair closer to the fire.

"Nothing, right away. The child was buried on the Beacon. Folks went back to their lives. The mother of the girl died after a sad, long life, and though I don't expect the Bowes have forgotten the story, no one spoke of it for years and years. Until the ship came back. It has been back to Lichport twice before, according to legend. Once each hundred years. And over those years and from wherever else it sails and takes on crew, it has grown swollen with damned souls. Maybe the ship is a part of hell itself—a piece of the Devil's own fleet, cut loose from its moorings—set upon the seas of the world by that Bowe woman's terrible vengeance. You can hear it coming. *Doom. Doom. Doom* is the sound of its heavy hull as it rises on the swells and crashes back down onto the sea. And when it comes here, it takes on another soul."

"Just one?"

"Tradition holds that to be the case, but it could be more. How could you tell? Perhaps your father would know something like that."

"And it's always a hundred years?"

"Yes, though I can't say why. Could be anything . . . that mother who cursed the ship could have said the captain's name a hundred times to bind him. No one knows. And how long the mist ship stays in harbor—well, that's a bit of a mystery. Once, when Joan was very young, she told me that the kids at school told her the mist ship would take her away to hell if it came, and that scared her so bad she couldn't sleep. I told her not to worry, there were plenty worse people in this town than her to take, but she wouldn't settle, and she asked me real quiet, 'what does it come for, Mama?'

"Well, I give it a good think before answering her. I don't care for lying, Silas, especially to children. But I don't think everyone needs to know everything just because they ask. So I tell her: 'Bad people. Real bad folk. That's who gets on that ship.'

"'Do they ever come back?' Joany asks me, maybe more interested now than scared.

"'No, child, they don't never come back, because to get on that ship, you got to be dead already. Ghosts get on that ship, real bad ghosts of real bad people, and they don't never come back. Not never.'

"So I hope that will suffice as an answer for you, Master Umber, because I ain't got another."

"I hope it is not here long."

"I do too, for the winds that blow from its sails bring madness to the living and dead. It causes to be felt what it is itself. Restlessness. Torment. And both the living and dead can feel it. Let it take what it's come for and be on its way. But as for how long it's here, I think that may depend on your good self."

"What? Why?"

"Just an old woman's intuition. In any event, Silas, unsettling as its arrival is, it is also a thing most rare and uncommon. Shall we look on't together?"

Silas and Mother Peale walked down from her cottage to the wharf. The high winds had cleared the sky, and the moon was bright and full and lit the surface of the sea like a lamp.

The wind worked the edges of the waves into tatters, and there was a loud crack of the surf as the wind pitched it to the sand. But below those sounds lurked another. A low song rose up from the churning sea, a chorus of the lost, rising and falling in hopeless strains.

"Master Umber, if you will oblige me by making use of your watch and taking my hand, we may see something more of this awful rarity."

With his left hand, he took up Mother Peale's hand. With his right, he reached into his pocket and opened the death watch to hold its small dial fast against the worn face. At once the sea before them went wild as if whipped by a furious storm. Spouts of water flew from the crests of great waves, and plumes of white water fanned out and up as if a great weight were repeatedly rising and falling on the sea. Silas watched the salt sea foam flying higher and higher into the air but could see no ship, not even a hint of its rigging as he'd seen from the Yacht Club. He turned to Mother Peale, confused, but her voice rose shrill and crested above the roaring gale. "Look down!"

And there, in the reflection on the sea's face, was the mist ship. Its tall masts stretched out on top of the surging flood. The ship's keel had rotted away, leaving only the hanging skeleton of the hull, curved beams like the ribs of some long-dead whale that had washed up on shore. The sails and jib were little more than thin veils of gauze, and woven into them were the faces of the damned, who wailed and cried, torn again and again by the action of the wind and the horror of their own perdition.

"Oh, God!" said Silas.

"Child," said Mother Peale, "this ain't got nothin' to do with God and that's for certain." She put her arm around him, but then patted him roughly on the back, saying, "Many are lost, Silas Umber. Not so bad as these, maybe"—she gestured at the terrible ship below the waters—"but lost just the same. And so it ever shall be, Undertaker, if you don't get on with your work!"

LEDGER

For whatsoever from one place
doth fall,

Is with the tide unto another
brought:

For there is nothing lost, that
may be found, if sought.

—Edmund Spenser, copied out by Amos Umber

All spirits, provided they are kept in
REMINDED OF their ruling love, can be
led wherever one pleases, and are incapable of
resistance. Their love is like a bond or rope tied
around them by which they may be led and
from which they cannot loose themselves.

—From Swedenborg's *Heaven and Hell*, copied out by Jonas
Umber, amended by Amos Umber

CHAPTER 53

FORWARD AND BACK

EVERYWHERE SILAS LOOKED, pieces of the past flew into his eyes like windblown dust.

As he walked the now familiar path through town that led to the mansion of the Sewing Circle, the road seemed longer than before, because everywhere he looked were reminders of the past. He would become fascinated with a carved stone column, or the worn bricks in a wall, or the ripple in an ancient pane of glass. Each door might lead into another world. He knew that now. And it made him worry that behind every detail might be something he'd missed before, a clue, a key to unlock the mystery of where his dad had gone.

But as he climbed the front steps leading to the mansion's door, a bell still sounded in his mind, ringing again and again: *Come find me. I am here. I am waiting.* Was it Bea or his father calling out to him? Or was it just some lonely portion of his own mind, telling him what he already knew: He was alone in a town more dead than alive? So in desperation he returned to the house of the Sewing Circle. Maybe since he'd now taken his first steps on the mistpaths of Lichport, other scenes had appeared in the tapestry. His great-grandfather had told him that he must know more of the town and its past, must go back to go forward. Well, then maybe it was okay that for every step he took, he ended up retracing his steps.

Silas entered their high chamber and found the three were waiting for him. They said nothing at his arrival, but continued on quietly with their work as he walked back and forth across the room. He would follow one thread for an hour, only to find that it ended at a wall, ultimately connected to nothing but itself. He followed the threads that spun away from town. As he looked closely at the tightly woven strands, he saw the millpond worked out in a strong twisted-knot stitch. The surface of the water was thick with cold-hued silks that seemed to hold that water motionless. He rubbed his eyes and looked closer. Down, below the stitches, there was a girl's form outlined in barely visible needlework. Her body was lashed over in red threads, and she appeared to be sleeping. Silas reached out slowly as though he might pull at the stitches.

"Stop!" said the first of the three. "Do not touch the tapestry!"

"What is worked there cannot be undone. Not by you. Not yet. Hold fast to your road, Silas Umber. The millpond is not why you've come here."

Silas dropped his hand and walked past the millpond. At last he came to stand before the silken marshes, before the portion of the tapestry that depicted the Bowers of the Night Herons. A place he had seen and visited before.

The second of the three finally spoke.

"If you tell us what you're looking for, perhaps we may assist?"

An idea had begun to form in his mind. A plan grounded in sympathy. He had felt the pain and losses of some of the dead. Maybe somewhere there were ghosts who could feel his pain and help him. Maybe there could be *an arrangement*. "I am looking for something connected to *this* place, the Bowers of the Night Herons. My visit there has left a feeling in me . . . I don't know what it is. But the ghosts who reside there are looking for people they've lost, children. In some way, each one of them has lost a child. I have lost my father. That means he has lost me. There is a resonance between us. I can feel it. Maybe if I can help the ghosts of these bowers they will speak to me and help me in return. But I want to help them anyway, even if I don't benefit from it. I think that the more use I am to others, the more I'll be able to help myself."

"He has taken up the father's fallen mantle!" trumpeted the third of the three. "Hail! Lord of January! Hail! King of the D—"

"Enough!" said the first, silencing the third. "We mean to say, it is well that at last you have warmed to the work."

"Maybe," Silas said.

"In that case," said the third and first together, "perhaps we may be more accommodating. Since, after all, we are now business partners."

"Look here! There is a thread—," said the third of the three.

"Do not!" said the second, but the third was already walking to the web.

"I think we may help him. I think we must. Look at the state of the web, the frayed edges, unknotted threads . . . on and on the work goes, because the grief in this place has no end. He may be able to bring about some resolution, and I am eager to cast off, if only for a moment," said the third.

"Resolution at what cost? You wish to help him. Fine. As do I. But he, most especially, should not come to *that place*," said the second.

"Enough! Show him," said the first. "Let him see and decide for himself."

With sharp fingers, the third plucked the thinnest thread from the tip of a marsh reed done in emerald flax and followed its length just a few feet away to a tangle of knots hanging in the air.

"What is it?" asked Silas.

"Look close," said the first.

Here was a square of rough cloth onto which had been stitched numerous knots. At first, Silas couldn't make out any details, but when he brought his face right up to the stitching, he could just make out small figures worked in beneath. Each seemed isolated from the others and was held down to the ground by numerous tiny gray binding stitches and knots. Below those were hidden hundreds of birds, almost invisible, also in gray thread. Wave after wave of little birds was lost in the knotwork.

"Why shouldn't I go there and try to help them? If I *am* the Undertaker, I believe that is my job."

"We can only sew what we know, and that is that there are lost children here. Your pain and theirs are not unrelated. You will have no trouble finding them."

Silas stood back and looked at the portion of the tapestry holding the two misthomes, the Bowers of the Night Herons and the other place where the lost children dwelled; they appeared to share a border. He wondered if each held the thing the other lacked. Maybe they could be joined, brought into accord, and both limbos relieved of their suffering occupants at once. Silas asked the ladies if they could just knit them together, pull the threads and draw them closer, make them one place instead of two.

"Oh, no!" said the first. "That would lead to ruin. You can't just pull threads together like that. It must happen out there first." She pointed out beyond the high window of old rippling glass. "Out there, in the places where the dead reside and gather. Changes occur, things take root, and we make it so on the web. This place, this room, is itself a shadowland, but the weaving is something else entirely. It is a reflection of all misthomes. We can only weave and stitch what is, not what we want to be."

"Have you ever tried?"

The second of the three turned away from the others. The first of the three raised her hand toward Silas.

"Do not ask. These places, these shadowlands and misthomes, are greatly isolated from one another. Although they may appear very close in our work, it is a false perspective. These two limbos you're looking at are separated by the deepest chasm of grief that can form in the human heart: to lose a child. Silas, what you ask cannot be done. Must not be done. We are not the only ones who keep a web, and our work is connected to innumerable others. Threads lead from this place to lands very far removed. All are connected. In the past, others have tried to force things, to bring together misthomes that were not in accord."

The second of the three appeared to be crying. Silas pressed, "What happened?"

"Terrible things," said the first.

"Not to be told." said the third.

"Not even to an Undertaker?" Silas asked again more pointedly.

The first, who was the oldest of the three, rose from her chair and walked toward Silas, her dress trailing frayed tendrils of silk and mist behind her, connecting her, perhaps even binding her, to the portion of the web she had yet to finish. Silas could see the weight of her work on her, and that whoever she had been while living, she was now a part of her weaving, bound to it, something far more extraordinary and powerful than whatever single name she once owned. Now she merely occupied a familiar form from a favored life, but she had become a constellation of forces and fates stretching back in time; a nexus of extraordinary power that had its source far beyond Lichport.

"Ladies," Silas asked with great reverence, "has my father ever visited this place?"

"No. It would never have been open to him. Always you were at the front of his mind and very much alive, so to consider such a misthome as this would have been difficult for him. Not because he was without sympathy, but because to imagine the causes that result in such a world forming is very awful for any parent. To imagine it terrifies them."

The first of the three came up alongside Silas and put a hand lightly on his shoulder. To his surprise, it felt warm. She drew him to the other side of the room away from the others, who had already gone back to their needlework. She walked with him to the window and stopped very suddenly as if something had snagged the hem of her dress.

"What you propose is very dangerous, and I will have no hand it in. Dangerous for me, dangerous for those souls involved, dangerous for you. Silas, there are mysteries within mysteries at work here, and I cannot pretend that in this place and at this time I know much more than I have told you. You know that what you say to the dead can have a profound, even painful effect on them?"

"Yes. I also know that the right words can set them free from their troubles."

"The challenge will not be, I suspect, extricating them from their losses. Like almost all the dead, they may leave their prisons whenever they wish to or acknowledge that they can. The problem will come when *you* try to leave. The condition of the souls bound to this place is very particular, because they are all young, all children. The young have not yet come to full knowledge while alive, and that makes coming close to them in death very perilous. Entering their shadowland will likely affect you greatly and in ways you cannot anticipate. They are lost, and so may cause that condition in those who are like them."

"But I'm not lost . . . I mean, not like that. I know where I am. I know who I am and what, I think, I am becoming."

"Oh, child, please—you have not even the barest knowledge of what the world has in store for you now that you have accepted the mantle of Undertaker. Now that you have returned to Lichport, forces have been set in motion, stitches that may never be picked out or cut. This is an awkward, delicate business all around. Just as you cannot wave your hands and reappear in your simple life before coming here, so you cannot merely clap them to wake up the dead from their troubles. Indeed, it would be very much like waking a sleepwalker. Where will they find themselves? Where did they dream they were? Who are they when they are woken? How will they find themselves? Walking? Dreaming? Dying?

"I will not knot two lands of shadow together, even when, as now, within one may reside the solution to another's grief. You must do this out *there*. You must help them see themselves. You'll have to find a way. But rest assured, when you puzzle it out, we will then do our part and make it so in the tapestry. Then, and only then, may the pattern of the web be changed. Resolve yourself. Set your mind to the task. Do not confuse your world with theirs, no matter how alike they may seem to be. You will have to use what you know to bring peace to the dead you encounter. In the work itself is salvation—for them, perhaps for you, but do not hope for anything in return. Silas, work such as this will require *sacrifice*."

"From them or from me?"

Each of the three was looking at him now and spoke in one voice: "From all."

"Will you tell me where to find them, these lost children?"

"I cannot, because the doors to that world are various," said the first.

As he looked again, Silas could see that there were other

threads, at first hidden from view, leading from the corners of this knotted bit of the web to many other portions, though none, not one thread, connected it to the Bowers of the Night Herons among the marshes.

"For everyone, the entrance to this misthome will be different and individual. You will know where to find it. You must follow your own particular pain to its threshold. Where was the place you felt the most alone, the most lost, the most frightened and miserable? In such recollections will you find it."

Silas didn't even need to think about it.

"School. The playground at school. But I went to school in Saltsbridge. Will I have to go back to Saltsbridge?"

"How tiresome," said the third. "I would not have taken him for a literalist—"

But the first spoke again, cutting off her sister.

"Any such place should be sufficient to provide an entrance for you, for many children share a common story and bear similar portions of sadness when it comes to regret and loss. By foot, you will not have to travel far to find the Playground." And as the first said the word "playground," a large portion of the tapestry shivered, like the taut thread of a spider's web when a fly becomes trapped in it. Very suddenly, the second began stitching a slide to the ground cloth where Silas had been looking, then swings and benches, and in the corner, the outline of a tree in rough nut-brown yarn.

"There!" cried the first. "You see! Already your mind hovers about this place, remembering, and already it is changing. Silas Umber, take great care! This shadowland is waiting for you. It knows you are coming."

THE DAYS OF YOUTH ARE MADE FOR
GLEE, AND TIME IS ON THE WING.

—transcribed in haste in the hand of Amos Umber, quoted
from "The Miller of Dee"

Once I saw a little bird

Come hop, hop, hop;

So I cried, "Little bird,

Will you stop, stop, stop?"

And was going to the window

To say, "How do you do?"

But he shook his little tail,

And far away he flew.

—Overheard on the Lichport salt marsh, March 23, 1924.
From Mother Goose

The hours must be endured and those who cannot do so in life will most surely do so in death. You say you cannot face them? Life's joys and pains both? You shall find them waiting for you, a world of ignored moments there to be explored. Then shall you know how long an hour can be, shall feel the awful depth and restlessness of even a single day, and all the days you fled from life while you were alive.

—From *The Sermon Book of Abraham Umber*, 1810

CHAPTER 54

ON MAIN STREET, near the edge of town, stood the old Catholic church, long since abandoned. Behind it, on the church's north side, by custom, was a small, derelict cemetery holding the mostly unmarked graves of travelers or strangers who died anonymously in Lichport before the Lost Ground graveyard had been consecrated. Unbaptized children were also brought to the church, and white stones lay deep in the tall grass marking those long-forgotten little graves. Directly across from the church was the school. Like the church, the school hadn't been used in years. Any children left in town either went to residential schools in Kingsport, or attended a small irregularly meeting classroom in the Narrows. North of the school, church, and cemetery was a weedy, fenced-in plot that was once the school playground. Rusted swings and a slide still stood there, and at its far corner grew a thick low tree, its trunk scarred with the names of children, which, though carved deep, were year by year vanishing below the thickening bark.

Silas had never explored these buildings, though he'd passed them many times. He had been a baby when he'd left Lichport and had never attended this school, yet the playground felt vaguely familiar to him. At one end, as on all playgrounds, popular children would have once gathered around the swings and worn benches to talk. At the other end, by the tree, one or two awkward kids would hide, talking quietly about their unpopular interests until the bell sounded to bring them all back to supervised activities in the bland, orderly world of their classrooms.

A small breeze whipped at the weeds that grew up through the cracks in the pavement, pushing and pulling at the swings that whined on their rusted chains. In the tree, and in the bushes that grew wild around the playground's fence, he could hear hidden creatures. The long, lone cry of a small bird pierced his ears, calling out again and again but never answered, though other birds seemed to move invisibly among the branches.

Silas opened the small rusted gate and walked onto the playground. He took the death watch from his pocket and held it for a moment without opening it. The sound of the wind grew louder. A plastic bag rose and fell on the air, hovered, then dropped to the ground, where it made spirals and scraped the pavement before leaping up again. Up and down it went, never blowing away. The death watch was heavy in his hand, and Silas could feel it tick in time with his heartbeat. It was as though it had become a part of him, this strange artifact; a second small heart that beat outside his body. When he felt it ticking like this, Silas knew that the watch *wanted* to be used, that it wanted to show him something, like a child begging for attention. He wasn't sure he entirely liked that sensation. But he had come to the playground with a purpose. He opened the skull and brought his thumb down hard on the dial until the clock's tiny mechanical heartbeat stopped.

At first, nothing stood out. The day remained gray. The weeds waved from their beds of broken pavement. The sound of the birds was getting louder, many of them calling out from their hidden perches, though none in concert. And in little pockets about the edges of the playground, the shapes of children stepped from the shadows. It was hard to make out faces, but their eyes, lidless and white as stones, shone from below their brows.

Silas turned in a full circle, and when he looked at the tree, one child hovered there near the trunk, slightly more discernible than the others, looking at him. When Silas took a step toward him, stooping slightly to bring himself closer to the child's height, the little boy drew back from him, scared.

The surface of the child's form was constantly changing, his skin a palette of shifting colors. He was covered in blotches of dark pigment, like clouds casting their shadows on his skin. Bruises, all the colors of bruises.

"Did someone hit you?" Silas asked, reaching out to the child.

"No one hit me," he said, recoiling back into himself, becoming smaller, the colors on his skin intensifying as he shrank.

"Did someone hurt you?"

"My stomach hurts. I want to go to the nurse. Why won't they play with me? I want to go home." The child was drawing farther and farther away from Silas now, and the air around his form began to darken like his skin, so it was becoming harder to see the child's shape. It was receding into the long, irregular shadow cast by the tree. "Why can't you leave me alone like everyone else?"

"Wait! Wait! I won't hurt you. I want to help," Silas called out.

"Please!" the child pleaded. "No more. No more words. They hurt. You're hurting me." The child moved in and out of the dusky air. When for a fleeting moment Silas could see him clearly, he saw that all the child's skin was now the plum-black stain of a bruise. The boy was defenseless and everything he heard hurt him.

"Where is my father?" the child asked pitifully, his eyes cast down, his shoulders making tiny jumps as he began to cry. "Do you know where my dad is?"

Silas had begun to grow very cold. At the edges of his vision, the gates of the playground were growing less and less distinct.

"What is your father's name?" Silas asked. "Maybe I can help you find him."

The child moved toward Silas very slowly and stood before him, a wave of freezing air rising up behind and breaking like a wave, crystallizing his features, making them sharper every second. The small boy raised his head to look at Silas, his white eyes bright and hanging in the air like two cold stars.

"Amos. My father is Amos," said the child, "and I can't find him. Where is he? I can't find my dad. Why won't he come for me?"

When the child spoke his father's name, Silas felt hands seize his chest and he stood stunned, unable to move or breathe. The boy's face was clearly visible now, even behind the bruises, and Silas could see himself in the childish features. He reached out and took the child's small hand and he could feel it, like it was one of his own hands holding its mate. In that instant Silas knew with complete certainty that he had unknowingly found his way into the limbo that awaited him at his death. Here, to this awful twilight, was where he would come at his life's end.

Papers blew and drifted over the shattered pavement. There were birds in all the trees, and each called out discordantly against the others so that no one song could be heard, but the air was full of noise and distraction. The equipment on the playground was now filled with gray shapes of children. They did not look at one another, their pale, unblinking eyes staring forward. Silas looked absently this way and that, trying to make out any of the faces, but no one held its form and no one would look back at him. And how could he know them? Here were lost children from many lands, many times. Silas felt very small and as though there were no weight to him anymore. A word from anyone, the smallest wind, would puff him away.

He sat at the base of the familiar tree, his once daily perch, its exposed roots polished from years of other children waiting there; waiting for a bell to ring, waiting to go home. He could see a few names carved into the lower trunk of the tree. None looked familiar. Nothing stood out.

Silas had crumpled into a posture of retreat and fearful expectation. Among the timeworn roots of the tree, he sat with his head on his upraised knees and his arms wrapped around, clasped together in front of him. There was cold metal clutched in his right fist. He couldn't remember what it was, but he knew he couldn't let go of it. Not ever. He was staring at the ground in resignation. When he heard a noise, his head would briefly fly up to see if someone was coming, but then quickly fall back down again, his eyes rimmed with rising tears. In the distance, he thought he heard a car. He strained to see, searching for a familiar shape: his dad's car, or one of his parents walking to the playground to find him. But his father wasn't there, and his mother had forgotten to come. So he waited, for a hundred years it seemed, and his father was not there, and was not there, and was not coming. He put his head back down and felt himself melting—like the old carved names—down into the bark of the tree. He could hear the other birds but not see them. The voices of other children were about him too but had become just an indistinct circle of sounds, isolating him from the rest of the world. *I am invisible*, he said to himself, at himself, trying to block out the noise.

I am invisible.

And I am alone.

They forgot me.

I don't want to be here by myself.

I don't want to be alone.

I want to go home.

I don't want to look at their faces. When I see them not seeing me, I feel sick.

My stomach hurts. I want to go to the nurse. I want to go home.

The kid from math I never spoke to walked past me.

I am not here.

Is that the girl who's been in homeroom with me for three years?

You know her. You know her name. Idiot. Say it.

There's Math Kid. Say his name.

He'll turn around.

I can't. He won't hear me. He'll ignore me because I am not here.

See? Invisible. No ones saves me a place at lunch.

Because when someone looks I look away.

They go on talking about something else. I'll never ask now.

Maybe at recess. Maybe they'll see me. Maybe someone will call my name.

I might get called. I might. Hey! You wanna play? No one will mind.

I'm Silas.

Hi.

I'm Silas.

Can I play?

Can I play with you guys?

The playground is loud with words, so many I can't hear myself anymore.

But no words for me.

Okay. Later, guys. I'll just say: Another time, it's okay. They don't turn around because I am not here. I am invisible.

I'll be over there. By the tree. If you need another player. I'll just be by the tree. But when I walk away, I disappear like I was never there.

Liar. I just lied. I told my dad I'd try to make friends, but I can't say their names.

There's something wrong with me. They know it.

I won't tell my dad about school, because he hates a liar.

Lies murder the world, he tells me. I'm a liar because I don't want to make him angry.

Maybe he knows. Maybe that's why he won't come to get me and bring me home. Because he knows I'm invisible too. It's not my fault they can't see me. He's mad at me because I don't have any friends and because he knows it.

If you're invisible, you don't count.

No one wants to be with someone they can't see.

My stomach hurts.

I want to go home.

Please.

Dad?

A child sits by the tree on the playground. Every day it is the same. He sits by the tree. He does not look up anymore. No one comes for him. He can no longer remember what he is waiting for or how long he's been waiting. There is only the tree and the cold earth below him and the voices calling out from the yard, but they never once say his name. He can barely remember his name anymore. He lays his head down on his folded arms and closes his eyes, and he doesn't know how long he's been there or how long it has been since he closed his eyes, and every second becomes a lifetime to him.

The child does not know how long he's had his head down.

But then, as his tears fall, the ground begins to feel different, no longer the frozen clay of winter, but warming now, even as he sits on it. There is movement in the branches, and the air around the tree stirs with unexpected heat, and from the brightening air behind the tree, these words fly to him, and he hears a name—his name.

Come outside and play, Silas! You've been inside too long! Come outside!

Silas lifted his head to look about him for the source of the voice.

It was Tom.

And Tom's name, like a key, opened a door in Silas's mind, and bright memories began to fill up the dark corners.

At first he could see Tom's face as it was on a Saturday afternoon seven years ago, when they played and played until the dark came, but then more of the past emerged. Silas watched Tom's face change, saw it pale and grow still as it might have looked on the day of his funeral. Silas wasn't allowed to go, but he'd had nightmares about seeing Tom in his coffin. And now that image rose again. Silas slammed his eyes shut and turned his head back to the roots of the waiting tree, the cold light falling around him once more.

But the voice spoke again, pushing back the graying air.

No, said Tom. *Not like that. Like this. Silas? Look! Say my name. Remember me.*

"Tom?"

Silas raised his head again and Tom was standing before him, smiling, holding out his hand. Silas reached up and took it, and as he stood up, the present enfolded him. As he remembered what had happened and where he was, some of the heaviness fell away from his limbs like dead branches shaken from a tree by spring winds. But as he awoke to himself, he was concerned now for Tom, worried to see him in such a place.

"Are you trapped here too, Tom?"

"I am not trapped here, Si, I'm waiting here."

"For what?"

"You, Silas."

Silas's eyes welled up at hearing his name spoken by someone who loved him.

"Why? I mean, how could you know? I don't understand."

"Nothing to understand. There is no great mystery in friendship. You brought yourself here, just as I brought myself here to wait for you. I don't even mind that you've kept me waiting." Tom was grinning now. "To me, it is hardly a moment anyway since last time I saw you. Just a breath ago we were playing. But why have you come to such a place?"

"I . . . I don't know."

Tom looked around and then lifted his head as though seeing something familiar in the distance. Silas couldn't see anything else, and he wondered if they were both looking on the same world. He saw the shattered concrete of the playground. A place where lines were drawn and some were out and some were in. A place he hated.

Tom saw Silas's face, fallen and unsure, and moved closer to him.

"While I waited for you, I've been running through our Saturday afternoon. That moment is ours to keep. Look, it's just there." At the far end of the playground, Silas could see the long stretch of grass that ran between the houses on their street back in Saltsbridge where he and Tom had played seven years ago, an island of light lying beyond a gray sea. Silas looked at his arms, his hands, his ashen skin, and then looked at Tom's golden hands and face. They were lit by the light of two different worlds.

"That world and a thousand others are waiting, yet here you are," Tom said, gesturing at the bleak landscape of the playground around them. "You should know better than anyone, Silas, better than anyone. We choose these things. These are our choices to make and nobody else's."

As Tom was speaking, the hard shadows of the playground's embankments and borders had become a receding tide. Silas could see the gates and the empty playground equipment again. The child-like forms had vanished, though the small branches of the tree were filled with birds and were shaking with anticipation. The air of the playground was changing, and the birds could feel it. They began calling and crying out all at once from the foliage, but their voices suddenly dropped off, becoming low, frantic chirps. The whispering world was holding its breath, and the small birds were waiting.

Tom was fading from the brightening air.

"Tom!" Silas called out to him. "Tom! You are my best friend!"

Tom, still smiling, was nearly indiscernible from the light rising from the land.

"See you soon, Silas. Okay? See you soon?"

In the space left by Tom's absence, Silas remembered how many times his dad had come to the playground to pick him up; late, because his mother was supposed to come but had forgotten. One time his father had driven all the way back from Lichport to get him. One of the teachers had offered to drive Silas home, but he had refused, saying he was sure one of his parents was coming. He had wanted them to come, but if they didn't, he was going to sit there until they noticed he hadn't come home. Had he been less stubborn, he'd have been home hours ago. His choice. It was nearly dark when Amos walked onto the playground and found Silas sitting under the tree. Silas didn't look up when his dad sat down on the ground next to him.

"I thought you'd forgotten me."

"No way, little bird. Did you forget me?"

"No."

"That's right, because we are stuck together. I might be late, but I'll always be there."

"I think being forgotten must be horrible," Silas had said, warming a little as his dad took his hand and pulled him to his feet, then walked with him away from the tree and toward the parking lot.

"Worst thing in the world, little bird. *The* worst," Amos had said.

Silas could still feel the death watch pressed hard into his palm. His thumb felt frozen to the dial, but he lifted it away and released the mechanism. He half expected to see his father, but he was alone on the empty playground, without even the sound of the birds for company.

No birds, Silas noticed.

Not flown away.

Just gone.

And quite suddenly he realized that the birds were not part of the waking world. Their world was the shadowland of the playground, and when the death watch continued marking time, they had vanished.

Steeling himself against whatever he might see, Silas returned his thumb to the dial of the death watch and time stopped again. There were children sitting, their legs hanging down from all the branches of the trees. He could see their faces now.

Silas turned around and around, his heart beating fast, looking at as many of the children's faces as he could, then called out:

"You have been lost here. Now it is time to go home. For some, kin are waiting. For others, there are safe bowers and the arms of mothers who wait to hold you. I am the Undertaker. I am Silas Umber of Lichport. I am here to help you. I am your friend. You are not alone."

As he spoke, the ghosts became clearer and clearer, until it seemed they could discern him as well. Silas could see some recognition on some of their faces. One was smiling tentatively, expectantly.

Without thinking, Silas began to sing the song his father had sung to him, amending the end to suit the need. He didn't know their names or what had brought them to this place, but he would help them if he could, and he knew where to take them.

Hush-a-bye, little ones, aye, aye;
Hush-a-bye, little ones, aye.
The night birds are singing,
And glad bells a-ringing
And it's time for you now to fly.
Little birds,
It's time for you now to fly.

Fly with me, fly with me, aye, aye
Fly with me, little birds, aye.
Your mothers are waiting,
For ages awaiting
Little birds to their waiting arms fly!

Then Silas shouted out with gladness ringing in his voice, "Little birds, fly with me. We love you, all this time we've been waiting for you, come with me!"

They rose from their perches in the tree, rising as birds again, each spirit moving on small wings. They rose together into the air above Silas's head, one great longing carried up by a hundred hopeful hearts. Some of the small birds flew in other directions, to homes long lost to them, to waiting family, to their rests. Others were truly lost and needed more time to remember what it was they once were, to make an account of their losses. Silas did not know their names, and they did not, or could not, speak. But he knew who would care for them tenderly. He knew who would keep them close until they could make their way on their own. It was these lost children who flew after him, following Silas to the marshes.

As Silas arrived at the Bowers of the Night Herons, the air above him was an eager tempest of swift-winged spirits. The night herons were already stirring, many standing on the edges of their high nests, looking frantically for the source of the cries coming from the small spirits flying above Silas. The women swiftly rose up as birds until there were two flocks turning about the tops of the trees. A great calling was heard, and the sky rang with bird-song. A sob of joy flew up over the marshes, and Silas could do nothing else but weep himself. And those bowers of absence and loss became the nesting places of peace.

With their deep mourning past, Silas thought many of the women and children would abandon the nests, move on, vanish into the contentment of their reunions. Yet many remained, glad for a time in each other's company, quiet children resting, secure in the love only a mother may bring to a child, even if the child was not hers in life. They were all at peace; not looking, in that moment, for any other place or any other thing. No past or future existed for them. There was only mother and child, and nothing else in all the wide world. And Silas knew that his plan to ask them about his own troubles was foolish. *Leave them to their long-overdue joy*, he thought. He turned away from the marshes and released the dial of the death watch.

Silas knew his troubles were his own, not the dead's, and he would settle them himself, one way or another. He made his way toward the Beacon, wanting to look out over the town. His heart was beating fast, briefly happy at the good work he'd done, but there was more and darker work ahead of him.

... Some men through the feebleness of their sight, beholding in the air near unto them ... suppose they see their own angels or soules: and so as the Proverbe is, they fear their own shadow. ... And we many times suppose those things which we see, to be far otherwise than indeed they are.

—Transcribed by Jonas Umber from the work of Lewes Lavater, *Of Ghosts and Spirits Walking by Night* (1572)

CHAPTER 55

FIRE WITHIN

Silas left the marshes and walked along the footpath toward Cedar Street, heading toward the Beacon, but as he approached the bridge to Fort Street, he turned instead and went to the house of his great-grandfather. *Fort Street for fortitude,* he told himself.

As he entered the large second-floor chamber, he found his great-grandfather still sitting in the chair, looking out the window.

"Ah! Silas!" the corpse said in a joyful rasp. "It is very good of you to come. Indeed, I suggest you make yourself comfortable and stay a while. Things that love the night love not nights such as these."

"But the sky is very clear . . . ," Silas said, but then understood his great-grandfather's meaning. "You're right. It's going to be a bad night. I just wanted to see you, too . . . you know, be with you again in case . . . well, anyway, it's just good to see you. I can't stay long, though. I have things I must do."

"Yes, I expect you do. There is trouble written right across your brow. How has it been with you?"

Silas told his great-grandfather about the shadowlands where he had walked looking for his father and about the ship and his fears about going back to his uncle's house on Temple Street.

"I think, Silas, you have known for some time that you'd need to go back to that house. Your uncle is, I fear, part of your father's unfinished work. In Lichport, we see to our own affairs, and settle them in whatever way the situation requires. There's a lot on your plate at present, I know. But some things you can do something about, while others may only get sorted out in the fullness of time. If it were me, I'd start attending to what I knew I could settle right now. Today. A man can't walk on two roads at once, at least, not if he's hoping to get anywhere."

"But how can I settle what I can't find? Bea is gone. And I don't even know if my dad—"

His great-grandfather interrupted him and said sternly, "Forgive me. You know where you must go. Kin must see to kin. Settle your family affairs before any other thing. You are the man of the house now. Act like it."

Now, as Silas walked quickly toward the Beacon, every sensation—the wind, the smell of earth, the beading of sweat on his forehead—made him feel more and more solid, washing away the mud of his immaturity, firing the clay of the man he hoped to become.

He could feel the soles of his shoes getting hot as he began climbing the hill. It was as if the soil of the Beacon had been mixed with embers, as if somewhere below his feet a fire was burning and warming the soil. Pausing, Silas leaned over and placed the cool skin of his palm flat on the ground. No illusion. It was warm, and now, with his head closer to the earth, he thought he could hear a kind of music below, a tune tapped out on slate and bone. Standing, he listened again for other sounds. Nothing stirred on the air, but still the drumming below continued, and with its rising rhythm, a vision engulfed him. He closed his eyes and was looking through the ground beneath him into the heart of the hill. Below was a great chamber, a massive vault of stone, and on the slabs of the floor, the dead of the town danced together, hands joined in dozens of interlocking circles, all the ages of Lichport moving with and through each other like the inner workings of a massive clock, turning, turning in a beautiful and terrible *danse macabre*. He could feel himself leaning toward them, leaning down into the earth. The music pulled at him, but as he began to reach toward the dancers, his grandfather's face rose up in front of him. He did not speak, but his expression was comforting and seemed to say, *Here are your earth-fast kin. They have always been here. We shall always be here. We are with you. On the earth or within it, we are with you.*

Silas opened his eyes. Heart racing, he moved quickly to the top of the hill. Never once during his whole life in Saltsbridge had he ever felt as alive as he did at this moment. Many times after his father had disappeared, Silas had thought of running away. How often had he starting walking, telling himself, *Get out. Leave. Who would care? I have nothing here in Saltsbridge now. I can go anywhere, get a job, live my life. Change my name. I could just disappear. Like him. Disappear.* But always, always, just at his side, or in his mind, a small, sure voice whispered, *Go home.* And now he knew the voice had meant Lichport.

This was where he was meant to be.

As he mounted the top of the Beacon, the wind began to show its teeth, slavering across the town like a pack of dogs, biting at his skin. He drew up the collar of his jacket and looked out toward the water.

From the top of the hill, with the dial of the death watch stopped, Silas could see the mist ship in the harbor, a patient and predatory animal waiting on the foam. It felt like the whole world was waiting for him to do something. Nothing would shift until he acted. No more questions now. Looking back over the town, he could see only a crossroads, a place of stasis, a ghost on every rooftop, just sitting there. Like the dead, Silas had made Lichport into his own personal limbo.

That time was over.

He released the hand of the death watch, and the mist came away from the land.

He was going to get his mother out of his uncle's house. And when he was there, he was going into his uncle's Camera Obscura, even if he had to break down the door with an ax. Whatever was in there, whoever was in there—his dad, his uncle's wife, even if it was an empty room—he would look at it straight on and then deal with whatever consequences his uncle might have coming to him. He wasn't running anymore, and the time for answers had come. Before the night was over, Silas would know what Uncle knew.

He was the Undertaker. He was responsible not only for his family but for the well-being of the town, its living and its dead. He would go back to his uncle's house. He would find a way to send the mist ship back to wherever it had come from. He would find his father, one way or another. And when that was done, he would find Bea, too, and help her if he could.

Silas felt the heat within the hill rising through him, as if all the dead of Lichport were filling up the gaps in his resolve. Every moment he stood there, he grew more certain that his hour was upon him. Hiding wasn't the answer. Neither was leaving the town's problems to someone else. Besides, Uncle was *his* problem. *Kin must see to kin.* Both his great-grandfather and his uncle had told him that.

So be it.

CHAPTER 56

CAN'T HIDE

WHEN SILAS GOT BACK HOME, he learned that his return to Temple Street had been anticipated, even expected.

The note was supposedly from his mother. "Come back," it read. "I need you. I am ill and I need you. Please visit as soon you can, Si. Please." He could feel the fear bleeding from the fibers of the paper as his finger smudged the dark ink letters, even though it wasn't written in his mother's hand.

He knew his uncle had written it, and the knowledge was fuel to the fire that now burned in him.

Mrs. Bowe was telling him not to go back to that house. She wrung her hands and worried the threads at the edges of her sleeves. She kept saying it and saying it. Like she knew already what was waiting for him there. But he couldn't be talked out of it. He didn't feel scared anymore, and he almost didn't care what he'd find or what might happen to him. If he opened a door in his uncle's house and found his dad's corpse, fine. He could cry later. Right now, he just wanted to know the truth. Whatever the answers might be, Silas just wanted all the blank spaces in his life filled in.

He stood very still. He looked at Mrs. Bowe, willing her to calm down, to stop talking, just for a moment. It seemed to work. She lowered her voice, the shrillness subsiding.

"I am going to get my mom," Silas told her calmly.

They both knew there was another reason he was going.

"Besides," he added, "who knows what else I might find in that house? And if I should die trying to find out the truth, well, I think now there are worse things than death."

He could see his calm was terrifying her.

Mrs. Bowe stood up so quickly that she knocked over the small side table next to her chair.

"Silas, I am asking you to wait. You have friends. People who care about you. People who want to help you. Let's call some folks over and figure things out. Your uncle is one man, he can't stand against the whole town. Maybe if some of us went over there together—"

"The whole town?" Silas interrupted. "How many people would that be, anyway? No. He's my uncle and my problem. Besides, were you planning on going over there *with* me? No one's died that I know of. We are not going to a funeral. Are you leaving the house now? Did I miss something? Are you accepting invitations again? Are you going for walks?"

Mrs. Bowe didn't answer, but only lowered her head, ashamed. Silas took her hand.

"I can't hide away like you. Do you think I should stay in the study for the rest of my life, maybe find some dark cottage down in the Narrows to hide in? Should I just hole up somewhere and watch the days and hours come and go like the tide? I could run from him, from my uncle, like you, just avoid him and whatever or whoever he's got locked up there in that workroom, but this is my town now and I won't be chased out of it, or made to feel like I should become invisible. Not again."

"Silas," she said, "I'm not arguing with you. You're right. You have a life here, and you shouldn't turn away from what you've made for yourself. I'm just asking you to think about what you're doing and wait before you do something foolish. Your uncle may be capable of terrible things—please."

Silas didn't want to talk anymore. He added pointedly and tenderly, "Mrs. Bowe, this is your town too, your home, and I don't think you need to hide from anything either."

He left her side and threw the front door wide open. "See? Nothing out there that isn't in here." He gestured to the room and then rapped his finger against the side of his head. "My uncle's in here, too! So no more hiding. I am going over there, and one way or another I am going to find out what he's been up to. I could feel it every day I lived in that house. He's hiding something, and I'm going to find out what it is."

He was sweating now, a coursing heat running along his spine, like when he lay against the bronze lion at the gates of Newfield Cemetery. And somewhere, deep in his chest, a low growl rose— made of anger and courage both—as if the lion had escaped its bronze sepulchre and was now crouching inside him, its free and fearless ghost running wild in his blood.

He had worked himself into a fury. Before he left, he ran over to Mrs. Bowe. He grabbed her hand in his and squeezed it tightly. Without another word, he pulled up the collar on his father's coat and then ran out the front door and down the steps, leaving the door open behind him.

All the fretting and arguing had worn her out. Mrs. Bowe sat in the quiet parlor of her house, trying to decide what to do next, what to do for Silas, afraid to move, worried that anything she might do would only make things worse. There was a familiar stirring in the air. Her man rose up from the floor beside her, leaned over her shoulder, and breathed words into her ear.

Immediately she rose from her chair. Through the still-open

door, the distant cries of seabirds came in off the sea.

She went first out the back door to her garden, to the mausoleum, to the hive, though she knew it was late in the year for the bees. She spoke quickly, and a gentle buzzing rose, growing louder. She explained and pleaded, telling them everything she could remember. "Please . . . ," she said. The swarm roused to her words, and the doorway of the tomb poured forth gold. The bees of the hive were flying fast. They hovered only briefly over the house, perhaps not liking the cooler air, then descended like a cloud of smoke and flew low over the warmer streets, away toward the Narrows.

Mrs. Bowe moved quickly. She went for her coat and tall boots, got as far as the front porch, and stopped. She told herself there was nothing out there to be afraid of. She took a step down, but then came back up to the porch, opening the door again and stepping back over the threshold into her foyer. She was breathing hard. Panic flowered in her like a hot flash. *Breathe*, she told herself. *Let it be no different from the garden.* "The world is my Eden," she said under her breath. She remembered, as a girl, wandering up and down the streets of Lichport. This was her town. She could go where she liked. Next to the door was an umbrella stand. She searched among the handles and drew forth a thick staff of blackthorn that had come with her mother's people from Ireland. As she tested its weight in her hands, she said:

"Yea, though I walk through the valley of the shadow of death, I will fear no evil: for thou art with me; thy rod and thy staff they comfort me. Thou preparest a table before me in the presence of mine enemies: thou anointest my head with oil; my cup runneth over. Surely goodness and mercy shall follow me all the days of my life: and I will dwell in the house of the Lord forever."

Mrs. Bowe walked out onto her porch and closed the door

behind her. She paused for a moment. She looked down, seeing her shadow on the stone, and then, without looking back, descended the steps to the street. She hadn't bothered locking the door. When she got to the sidewalk, she paused again. She wasn't sure which way she should go for help. The flight of the bees confirmed that possibilities lay in both directions. She looked briefly east, toward the Narrows, and prayed that the bees had carried her message there. Then she hurried off, slowing often to a sort of trot, then walking as fast as she could, all the while trying to catch her breath. West and then north her brisk stride carried her, on, on, toward the marshes.

CHAPTER 57

HOMECOMING

THE MOMENT HIS FEET STRUCK Temple Street, Silas's stomach tightened.

He went first to the garage and got the ax, then walked quickly to the porch, leaning the ax against the house next to the door frame, just out of view.

Silas knocked on the front door. He could have entered with the key he still had, but he wanted his uncle to come downstairs, away from his mother, or anything or anyone else that might help him.

When Uncle opened the door, he was disheveled, clothes and face filthy, hair unwashed, but when he laid eyes on Silas, he became elated. He looked frantically over his shoulder toward the stairs and then back at Silas, whose own wild hair was like a mane about his face. Uncle held out both arms. His hands were shaking.

"Silas! My son! Welcome home! Come in, come—" But he didn't get to finish his welcome, because Silas swung at him hard, hitting Uncle solidly in the side of the head, knocking him to the floor of the entry hall, where he lay dazed, his head moving slowly from side to side.

Silas crouched down by Uncle for a moment—he was still breathing—then stepped quickly over him and retrieved the ax from near the door. His hand throbbed from the blow. He flexed it open and closed as he strode back over his uncle's body and leapt for the stairs.

He could see from the landing that a lock had been put on the outside of his mother's bedroom door. Silas prayed that it meant she was safely inside.

He passed quickly through Uncle's stale-smelling bedroom and the outer chamber, and found the door to the Camera Obscura open. The room was dimly lit by a small lamp.

In the middle of the room was an enormous bottle, some huge industrial glass ampoule. Over six feet high, it flared slightly at the sides and had an open top. It was resting on a large, low wooden table and a short ladder stood on the floor next to it. Silas lit a candle, and its light threw strange reflections across the curved surface of the glass. Fearing the worst, he stepped forward and looked intently at the glass, trying to see past its light-strewn surface into its darker depths. At first, all he could see was his own distorted reflection, magnified. The glass caught everything before it, held the room on its surface. The closer Silas looked, the more distortion he saw, no matter which angle he tried. Slowly his incessant stare began to pierce beyond the surface and into what lay beyond. His heart beat madly in his chest as terror and confusion coursed through him like an electric current.

Blood pounded in his ears, and he was unable to look away from the strange corpse floating in the glass; so he did not hear or see Uncle stumbling into the room behind him. Quickly Uncle put an arm around Silas and tightened his grip around his neck. Silas struggled, but his uncle's arm was made of stone and held him fast. He could hear Uncle's voice, raspy and only slightly slurred from the blow to his head.

"I am sorry, Silas, that Lichport has let you down in so many ways. You have come seeking something, and I fear you are to be disappointed. But that doesn't mean there isn't business to attend to. Still, I know how very much you have wanted to see my little study. Well, here you are."

At that, Uncle pushed a cloth sodden with chemicals to Silas's face, covering his mouth and nose.

Silas looked about the room, kicking frantically.

Uncle's hand was immovable.

"Calm yourself, son. There is no rush, I assure you. You will be here for some time."

Silas succumbed to the fumes. His head tilted up, his eyes rolled back, and in a blurring instant, he found himself looking backward, right into the dark inside of his own skull as he hit the floor.

Silas awoke to find himself tied to a chair directly in front of the glass vessel. Another lamp had been lit and hung from the ceiling, its light making the golden liquid in the glass glow like amber.

"What is this?" Silas coughed as consciousness returned to him. He could barely speak. His eyes were wide open, searching again for recognizable details among the pale limbs of the body beneath the glass. "Who is this? Did you do this? Did you do this to him?"

"Do you mean did I kill him?"

"Y-yes—," Silas stammered. His whole body was shaking, and sweat was coursing into his eyes, mixing with his desperate tears.

"No. Of course not."

"That's him, isn't it? It's my dad!" He could hardly imagine what it would have taken to do that to his father's body, what horrible efforts it would have required to render him into the contorted, preserved relic he saw before him. Sickened, Silas closed his eyes to block the sight of it. He hung his head and sobbed.

His uncle reached out to him, tenderly putting his hand on his nephew's sweat-soaked head before Silas violently jerked away.

"No. No. Your father is not in this room, though rest assured, he will not trouble anyone again. A family needs only one father, after all. But you should know, son, that Amos—the man who presided over your *first* birth—is dead and shall not return."

A soft moan came up from Silas's throat, an exhalation of air that sounded like life itself was escaping from his wracked frame.

Uncle moved closer to the enormous glass apothecary jar that held the preserved corpse. He climbed a few rungs of the ladder, then reached his hand over and into the liquid, and gently brushed the face's cheek with the back of his hand. "Silas, this is Adam, *my* son."

Uncle said these words with such pride, such tenderness, that for an instant, Silas forgot where he was and what he was looking at. But then he began to look closely at the corpse in the glass vessel. Silas could see that the body was too small to be his dad. Uncle's words held in the air for a moment. They rang true.

Within the enormous ampoule, he could see a face. The nose was pressed up against the glass, one eye larger than the other, as if trying desperately to see out. Through the thick, curved glass, Silas could just begin to make out the familiar features of the face that had stood over him that night, breathing, in his room.

"What did you do to him?" demanded Silas, becoming hysterical.

"I didn't *do* anything to him, Silas. He is as nature made him. What you see is the work of corrupting nature. I did not kill him. I kept him, and let me tell you, every day of his short life was like a century to me, and when the blessing of death came to him on its own, I only preserved him, maintained the vessel, in a vessel. And because of my careful work, *he is still here*. Can't you feel him in this room? He has never left this house and he never will, for, being as he was, he will never come to full knowledge. But here, in this chamber, he will be assured the comfort that nature denied him in his brief life. You are that comfort, Silas. You are nearly brothers, you two. Both now my sons. Adam already knows and loves you well. I have realized, at last, that your shared blood binds you, and that kinship will allow you to perceive each other, be a friend to each other in, well, in what comes next."

Silas tried to reach his pocket to get at the death watch, but his hands were bound behind his back.

There was no need.

His cousin's ghost began to take shape and crouched by the leg of the table that held his corpse. Adam's ghost cocked his head to one side, looked at Silas with an uneven smile, and began to gibber and shake in excitement.

"My son lived his entire life in this room until he died two years ago. After he died, he had the run of the house, but that was a difficult time. So again, he was bound in this room. But what problem exists that cannot be solved by the application of learning?" Uncle gestured to the shelf and tables piled with books— tomes of magic and demonology; bindings and protective charms like the ones on the Camera's door; a copy of *Good Parenting* magazine; several open, waiting tins.

"So here he remains. Waiting only for—"

Silas interrupted, "What became of Adam's mother?"

Uncle looked up and away from Silas.

"Unable to bear the responsibility of what her corrupted blood had wrought, she fled. Disappeared."

But at the bottom of the glass jar were bones, forming a kind of nest below the honeyed corpse.

"Lots of people seem to disappear from this house." Silas said, full of implication.

"Some people are the cause of problems," Uncle said, looking at the bones, "other people resolve them. I am the latter type. I live only for resolution. Silas, I am a *helper*. It's in my nature, part of my parenting instinct."

Uncle began to walk in circles around the room, then stood behind Silas and continued.

"Who else but the most loving father could perceive the lasting perfection a son such as this might achieve despite his shattered form? The form, his body, was a gift from his mother. But he carried my blood as well—our blood, I should say. So you see, by excellent parenting and the vigor in our shared blood, death was cheated for a time, for surely my son should not have enjoyed even a moment of life, not if there ever were a God of mercy. I will not lie to you, Silas; while he lived, Adam was not an easy child. He was not like other children. Of course I tried to make him comfortable, but, oh Silas, his poor tortured soul. You cannot imagine the terrible length of every day while he lived. But I knew it was my task to keep him here for this great experiment. I patiently waited for his miserable life to end, and life everlasting to begin. That took sixteen years—"

Silas knew that he and his cousin were nearly the same age. He began to understand that his uncle would never let him leave this house again. But instead of pleading for himself, it was the Undertaker in him that spoke. "You must let go of your son! Let him have some peace . . . the peace he didn't have in life. Why keep him here, as a prisoner? You have to let him go. I can see him. There. In this room, still trapped in the hell you've made for him. Let me help you. We can bury him. Honor him together—"

Whatever remained of Uncle's composure finally broke, and

he struck Silas hard in the face with the back of his hand.

"After everything I've told you, you sue for *more* corruption? Bury him? When he shall live forever? Do you really think you're qualified to lecture me on how to raise a child? What I do, I do for both of you, for the peace of this family. Can't you see? He has no rest while he is alone. My son wants for a brother. It took me some time to see the truth of it. I thought he wanted a father in spirit, another parent to rest beside him in eternity. But my son already has a father. What matter if I am not yet joined to him in a more eternal form? Perhaps, then, a mother? That, alas, did not work out. But a friend, a *brother*. That's what everyone needs. Is that not so?"

"You killed your brother!" Silas screamed.

Slowly Uncle nodded.

"Yes. That was very unfortunate. But Amos did not approve of my parenting. He suspected that when Adam died I had not dealt with him in the—*accepted* way. How that infuriated my brother. But who was he to sit in judgment over me, over the dead? Was he become Hades himself? No! Not yet. Not even for all his skill and arrogance. I could not let anyone disturb the plans I had set in motion. For my *son's* sake, you understand. This is all for him. I had hoped Amos's spirit would remain here, someone to watch over Adam, but I had not yet fully understood the use of mummiae in restraining the dead. Amos's spirit fled in the instant of his demise, and I could not bring it to heel. So you see? Even in death he continued to avoid responsibility."

"Where is his body then? What have you done with him?" Silas pleaded.

"Oh Silas, do not think on him again. Indeed, if you were to see him now, you would find him not so pleasant to look at. Nature, who ravishes all she touches, has had her way with him.

"I am sorry to upset you, but consider: Amos was to me a brother only in flesh. I have never known the comfort of a *true* brother. I speak of brothers *in spirit*. What you and Adam shall soon be. Only spirit endures the ages and is a holy and mysterious thing. Very shortly, you shall know much more of this sacred matter even than I. This is a hallowed business, a thing that most people could not aspire to, could not dream of. Let kin keep kin and let the dead keep the dead. I am sure you must agree this is the best way."

Silas was now aware of exactly what his uncle was capable of, and the fear-taut muscles of his legs began to loosen with terror. He frantically considered the implications of what his uncle was saying, and of what he was preparing to do. The idea of dying was a small thing compared with the possibility of being trapped, forever, in his uncle's Camera. This room would become his tin.

Uncle came around the table and stood again in front of Silas. From his apron, he drew out a small, thin scalpel.

"You should prepare yourself. We are family and I love you. I will take care to be sure this causes you as little pain as possible. One brief moment, a pause at the threshold, a mere comma in your life's tale, and then you'll feel no more pain, ever."

In his rising panic, Silas saw how little his uncle understood about death and what might follow it. The walls of the room seemed to press in on him, and he heard himself begin to scream.

Uncle hummed quietly, preparing a large cloth around Silas's feet, perhaps to catch the blood. Silas thrashed his head from side to side, and the feet of the chair he sat in began to rock on and off the floor, but the ropes and knots held him. As Uncle drew the scalpel close to the light of the lamp to inspect its edge, a great booming noise was heard downstairs. Then there was another. Uncle's face knotted in anger.

"Oh, eternity! How long must thou wait?"

Uncle picked up the fallen ax and, checking Silas's bindings once more, excused himself and went to see who was trying to break down his door at such an inconvenient moment.

CHAPTER 58

STORM

MRS. BOWE STOOD AT THE EDGE of the salt marshes, below the stick-woven nests. Before her gathered the mothers of the lost, the Night Herons. Out of deference to the Wailing Woman, the ghosts appeared, high in their bowers, in maternal raiment. Tall women in dark gowns that spilled like tattered banners from their nests into the reeds of the marsh.

Mrs. Bowe spoke quickly, but there was little need to say anything more than Silas's name: Silas, who had brought the lost ones home. Silas, who had brought them heart's ease and freed them from suffering. Silas was in peril, and they would come. Instantly the air of the marshes began to churn with a great wind, whipping the reeds in frantic circles. When the women of the marshes descended from their bowers, they were terrible to behold. Some moved as tall, impenetrable shadows, cowled still in their mourning weeds. Others took less discernible forms, anthropomorphic nightmares whose features became the blurred masks of horror-birds, beaks sharp and tipped in flame. Many of their lately restored young accompanied them, eager to repay their debt to Silas Umber. These cut through the air as a host of daggers, their small wings edged all in bloody hues, their eyes as fiery jewels burning deep in their sockets.

As Mrs. Bowe walked from the marshes, the air behind her rose in wrath like a mighty wave cresting on the surface of a storm-churned sea, and it followed her like the tide in flood as she made her way toward Temple Street.

Mother Peale and a host of men from the Narrows were turning from Prince Street onto Fairwell when they saw Mrs. Bowe and the dreadful storm that followed at her heels. The heavy air was filled with frightful sounds. The calls of birds and angry wails rose together into a vengeful chorus, and Mother Peale bowed her head and raised her hand slightly, saying only, "We are with you," then joined the nightmare procession as it moved toward the Umber house.

Mrs. Bowe and Mother Peale climbed the front steps of Uncle's house. Mrs. Bowe struck the iron door with her walking stick. The knock rang hollow through the house, but there was no answer. Mrs. Bowe could feel Silas somewhere inside, as sure as she knew her own name. She looked at Mother Peale, and in silent acknowledgment Mother Peale raised her fist and hit the door with it, shouting a name in a voice that rattled the glass in the windows:

"Grey Lady of the house, the mother of the Narrows calls you! Sister, open the door!"

For a moment, all was silent. Then Mrs. Bowe and Mother Peale could hear the draw of the lock, metal against metal, and the door opened. Mrs. Grey stood far back in the entrance hall at the foot of the stairs. Her head was hanging down as if in shame, and it was hard to see her face. She was mumbling confusedly but said to Mrs. Bowe and Mother Peale as they came through the door, "I serve the house—"

"And you shall continue to do so. Be easy, now we are come," Mother Peale said as she mounted the stairs. She looked back toward the door. The men of the Narrows poured in, filling the hall. Beyond them, the front of the house was torn by frantic winds risen from the beating wings and billowing mourning gowns of the Night Herons. Feeling the rising wrath of the apparitions, the men parted to either side of the door and only watched as the ghosts stormed into the house, following Mrs. Bowe and Mother Peale up the stairs.

Halfway up the stairs, Mother Peale turned and called down to her folk, "Until it's done, no one leaves this house!" Below, the men closed the iron door and locked it again.

From the landing, Uncle saw Mrs. Bowe and Mother Peale coming up the stairs. The air about them bristled with fury, and though the front door had been closed, a wind whipped up the leaves and dust behind them as they climbed the stairs. Fear rose fast in him, and Uncle turned and ran back to the Camera Obscura. Crossing the threshold, he quickly closed the door behind him and tried to lock it. The locks resisted him, so he left the door open and turned back to the room. What he saw set his hands trembling so hard that he dropped the ax.

Silas was standing now. The chair he'd been tied to was shattered into kindling, and the rope spilled uselessly around his feet. His fists were clenched, and next to him a form took shape in the agitated air, framed of dust and motes of amber light. The golden thing moved in front of Silas, as if to protect him.

Uncle's whole body began to shake, and his mouth moved but no words came. "Adam," he tried to say. Then, without warning, he threw back his head and laughed triumphantly. "See? He has risen forth in eternal gold!" He began to sob, and then laughed again in mad elation.

Outside the Camera Obscura, a great roaring came upon the air, like a train streaming down the hall, and the door burst and fell away from its hinges. Uncle's head and neck snapped up into a straight line, and then he fell to the floor, frantically scrambling for the ax. Holding it above his head, oblivious to what was happening in the room, Uncle stood and moved toward Silas through a blizzard of dust and papers that had been whipped up into the air. His voice rose above the wind. "A golden Eden awaits you, and today shall be the first morning of all the world!" Uncle ran at Silas, but three steps were all he took before the furious air held him fast.

Silas strode over to where Uncle was suspended just above the floor, unable to move. He reached out and put his hand around Uncle's wrist where it hung motionless, held by an unseen force.

"I want to show you something," Silas said, tightening his grip. "I want to show you something of the world you've made and the world you're going to."

He clutched his uncle's wrist, and with his other hand, he reached into his pocket and opened the death watch.

"Let the dead keep the dead," Silas said, repeating Uncle's own words. He pushed down on the watch's hand.

The air in the Camera Obscura became a tempest.

Uncle could now see the Night Herons in all their terrible wrath as more and more of them rushed forward to take hold of him. Uncle's eyes were wide with what he beheld, and he began to scream. Silas stepped away to stand next to Mrs. Bowe and Mother Peale. In the far corner of the room, a tall woman, her features soft but veiled, held Adam close to her, her arms about his neck and shoulders, protecting him. The ghost looked once at his father and then hid his face in his mother's voluminous gown.

Uncle's still-screaming body was dragged across the room, the heels of his shoes thumping at each gap in the old wooden floorboards. Flanking each side of the door, Mother Peale and Mrs. Bowe cast their eyes down. Without looking up, Mother Peale said, "Let it be done," and as the words left her mouth, the nightmarish regiment of women from the marsh lifted Uncle higher into the air. His body jerked as if pulled by an invisible rope, and was flung through the covered window. Many of the wraiths continued to tear at him as he fell, screaming as they plummeted in a single dark writhing mass. Silas ran to the casement and saw his uncle's body strike the earth below, utterly broken.

The wind rose up in the west, and a great, deep, tolling bell rang out. Silas, Mother Peale, and Mrs. Bowe moved quickly from inside the house down to where Uncle's body lay. Still clutching the halted death watch, Silas saw the Night Herons circling his uncle's corpse, their wings lashing at it like scourges. A mist rose from the body, and Uncle's ghost was set upon by the wraiths, the marsh women and their children both. A great cry went up from the avian-formed dead and as Uncle's ghost fled, they pursued, lashing him this way and that, down and down toward the sea.

Mrs. Grey stood in the doorway of the house, watching the living and the dead moving away toward the Narrows, before fading back into the dark interior.

Down through the Narrows, the hunt coursed ever closer to the sea. The Night Herons were relentless, never letting Uncle's ghost veer from the path they drove him hard upon. As the chase emerged from the alleys and poured out along the harbor, Silas could see the mist ship, horrible in its resplendence, towering over the sea. It had sailed in right up to the harbor's seawall, and the bowsprit loomed over their heads and jutted into one lane of the Narrows. He looked closely at the ship and could see that the horror-drawn lines of his uncle's face had been burned like a medieval shroud into the wind-torn spectral fabric of the ship's great sail. Silas frantically looked among the other contorted portraits of the damned, but saw no other face known to him.

An awful cry crawled its way into the air, first in his uncle's voice, but soon that wailing strain was lost in a rising chorus of all those tortured souls who had been stitched tight by their sins into the rigging, and crushed into the wood grain of the mast, and nailed fast to the boards of the skeletal hull. Just as those voices rose into a stormlike crescendo, somewhere in the deep water beyond the boiling harbor a horn sounded, muffled at first, but then sharply breaking over the surface of the sea, its deep conch-call flying up from the depths and blasting through the damp night sky.

The folk of the Narrows fell to their knees, and the spirits of the marshes hung on the air like wind-blown pennants.

And to these sounds, one other was added. Mrs. Bowe screamed as she stood at the edge of the harbor wall, wailing the words of that terrifying curse her ancestress had spat out long ago at that same ship. Words of binding and wandering. Words of curse and imprisonment. Words of wide, harborless waters without ending. And when she was finished, the ghosts of the marshes had vanished, and all the folk of the Narrows were standing once more. Below them, little waves from the now peaceful sea lapped at the harbor wall.

The harbor was empty. The mist ship had gone. Folks had returned to their homes. Silas walked next to Mrs. Bowe as they made their way back toward Main Street.

"Joan Peale will see to your mother. Don't worry. What she needs, she'll have. Though now, there's no reason why she can't remain in that house, if that's what she desires. You can go to her tomorrow, when the dust settles a bit."

Silas could barely hear her. He was walking faster now, leaving Mrs. Bowe behind as he leapt up the front stairs of his father's house two and three steps at a time. Uncle was gone. The mist ship had sailed. Silas knew that when he opened the door, his father, in some form, would be standing there, waiting for him.

The door was still ajar from when he'd left earlier. Silas spoke his father's name into the mouth of the empty house. He stepped across the threshold, but nothing stood out. Silence. Motes of dust in the light of the lamp. A thought slipped into his mind, one that for more than a year he had tried to push away: *I will never see my dad again.*

Mrs. Bowe came up behind Silas and put her arms around him.

"I don't want to be alone," he said.

"Child, I'm here," answered Mrs. Bowe, misunderstanding him.

"All my folk are gone. My mom might as well be gone. Everyone I know is dead. I am alone here."

Mrs. Bowe only nodded, knowing it would be best not to argue with him, or coddle him. She took his face gently in her hands and said, "You must take up where he left off, whether you find him or not. I wish you'd spent more time here in Lichport growing up. You'd have become more accustomed to the ways of the sea, more accustomed to people setting sail and sometimes not making it back to port.

"But like all the living and the dead, Silas, you have your work," she said, brushing the dust from his jacket. "And for the moment, that will have to suffice."

◆ ◆ ◆

The next morning Silas woke early and walked slowly to Temple Street to see his mother. As he approached the house, the front door opened and she emerged, as if she had been waiting for him. Dolores came to the edge of the porch, pausing briefly, before coming down to the front walk to stand in front of her son.

Words failed him. All he could do was look at his mother.

When Dolores tried to speak, her voice was barely audible.

"I didn't know. Silas, I didn't know—," she started, but then went quiet.

Silas stepped forward to hug his mom. She didn't pull away, and he put both his arms around her and pressed his face against her cheek. She didn't move. When Silas drew back, he felt her hand touch his back as if it had been hanging in the air, waiting but unable to move closer. He quickly kissed her cheek and said, "Soon," before turning to walk back home.

CHAPTER 59

LOST AND FOUND

MRS. BOWE HAD SET AN ORNATE mahogany chest in Silas's front hall, just by the door. Each day, when the letters came through the letter slot, she would collect them, date them, and place them in the box for Silas to read.

Everyone in Lichport knew Silas Umber was the new Undertaker. And yet he remained hesitant, still nervous about the protocols.

Each day he brought some of the letters into his study and read them. They were all of a kind: requests for help. Troubled houses. Cold rooms. Noises in the night. A grandparent who'd passed peaceably enough, but wouldn't take to his road. Unsettled business.

Some people just left notes in his mailbox, brief missives quickly scrawled on scraps of paper, as if the sender assumed that the Undertaker would already know the history of the house and what the particular details were. Perhaps his father would have known what to make of notes like these:

147 Queen Street. Knocking resumed. AGAIN. Three sightings of HER. Will await your arrival any weekday evening between hours of eight and ten p.m.

Most of the notes and letters were from Lichport or houses on its margins. At first Silas was unsure of what exactly his responsibilities were. Did he have to respond to every request? There were notes in his father's desk and in the Undertaker's ledger about some of the homes and the more familiar and recurrent hauntings in the town, but not all of them, and from what Silas could make of his father's notes, there had been more and more problems of this sort in Lichport, even though the town's population had been steadily shrinking. Certainly, by now, the dead far outnumbered the living. Though resolved to help, obligated even, Silas wasn't sure exactly how quickly he had to respond. Was there to be a fee for his services? How much did his dad get paid for each ghost? Were some worth more than others? He needed a menu.

Mrs. Bowe had tried to be helpful since Uncle's "departure" from Lichport, but she seemed withdrawn, spending most of the time in her own part of the house, quiet, except at evenings when her visitor would still come. Since the departure of the mist ship, it seemed everyone in town was lying low. His mother never left the house on Temple Street, and he hadn't seen the Peales much either. Bea was still nowhere to be seen.

Mrs. Bowe noticed his confused looks as he sifted through the stacks of unanswered letters. "You will need to answer them, one way or another."

"I don't know what to say, or what to ask them for. Is it rude to ask for payment?"

"Silas, you are not a plumber. There is not a fixed wage for such work. I believe people paid your father whatever they thought was appropriate. To my knowledge, he never asked anyone for any money. Some paid cash, others paid however they could, in food or supplies. For that matter," she added, gesturing at the stack of papers and deeds that had lately arrived from his great-grandfather's attorney, "it's not as though you need the money now."

Silas looked around his father's study. He could now see how his dad might have come by his extensive collection of books and art. Lichport was filled with people living in large old houses, families who might now be poor but were still surrounded by the remains of once-opulent estates—libraries, paintings, sculptures, curiosities from abroad—and here, in this study, sat payment for the settlement of some of their ancestral troubles. Silas began to wonder what else his dad might have accepted as payment over the years, from folks less well bestowed in family relics. A car? Clothes? Food? A drink at the Fretful Porpentine? He would have to figure it out as he went along.

"You are only obligated as far as you wish to be, though if you help one family, others would take it very poorly if you didn't answer their request. Your father found it very hard to close the door in the faces of people who needed his help. I expect you'd feel the same, no?"

"I would. But what about my life?"

"Your life?"

"I mean, what about time to myself? For what *I* want to do?"

"And what would that be, dear?" Mrs. Bowe asked in a patronizing tone.

What else did he want to do, after all? He looked at the Undertaker's ledger open on the desk and could easily see himself written into its pages, becoming, year by year, more a part of the world left to him by his father. It was no accident that this was a family business. There was something about him that rose to the work, that came more alive in the presence of the past, in the presence of the dead. And so he said, "I see your point."

Mrs. Bowe smiled. "Of course you do, dear."

She was knitting a long scarf, nearly done. She looked up and asked Silas if he'd had many curious inquiries lately.

"I've had lots more," he said, "since Mr. Peale's wake. I haven't gone through them all, but one just arrived from Saltsbridge."

"Really, that is a rare thing. It must be a Lichport family. May I see the letter?"

Silas found the letter in a small stack on the desk and handed it to Mrs. Bowe. "There's no address on the envelope or in the letter, just the postmark from Saltsbridge and a telephone number."

Mrs. Bowe turned the envelope over and then retrieved the note from inside. "That's not unusual. They'll expect you to call and then they'll send a car, most likely."

"Really?"

"Oh, yes. It is traditional to provide transport, unless the Undertaker specifically declines it. You know how it feels when you . . . well, when you do what you do. Best not to drive after. Safer. Your father usually walked when it was in town." Mrs. Bowe read the letter, raising an eyebrow as she finished. "Northend . . . Northend . . . yes, that is a Lichport name. Most of the family left some years ago, but there were a few of them still living in town until, oh, about the time you and your mother arrived. They would certainly have known about your father's work and may still have friends or acquaintances in town, so they could easily have heard about you. I don't believe your father ever had any work in Saltsbridge, and most of his work out of town was for wakes, families here and there still wanting something traditional. Are you going to help them?"

"I think I'd like to help them, yes. Maybe I'll just go to the house and have a look and then decide what's to be done. You saw in the letter they're not staying in the house now, so it must have gotten bad." Silas decided that he would call them and make arrangements.

The next morning he dialed the number, and as Mrs. Bowe

predicted, they had indeed once been a Lichport family, and they would send a car for Silas.

Later that afternoon, when the hired car pulled up, Silas was surprised to see that it was the same driver who had brought him and his mother to Lichport.

"Going home, huh?" the driver asked, recognizing Silas.

"No, no, just visiting back in Saltsbridge. This is home now."

"Funny," said the driver, "it's usually the other way around."

Though he was nervous about the job, Silas enjoyed the drive over the marshes. But as they approached Saltsbridge, it began to feel odd to be back in the neighborhood where he grew up. Familiar sights, the school, restaurants, the library, held little for him now. They were just places, no more, no less. That part of his life was over.

And how strange it all looked after the time he'd spent in Lichport: the bright lights of the streetlamps, the people, all the cars, traffic. He realized, driving through Saltsbridge, that he'd been living in another world entirely, one with very few connections to the lands beyond its borders. Surrounded by the sight of other cars on the road, and hearing all the noise from the street, he felt uneasy, unable to hear himself think clearly. He had changed. He had become accustomed to quiet and stillness and ruined streets and the colors of faded, forgotten buildings. All around him, from well-kept street signs and stores and the lights coming from the wide windows of the houses and small shops, was an awful electric glow, making every hour in Saltsbridge into an overlit candy-colored blur.

As they wound their way through the suburbs, Silas reviewed the letter and his recollections of the conversation with the family. They'd said the house had never been "quite right" since they bought it. Upsetting noises got worse the longer they stayed.

Sometimes they'd see a shape, some hunched thing come out of one of the walls. It would wail, and darkness poured from its eyes like ink or smoke, and it would feel along the walls with its hands like it was blind. And their kids would see things and start screaming, and well, who could live like that?

It was supposedly a newer house, built sometime in the last twenty years, and that worried Silas. The problem would more likely be related to something terrible that had happened there, a murder, maybe. No point in speculating, but it was hard not to. It might be older than the house. Something buried beneath it. Something older than Saltsbridge. He was making himself nervous, and so he conjured up Mrs. Bowe's calming voice in his mind: *Don't borrow trouble*, the voice told him. But then another voice—his mother's—said softly, cruelly: *No need to borrow what you've already got coming in spades.*

It was dark as the car slowed, and Silas looked up to see they'd turned down an overgrown driveway. As the car parked in front of the neglected home, his heart nearly stopped. Without another word to the driver, he got out of the car and stood staring at his old house.

Silas approached the front door. He turned the handle and found the door unlocked. He reached in and turned on the light switch. Two exposed bulbs in the small foyer cast hard light toward the front room. Inside, the house was almost completely empty, the family having moved out the previous week. As he stood in the living room, it was as if no time had passed since moving day. The house was cold, far colder than it was outside. Wind was blowing down the chimney, making a low, endless moan. Silas stalled the hand of the death watch, and the sound took on more depth, clarified, and grew louder.

A man cried somewhere near the door. He was waiting.

Silas didn't want to turn around. He looked down at the floor, scared of what he might or might not see.

Then he heard his name from within the walls.

He turned and lifted his eyes.

By the door, looking out the window, stood the ghost of his father. The ghost was close enough to touch, yet Silas felt like he and his dad were standing on opposite sides of a crevasse. The ghost was saying his name, "Silas? Silas?" over and over, as if asking the wind outside to give him back his child. Thick black smoke poured down from his chest, like a bleeding wound above his heart.

Silas's breathing quickened, and the shape of the ghost solidified and sharpened and seemed to take on more presence in the room. Silas saw that he and the ghost were wearing the same jacket.

"What are you doing here?" Silas said, choking back a sob.

"I'm waiting for my son to come home," the ghost said absently. "I've called the school. No one knows where he is. Something has happened to him. I know it."

"Dad," said Silas. "I'm right here next to you."

"No one can find my son. He hasn't come home. Where is Silas?"

"I've been in Lichport, Dad. In your house. Come home with me. Let's go home."

"I can't leave until Silas gets home."

Silas knew then that he and his father were not part of the same room, or the same house. They were barely even part of the same conversation.

"Why are you here? Why are you waiting here, in this place? Can you tell me?"

And the ghost wailed and then said in wracking pain, "Because I was *not* here! I didn't come home, and now my son is lost. He is gone and I'll never find him."

"Dad? We're both here. Silas and Amos. I followed you. Followed the path you left for me. I'm okay, Dad. I promise."

"Where are we?" Amos asked, never looking away from the window.

"Where we were."

"Then we're lost."

"No. We're right here. Together. But we can be someplace else if you'd like to be. You can come with me now. We can leave this house together."

"I am trying to get home."

"No. We are home. Right now. You and me. Where we are together, *there* is home. Look at me. I am not out there. I am here. With you. Always with you."

And Amos turned away from the cold glass of the window to face his son.

"Oh, Silas . . . I am so sorry." Amos's whole form began to shake as he cried, saying his son's name over and over.

"No, Dad, it's okay—"

Amos's voice was broken, but he spoke through his sobs. "You've gotten so big. I forgot how much you'd grown. There was a child here once. You were smaller. I was looking for a child . . . it is as though no time has passed."

"Dad, it's okay. I'll stay here with you as long as you like. We can live here like we did, if that's what you want. Please . . ." Silas began to cry. "We can go anywhere. There's no reason for you to be bound here, not now. Come away with me."

His eyes filled with tears, and the ghost wavered on the air. Silas held the death watch up in front of his chest as he tried to push the dial, not trying to halt its motion, but to reverse it, to push the dial backward.

"Son?" said Amos. "Son?"

Silas looked up, his face streaked with tears as he pushed hard at the tiny immovable dial with both thumbs.

"It doesn't work like that, Little Bird. You may stop its hand, but there is no going back. What's done is done." The ghost was becoming dimmer, as though he was lit by only the smallest candle.

"Dad? I love you. Can you hear me? What's happening?"

"I can feel what's become of me. I am lying on cold earth. I must go. I can't explain."

"Tell me where. I'll go there. I'll—"

"No, Silas. Leave it. I don't want you to see me like that. Remember me as I was. I will come again. Remember me. . . ."

And Amos Umber walked through the veil of the wall and into the night air, and was gone.

CHAPTER 60

STREET SCENE

WHEN SILAS RETURNED FROM SALTSBRIDGE, Mrs. Bowe was waiting for him on the porch of his house.

Before he could speak the words, she said, "Yes. I have seen him. Preparations are being made. Friends have gone to his side and will bring him home. Tend to your own heart now, and those of your family. We will see to the rest."

She left him, making her way out to the garden and the tomb, for there was much to tell the bees.

The next morning Silas walked to Fort Street to tell his great-grandfather what had happened. As he walked up the path through the front yard, he was surprised to see his mother, who had just come out of the front door and was standing on the porch, leaning hard against the rail.

"I was just paying my respects, Si. I thought he should know, and I thought I should tell him."

"I understand," said Silas, joining her on the porch.

"Yes, son. I expect you do. Your sense of obligation comes from my side of the—well, you come by it honestly on both sides. I suppose my mother would have been pleased to see you here. Your great-grandfather is very impressed with you. Very proud."

Silas looked at her and nodded.

Dolores leaned forward and kissed him on the forehead. She turned away quickly. It was still uncomfortable, but there was a truce and they both could feel it. A truce, and a chance at maybe a little more, so they were both careful and protective of the lightening of the air between them.

"Si, I'll be needing some help at the house. I know you're busy, but when things settle down, could you come by and give me a hand? I plan on making a few changes, and there are some things I'd like out of the house as soon as possible. Maybe you'd like to see if any of them would be of use to you before I get rid of them?"

"Of course. Thank you. Mom, you know, if you want, you can come and live with—"

"No. I will stay where I am. Thank you, Silas."

"Okay, but if you change—"

"Silas, I have no intention of leaving *my* house. It's *mine* now, and I'm staying in it. That house should have been ours anyway, and if you think—" She was becoming agitated, but she caught herself and paused. She looked up, allowed herself to be distracted by the sound of a distant bird, and said, "I suppose now there will be a funeral?"

"Yes."

"Will you be—*overseeing* things?"

"I will. Though the Peales and Mrs. Bowe are helping with the preparations."

"Of course. Fine. When it's time, maybe you could come by and get me? We could walk together."

"Sure, Mom. I will."

"That will be fine, Si."

"Good."

"Good."

"Silas?" his mother asked, her voice tentative and falling quickly to a whisper. "I have spoken with Joan Peale. I know that

. . . oh . . . I don't know how to say it. There was something in the house. I've closed off the north wing. I can't bring myself to go into that room. Silas, what's become of the son? Of Adam?"

"I've seen to it." said Silas slowly. "The Peales brought his body out of the house that night. The peace is on him. He is at rest among our relatives and his mother."

"My, you sound so like your father." Dolores nodded her head in relief and resignation both.

"Mom?"

"I know," she said.

Dolores put her hand on her son's shoulder, then turned away and walked down the stairs of the porch, heading home. She wobbled slightly as she made her way down the uneven sidewalk in her high heels past the houses of the Restless, but her back was straight and she held her head up like she owned the street.

A MAN DIETH NOT GLADLY THAT
HATH NOT LEARNED IT, THEREFORE
LEARN TO DIE SO THAT THOU SHALT
LIVE. FOR THERE SHALL BE NO MAN
WHO LIVES WELL BUT HE WHO HATH
LEARNED TO DIE WELL . . . THIS LIFE
IS BUT A PASSING TIME . . . AND
WHEN THOU BEGINNEST TO LIVE, THOU
BEGINNEST TO DIE. NOW HEARKEN AND
UNDERSTAND. DEATH IS BUT A PARTING
BETWEEN THE BODY AND THE SOUL
AND EVERY MAN KNOWS THAT IS WELL.

—From "Lerne to Dye" by Thomas Hoccleve (c.1421–26)
Translated by Amos Umber

As hard pains, I dare well say,

In Purgatory are night and day,

As are in Hell, save by one way:

That one shall have an end.

—From *The Last Judgment* (ca. 1475)

CHAPTER 61

PASSING BELL

AMOS UMBER'S BODY HAD LAIN in a shallow grave in an overgrown corner of the old Temple Cemetery since the night he had disappeared. These circumstances would not allow Amos's body to be displayed at home as was still the preferred custom in Lichport, and Mother Peale and Mrs. Bowe thought it best that Silas not look on the body, all things considered. So Amos's remains, wrapped in good linen, had been kept in an icehouse overnight with Mother Peale sitting the vigil, and then put right into the coffin. Even though the body would not be brought into the house, no one in town would be denied the wake, and as if by instinct, people began arriving at Silas's house that afternoon, many of them walking up just behind the cart that was carrying Amos's coffin to the Beacon. Joan Peale was driving the horse-drawn cart that had been hung with black crepe and ropes of ivy.

That morning Silas had walked to his mother's house on Temple Street to fetch her. She would wait with the folks making preparations. Silas and most of the others waited quietly outside to follow the cart from the house where Amos had lived in Lichport, to the ground where his body would rest. As Silas climbed into the cart, a wail rose up from Mrs. Bowe, who had been standing with him on the porch. That wild strain rang in the cold air, piercing every heart that heard it. To its sound, Silas rode off with Joan Peale to the Beacon to bury his dad, a company of mourners trailing behind them. No one asked why Silas had preferred the Beacon to the old Umber plot on the other side of town. They all knew, as Silas did, that Amos would prefer the communal Beacon to the formal family plot, for the view over the sea if nothing else.

They carried the coffin up the hill, feeling its weight with their hearts and hardly at all in their arms and backs. With the sexton looking on from the long shadows of the trees, and with his father's own spade, Silas and some of the men of the Narrows dug a grave near the top of the Beacon. Then, with little ceremony, they lowered the cedar coffin into the waiting earth. Silas knelt by the grave, but offered no words. Not yet.

After the burial, most of the mourners returned directly to Silas's house to begin the funeral revels, but Silas went to the little chapel of the Narrows with Mother Peale before going home to the comfort of his friends and neighbors. He'd insisted that the Passing Bell should be rung for his father only after his body had been laid to rest, and he wanted to ring it himself. At the chapel, Mother Peale unlocked the heavy door with a large iron key and lit a lantern as they entered, for the windows were small and the day was nearly spent.

"You go on up," she told Silas, putting her hand to the side of his face and handing him the lantern so he could see his way up the ladder. "Go up into the tower and ring the bell by hand. Put your hand to the bronze and give it a push to send it swinging. That is the old way."

So Silas climbed awkwardly up the ladder with the lantern. The walls of the tower were close in about him as he ascended, a small orb of light moving up and up through the clutching darkness. At the top of the ladder, he stepped off into a small room with four unglazed windows that looked out over the town. Just in front of him, the bell hung from a short, thick beam that spanned the small chamber. Silas held up the lantern to better see the tarnished surface of the bell. He could see there was an inscription commemorating its installation here in Lichport, for the bell had been brought from across the sea hundreds of years ago. The inscription was deeply and ornately carved and still clear, even in the low lantern light.

> Lichport's bell rings o'er the tide,
> And to its call the dead abide.
> They hear its chime and dream of home,
> And leave behind this bed of loam.
> Come Young or Old, your time is past—
> Here is thy final song at last!

Silas set the lantern on the floor. He put his hands on the bell and pushed against it, briefly feeling the cold metal on his skin. The bell swung away from him, then came back, its hinge creaking and the clapper striking its first note. As it swung toward him again, he moved in rhythm with the bell, leaning back, then forward, pushing it, gracefully, with only a finger now, as it made its way out and back, out and back, its song ringing across the Narrows, out over the water and along the lanes into the upper part of Lichport.

The sky was deep azure, and the little room was lit only with the light of Mother Peale's lantern, for the moon had not risen. The Passing Bell had been ringing for some time when Silas turned and saw his father standing in front of him. As the song of the bell grew softer and softer, as its arc slowed, Amos and Silas spoke to each other. It was nearly time to go.

Silas was crying.

Amos stood looking tenderly at Silas, as if wanting to

remember everything he could about his son; his face, the way his hair hung a little in his eyes. Then Amos leaned in close and whispered into Silas's ear before becoming indiscernible from the air and leaving Silas alone in the bell tower.

The ghost's voice wasn't loud enough to be heard below, and Silas Umber never told anyone what his father said to him that night. And when, many years later, he went to his own grave, he took those quiet words with him out of this world.

Silas went back down the ladder and walked with Mother Peale from the chapel back to his house, where the revels would be well underway. Mrs. Bowe and his mother would be waiting. All day, people had been arriving, bringing flowers and food. Silas could see the room in his mind, filled with the people of the town, and he longed to be with them. While there would be no waking of the ghost, the rest of the traditions would be upheld. And Silas knew people simply wanted to be with him, wanted to share their sadness at his loss and share their memories of his father in his house, surrounded by Amos's things. Good words needed to be spoken, then all would be well done.

The wake lasted for three days, with people drinking night and morning and sleeping all over the house whenever sleep took them before getting back up to join the company again. Late in the afternoon of the third day after Amos's burial, Mrs. Bowe and Mother Peale began putting things away and packing food into the refrigerator. With only a little help, even the drowsiest of the company began making their weary way home. At ten o'clock, Mother Peale rode home to the Narrows in the cart with her daughter and a few friends, and Mrs. Bowe had left Silas to the quiet of his thoughts.

Midnight found Silas so tired he couldn't sleep. He sat in the study among his father's things. The evenings had turned cold. He built up the fire on the hearth, took his dad's jacket from the back of the chair, and put it on, pulling it tight about him. In the house next door, he could hear the music through the wall and knew that Mrs. Bowe and her man were beginning their nightly dance.

> Just a song at twilight, when the lights are low;
> And the flick'ring shadows softly come and go.
> Tho' the heart be weary, sad the day and long,
> Still to us at twilight comes love's old song,
> Comes love's old sweet song.

Before him on the desk, the town's death ledger lay open to the beginning. Silas read down the list of names of Lichport's dead, and their death dates, many of the departed now as familiar as his ancestors and kin. At the bottom of the list, he saw again where his dad had written his own incomplete entry: "Amos Umber, d. _____." Silas took up a pen and inscribed the date of his father's funeral in place of the death date. On the next line, he wrote his own name in the ledger before laying down the pen and closing the book.

And away toward the marshes, a single small flame hung in the air over the cold water of the millpond. It flashed, but only for an instant, then wavered and went out.

Acknowledgments

A book takes on a life of its own and if anything at all is to become of it, a book (not to mention its author) needs friends. I have been very fortunate in this regard, for even before *Death Watch* had a title, it was befriended by exceptional people, and to them I am exceptionally grateful . . .

Eddie Gamarra, friend, manager, ship's rudder, and guardian of my writing career, offered always sage and sober guidance. Were it not for his confidence in me, this book would never have been written.

Tony and Angela DiTerlizzi have walked with me through the landscape of this book, offering suggestions, critique, and the kind of support that is a rare thing in this world, even from dear friends. I owe them such a debt of gratitude. GD.

Holly Black has given me more encouragement and help than I suspect I am entitled to. Her comments on the first complete draft were timely and challenging.

Navah Wolfe, my editor, always had smart questions and suggestions, and was Silas Umber's best friend from the beginning of this adventure. This book is so much the better for her good work. The rest of my Simon & Schuster family: especially Justin Chanda, Laurent Linn, Katrina Groover, and Michelle Kratz, who have in various ways helped this book find its place in the world. Drew Willis made the excellent map of Lichport. And I thank Valerie Shea, my copyeditor, for her meticulous work and hawklike eyes. The book you're holding simply would not be here if not for the Simon & Schuster team.

A few brave souls read very early drafts of this book; their help, suggestions, and conversations helped shape it in innumerable ways. Tracy Ford read it more times than anyone and his friendship, insight and support were always there when I needed them. Nancy Berman provided elegant comments and delicate corrections early on. Maggie Secara found some hidden trouble spots and also told me what she loved.

Matthew Roberson and Gretchen Papazian were more encouraging than they know. Anne Alton smiled at just the right time. And Larissa Niec and Honora Foah gifted me with their ideas and initial thoughts when the book was in a highly metamorphic state. Erin Parker's thoughts after reading this book have earned her a fine supper and my thanks. Deb Shapiro gave excellent advice as well as drafting the excellent reading group guide.

My colleagues at CMU have always been surprisingly supportive of my strange "other" work, Marcy Taylor and Pam Gates especially so. For the priceless gift of camaraderie, I am so very grateful to Mark Freed, Brooke Harrison and Jacob Harrison-Freed, the Weinstock family, and Talat Halman.

John and Caitlin Matthews, my brother and sister in Art, have since I was twenty been incredibly supportive of me as a writer and in most other ways too. They are there at every turn, and our many adventures together—both philosophical and topographical—have inspired this and other books of mine besides. I thank them too for those golden days, surrounded by sea and stones, upon the northern rim of the world. We'll always have Orkney. This book really took shape on those trips and in their excellent company.

Adam Barrett, explorer and chronicler of ruins, has allowed me to use his excellent photographs of urban decay for inspiration. Lichport would be far paler in its descriptions but for his fine eye for the abandoned.

For my own selfish purposes, I convinced Jim Ryan Gregory to become a medievalist. His Latin is excellent, and because of that, so is mine.

I thank Stacy Burnette for the marvelous distraction of his friendship, and for showing me time and time again the wonders of the rural.

The dead have also played their part in the making of *Death Watch*, lending me ideas, encouragement, inspiration, and occasionally their own words to light my way through the labyrinth of ghostly lore. John

Donne, Robert Burton, Thomas Browne, George Herbert, Emmanuel Swedenborg, William Shakespeare, Lewes Lavater—to them and so many others: my undying respect and gratitude.

But above all who have helped and befriended this book, both living and dead, it is my family to whom I owe the greatest debt. My parents, Susan and Mike Berk, put books in my hands from an early age, many of which became the bedrock upon which this novel has been written. They knew I would write this book long before I did. My brother Jeremy, sister-in-law Rebecca, and their children, Madeleine and Spencer, added laughter to my writing days in the West. My aunt Joan introduced me to the gothic when I was very young and this, it appears, has stuck. My grandparents, all dead, were much in my thoughts and often at my side while writing this book. Suzanne McDermott, my beloved mother-in-law, taught me anything I know about graciousness. Her death, which occurred while this book was being written, showed me that a good life and a good death go hand in hand and can be a blessing to everyone. I think about her every day.

Robin, my son, you show me day after day how wonderful life can be if we look to small things for joy. I love you with my whole heart. This is your book.

And my dear Kris: there are not words. You are my rock in everything I do. You is my darlin' girl, and I loves ya.

READING GROUP GUIDE

for *Death Watch* by Ari Berk

1. What does the title Death Watch mean to you?

2. Silas Umber is like a detective; he's searching for clues to unravel the mystery of what happened to his father, as well as what the reality of his work entailed. What do you consider to be the key evidence he uncovers?

3. If you were to read Death Watch following the story of Dolores Umber, Charles Umber, Beatrice, or Mrs. Bowe instead of Silas, what aspects do you think would be different? The same?

4. What, if any, aspects of Silas's life do you relate to? What feels completely foreign?

5. Silas's mother did not want him to return to Lichport and learn about his family's history. How do you think Silas's life would have been different if he never returned? Likewise, what do you think would have been different if at any point he chose not to follow in his father's footsteps, and/or had stayed with his Uncle, instead of following the path he did set out on?

6. Lichport is divided into different neighborhoods—both for the living and for the departed—each with its own seemingly different attitude toward death and dying, as well as humanity. Why do you think this is? How would you describe these differences? Do you see any similarities?

7. Amos and Charles Umber were very different—in many ways they were even mirror images of each other. Good vs. evil; selfless vs. selfish; and needy vs. affluent. What other parallel personalities or events did you find in the novel?

8. Upon Silas's arrival in Lichport, Uncle Charles says: "Metamorphosis. All will change." (p. 67). What do you see as the major transformations in the novel? D you think these are the changes Uncle Charles meant? How so?

9. What is life and what is death? How would you answer this question? Do you think your answer would differ if you had not read Death Watch?

10. If you could have the death watch for a day, what would you do with it?

11. Uncle Charles collects artifacts and only serves preserved food in his home. Why do you think he has an aversion to new and fresh?

12. Uncle Charles is obsessed with photography and his camera obscura, both of which allow the user to focus on the image they wish to capture and present to the world. Do you see other literal and figurative ways Uncle Charles is trying to manipulate what people see?

13. Do you think this story and the history of the community would be different if it were set in a land-locked place? How so? Water and tide, storm and mist all figure prominently in the novel. What do you think they symbolize?

14. What purpose do you see Beatrice serving? What does Silas find so attractive about Beatrice? Does he see her as a person or as a part of something larger?

15. Do you think the three ladies of the Sewing Circle are controlling the fate of others or just responding to the actions of others and helping them tell their stories? Why?

16. The author, as a storyteller, is similar to the ladies of the Sewing Circle, weaving several people's stories, as well as bits of folklore and mythology, into a larger narrative tapestry. Some of the threads have been left dangling. What are they, and how would you stitch them together? What is the purpose of leaving dangling threads in a story?

17. Aside from the tapestry the three ladies weave, trees also play an elemental and metaphorical role. Is there other imagery embedded in the story that plays a similar role? If you had to select an image to represent you, what would it be?

18. If you were directing the Death Watch movie, whom would you cast in the roles of the main characters?

A CONVERSATION WITH ARI BERK:

Q: What inspired you to write Death Watch?

A: I was inspired to write Death Watch when I saw the actual timepiece that inspired the death watch. It is several hundred years old and is kept in the Ashmolean museum in Oxford, England. It's rare, but not unique. Long ago, little pocket watches and other jewelry used to include skeletal imagery (called "memento mori" meaning *remember, thou shalt die*) to remind people that death was always close at hand. The moment I saw that watch, I got the idea of the book, for a timepiece that if stalled, would enable you to see the spirits of the dead.

Q: How has your interest in mythology and folklore informed your writing of this series?

A: Well, honestly, my interest in these areas informs my whole life! I grew up reading myths and legends. They were what began my interest in both reading and writing. In The Undertaken trilogy, it's really the pieces of lore that bind together the other elements of the books (plot, characters, etc.) and that frame the world of the novel. I have always been fascinated by folklore relating to death customs and ghosts, so I set out to create a world where such beliefs were not only present (as they are in ours), but central to a whole town, the lives of most of its inhabitants, and their world-view. I asked myself, if I lived in a necropolis (like Lichport) what would my beliefs be? Generally speaking, I have just always wanted to learn more about the things people used to believe in, and sometimes still believe in; rituals, legends, even old phrases. I have a very large library and have been fortunate enough to have had access to many strange and rare books in archives around the world such as the Bodleian Library in Oxford (where I once spent a day reading an Elizabethan magician's personal diary written in the margins of a sixteenth century ephemeris). *Death Watch* is woven through with some of the things I've found on my many literary expeditions–for example, I've seeded the Undertaker's ledger with some of the more intriguing texts I've found over the years (and a few that I wish really existed!). I have spent much of life looking around corners for the arcane, so it's natural for me to give my characters and my readers the same chance to experience something of the wondrous and the bizarre.

Q: Do you see yourself in any of your characters. If so, whom and why?

A: When I finished the book and read through it again, I was a little surprised by how personal some of it felt to me. I am very close to both Silas and Amos. Some of Silas's experiences in Saltsbridge (such as ditching school and giving unofficial tours of the cemetery) were borrowed portions of my own past. His interests in lore are something else he and I share. As a father, am I constantly thinking about how my son sees the world and experiences both the present and the past. Amos's fears of one day being absent from his son's side are mine too.

Q: Do you believe in ghosts?

A: I do believe in ghosts. But really, the better question is *what do you think a ghost is?* Of course, everyone has their own opinion on this matter. For myself? I believe a ghost is little more than an unfinished conversation. When words are left unsaid, when final wishes are not followed, when familial obligations are not met, when someone dies suddenly, or in an unexpected way, when words or the natural completion of a life hang unfinished on the air, there we find a ghost.

Q: You've written about a wide array of subjects, including the secret history of giants, mermaids and hobgoblins, as well as William Shakespeare and Vikings. Has the writing of *Death Watch* differed from the writing of those books? If so, how?

A: In some ways, perhaps on the surface, the subjects of my various works may seem quite different, though all of them tend to speak of things that happened long ago, and events or accounts of the past that have shaped the present in some way. Ghosts are often very personal, a very intimate kind of manifestation of the past. Ghosts are about family and ancestors and conversations that trickle down through time. The tales of giants and mermaids are about conversations with the land, with the places we find ourselves living. But ghost stories are also conversations with place and time, so perhaps it's best if I just say that all the things I write about are somehow connected to the ways we perceive history and how we use (or choose not to use) our memories. My books are also, fundamentally about my deep respect for and love of the past, and my delight in (and sometimes, fear of) how it continues to weave its way into our own times and makes itself known in often-unexpected ways.

Q: What were your favorite books when you were Silas Umber's age?

A: Like Silas, I loved (and still love) old books on folklore, myths, and ghost stories. I read lots of myths. When young, I especially enjoyed accounts of monsters, sea serpents being among my favorites. When I was seventeen I was really into Egyptian mythology and was reading lots of Egyptian funerary literature, such as *The Coffin Texts*. I was also fascinated by an Elizabethan scholar and mage named John Dee, so I read a lot about the sixteenth century world and its literature, voyages of exploration, and magical beliefs.

Q: When you're not writing or teaching, what do you enjoy doing?

A: Writing and teaching takes up a good deal of my time. I'm also an artist, so I draw and paint as time allows. If possible, I'd almost always rather be traveling. It will not surprise anyone to learn that I enjoy places with long pasts. Ruins, overgrown cemeteries, old woods, ancient buildings—places where the past and present converge . . . that's where you'll find me. In places like those, I get a lot of ideas for things that later end up becoming parts of my books. Some of my art as well as images from my travels can be seen on my website: www. ariberk.com

Q: What do you hope readers take away from their reading of *Death Watch*?

A: Reading a book is always a personal experience. Every reader will have, I believe, a unique take on this, or any book they read. If I could point to one thing that for me is central to the story, it would be the importance of listening to the past. There is an ancient custom for banishing ghosts, and the crux of that custom is to simply ask the ghost what it wants. Then the ghost speaks and once the ghost tells its tale, it vanishes and no longer troubles the living. Well, there is a lot of talk about ghosts these days, lots of late night television shows with people in night-vision goggles running around old houses and ruinous asylums shouting at the dead. In the many stories I've read, when people talk to ghosts, they are really talking to the past of that particular place. In our modern society, we look ahead and seldom back. We make demands of everything but seldom ask others "what do *you* need?" But what is lost when we close our minds to both our obligations to the past, and to others with whom we share the present? We are surrounded with wonders, every moment of our lives, if we only take the time to look and listen. People will make of ghosts what they will, so really, my only is wish is that any reader of *Death Watch* will consider their time well spent in reading it.

HERE'S A SNEAK PEAK AT THE NEXT BOOK IN THE UNDERTAKEN TRILOGY

From the ruined lighthouse clinging to the rocks stacked high above the sea, a gray ghost-light swept out over Lichport.

Every evening, for over a week, on the very edge of town, the miasmic beam shone down from that tower. Grim weather descended with that light: furious winds and buffeting rain. And when the storm rose into a gale and screamed from the cliffs and whipped the surf into flying sheets of foam, that's when the bad dreams began. It was mostly in the Narrows, where folks lived closest to the lighthouse; they would wake, terrified, from awful dreams of drowning and shipwrecks and muted voices crying through slowly rising bubbles far beneath the surface of the sea. Even in the upper part of town, people were affected.

But not Silas Umber, the Undertaker of Lichport. He wasn't sleeping anyway. Not since a few nights ago, when someone burned the name of the old Umber family estate into his front door. Silas had spent the rest of that night pulling books and records from the shelves of his study, anything he could find that would tell him more about the house called Arvale. He had a large pile of these on his desk, awaiting his attention. But the lighthouse would have to come first. People were talking. Letters requesting help had been coming in every day since it started. Nights were bad for the rest of the folk in Lichport, and Silas knew they expected him to end the trouble.

Mrs. Bowe, who lived in the house attached to his, woke screaming six days ago and hadn't had a good night's rest since. Silas's mother called him two days before to say the dreams were so bad that she had resorted to only napping in a chair during daylight hours. Silas had spent several evenings at his mother's house across town, playing cards with her from midnight until morning because he was worried she'd go back to drinking to calm her nerves. Things had eased a little between them. They were talking *to* each other now, not *at* each other. He knew his mother was proud of him in her way. She still had trouble saying it, Silas could tell, but things were better. She had come to his dad's wake and had begun talking about Amos civilly again. Silas had even invited his mother to move in with him once more. And although she declined, saying again the house on Temple Street was *her place* now, and the only way she was leaving was *feet first*, she took her son's hand warmly and kissed his cheek for having asked.

But the nightmares were fraying the edges of everything.

Now Silas looked out from a high window in his house. In his hand, the death watch was silent, its ticking stilled by his thumb against the dial. Silas could see, clear with the ghost-sight the watch bestowed, the beams of sickly gray light turning out from the lighthouse and falling like a pall over land and sea.

At first, Silas thought the light might have been one of the occasional phantasmal glimmerings seen near the ocean. These were not uncommon, and while they might be related to sunken ships, or some poor soul lost beneath the waves, no ghost ever manifested, and the lights would usually vanish almost as soon as they appeared. But this was different, and people in town, *his* town, were suffering.

Enough, he said to himself. *Enough.*

He opened the enormous funereal ledger that contained everything his father and the other Undertakers of his family knew about ghost lore and death rites. Scrawled throughout the book and upon its margins were the notes, instructions, and gleanings of his ancestors, those previous Undertakers who, like him, sought to bring Peace to the unsettled dead.

The ghost of the lighthouse had been known to his father, but only through secondhand accounts. Silas had read an entry in his father's handwriting that explained that the ghost of the lighthouse would never appear to him, though he had tried to speak to the spirit on more than one occasions. For several days, and as the nightmares continued to run like wild things through the town, Silas read and read, making an especial study of the lighthouse and its sad history. He devoured newspaper accounts, memoirs, notes, rumors: everything he could find in the ledger and in the large collection of books on local history that spilled from the shelves of his father's home library.

When he had learned all he could on the subject of the lighthouse and its last occupant, Silas set out for the cliffs, a little before dark. In the months since his father's death, he had diligently applied himself to Undertaking, reading widely, and practicing the arcane rites he'd read about in the ledger when and where he could. And while Silas wasn't even sure if he'd be able to help, he was resolved to try. In his mind Silas carried a name, held it like a talisman with which he might be able to settle the dead within that spindle of brick perched upon the rocks. He prayed the name would be enough.

The sky was pouring down pitch as Silas walked quickly along the cliff toward the old lighthouse. He wore an oilskin cape over his father's jacket and held a small lantern. As he approached the high tower, he reached into his jacket pocket and took hold of the death watch, that ancient timepiece that when stopped, compelled the dead to become visible to the living. Silas drew no comfort from how quickly the silver warmed in his hand. It was as if the death watch wanted to be held and used. It made Silas feel uneasy.

Before even reaching the door, before stopping the hand of the death watch, he could sense the past of the place weighing down on him, more and more with every step, pulling at his feet as though the earth itself were trying to hold him back. He picked up his pace and when he reached the door, he took out a large iron key lent to him by Mother Peale, who had taken it upon herself to keep an eye on the place many years ago. She had been only too happy to hear that Silas would try his hand at bringing Peace to that haunted tower.

"You take this key and do what you can, Silas Umber," Mother Peale had said. "You know we're all for you, no matter what happens. And remember, if you don't come back, your funeral is paid for by the townsfolk, as is customary, so don't you worry. It's all taken care of should it come to that." Mother Peale had smiled and winked at Silas then, attempting to rouse his good humor. Silas had smiled back, but hadn't found it terribly funny.

At first, the key wouldn't turn in the lock. Silas twisted it back and forth, worried that it might break. Finally, the rust gave way and the lock turned, but when Silas pushed the door, it wouldn't budge. He shoved it, then struck it with his fist as though the door might fly open by the sheer force of his rising aggravation. Finally, in anger, Silas threw his full weight at the door, hitting it hard with his shoulder, and the door relented. A damp, salty smell flowed out from the darkness beyond the doorway as he stumbled inside. He held up the lantern, its weak light barely making an entrance into the inky black of the room, and then closed the door behind him. He walked to the center of the room, set the lantern on a small uneven table, and took the death watch from his pocket. Opening the jaw of the small silver skull, he brought his thumb down hard on the dial. He could feel the watch's little heartbeat slow and then stop. Silas closed his eyes, drew in a breath, and opened them again.

Where only a moment ago there had been an abandoned room with a few pieces of rotted and broken furniture, now a new scene glimmered before him. A wood-burning stove glowed on the far side of the room and a few toys lay scattered on the rug. In the middle of the room, a table was set with a cloth and candles. A hutch against the wall bore dishes and mugs. Here was a comfortable family home.

A sudden movement caught Silas's eyes. A shadow was drawing away from the wall. Slowly it lengthened out across the floor, and began to rise and take shape. The shadow moved against the light to place itself in a chair across the room from Silas. There, now, smiling faintly, was a young man, perhaps in his twenties. His body gave off a gray ineffectual light, as though he were a candle seen on the screen in an early film.

"Good evening," said Silas to the ghost, breathing slowly, steadying himself.

"Is it evening? I hadn't noticed," the ghost replied absently.

"Almost. I am looking for the keeper of this lighthouse. Is that you?"

The ghost looked away. "No. That is my father."

"May I speak with him?"

"I am afraid not, sir. He's not here at present."

"May I ask where he is?" Silas inquired.

"My father's not here. Just me now. The son."

Silas was surprised. He knew that the lighthouse keeper's son, who had died with his mother in a shipwreck, had been an infant. So who was this? Was there another son? Had the records he'd consulted been incomplete? There was something in the ghost's voice—a knowing hesitancy—that made Silas uneasy.

"I need to speak with your father," Silas said again, this time putting some iron into the words.

The ghost began to shake. He looked at Silas, then toward the window.

"I think I know you. . . . I've seen you, sitting out there, with a girl." The ghost smiled wanly then. "You were with a strange girl. Her skin was like the moon—"

"I don't remember," Silas said. While he couldn't recall the particulars, he knew the ghost was right. He'd been there with a girl. What was her name? No. He didn't want to start on this topic. Not now. Memories of her . . . of the girl . . . made his heart ache, and he hadn't come to the lighthouse to talk about his own losses. "But," he said instead, "I am pleased to meet you. I am Silas Umber. I am the Undertaker. I am here to help you."

"I am Daniel. Daniel Downing." As the ghost spoke the name, he seemed to dim and lose the definition of his form. His edges blurred.

Now Silas was confused. Daniel had indeed been the lighthouse keeper's son, the very son who had died out upon the reef with his mother when their ship struck the rocks. Thus far, Silas's experience had been that ghosts appeared as they were in at the time of their passing, or as they had been at some especial point during their life. Ghosts only had full knowledge of what they had been and what they had done during their lifetime. So how could a child appear as the man he had never become?

"Now, if you please. I would like to speak with your father."

The ghost looked down at the floor and shook his head.

"He's not here. I told you."

"Are you sure?"

The ghost looked up, his eyes rheumy and unfocused. "It's time to light the lamp," he whispered.

"All right," Silas said, trying to encourage him. "Let's have some more light."

But the ghost looked frightened and only repeated, "Time to light the lamp." The ghost began to open and close his hands as though he were giving some kind of frantic semaphore to the floorboards. "It's getting dark."

"It is. Night is coming."

"Oh, God," said the ghost.

"You don't want to light the lamp? May I help?"

"I do. I must. It's just that . . . the light affects me badly . . . my head."

"Let's climb up together. I will help you."

"All right," said the ghost passively. The color of his form deepened and darkened, becoming more present, the buttons on his clothes coming into focus, and he added, "If you like, I can show you the spot where my father jumped."

"Thank you," replied Silas, his nerves prickling at the ghost's mention of the suicide. "That will be fine."

They climbed the steep stairs of the lighthouse together. When they reached the uppermost chamber, the great lamp of the tower burst into spectral flame and began to turn, casting its grim light over the sea and land and the tower itself. As the beam passed through the ghost, Silas could see another aspect, another face, hiding just below the glimmering ashen surface of the ghost's skin. It was older, but not vastly different from the one Silas had seen only a moment ago. When the beam swung away, the older face vanished, and the young man was there again.

"Let me show you where he jumped, Silas Umber. Just here. You see, the rail is not so high. Just here, the waters below are churning and churning. They never stop. How restless the sea is . . . that's where you'll find him. Down there."

Silas tried to turn away from the rail, tried to focus on something, anything other than the dizzying descent and the noise of the waters crashing on the rocks. He looked at the lamp room and found it changed. The piercing light now seemed to pass through the solid walls of the building. And just as the death watch had altered the appearance of the room below, now the beam illuminated a space different from the one Silas had first seen; the room appeared in the full flush of its heyday long ago, long before the lighthouse was abandoned. This spectral effect was taxing on Silas's eyes and the repeating flash of past, present, past, present made him dizzy and disoriented. He knew the spectral effect was a warning, but Silas could not yet perceive which way lay hidden rocks and which way the safe harbor. To steady himself, he ran his own name through his mind: *I am Silas Umber, Silas Umber, Silas Umber.* As he did, he remembered what it was he came to do, and his face flushed with resolve. By speaking his name, by saying the word "Umber," he could sense his father's steadying presence. Silas stood up straight and pushed back his shoulders, feeling, in his blood, that a part of his father was always with him.

The ghost stood at the rail, looking out at the sea.

Silas stepped close to the ghost and said, "I believe I know who you are. You are J—" But before Silas could continue, the ghost began crying out in a rapid circle of words.

"Gone . . . all gone. I have nothing now. No one. All my fault. Now all is lost. All is lost. All is lost. . . ." And like the rising of a sudden gust, the ghost lifted quickly into the air above the railing, his eyes darkening, their sockets becoming black and empty.

Over and over and over like a prayer, Silas called out the ghost's true name. "Joseph Downing! Wait! Joseph Downing, be still!

The ghost stood upon the cold air, holding himself in the posture of an angry child, fists thrust up over his ears.

"No!" cried the ghost. "My father is below! I am his son. This is my home."

Standing his ground, Silas shouted back. "You are Joseph

Downing! Hear these, my words! You are Joseph Downing, the keeper of this light—"

The ghost fell upon Silas, trying to push him from the tower, his blurring form buffeting Silas with a freezing blast of air. The great wind took Silas off guard, raised him up off his feet, and made him lose his balance. He fell forward, nearly over the rail. Looking down, Silas wove his arms through the railing and held it fast. Silas looked up. The ghost was hanging in the air before him out beyond the protective rail. And all the while, the dark light continued to go around, washing the world in successive veils of its dismal nightmare-light.

When the lamp beam poured over Silas, his own name began to unravel. In that light, he heard only the call of the waiting rocks below and the deadly churning of waters. He arms loosened on the rails. He stood at the edge of the tower as the ghost swayed back and forth against the backdrop of the black sky, crying with a throat of storm, crying shards of a lie, a tale grown twisted and false.

"My father is lost. He is lost down there!" The ghost turned in the air, thrusting a finger toward the rocks and sea. "Even now. Lost among the waters. Dark places. Below the kelp. Cold. Cold. Cold. My father is—"

But Silas cut him off. "Joseph Downing, enough!" he said.

"I am Daniel Downing," the ghost moaned piteously, desperately, hiding in the name. "I am the son—"

"Enough! Here is your story and your name!"

And while the ghost continued to sob, Silas told the ghost his own sad tale.

"Their ship was coming back to Lichport, returning from up the coast, where they'd been visiting family. Your wife. Your child. They were coming home. All day you'd been waiting, but how were you to know the ship had been delayed? Only two days, due to bad weather. But when the ship did not come in, you waited. All night you waited up on this tower, straining to see through the night. Hoping to see the silhouette of their ship against the moonlit sea. But the ship did not come. The next day, twilight found you still up on the tower, sitting, watching. And as the day ebbed, so did you, and for only an instant, you told yourself, 'I'll close my eyes.'"

The ghost stood frozen on the air, his eyes wide and fixed on Silas. He muttered, "I did not sleep. Only rested. I did not sleep. . . ."

"Nor has anyone in this town slept. We have all kept vigil with you. But Joseph, that night, you did sleep, and evening stole in and the lantern had not been lit, and so when their ship approached, there was no candle to guide it home. The ship struck the reef and all aboard were lost to the sea. Your wife. Your child. Both lost. On this very night, long, long ago."

The ghost wavered and began to dissolve, falling away into his own misery and shame, but Silas spoke again. "Wait, Joseph Downing, one moment more."

The edges of the ghost's form sharpened and took hold of the air again.

"Now, Joseph Downing, tell me what happened next. Speak."

Slowly, the ghost began to move his mouth, then the words came.

"A boy from town told me what had happened. Everyone knew there had been no light. My son and wife were gone, gone below, and . . ." The ghost's voice began to waver.

"Go on, Joseph. It's all right now. There is nothing left to lose but your own good self. Speak your name and tell me what happened."

"I am . . . I am Joseph Downing. Yes. That is my name. And

when I learned what had become of them, I tried to put myself low, to be with them in the sea. I jumped from the lighthouse! But, oh, I fell upon the rocks, there! Oh, God . . . even in death I was denied them. . . ." The ghost pointed to where Silas was now standing. Silas looked toward the railing, but when he looked back, the ghost was standing by the lamp room and had started walking toward him.

"Wait! Joseph! Abide!"

The ghost's eyes had become flat, black stones. He walked past Silas and through the railing and fell like a thing of substance down into darkness.

Silas stood by the rail, looking down, unsure of what had happened. Was it over? The ghost had said his own name. Had it been enough? He must not assume. He straightened his back and called out over the water. It felt unfinished. Should he summon the ghost back, compel him to return? But Silas thought about the ghost and his family, his wife and child, lost in the waters. Perhaps there was something he could do for them all.

"Who will come for this weary soul?" Silas intoned. "Who shall abide with Joseph Downing and keep him?" Silas closed his eyes. With his words, Silas sent his mind's eye out into the sea, searching along the bottom for the bones of those who had been lost so long ago. And as he'd learned from his father's writings, he imagined his words stirring the remains, lost, sinking into them and waking, gently waking, those who had so long waited to find the Peace their awful deaths had kept from them. *Mother and child,* Silas said to himself. *Come, now, for here is restoration. Mother and child, bring peace to this lost soul. Mother and child, carry him to peace. . . .*

Silas closed his eyes and tried to feel the words flowing out across the sea, though a small voice in the back of his mind held back and whispered to him. *It is wrong to summon the dead.*